PAST TENSE

B. J. Gradney

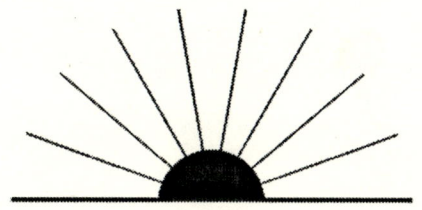

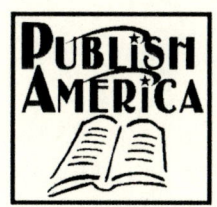

PublishAmerica
Baltimore

First printing

ISBN: 1-4137-6549-1
PUBLISHED BY PUBLISHAMERICA, LLLP
www.publishamerica.com
Baltimore

Printed in the United States of America

To my daughters Amber and Kristin and my niece Angela who've always given me courage. Thanks!

And thanks to my mother Mrs. Bernice Gradney.

To Joyce,
Thanks for your support & being a good friend!
B.J. Gradney

BOOK ONE
CHAPTER ONE

"Again."

Dr. Williams knew he should stop but he wanted to try once more. The nurses moved back a little. The doctor placed the paddles back on the patient.

"One more time," he said.

Silence followed, they have all been involved in cases when a patient died, but it never got any easier.

Dr. Williams sighed. "OK. Time is 17:31. I'll go and speak with the family."

As he walked out of the room to find the family, Dr. Linden told him they hadn't been located yet.

He stopped and turned to the nearest nurse. "Nurse Copper, please have me paged should they arrive before six. If after six, Dr. Linden will attend to them," relayed a weary Dr. Sean Williams.

Dr. Williams walked down the hall to take the elevator to the locker room. As soon as he entered, he saw his brother, a doctor also, lounging in one of the recliners. He wanted to turn around but it was too late, Thomas had seen him. Sean was not in the mood for one of his brother's word games again.

"Say, Sean, if I didn't know better it looked as if you were going to leave when you saw me," Thomas smirked.

Sean tried to hide his emotions, losing patients always upset him. He hoped Thomas would take the hint and leave him alone, but it was not to be. Reluctantly, Sean answered. "What kind of a brother would I be if I purposely avoided you?"

Thomas looked closely at his brother. He could see he wasn't in a particularly good mood. He knew he should just leave him alone, but he couldn't pass up the chance to get under his skin. So he asked. "Did you lose another patient today?"

Thomas was well aware of the fact that Sean was one of the best doctors in the United States. In all honesty he was proud of him, but he wouldn't let his brother know.

Sean looked at him and wanted to strangle him, but he admitted to losing a young woman a few minutes ago. "Yes, I lost an accident victim," he answered.

"I'm really sorry about that, but how are you doing?"

Well, Sean thought. *This is about as sincere as he's been in a long time, or is it?*

Thomas noticed the change in his brother's face. *He's just not a challenge anymore, must be getting too soft.*

"Well, Sean, don't be too hard on yourself. You know I've worked emergency longer than you. You're a top specialist. Go over what you did and I'll try and see if I can help you for the next time."

"You've got to be kidding, Thomas. I don't need your help. I am more qualified than you are."

At this point, Sean's voice rose in volume. He started to say something else and thought better of it. His brother was the only person in the world that could make him revert and start acting like a child.

"Look, Sean, I didn't mean to upset you. I was only trying to help. I'm sorry if what I said offended you."

"Oh forget it, Tommy. I'm just a little touchy today. No doctor likes losing patients."

Thomas tried hard to hide his smile from Sean. He replied, "Yea, I know, but my offer still stands if you want it."

He delivered this little put down as he got out of his chair and headed toward the door.

"I can't believe I allowed myself to fall into his trap again. When will I learn?" Sean shook his head.

He collected his things out of his locker, looked at his watch and started down the hall toward the elevator. He got off at the doctors parking level and slowly walked toward his car. Once he reached his car, he threw his bag in on the passenger seat and sat down for a minute shaking his head. He started the car and peeled out of the garage as fast as he safely could. He wondered why he let his brother get to him the way that he did. He knew Thomas was trying to rile him, but he took the bait anyway. It seemed his brother had a thick skin and nothing bothered him; but then again, he would've had to have a conscience, wouldn't he?

Thomas had always been a little coarser around the edges just like their father. He was the one who always got into fights at school or slapped by girls. It didn't bother him to lose a fight. He would just keep coming as if he didn't know any better. Sean knew he did. Thomas always wanted to appear tough to their dad, who was a career marine sergeant. Their father Phillip was retired for thirty years from the military when he died.

Thomas had overheard a conversation between his parents when his father said that he thought he was too pretty for a boy. So of course, he tried to be as physical as he could. Where Sean was six feet four inches tall and about two hundred twenty-five pounds as a high school senior; Thomas was the same height but was a bit thinner at one hundred ninety-five pounds.

The brothers were only eighteen months apart. That in itself made them rivals for everything from who got the biggest piece of cake at dinner; to who could score the most touchdowns. In football, they were known as the Assassins. If one didn't get you for a touchdown, the other one would. Sean made all-district and all-state every year he played. He was the only freshman in the state of Texas that made the all-national team, best receiver in the nation. There was a lot of talk in the barbershops his whole high school career that he would play in the professional league.

Thomas knew Sean didn't want to play football all his life. He wanted to become a doctor, he always had. Thomas felt all of that athletic ability was wasted on Sean when he wanted it so much. To give Thomas his due, he was no slouch. It was just that Sean was the proto-typical wide receiver that coaches wanted.

The closeness in their age set the pattern of the brothers' lives. The younger always trying to top the elder. Thomas worked hard at what came easily to Sean. Both got scholarships to major universities. Thomas went to Texas A & M, while his brother went to the University of Texas. Once again, Sean went to the school that he wanted to go to. He could have gone there also, but he refused to play in Sean's shadow. He had to be his own man. He excelled at A & M, being their best go-to receiver in tight games. Sean turned out to be the star his hometown knew he would be. After college, the Dallas Rustlers drafted him in the first round, but he turned it down to go to medical school. The team also drafted Thomas the next year. He played for two years before getting a career ending injury. After that, he went to medical school.

As Sean pulled into his driveway, his cell phone started to ring.

"Hello, who's calling?"

A female voice on the other end asked, "Can't you recognize my voice by now Sean? We've dated off and on for a while now. I think I should be offended."

"Oh, hi, what's up?" he asked already dreading the answer.

"Well, I was saying to myself this morning, Becky, why don't you call Sean today and invite him over."

"Not tonight, Becky, I'm tired and I just finished a double shift today. Anyway, we agreed to go our separate ways after that last disastrous date. So my question to you is, why are you calling me?"

Sean had gotten out of his car by this time and was trying to find the key to the back door. Finally he found it and walked into the kitchen. The first thought that crossed his mind when he entered was, why is this place still a mess? What happened to the cleaning crew today?

All the while he was thinking to himself and looking around his kitchen, Becky went on and on about how much she wanted to see him. Sean finally got a chance to interrupt her after she'd been talking nonstop for the last five minutes, and said that him seeing her was not a good idea.

"Becky, look, we decided not to see each other for some very good reasons. For one, you can't be faithful and I've caught you in several, let's just say, half-truths. I don't have time to spend on a relationship with a person that I can't trust. So please make it easy on yourself and lose my number. Just tell yourself that it's me, I'm not good enough for you, OK?"

By now, Sean had crossed his fingers hoping his little speech would be enough to make her forget she ever knew him.

Becky sighed. "Alright Sean, if that's the way you want it, I'll see you around. Bye."

With that, Becky hung up at last and he breathed a sigh of relief.

Sean spotted a note on the counter from the cleaning crew. It seemed the van had a flat tire and they didn't get to his house until it was too late to finish. They would be back at ten the next morning.

Well, he thought, *it's not like I haven't lived in a pigsty before. I did for years in med school.*

While looking in the refrigerator for something to eat, he found beer, bad lettuce, no juice, and a bad smell.

"Dang! That smells awful." He quickly closed the door.

Sean made a mental note to leave instructions for the crew to clean his refrigerator.

"Mmm, nothing in the cabinet either. Pizza again."

After the pizza man left, he readied himself for a shower. As Sean walked into the bathroom, he took a good look at his image in the mirror.

"Not a bad-looking chap," he said aloud. "Why is my track record with women so lousy? As soon as they find out I'm a doctor, they dig themselves in for the long haul or they are completely without an intelligent thought."

Sean hunched his shoulders. He'd resigned himself to the fact that maybe he was looking for someone that doesn't exist. He was looking for a dream woman, someone who couldn't possible be real.

He stepped into the shower and turned on the water. He was beginning to feel that Thomas' way with women was the right approach after all. He did what they would allow; when he tired of their games, he left and went to the next woman. But he wanted more than a bed partner. He was ready to settle down, if he could find the perfect woman. The water had gotten hot, so he turned his back into it and moaned.

"Aah, that feels soo good."

As he was washing his hair, he remembered he'd had another one of those dreams again last night. The dreams he now felt were part of a life he believed he actually lived through. They were so real and authentic he started seeing a psychiatrist. It was that or a psychic.

He was experiencing déjà vu more and more lately. In his dreams, there was his brother, a very beautiful black woman named Me'na, and a host of different players in every dream. They were sometimes powerful people and some of them were dangerous people. There was always a person or two whom he thought he'd seen before, but their faces were always vague or they would turn away if he looked their direction. His dreams all had him and Me'na in a great love affair with his brother always in the way. Many obstacles were placed in his path to her, as he overcame each obstacle, Me'na seemed farther away. She kept getting away from him until he couldn't save her life and she died. She always died. If he could find her, he would do his best to rescue her and love her.

Sean walked out of the shower reaching for a towel to wrap around his waist. He once again took inventory on his looks. He was still the same weight he was in high school. Green eyes, lashes so long they were ridiculous, but deep inside him he knew his looks weren't his problem. He was coming to understand that maybe he lived a previous life he had yet to come to terms with. He didn't know how to resolve this dilemma and he couldn't talk to his brother about it.

Sean walked over to his super king-sized bed and plopped down in the middle. He folded his arms behind his head and looked through the moon roof above his bed.

I could move back home to Beaumont and take life slower but Thomas might follow me out of spite. I know he'd do it just to get under my skin.

As he fell asleep, he started to toss and turn a bit. Mumbling to himself in a foreign tongue he did not know when he was awake.

Sean dreamt one of his earlier dreams, faraway in another lifetime, in early sixteenth century Fastonia.

BOOK TWO
CHAPTER ONE

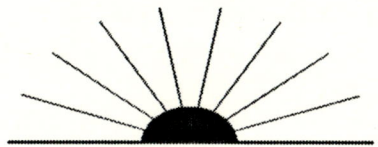

King Sean Phillip Winslow of the seafaring kingdom of Fastonia sat in his chamber with the Minister of Finance Lord Edmund Hightower.

"Your Majesty, you know I understand why you established the Holiday of Plenty last year. But must we give away a whole cow to the families that appear? How about a fourth of a cow? It will save you a great deal of money. Please reconsider, Your Highness?" he pleaded with the King.

"Edmund, how can the day be called Holiday of Plenty if we treat the masses poorly? Those are our people out there. Don't you agree they need at least one good milk cow for their children? You drink milk whenever you choose, don't you?" the King asked.

"Why yes I do, sire, but next year why don't we give spread seed away?"

The King smiled at his beleaguered minister. "Edmund, each year the grant will be different. We just happened to have been able to purchase several large herds of cows from Saint John. We will hold on to fifty cows for the palace's use and portion out whatever left over milk there is on a first-come-first-serve basis." King Winslow stood and stretched his long frame. His back had become cramped with sitting at his desk.

"So rest easy. Many may not show up. The peasants do not know that cows are to be given."

"I sincerely hope, Your Majesty, it rains today. With your permission, there are letters I must attend to. I will take my leave."

The King nodded his head. Edmund backed a few steps from him, bowed and left the room. On his way out he bowed to Prince Thomas who was on his way in to see his brother.

"Good morning, Your Highness," Prince Thomas greeted his brother upon entering his chamber. He did a polite bow and seated himself across from him.

"What have you been up to this morning, Thomas?" Sean asked him.

"Nothing as yet, but it is still early," came the impudent reply.

"Mm, huh, have you forgotten what today is, brother?"

The prince remembered why today was special, but he pretended it slipped his mind. "Monday?" Thomas asked with a quizzical lift of his brow.

Sean, exasperated once again with Thomas could only wonder at his motivation. "You are to sit with me on the balcony nearest the street in about one hour. What happened to your clothes? Did you sleep in them again?" he asked.

Thomas looked around the room to make sure they were alone. "Well Sean, I didn't exactly sleep in them. In fact, I haven't been to sleep at all." Thomas rubbed his new growth of beard and smiled slyly at his elder brother. "I dropped them on the floor and they kind of got stepped on a couple of times, I think we even rolled over them."

"Whose wife is it this time? Who is to be paid off now?" The King really didn't want to know. He knew too much already. "Why weren't you born a girl? That way I could marry you off. Your constant bed hopping is costing too much to satisfy the wronged husband." Sean was trying very hard not to be angry with his brother.

Thomas erupted into laughter. "You know, sire, if you socialized with me more often, you might be more understanding and not so tensed up all the time. I know a couple of ladies of the court that are real easy to get to know, even for a proper King as you."

The King straightened up in his chair and leaned toward his brother. "Thomas, if I needed you to get me a woman, it wouldn't be one of your cast-off friends. Any lady I have a relationship with is discreet and above reproach."

Thomas was finally able to bring himself under control. He stood and touched Sean on the shoulder. "Must I change my clothes now or do I have time to break my fast?"

"Change now, please, and do shave. I expect you on the balcony beside me in an hour."

Bowing slightly as he prepared to leave the room, Thomas allowed a soft chuckle to escape. He meant for Sean to hear him. He always thought Sean took himself too seriously.

The King and prince stepped out onto the balcony to the many cheers of the gathered populous. Their kingdom consisted of many different nationalities and races. Sailors often brought home new wives from faraway lands. Their country was very diverse.

"Thank you for coming out to celebrate our second Holiday of Plenty Festival," the King began. "As long as we live in this blessed kingdom, we will share the bounty with the people of Fastonia."

"God save the King!" was shouted out.

Sean smiled and waved to the people. The people loved their ruling family. There had been peace in their land for the last eighteen years. They were a strong nation.

"Long live King Winslow and Prince Thomas!"

Both brothers smiled and waved to the crowd. Thomas threw candy to the children in front.

"Long may the King rule!"

The King had to raise his hand for the crowd to quiet down. This was a day free from labor for everyone; naturally, they were going to make the most of it.

"Everyone, please enjoy the carnival and the food. In a couple of hours, Lord Hamilton will have the horn blown and every male head of household and single male must go to the northern edge of the square. Please allow the widows to go in front of the line. There you will be given this year's grant. If there is not enough to go around, he will instruct you further. Thank you very much," he finished.

His people were still shouting. "King Sean! King Sean!" so loud the roar was somewhat deafening.

Prince Thomas leaned over to his brother and said, "You love that, don't you?"

Sean replied, "I'd rather that than off with his head!"

They walked back together, laughing with their arms around each other's shoulders.

They sat and talked for hours. The brothers hadn't talked this way in a long time. Usually Thomas was trying to get Sean to help him out of a love affair gone wrong. Not this time. They spoke as the brothers that they were. A couple of times a page or minister would try to disturb them, but Sean would tell them to go away.

Lord Hightower wanted to break up the conversation. He knew the King's only weakness was his love for his brother. With any other brother that would be fine, but the prince was no ordinary brother.

Thomas was the fiercest knight in the realm. His bravery was unquestionable as was his skill with all weapons. He was often called Thomas the Dark, for he was as dark as Sean was fair. Thomas had the blackest hair, the same as their father; while Sean was fair as their mother had been. Thomas was broad of shoulder with a warrior's build. His right arm was larger than his left. That was the deadly sword arm. Not many men could stand against him for long. He was at home on the battlefield with the same ease in which he lounged in the palace. The only difference was that when in the palace, his eyes were always surveying the incoming crowd. One never knew he was watching. On the battlefield you could see your enemy coming towards you. There was usually time to prepare for a fight and let them feel your blade. But in the social settings that he had to participate in, the enemy was cloaked. You never knew who they were. He and Sean might not see eye to eye on most things, but he would protect his brother at all times. He would guard against treachery.

The last war that Fastonia fought was against Candea, King Sardin's domain. That war took their father away, but he would die before allowing anyone to assassinate his brother. The chances of that were slim, but one never knew. Prince Thomas loved his brother very much, but he wanted to be king also. Thomas felt his brother was too free of spirit, like the holiday that was celebrated today. He wouldn't have given the peasants cows. He may have passed out coins to them, which was less expensive, but he believed the treasures belonged to the ruling family alone. What did the common folk know to do with riches anyway?

Thomas was certain; Sean didn't now he felt this way. The only person who could see his true character was Lord Hightower. If the chance ever came, he would kill him himself. Lord Hightower stood between him and his imaginary crown.

Thomas did his best to keep Sean unwed. If he died without issue, then the kingdom would be his. Sean was only eighteen months older than he was. That just didn't seem fair to him. He was torn between his desire to be king and the immense love he had for his brother. He didn't wish him harm. He loved him as much as he could love anyone. But if an accident befell Sean and it couldn't be tied to him; then it was out of his hands, wasn't it?

Sean was a very easygoing person. He was the best diplomat visiting princes and other emissaries had ever dealt with. He was very fair. If Thomas had been king, he would make the tribute visiting ships paid much steeper than they were now. The diplomats would not like to deal with him. As it was, they cut a wide path when he was around.

Both brothers were about the same height, but Sean was a bit leaner than Thomas. He was a very good swordsman; he could almost beat his brother. But he couldn't get Thomas to practice with him often enough. Sean was left-handed. Thomas always teased him about looking awkward using the sword when they would first begin. It didn't take long to wipe the smile off his brother's face.

At thirty-four, the King's ministers were trying to get him to marry. The kingdom needed an heir. There just wasn't anyone that attracted him. He knew he'd have to marry for political and strategic reasons, but just not now. He would find a young princess who could provide a military alliance to satisfy his minister of war, who was also his brother, along with a reasonable dowry to satisfy the Lord Hightower, the minister of finance.

Neither brother had ever been in love before. Sean had only been infatuated with several women, but not enough to marry them. He wanted a wife that would set his blood on fire, not a political pawn. There were several offers from neighboring kingdoms, but the women were too old for him. He wanted a young wife who could bear him many children. Sean had always known he would know his future wife from first glance. He would be able to feel her presence the moment she stepped into his world. If the fates waited much longer, he would have to accept one of the offers he now had. That would not be a good thing for him. The King never shared these emotions with his brother. Thomas thought he was too soft anyway. He wasn't going to give him any more ammunition.

As they walked out of the solar, laughing together, the greedy nobles that were there to beg for a favor knew this was the right time. The King and his brother were often seen together, but not necessarily both enjoying the same antidote. Since they were laughing collectively, that meant the King was in a very good mood. The perfect mood for begging they thought. There were some nobles who wanted to widen their borders, but there was nowhere to go. The only way for them to increase their holdings would be to start a war. These nobles curried favor with Prince Thomas. It was assumed since he was a great warrior he would rather be fighting than dancing in the palace after supper. Most of these nobles wanted to invade Candea, not many Fastonians liked King Sardin. He was the cause of the last war Fastonia fought on their soil. King Phillip was lost in that war of greed. The nobles were in for a surprise if they thought Thomas would want to go to war. He didn't believe greed was enough of a reason to start a war. After all, it was King Sardin's greed that took their beloved father from his sons.

After the King sat on the throne to begin afternoon court, a dusty sentry walked swiftly into the public room. He begged for an audience with Prince Thomas his military commander. He was shown into a small closet to await the prince. As soon as Thomas walked in the young man sprang to attention.

"Begging your pardon, Highness, but a detachment about the size of a small infantry unit has crossed onto our land."

"Slow down, soldier, take your time," Thomas told him.

"Thank you, Your Highness, I was trying to get here as fast as I could. My patrol was riding the borders connecting Fastonia and Candea between the mountain pass closest to Winslow Town. We watched from the mountains as they crossed into Fastonia. They were moving very fast. We kept up with them for about an hour; we then approached them with caution. We rode into their camp as we normally do all travelers. I was shown into Duke Bolwin's tent. He asked me to come and deliver a message for him. The message is Highness; that they were sent by King Sardin to speak with the King on business that was all he would say."

The young soldier was out of breath when he finally stopped. The prince asked him if he could determine if an advance rider had been sent ahead to announce their arrival.

The soldier answered, "The duke said he was going to send someone ahead, but since we ran into each other he'd appreciate it if I would deliver the message for him."

"Is this everything, Sir David?" Thomas asked.

"Yes, Your Highness, it is."

"Go then into the King's household guard's kitchen and tell them that I said to feed you and give you drink," the prince told him. Sir David bowed, turned and left.

"Mmm, what is the duke doing here early? I must go to Sean and tell him this news," he thought aloud. He turned on his heels to go talk with the King.

The Candean ambassador was not due to arrive in Fastonia for another six months. Their tribute had not yet expired. Duke Bolwin was the personal friend of his King and therefore knew the real reason for the early visit. The Candeans wanted to control Fastonia's ports. There was a port in Saint John, but it was small and insignificant when compared to Fastonia's. Candea was completely land bound. The ride to Fastonia's ports was longer because one had to pass through the mountains to reach the nearest one, but it was worth it. Their ports were many and foreign vessels arrived there almost daily. At least three-fourths of Fastonia's borders were water. It was a very rich kingdom and King Sardin wanted to try young King Winslow in a game of cat and mouse. Fastonia's army and their navy were supreme in the region. He knew they couldn't be beaten on the battlefield; so, he was going to try and steal the kingdom by guile.

Candea had spies in the capital city of Winslow Town. They reported back that maybe Prince Thomas' escapades with married women might be a lever they could exploit. There were many husbands whom he had made a fool of that might like a little revenge. They would not know what was actually going on behind the scenes, but the duke was confident a husband could be found with little trouble.

His spies knew of a husband they might be able to persuade to help them; but he was a fool and could spoil their plans. The duke didn't want to have to kidnap the prince and force the King into battle in the city, Prince Thomas was not an easy man.

There was always the secret weapon that could part the brothers and make them enemies he thought. He was willing to wait and see which plan had the best potential. They should arrive in Fastonia within twenty-four hours.

BOOK TWO
CHAPTER TWO

The King enjoyed his morning meal alone as was his custom. He needed the time to clear his mind and to relax. The different ministers kept him busy from the time he arose to well past midnight sometimes. Being the sole ruler of a busy and important kingdom often gave him no time for pleasure.

He suffered from headaches now and again. His physician wanted him to take his ease when possible. His crown weighed heavily on his shoulders. More than anything he really wanted to be the warrior his brother was. He accepted his destiny. His fate was to rule wisely, this he did to perfection.

Lord Hightower taught Sean everything he knew. His father trained him from birth to be king; but, policies and military knowledge he learned from Lord Hightower. Sean became king when he was eighteen, during that time; all he wanted to do was fight. He'd recently become a knight and he wanted to pursue the lore of the romantic version told by traveling minstrels. Lord Edmund Hightower steered him in the correct direction for the kingdom.

As the King was eating, a bloodied knight on a limping warhorse came through town. A shopkeeper's son found the knight and cautiously brought him to his father. He had never seen a man hurt as this one was. There had always been peace in his lifetime. The boy's father was the town's clockmaker. When his son Joshua brought the knight to him, he sent him straight away to the palace for Captain Lovett.

Captain William Lovett and a small detachment of men approached the shop. A large crowd was gathering too close to the warhorse. The soldiers moved the crowd back. Even though the horse was injured, he was still a dangerous weapon. The men took the knight off the horse as gingerly as possible and placed him on a waiting stretcher. Sir Timothy broke the arrow shafts down as far as he could without reinjuring the knight. He handed the tail of the arrows to his captain who closely examined them.

The knight's helmet and armor were removed. Captain Lovett recognized him as Sir Benjamin, Lord Geoffrey Blackmon's younger brother.

Sir Benjamin was brought to the palace guard's infirmary and the physician was sent for. Captain Lovett beat a hasty path to the palace in search of Prince Thomas. He saw one of the prince's squires lounging with the other court squires in a corner.

"Ian, come here. Go and get the prince quickly."

Ian ran to the captain with a smile on his face until he noticed the grim set of his mouth. He schooled his features accordingly. He started running to the prince's private quarters. Once there he beat upon the door.

"Highness! Highness! I have a most urgent message for you," he fairly shouted. Ian heard voices in the room speaking low.

"Go away, Ian, I am attending to important business," Thomas replied.

"Highness, I cannot, Captain Lovett has sent me in search of you. He says it is most important."

Thomas left his important business reclining on the bed to talk with Ian. If Lovett sent him here, it had to be an emergency. He opened the door a crack.

"Calm down, Ian, let me dress and I'll go with you shortly." Thomas closed the door to put his clothes on. Ian heard giggling and laughter inside. He stuck his chest out. His prince was indeed a legend among men.

Thomas dressed and joined Ian in the hall. He asked if he knew what had happened.

"No, Highness, I do not. Captain Lovett only told me to make haste."

Thomas really worried now. Captain Lovett was not a man who needed assistance often, he knew his job well. As they approached the captain he bowed to Thomas.

"Your Highness, I am sorry to intrude upon your day. Sir Benjamin Blackmon was found this morning badly wounded." Thomas listened closely. "He was bloodied and his horse was injured. It appears he was ambushed. We found two arrows on him, there were no markings. As you know, that's usually the trademark of assassins or hired mercenaries."

"Yes, Captain. Was Sir Benjamin still alive when you left him?"

"Yes, Highness, he was."

"Where is he now?" the prince asked.

"We brought him to the infirmary. I sent for the physician, he is there with him."

"Come, Captain, let's talk as we walk."

They walked very fast out of the palace, they were almost running. It was causing quite a commotion among the afternoon court hold-overs. The palace was usually a quite place after the king dismissed court for the day.

They arrived in the infirmary as the physician was sewing the wounds close. Thomas hurried over to see how Sir Benjamin was. The men around him bowed and cleared him a path.

"Old friend, is he going to make it?" he asked the physician.

"Only time will tell, Prince, he needs rest and peace. Beside that I will do all in my power to help him."

Thomas patted him on the shoulder and thanked him. Their physician, Sir Tallmadge, was good at his job. Thomas looked at the unconscious Sir Benjamin. He wanted to try an awaken him. But he decided to wait and ask his questions later. He needed to know who attacked a Fastonian knight on their soil. Captain Lovett had guards in place at the doors and windows just in case his attackers wanted to finish the job. He left orders with the captain to send for him as soon as he awakened.

Thomas went off to find his brother, but he was nowhere in sight. He turned and headed toward the King's private chambers. There he found him.

"Highness, I must speak with you privately."

Sean looked toward the Duke of Hamshire who bowed. He backed away and told the other men to go into the outer room. The brothers were alone. "What is it, Thomas? Something has you worked up this morning?" Sean asked him.

"Sir Benjamin was found wounded this morning. He is in the infirmary now. We don't know who attacked him or if he will survive."

Sean was astonished. "What are you saying? Someone attacked a Fastonian knight here?"

"Yes, brother, I am. I wanted to let you know what has happened. I will lead some of our knights out of town to look for clues. I will return as soon as possible with your permission."

Thomas bowed to his brother, and quickly left without waiting for an answer. Sean turned and bellowed for someone to come and help him finish dressing. He was going down to the infirmary to see Sir Benjamin for himself. His elder brother was a good friend of Thomas.

As he was preparing to leave, a page informed him the minister of finance awaited his pleasure. Sean looked upward and thought, *What else?*

"Tell him to give me thirty minutes and await me in the treasury room. Page, before you go, have Lord Hamilton meet me there also."

"Yes, Your Highness," the little page answered.

When the king returned from the infirmary, Lord Hamilton and Hightower were there awaiting him. Both stood as he entered the room.

"Good morning, Your Highness. I trust you slept well," Lord Hightower said.

"Yes, I did, Edmund, thank you for asking," replied the King.

"Sire, how may I be of assistance to you?" asked his old friend Lord Hamilton.

"Gentlemen, as you both know Duke Bolwin has entered the countryside. I have tried to understand why King Sardin has sent his emissary to us so early in the year. Candea is not scheduled to renegotiate their contract with us for another six months. Is that not so, Edmund?"

"Yes, Highness, you are correct."

"I don't like the smell of this. Whenever we deal with Candeans my skin starts to crawl," the King admitted.

"Sire," began Lord Hamilton, "If you believe something could be going on, I will help in any way I can. I can speak with the prince and have all available men assigned to extra duty."

"Yes, Edward, please do. I have the same eerie feeling I had when my father was murdered." The King had a faraway look in his eyes. Both men remembered the bitter pain everyone felt when King Phillip was killed in battle.

"Highness," he began, "we have spies in the Candean court. We have a spy that's very highly placed within King Sardin's personal court. Word reached me this morning that he is to arrive sometime this afternoon. He is believed to be traveling swiftly. He may have news that can shed light on the true reason for the early visit."

"Do you know how soon he will be here?" the King asked.

"No, sire, I have learned he is traveling by an alternate route so as not to run into the duke."

Sean turned his gaze to Lord Hamilton. "Edward, have our best scouts on this. Prince Thomas is unavailable for the time being, I need your assistance. You have my permission to do whatever is needed."

Lord Hamilton bowed to his king. "Highness, do you have any one reason or is it merely a feeling we could be attacked?" Edward asked.

"It is more a feeling than anything else. I would rather we be over zealous than caught napping," the King replied.

Lord Hightower looked into the King's eyes. They had glazed over. King Winslow hadn't had that particular look in almost eighteen years. He had sensed his father would not be returning from the war. He had been right.

"Edward, Edmund, you both know what King Sardin is capable of. He is the lowest of God's creatures. He wants our ports for himself. That was the reason for the last war between both kingdoms. Our ports are the best and the deepest in the region. Without them, he would have to travel to Saint John and wait for docking space to open. There the ports are much smaller and in some places too shallow for ships." The King turned and started pacing in the small chamber. He needed to do something, anything but stand in this room. He stopped and turned toward them.

"King Sardin is still smarting from his defeat at the hand of my father. Even though my father was taken from us, we still won the battle."

Both men nodded their heads.

"As you know, Prince Thomas still has not forgiven himself for being too young to fight beside father. He wanted to guard his back as he'd been taught. He will never stop blaming himself over something he had no control over. That is why today, he is our best warrior."

The King smiled remembering how hard his brother worked on his skills. After their father was killed, Thomas made it his primary duty to protect Sean.

Lord Hamilton interrupted his reminiscing. "If you will excuse me, sire, I want to get our men started as soon as possible. Knowing the prince as I do, I'm sure he already has the ghost patrol on it. I will make sure that all is as you desire." He bowed and left the room.

For a man in his late fifties, he was very active and hands on. He worked under Prince Thomas as an advisor or took command when necessary. They could hear him in the hall bellowing orders to the nearest pages to go and get this man or that man.

"Highness, do you really expect duplicity from the duke?" Edmund asked.

"Yes, I do. A storm is approaching, we must be ready."

Lord Edmund Hightower bowed to the King. "Well, Highness, you were correct when you told me your father was not going to return. I assume this to be the same. Your judgments have always been clear and unaffected by your personal feelings. I am not one to question your wisdom, I merely wait to serve." Sean looked at him and smiled.

"With your permission, I will go and await my contact." With that the cagy old minister backed out of the room.

After Lord Hightower left the room, Sean went to his chamber to dress for court. When he arrived in his rooms, he found his favorite doublet with the rich gold trim laid out. The softest undershirt his mother made for him was there also. He had dozens of undershirts, but this was the last one she made before she died. With the King's secret desire to be a warrior still in his heart, he chaffed at all the unnecessary clothing men had to wear to be presentable. As long as his body was covered by a single layer of clothing and he had his favorite hunting boots on, he was satisfied. He and his brother made fun of the men in his father's court. Most of them had more clothes on than the women and wore more jewelry. They looked more like peacocks than gentlemen.

His mind was on his brother and the goings on within his kingdom. He wanted to ride out himself and investigate the happenings. The last thing he wanted to do was dress for court. Still the King went to his chamber to dress. After he was dressed and arrived for court in the public room, his brother had returned. Thomas pulled him aside.

"Sean, there is a somewhat larger force accompanying the duke. It's not extremely large, but too large for a simple meeting. We have extra men at the borders or are almost there now. Lord Hamilton told me that the ghost patrol is already on their way to do what they do best."

Sean put his arm around his brother's shoulder. "Let's walk." They started slowly walking and talking, so as not to be overheard.

"We have extra soldiers in the city. The normal patrols have been increased for as long as the duke is here. We did not find out who ambushed Sir Benjamin. We will have to wait for him to awaken. The only thing we found was blood and signs of a struggle." Thomas stopped walking and looked to Sean. "Is there is anything else that you want me to do?"

"No, brother, I yield to your judgments on what to guard against. I trust you above all others," a smiling King told him.

Praise coming from Sean still made him feel good. It had been that way since they were kids. The prince took his position as minister of war very seriously. He just couldn't be a prince and do nothing all day. He had to be busy and on the move, he needed to make things happen. He may have felt he would make a better king than Sean, but he always followed his brother's instructions to the letter. Sean had a cooler head than he had. If he were king, he'd probably have already ridden out to meet the duke. But his brother the diplomat would wait and see. When it was the appropriate time to spring a trap, he would catch whatever it was he wanted.

"Thomas, we have a rich heritage here. We have much to lose if we are careless," the King said. "Our family has ruled a long time with no break in lineage. You and I have much to be thankful for." They were both silent for a moment as they reflected on their family history.

The Winslow family had ruled Fastonia for the last five hundred fifty years. No one was going to change that, not now or ever. The King might not have any legitimate or illegitimate heirs, but the prince had plenty. Per the kingdom's charter, if both brothers died without issue, an illegitimate male may rule. In Fastonia, an illegitimate male could rule as long as the father recognized him. But he had to be born on Fastonian soil. If there was more than one, then the eldest would be king. The only way a female could rule was if she was the only living relative alive. The brothers continued to walk for a moment.

"Thomas, where is the duke now?" Sean asked him.

"His entourage is about an hour outside the walls. Do you want me to have him stopped before he enters the city?" he asked.

"No, we don't want to alarm them. Let them enter as they always do. I don't want them to suspect a thing. With your network of men out there, I'm sure we are protected." They stopped for a second, the public room was busy today. Just what the King needed today, more arguments to settle.

"Come, Thomas. There's Edmund, his man must have arrived."

The brothers hurried into the minister's office. There they met a very weary and travel stained middle-aged man. He didn't look the part of a spy, but if he did, he wouldn't live long.

"Your Majesty, allow me to introduce your loyal servant, Lord Adam de Walt. He has been in my employ for many years."

Lord de Walt bowed as low as he could to his King. To him this was the highest honor that he could ever wish for. He'd never met the King or prince before, but he greatly admired them as men. He'd fought with their father King Phillip in many battles. It had long been his desire to serve the sons as he had served the father. Since this was the first time he had met either brother. He was understandably nervous. Sean bent down to help him rise; he appeared to be stuck in his bow.

The King ever tactful said to him, "Rise. You do me great honor. Come, sit and refresh yourself."

Sean kicked Thomas on his way to help the poor gentleman. Thomas, the insensitive brother, was suppressing a smile at Lord de Walt's plight.

The King served him wine and took a seat across from him. All waited for him to catch his breath. You could just look at him and tell that he had rushed all night and day to get here.

"Thank you, Your Majesty. This is the best wine that I've had since leaving home."

Lord Hightower looked toward the King. Sean asked everyone to be seated.

"Your Highness," he began. "I was instructed to report everything I heard and saw to Lord Hightower, no matter how insignificant it seemed to be."

"Go on, please," Sean asked him.

"Well, sire, as you probably know, King Sardin is very jealous of our kingdom. There isn't anything he wouldn't do to get his hands on what we have here. He does not believe in taking care of his people as your family has always done here. I heard him tell Duke Bolwin a fortnight ago, you wasted money on the people when it should be kept in your private chest. He could not understand why the Winslow family cared so much for the common man. The prevailing thought among the Candean nobles is to keep all riches to themselves. They feel the people won't know what to do with riches. I sent this information to Lord Hightower as soon as I heard it. It was not something that I hadn't heard before; but I followed my orders." He turned toward Lord Hightower.

"Did you get my missive, my lord?"

"No, I did not. I thought something had gone wrong when I hadn't heard from you within a month. It was assumed you had been discovered until I received the latest encoded message."

Lord de Walt told them the first message was sent to him via merchants coming to Winslow Town to trade. They were to deliver the note to his usual contact in town who would in turn deliver it to his contact. The message was supposed to go through at least three agents before arriving in Lord Hightower's hands.

"Your Highness, I believe King Sardin may have found out who our spies are. I was being watched everywhere I went. Each Fastonian agent there only knows his contact person. If one of us is caught, we cannot bring down the whole network." Lord de Walt stood, he appeared to be agitated.

"Duke Bolwin was told to try and locate any dissatisfied Fastonian noble who would support a rebellion. He was to promise them anything they wanted to win them over. Of course, whatever was promised would not be given, they could not be trusted. If they betrayed you, how could he trust them? They would turn against him at the first opportunity that was presented to them."

Lord de Walt had finished his report. He went to sit back down, but thought of something else. "Sire, may I add something?"

Sean nodded his head yes.

"The duke and only his most trusted agents are going to approach nobles they believe to be leaning away from you. He and his soldiers are going to walk around town as they usually do. They will shop and trade so as not to arouse suspicion. They will do this for many nights until the perfect opportunity presents itself. They will be waiting for the last quarter of the moon. If I am not mistaken, that's when the southern garrison has the least amount of viewing time. I believe the moon should appear that way in about five days."

Thomas looked Sean's way. He couldn't believe what he was hearing.

"A ship left the port of Biscayne in neighboring Saint John about two days before I was able to leave. The hold is reported to be empty. I heard they were going to pick up supplies here in Winslow Town. We all know they never pick up supplies here unless they were ordered ahead of time." He paused to take a drink of wine.

"I checked with the secretary in charge of orders. He said there were no supply orders for anyone. He told me that Candea was good for another five months at least."

Sean asked him, "Can this man be trusted?"

"Yes, sire, he is a cousin of mind. No one in Candea knows of our connection."

All four men looked at one another. The King's hunch was correct as always.

"Lord de Walt, is there anything else?" He hoped there wasn't. This was enough to digest at one time.

"One more thing, Highness, about seventy-five to one hundred men were seen marching toward Saint John over a week ago. They could very well be on that ship," he concluded.

"It took you about two days to get here traveling all night?" Thomas asked him.

"Yes, Highness."

"So, that means the ship should be here in about three days or so. Perfect timing. They will probably sit out to sea about two days then come in."

The entire room was deadly silent. It was a moment before the King could speak.

"Lord de Walt, does this conclude the report you have for me?" the King asked. Lord de Walt stood and told the King that it did. Lord Hightower stood with him and prepared to walk him to the door, but Sean stopped them.

"Lord de Walt, I want to thank you for your patriotism to your homeland." Sean had a hand on his shoulder, and tried to make him feel he was a valuable asset to Fastonia.

"You put your life at risk for the sake of your homeland. I know it must have been very hard being away from home. I would speak with you again when this awful business is behind us. We will have dinner together, just you, me, and the prince. I would like to discuss your future serving the crown here at home."

Adam de Walt straightened his stance at the pleasure he felt from the King's heartfelt words.

"It goes without saying that you cannot go back to Candea, it is no longer safe for you to do so."

Sean walked with him to the door, his hand was still on his shoulder. "On your way out, please speak with my personal secretary Sir Galen. Tell him I want you to have the best accommodations we have to offer in the palace. Also, give him a list of all household items you were forced to leave behind. Include whatever animals you owned. After we have finished with the duke, a nice estate will be awarded to you for your service to the crown," the King told him.

Lord de Walt didn't know what to say. So he simply fell to his knees and grabbed the King's robe to kiss the hem of it. These types of displays made Sean uncomfortable, he leaned down to help him up and gently send him on his way. After he'd gone, they could hear him praising the King's goodness to any that would listen. Prince Thomas told him he'd made Lord de Walt the most loyal man in the kingdom if he wasn't already.

Sean smiled. "Loyalty should be rewarded, and he could have been killed in Candea. He is and will remain a very loyal subject."

"Well, brother, as always you are right," Thomas told him. "I will send for my undersecretary of war. I shall be right back, Highness."

He left the room and walked swiftly into the public room. He sent pages looking for Lord Blackmon. He was not to be found anywhere in the palace. Thomas sent his honor guard to look for him. He hoped Geoffrey was not visiting one of his regular haunts in the daytime. He was supposed to be on duty. He had not been found to tell him of his brother's injuries. No one had seen him in several hours. He was a good man, but had a weakness for pleasure; it would be his undoing one day.

Prince Thomas arrived back in the minister's private room. He hated having to inform his brother he had to send a search party out. He assured Sean that Geoffrey would be found directly. Sean looked doubtful, he knew Geoffrey well also. He was probably with a woman.

"Thomas, do you know how many war ships we have in the harbor today?"

"Yes. There are five that are docked and another three are due back within a week. They are making the long patrols outside of our territory. There are ten that are in the international waters looking for pirates. We are still trying to find the ones who have started to plague us lately." Thomas leaned back in his chair. "Only half those numbers are due back within the month for supplies and to change places with the sailors that are now home," Thomas finished.

"Where are the rest of them?" Sean asked him.

"We have five that are being refitted and the last five are escorting your flagship *The Warrior King* to Warpolling for trade talks."

Thomas did not want their ships going there. He was convinced they were the pirates who'd tried to raid them. The Fastonian navy was too strong for them and they were always chased away. But, they sent special flags for Fastonia to fly on their masks to supposedly protect them from pirates.

Lord Hightower wondered aloud. "How do they expect to pull this off? They know we have more soldiers and ships than they have. There must be a spy among us."

The King turned toward his brother. "Have you noticed any of your officers spending more money than before?"

Thomas was quiet for a minute. "I haven't gone out to the local spots with them in a while. I've had to keep company with a friend in need lately."

He looked around the room, he felt as if his father was there shaking a disapproving head at him. Sean knew the friend in need was his latest lady friend. He was pretty sure the other men in the room knew it too. He recovered quickly, but Sean enjoyed his embarrassment.

"I will ask around discreetly. Maybe someone's been gambling that never did before."

Sean turned his attention to Lord Hightower. "Edmund, has there been any large purchases that would come under your office's notice?"

Lord Hightower said no one registered any land purchases within the last six months. At least no large purchases had come to his attention.

The King looked around the room. "Well, gentlemen, it would appear we may have a clever spy in our midst. Either he or she could be clever or they are doing this to get back at the crown for some imagined slight."

The King walked back to his seat. "Edmund, check through the records. Look for any decision that was made in the last year that was greatly objected to by anyone. This may well be a simple case of revenge, with no financial profit."

Thomas leaned back in his seat, trying to think if anyone could be trying to get at him. *Nah*, he thought, *not me.*

"Thomas, are you listening?" Sean asked him.

"Yes, I'm sorry, sire. Did you ask me something?"

"At this point, I don't think you should tell Lord Blackmon more than necessary. The spy could be anyone. The castle on the southern coast, is it fully staffed?"

"Yes, we are fully staffed at this time of the year. Only a few men have gone to visit their families in the countryside. As you know, Sean, the southern garrison sits on top of the hill. No ship can enter the port without the lookout seeing it. Since most of the southern coast is jetties and can't be docked with ships, a long boat could put to shore there. The lookout can see for miles even pass the curve in the coastline on a clear day or a full moon."

As soon as he said that, everyone remembered what Lord de Walt said about the upcoming cycle of the moon. It seemed as if some of the pieces to the puzzle were starting to fit. The only thing they had to do now was to hold their hand close to the vest. Duke Bolwin couldn't know he was suspected. It was going to be hard enough just sitting across from him at dinner and not slitting his throat.

Sean asked Lord Hamilton to stay in contact with the prince. They may need the old warrior's keen sense of strategy. He asked Thomas to walk with him in the garden. His personal guard followed at a discreet distance. Thomas insisted on this security after their father died.

"Sean, is there anyone in particular you want me to investigate?" he asked. Thomas couldn't take not doing anything, it was killing him.

"Well, I'm not sure," he started. "Do you think our spy was purposely misled? It would be folly for Candea to think they could surprise us if they came by sea. Lord de Walt did say that our citizens in Candea were being watched didn't he?" Sean asked.

"Are you thinking King Sardin could have been careless on purpose, hoping someone would pass on bad information to us?"

Before Sean could answer him he said, "I don't think this is a ruse. He could be trying to draw all our attention to the coast. I believe de Walt, he seemed to be a very intelligent man."

"I agree," Sean replied.

"But even though there is a mountain range on most of the border with Candea, I will watch all borders brother. We have a lot to lose." Thomas concluded.

"That, my brother," the King began, "Is why I have you over the war department. I trust you above all people. We both have the same love for this kingdom. I know you will do everything in your power to protect Fastonia."

They stopped walking for a moment. "Whatever you need, Thomas, no matter what it is, you have but to say the word."

Thomas embraced Sean. Their relationship was more informal than most monarchs had with their siblings. Even though both wanted to be king, for now, only one would be. They continued their walk in the gardens silently thinking on the future of their world.

BOOK TWO
CHAPTER THREE

Duke Bolwin and his men marched into Winslow Town as if their reason for being there was the same as always: a new trade agreement. Only his specially handpicked officers knew this was not an ordinary meeting. The regular soldiers didn't know more than they needed to know.

There were always volunteer soldiers to make this trip. Everyone liked Fastonia. It was a clean place to visit. There was no odor here as there were in other kingdoms. One could shop, walk around with friends and maybe eat without worrying at any moment they would be robbed. All the townships and villages had law enforcement officers that were honest. They had to be. The King would not tolerate anything less. In the larger towns, there was a small garrison of soldiers. Prince Thomas or his agents made regular visits to ensure all was well and none suffered unduly.

Traveling with Duke Bolwin was two of his childhood friends. They had served as pages in the old King's court. With him, there was transplanted Fastonian Charles, Earl of Greenfield, a most attractive man. He encountered no problems with the fairer sex, which was the main reason Bolwin became his friend. He attracted girls as readily as Bolwin's face repelled them.

Where Charles had laughing brown eyes, Richard's were black and beady. They were always on the move looking for his next victim. Charles was tall and well built while Richard was short and slight. The noble women of the court reminded him of his small stature quite often. To overcome his lack of height, he was filled with an undeserved sense of importance. He was a cruel man, most avoided him if possible. The only thing he had going for him was his ability to talk any unwitting person he encountered into doing something he wanted them to do.

Charles was his pawn. He only saw the good and refused to believe what other people saw in Richard. He tried to bring out what he thought was Richard's good side, except there was none.

Duke Bolwin's other companion was Martin, Earl of Langley. Here stood the enforcer of whatever Richard was doing. Martin was a brute of a man. He had red hair and legs that were as thick as tree trunks. He was the only one of the trio that was married.

The citizens of the diverse capital city Winslow Town appeared to be well fed and remarkably happy. The happy part in itself was unusual for the period in time. Most peasants were a poor and filthy lot. Usually disease was rampant in the poorer sections in most kingdoms. In most cities, there were bands of roving thieves working the neighborhoods and the dock area. Not in this kingdom. For a kingdom as large as Fastonia and with such a rich mixture of the races, the people seemed very tolerable of one another. Everyone worked in harmony with the soldiers to ensure a safe city. There were patrols of soldiers walking through the town at all times of the night. Along the dock, the sailors kept watch. There were still pubs and the houses of fallen women as in any other port. But order was kept. The royal family made sure Fastonia was as safe as they could make it.

As they approached the palace, the Duke stopped and looked upward. This had to be the biggest palace he'd ever seen. It was more that the eye could behold in just one glance. As he stood there, a small detachment of soldiers approached them. His men were led away to be quartered and fed. This was an added benefit of coming to Fastonia. They ate well and didn't have to sleep out in the open.

The duke and his companions were going into the bailey when Lord Hamilton came upon them and offered assistance. Lord Hamilton had been a good friend of the late King. He almost lost his life defending his King. He was left for dead on the battlefield until a scavenger found him and brought him to the palace. Since then, he had become a favorite of the brothers and had their complete trust.

Duke Bolwin and his companions were led into the public reception room. Once the King had officially been informed of the duke's presence, he was asked to state his business. He did, but the urgency in which he stated it did not move the secretary. He was told maybe in forty-eight hours he could be seen. If that wasn't soon enough for him, he could go back to Candea and make an appointment the official way. The duke's temper was inflamed. How dare he be put off as if he were some unimportant baron? He was Duke Richard Bolwin, the Candean King's emissary. They would pay for this insult if it was the last thing he did.

The surface of his face showed none of this, he was cool and calm. Beneath the surface, a volcano was erupting. Charles looked at him. He knew Richard was seething inwardly. He reminded him they were not expected for a visit for at least another six months. They should be grateful to be seen at all. Charles did his best to balance Richard's outlook on things out of his control. Martin acted out his dark side. They were given suites in the palace as usual, but this time they were separated. Each was in a different wing of the palace. Martin was placed the farthest away as he was the most dangerous. Charles was considered a friend.

At first, the duke thought this arrangement was strange, but he noticed an unusually high volume of dignitaries there. The King's best friend, Prince Kristoff from neighboring Mayfair, was in attendance. He hated that smug man and his equally smug wife. There were also many trade negotiators with stacks of papers running from room to room.

"Charles, I believe that you are right. We weren't expected and so I should be more tolerant, and not get upset so easily," he said.

But inside his mind, he was thinking this was a very rich kingdom indeed. He had never been in the palace when there were so many deals being made. In his mind's eye, he envisioned treasure chests overflowing with gold, silver, pearls, and precious silks. He saw himself sitting on the throne instead of King Sardin with hundreds of people begging him for favors.

"Richard, are you alright?" Charles asked him.

Shaking his head as if he was clearing out cobwebs he said, "Yes my friend, I am good."

There was a malevolent look in his eyes when Charles turned his head and he made eye contact with Martin. He shrugged his shoulders and decided to really look around his future home.

Richard Bolwin sent his personal attendant to check on the supply wagon. It traveled at a slower speed and should have arrived by now. His manservant, Adam went to check on the progress and to make sure that the cargo was safe. The wagon's guards were told to not let anyone come too close or the occupant out unless it was necessary. The occupant was told to stay hid and not to come out unless answering a call of nature. The duke's guard would bring food and water.

That night after everyone had eaten, the King, his brother, Lord Hamilton and Lord Hightower met in private. Prince Thomas related to Sean that so far, no ships had arrived that had not been searched before they put into port. The Fastonian Navy was meeting and boarding all incoming ships. The fleet of ships was under the command of Lord Geoffrey Blackmon who had finally turned up the next day. He checked on his brother who was still unconscious. For now, he knew the King had a new policy: all incoming foreign ships were to be boarded and searched. If any ship refused, they were immediately surrounded and boarded. Whoever fought them was to be arrested. Geoffrey didn't know what he was looking for, but Prince Thomas told him whatever seemed out of the ordinary, no matter how small must be brought to his attention immediately.

While Geoffrey patrolled the coastline, Lord William Chaney sent out additional soldiers along the mountainous borders between Candea and Fastonia. He was the prince's right hand man. He had trained in the art of war with Thomas and Sean when they were young men. His ability was well known. Men didn't cross him often. Once was usually enough for anyone. He was not Thomas' right hand man for nothing. Everyone was in place or soon would be by midnight. The men going to the border were told to ride as if Satan himself were after them. They did.

The King asked the assembled men if they had any thoughts and if they did to please share them. Lord Hamilton started, "Sire, the duke appeared to be upset when told that you could not see him for two days. His friend Lord Ainsley, took him aside, and could be heard telling him that they were not expected nor did they send word ahead. So for, Ainsley is still the only cool head among them," Lord Hamilton finished.

Thomas told them that whatever was going on, he just knew that Charles Ainsley didn't know anything about it. He was an honest man, a patriot of his homeland and from all reports on him had never been in any trouble when away from Bolwin. His only fault was his loyalty to a childhood friend that didn't deserve it. Charles would not betray his friend. He would defend him to all comers. He was honorable that way. Bolwin would not defend anyone unless he could profit from it. Martin Beaumont on the other hand was a ruthless cutthroat. There were rumors in Candea that he had had his elder brother murdered so he could inherit the earldom.

All decided everything that could be done was done or would about to be. Prince Thomas doubled his brother's personal household guards. His bedchamber was guarded from the inside as well as the outside. The King decided that tomorrow he would only appear in public for the evening meal. Everyone would be told that he was in meetings all day and could not be disturbed. He would only see the prince.

It was hard for Sean to rest that night. He hadn't spent a night like this since right after his father died. At that time, it was thought that since King Sardin had been defeated at the Battle of Foster Field, he would try to send his agents to murder the princes. Lord Hightower and Lord Hamilton stepped in to protect them. Lord Hamilton could barely move, his injuries were most severe; but he insisted that he be placed in the prince's suite to guard over them. His bed was placed in front of the door inside the room every night. He would stay awake as long as possible; if anything, none could move his bed from outside the door to come in.

There were soldiers outside on the balcony and all around the palace. Neither Sean nor Thomas could sleep much back then, they were too angry with Candea. Their father, King Phillip, didn't want his boys in this fight. His wife had died just eight months before and he couldn't take any chances on losing his sons. He knew he could defeat King Sardin, for Sardin had no honor. If his horse hadn't fallen and Sardin's mercenaries been so close to him, Lord Hamilton could have saved him. As it was, their father died fighting for his kingdom. He almost made it to the end of the battle. When his standard bearer's horse was hacked with an ax, that horse fell against their father's horse. The mercenaries were on top of the situation, he didn't have a chance.

Candea paid the highest tribute tax for the opportunity to dock their ships in Fastonia. It took ten years of sensitive negotiations between the two kingdoms before the King would allow them to use his ports. The higher tax didn't matter to the brothers. They were uncomfortable when Candeans were around. King Sardin had been allowed to use their ports now for the last eight years; it was still a shaky alliance at best. Security was naturally tightened when their ships were in port. The Winslow brothers just couldn't forgive King Sardin. The entire war was about greed alone.

There were many citizens from Candea who lived in Fastonia. They had to register with Lord Hamilton's office first before they would be allowed in the country. Lord Hamilton found out that many of the Candeans that lived in Fastonia before the last war were spies. This may have seemed a little extreme to some, but they brought this upon themselves. The Candeans without anything to hide had no problems with the approval process.

Upon rising the next morning, the king wanted to see his brother after his bath. He told the Duke of Richmore, to send a page with his request to his brother and invite Thomas to breakfast.

While the brothers were breaking their fast, they spoke of inconsequential topics since they were not alone. The gentlemen of the bedchamber were present on the opposite side of the room. When the meal was finished, Sean released his gentlemen to enjoy the remainder of the morning. They were told to stay within the palace grounds since the King didn't know if he would need them further; he would send for them if necessary.

"Sean, let's go riding on the grounds, we haven't ridden together for ages," Thomas said to him.

The King thought this was an excellent idea. The horses were ordered saddled and off they went. Sean owned a jet black Arabian stallion he called Sunrise. The prince rode a wheat-colored stallion that was the grandson of his father's horse Conqueror. He called his horse Firestorm.

Both men galloped along at first enjoying the sunshine. Then the old competition started again. Before they knew it, they were racing at breakneck speed across the meadow. Around the grounds, they went until both reached the starting point almost at the same time. Sean won the race by the tip of his horse's nose; it was a very close call.

Both were laughing and breathing hard, Thomas had forgotten what it was like to just be a brother. They were more alike than he would admit. Sean was very physical. He liked keeping his body fit for war. He had an unleashed quality about him hidden beneath the surface. Sometimes it was like watching a caged animal pace around in a too small cage. Thomas knew Sean would rather be a soldier, able to be free to fight at a moment's notice. That was all he talked about as a boy, him and Thomas fighting along side of their father.

King Phillip tried very hard to prepare Sean to be king one day. But he didn't want to talk about it, if he had to be king, why not a warrior king. His father tried to explain to him that as king, he would fight only if it was necessary, to boost moral among the soldiers. If he died in battle, who would rule in his stead? But, Sean took being king very seriously. He would do nothing to jeopardize his kingdom, or his people, so he paced instead of fighting. Thomas on the other hand was free to be the soldier that both wanted to be.

They rode for hours until the horses were tired. By the time that they stopped riding, it was well past the noon hour, but neither brother was hungry. They stayed in the courtyard talking.

The prince asked his brother to practice his skill with the swords with him. This gave them both a chance to work off the anger they felt toward Candea. Sean stripped off his shirt, Thomas followed suit. To the ladies eyes, they were two fine specimens of male flesh. All these two needed was to get married. That's what all men needed, a wife, children with all the trappings of wedded bliss. That was the way they were brought up to think, for there was little else a noble woman could do.

Lord Hightower came into the King's private courtyard and watched the brothers for a moment. He decided that he would leave them be, his news wasn't new and it could wait.

Swords were clanking loudly and some of the king's household guard started to watch the activity. The brothers were closely matched. What Sean lacked for in strength, he made up for it with finesse. Thomas was naturally stronger since he worked out daily, but he was impressed that Sean was still an excellent swordsman. Any man could win on any day. Sometimes the thinking man won over the man with the brute strength. It was about reflexes and smooth moves.

Thomas was satisfied if a fight should ensue Sean could and would protect himself if he didn't have his back. The king had his household guards who would surround him during a battle. The last thing that Thomas wanted was for Sean to be in a fight. If it came to that, Thomas would make sure that the king's guard did their job well. They numbered at least two hundred skilled knights and squires. Sean had a tendency to forget himself and run right into the heart of the matter. The men called that blood lust; no one was immune to it.

After going at each other for about forty-five minutes, both stopped, they were exhausted. The men gave them a rousing round of applause. It was good for them to see their King was still a soldier at heart, and still one of the best swordsmen they had ever seen.

Each was given a pitcher of water, which was promptly poured over their heads. Squires handed them towels. After they dried their faces, both drank down a large goblet of wine.

"Tommy, I really appreciate you staying cooped up with me, it was good to whip you again." Sean smiled.

"Whip me, begging the King's pardon, I think I let you win to make an old man feel good," Thomas laughingly replied.

"Eighteen months does not an old man make, little brother," responded Sean. "Come, Tommy, let's clean up, I am starving." They walked out of the courtyard and into their rooms to bath and dress for dinner.

The gentlemen of the bedchamber were waiting for him with a hot bath and clothes already laid out. The Duke of Hamshire Lord Carrington commented on how rested and relaxed the King appeared after his workout.

"Yes, I feel invigorated," Sean answered him. "I should do this more; Thomas is always nagging me to workout."

Sean told his gentlemen that he would go to the dining hall in a moment. First, he must meet with Lord Hamilton, Lord Hightower, and the prince in his private solar. The Duke of Richmore, Lord Ramsey sent for a page to deliver the king's message.

"Connor," the King turned and looked to his left, "Have my gentlemen await me in the dining hall, the Prince will escort me there after my meeting."

"As you wish, sire." With that, the duke bowed and left to gather the others. Sean called his gentlemen of the bedchamber his companions. The title was a bit stiff. He and Thomas were raised with half of them in the palace. A group of naughty little boys of royalty and the peerage reeking havoc everywhere they were allowed to go. No one dared to chastise them, especially the princes, who were always the leaders. Sean and Thomas were seated in the solar waiting for the others.

Both were getting on in years, Lord Hightower was the elder by seven years. Neither man would admit they were getting older. They wouldn't even talk about retiring to their country estates. They entered into the room together and bowed to their king and prince. Sean stood up to greet them and asked them to be seated. Lord Hamilton was asked if there was anything new to report.

"No, Your Highness, Duke Bolwin and his men have acted as they usually do, they have bought trinkets and household goods," was the reply.

"Edmund, anything new?" the King asked.

"No, sire, they are sly, but the duke does appear to be looking around the palace as if appraising it. They are being discreetly followed by the ghost squad."

Thomas waited patiently for his turn. "Highness," he began, "Geoffrey reported that a ship was stopped before it reached the harbor. They boarded and searched it; it is still there. He sent word asking what do you want him to do?"

Thomas leaned back in his chair and crossed his legs. "The ship had about seventy-five sailors on it. No cargo. He is not allowing them to disembark until he hears from you. I got this message as I was leaving my room." He leaned over to his brother and touched him on the arm. "One more thing, he asked the captain where his cargo was and if they were picking up a shipment. The captain had no feasible answer. He said if Geoffrey had any more questions he would have to speak with the duke."

The King slammed his hand against the table. "Who does this man think he is dealing with. I'm not a child king anymore," Sean fairly shouted. "Thomas, I want this captain brought to the northern garrison and questioned until he talks. Have someone who knows how to get at the truth, someone who can control himself and not get carried away. He must know when to stop. The man may not know anything."

"I know just the man. I'll be right back," he told them.

Thomas got up and left for about five minutes. When he came back, he told them he sent for Lord Chaney's man. He was a Candean refugee who hated King Sardin. King Sardin had wooed his daughter and ruined her. After he refused to marry her when she got pregnant, she committed suicide. Her name was Camille. She was eighteen, the last living relative of Lord James Stanley, former Earl of Landsend. The King asked Lord Hamilton if the duke was going to be in the dining hall tonight.

"He is there already, Highness," he replied. "His friends are seated beside him."

The King did not like being tested; he felt this was one. He allowed his rage at everything Candean boil over inside him. Sean stood up abruptly, overturning his chair. His face was livid. Thomas looked down to his hands and saw that Sean was tightening and relaxing his fists repeatedly. It had been a long time since he had seen his brother like this.

Sean turned his back to the group, trying to collect himself. He would not go into a rage as his father was prone to do.

Lords Hamilton and Hightower looked to Thomas for help. After all, the King was his brother. Thomas motioned for them to leave the room. He wanted to be alone with Sean. Both bowed to the King and prince and left the room quietly.

Thomas stood up and went to where Sean was standing. He put his hand on his brother's shoulder. "I know how you feel, and we both harbor deep feelings against Bolwin. We both remember that he was one of the suspected spies living here before the war. We were unable to prove our suspicions about him though."

Sean turned to look Thomas in the eye. The prince continued, "You and I together will not waver in this. We will ferret out the stink here and extinguish it once and for all. You are the responsible one, remember? That's why you are eighteen months older and King." At this, Sean smiled at him. Thomas smiled back and said, "I don't know how to calm you down. That's your job with me the hothead, and let's not change positions this late in life."

With that said Sean responded, "Well, let's not keep them waiting brother."

They left the room with arms on each other's shoulder, letting all who would see, that they were a united front. It did not go unnoticed.

As the King and prince entered the hall, the assembled nobles and visiting dignitaries stood until they were seated. All sat down and the King apologized to his table guest for his tardiness.

The King's table was made in the shape of a cross. In the upper portion where the King sat, the prince and any visiting royalty also sat there. Also included in this honor were dignitaries that were representing kingdoms important to Fastonia's trade or a personal friend of either the King or prince.

Tonight seated were Lords Hightower and Hamilton, the prince from neighboring Mayfair with his wife and Thomas' friends Sir Adam Downing and Colin, Lord Firth. Their cousin Henry, Lord Stowell, along with his wife Cynthia was also present. There were still several open seats, but the King was not in the mood for a large crowd. He was mentally preparing himself for tomorrow night when Duke Bolwin would sit with him and Thomas. He needed a reprieve from his reptilian face.

The meal progressed as normal. Prince Kristoff of Mayfair was a very entertaining fellow. He was about three years older than Sean and the heir to his father's kingdom. He and his wife Princess Edwina were frequent visitors to Fastonia. If Sean had a best friend, Kristoff would be it. They had a lot in common.

Duke Bolwin stood up and made a toast to the King's continued good health.

All arose with goblets held high shouting, "TO THE KING!"

Sean acknowledged the toast with a smile and a nodding of his head.

Thomas whispered to him, "Do you think the duke seeks to mollify you with this very obvious display?"

"Yes I do, he knows that I am not pleased with this early visit. We will see what brews with him in the morning. He has been given an appointment for eleven. Then we lunch together and you must be there."

At this, Thomas started shaking his head no. "I know that you do not normally appear at the noon time meal, but it will be very informal and short. Think you can get away from your lady friend early? Your King needs you."

"Excuse me, sire." Thomas was purposely teasing. "Since when did you need the services of a lowly prince such as myself?"

"Come, brother, give over. You know I need your opinion." Sean smiled at him.

"Well, since you put it that way, I'll be here."

Sean leaned over to Thomas and whispered, "but will your lady friend let you?"

"Sean, when have I ever allowed a woman to dictate anything to me, let alone whether I join my elder brother in a meal? Methinks, she may have a husband, but husband or no, she'll be kicked out of bed before sunrise."

"How do you do it, Tommy? Shouldn't you have asked her if she was married?"

"Well, if she is, shouldn't she worry about that and not me? I'm not the one that's married."

Sean burst into laughter, and slapped Thomas on the back. "Tommy, one day, someone is going to put a dagger in your back. There are dozens of single ladies here that you can choose from. Look there's Lady Jane. She's pretty enough. She's petite and has nice figure. I've seen her looking at you several times. Why not dance with her tonight?"

Thomas answered him, "the only reason she looks at me is because she wants a husband, I am not husband material right now. Wait until I'm through having fun, then we'll see. What about you, big brother? Why don't you marry?"

Sean pretended his feelings were hurt and made a face. "Why did you have to ruin a perfect evening, bringing that up? You know the women that the council has proposed for me or either too plump or too skinny. I think I need younger men on this marriage council."

Thomas almost fell over laughing so hard that he had to wipe tears from his eyes,

Sean just shook his head. "Well, Prince Thomas, since you are being so rude in bringing up that dead subject again, I will let you be for now." With that, Sean turned to engage Prince Kristoff in conversation.

The remainder of the evening went the way that most did. There was dancing in the ballroom. This was the time the young looked forward to. The single ladies of the court kept a constant buzz around Thomas. They figured he had to marry someone, why not try to make it happen while dancing? The King was less accessible. It was already a given that he would have to marry someone to benefit the kingdom. They expected that he would marry soon. Fastonia was rich enough. Sean didn't have to marry for money. His kingdom was in no financial trouble. They owed money to no country. His military might was well known. One would have to be a fool to attack them, especially by sea. He wanted to marry most because he needed an heir, if he and his wife cared for each other that would be a plus.

The King had managed to avoid Duke Bolwin most of the night until he was cornered near his chair. "Your Highness, may I speak with you for a moment?" he asked. Sean nodded his head.

The duke began with apologizing for the untimely visit and thanked him for being able to see him tomorrow.

Thomas watched from across the room. He'd been trying to get away from Lady Jane and Lady Margaret all night. His brother was always a good excuse. After all, he was the King. No one could say no. By the time he got there, Bolwin had departed.

"What did he want, Sean?"

"Well, he wanted to thank me for seeing him even though they were not expected. As usual, just looking at him made me want to slice him from head to toe. He is up to something. I saw you talking to Charles, did you learn anything?"

"Charles does not know why they came early. He said he asked the duke, but he was vague. The vagueness is not unusual. He's always like that. Charles always knows about the offers that King Sardin has given Bolwin to make, but not this time. He is perplexed. I still believe he doesn't know what they are up to."

They started walking around the ballroom, nodding to people and shaking hands as they made their way back to the throne.

"Bolwin may have asked him to come because he always comes. It would be strange if he didn't. Besides, Charles is a strong sword arm in case of a fight. Bolwin couldn't skewer anyone face to face. Martin Beaumont is just strong with no skill. Charles did tell me he wanted a private audience with you as soon as it could be arranged. He will make an appointment with your secretary in the morning."

"Do you know what he wants to talk about, Thomas?"

"No, he didn't say, but he looked strange."

"Where is Lord Beaumont? I haven't seen him for some time," the King asked.

"I don't know. The ghost squad is following him, I expect a report from them in the morning. I'll bring it with me to give to you before the noon meal." As Thomas spoke he was looking around the room for Beaumont himself. He was not in the ballroom. One could only wonder what he was up to. The ghost squad was good. They would be able to find him and keep him under surveillance.

"Sire, first thing in the morning the captains will make their reports. A scout will be sent right after sunrise from each of the checkpoints utilizing our relay system. Once the reports are at hand; if there is anything to report, I'll get it to you immediately. But they are smart. We haven't had a war on land in eighteen years. Nothing but peace and prosperity."

They had made it back to the throne. Sean sprawled his frame in the chair. He was restless tonight. He didn't know what was wrong with him.

"Sardin thinks that we have grown fat and lazy, ripe for the picking. Instead, we have grown stronger since father died. You have strengthened our coastline with an additional castle on the southern coast. We've built a fortress on the border of each of our neighbors, we are safer," Thomas finished.

"Everything you said is true. We can but only wait for them to show their hand. I'm going to close the dancing tonight. I am tired of all these smiling faces. What I need from you brother is for you to meet me in the garden. Bring your rapier. I have a need to fight tonight. You had best bring your chest plate."

BOOK TWO
CHAPTER FOUR

Sean and Thomas had breakfast together that morning on the balcony overlooking the garden. The atmosphere at the table was less than happy. Both brothers had their minds on Duke Bolwin and the wounded Sir Benjamin.

They enjoyed a good and vigorous workout last evening. Sean was antagonistic during the whole time that they were fencing. For once, Thomas was not trying to outdo him. He knew that his brother had a lot of frustration to work off. He allowed Sean to be the aggressor. He just gave him the avenue he needed, so that he could make better judgment calls in the days to come. He didn't want his brother to make a bad decision and later regret it because he was so angry.

The King and his brother went to Thomas' military compound office to await the incoming reports. The scouts reported seeing a build up of troops on the border with Candea. The Candeans, when asked told them that they were playing war games. It was a brand new unit of farmers that didn't know how to fight a war. They were teaching them how to protect themselves. When asked from whom, the officer said from anyone that attacked them. They were told that King Sardin was trying to show the farmers how to protect his borders.

With the supposed war games on the border and the ship that had not been allowed to dock, they were convinced that there was a conspiracy under foot. Prince Thomas sent word to Lord Chaney to camp as close to the border as possible in plain site. He was to have several ghost squad members' camp on the Candean side of the border. They knew to run a cold camp.

Soon after the scouts left with their new orders, the King and prince went to check on Sir Benjamin. He was awake at last and taking a little broth from the physician. When Sir Benjamin saw the King walk through the doorway, he tried to rise up but fell back upon the bed. Sean went immediately to his bedside.

"No, Sir Benjamin, lie still, you are grievously wounded."

"Your Majesty, I regret that I cannot get up to greet you proper. This is a great honor that you pay me. I am afraid that I failed you and the prince. I did not see my attackers' faces for they wore masks," Sir Benjamin told them.

Prince Thomas asked him, "How is it that you were alone when you were attacked? We always ride in twos."

"Sir Robert Temple awoke ill that morning, and there was no one in which to be paired with in so short a time. So, I thought that it would be fine if I rode alone; it is always peaceful on the particular route that we patrol. They came out of nowhere. I didn't see them until two of them jumped from above me. I believe that there were five altogether, two were killed."

Thomas looked to Sean. "Yes, we found traces of blood and a slight trail that looked as if someone had been dragged. They were trying to cover their tracks. The trail that we followed ended abruptly."

The King asked Sir Benjamin how he felt and told him not to worry about anything that all would be taken care of. Benjamin inquired if his brother had been told and was told that he had. Thomas told him that Geoffrey would be in to see him as soon as he finished his duty in the harbor. Benjamin was exhausted and they left him in the physician's care.

"Thomas, I must go and open court now and speak with Lord Hightower. If anything else happens, please come to me."

"I will, Sean, never fear," Thomas responded.

The King went first to Lord Hightower's office. Edmund rose up, bowed to the King, and offered him tea. "No thank you, Edmund, please sit." Lord Hightower sat back down behind his working table. "Exactly what are the terms of Candea's present contract with us?"

"Sire," he began, "the Candeans pay the highest tribute of fifteen percent per ship."

"Fifteen percent is a large amount," Sean said, "but they should be happy that I allow them to use our ports at all. We will let the duke make his pitch in thirty minutes. I will allow him to think that whatever he presents to me, I will take it under consideration. Thomas is having our infantry camp as close to the border as possible."

The King walked around Edmund's office. He felt cornered. There had to be something with a physical release for him to do today. *Ah, Lady Deborah is back in the palace tonight,* he thought.

"Your Highness," Edmund interrupted his thoughts.

"I'm sorry, yes. I was talking about the prince. He sent a rider to the northern garrison. There the instructions will be sent via falcon to Lord Chaney. We sent scouts earlier with a message, but this intelligence will place several of the ghost squad commanders in the Candean palace with instructions to slit Sardin's throat if war breaks out. I will take no chances and let him live if war occurs, my decision is final." As he said this Lord Hightower stood and approached him.

"Sire, I understand how you feel, I really do. But are you sure that you want to take this type of action?" Edmund asked him.

"I am positive. He will not live out the remainder of this year if there is aggression against Fastonia. Not this time, I will not yield!"

Looking at the King as he said this, Edmund thought he was seeing a ghost of King Phillip in Sean. Lord Hightower really looked at his King, and for the first time he saw that, he was a boy King no more. He was a man full grown, full of the righteousness of his convictions. He would not falter in his duty.

"You have but to command, Highness, all will be done according to your will." He realized that Sean had actually surpassed his father. He seemed more regal than either the prince or the former king. All was as it should be, Edmund was proud of his protégé.

The duke appeared promptly at eleven, accompanied by Lord Ainsley and Lord Beaumont. The king was sitting on the throne looking very much in command. Prince Thomas was sitting in his seat on Sean's right just one step below the King. Duke Bolwin approached with many important looking papers in his hand. The trio bowed low to the King, then Richard Bolwin stepped up to the throne alone.

"Your Highness, thank you for seeing me, I know that we were unexpected. We apologize for this untimely and early visit to Fastonia. The king of Candea wishes to convey his thanks to you on allowing this early renegotiation of our contract with your kingdom. It is asked that you consider lowering the tribute that we pay per ship by five percent."

Sean asked, "Why would I want to do that? We have an excellent contract with Candea. It is very lucrative for Fastonia."

The duke turned pink at the comment from the King. "Well, Your Highness, we are trying to improve the lives of our peasants. King Sardin is determined that if he made things better for the working class, they would stop leaving

Candea for Fastonia, Mayfair or Saint John. We are losing too many of our citizens. It is thought the extra five percent per ship that we could save could be used to clean out the disease infected quarters of our townships. We would even like to try and help build cottages for the farmers as you have done here," he finished at last.

Sean looked through him and said, "That is an admirable task that King Sardin has set. What really brought about this turn in ideology?"

The duke was at a lost for words, he never expected Sean to question the Candean King's good intentions. He thought because Sean was a young man and had never been tested that he was too soft to rule and would jump at the chance to help Candea change. He was sadly mistaken. He and Sardin had misjudged Sean's character completely.

Thomas looked up at his brother. He knew how Sean felt about the people, anyone's people. *So, this is the reason they were going to use as their cover. Bolwin knew if Sean had a weak spot, it would the people. But this new Sean, this one is a force to be reckoned with.* The King looked at his brother and stared into his eyes with purpose. He knew Thomas thought he would forget everything because Bolwin talked about the people.

Thomas stood up and looked at the duke. "Excuse us for a moment, Duke Bolwin, I must speak with the King."

The duke and his companions bowed and backed away a little.

"Sean, you seem different somehow. What is it?"

"You know, Tommy, I've never flexed my royal muscles before." He smiled at his brother. "I think that it's about time I did. I will not forget our purpose, do not worry. I know that this is a ruse to try and sway me. I will tell them that we need time to go over their proposal with the finance minister."

As the brothers were speaking quietly to each other, Duke Bolwin made eye contact with Lord Carrington who was standing to the King's left. Lord Carrington quickly looked away. He wasn't sure anymore that he wanted to go through with his part in this scheme to kill Prince Thomas. The prince had slept with his young wife and gotten her pregnant. His wife Cassandra told him the prince didn't know she carried his child. Thomas had probably forgotten about her. She was just another feather in his crown. Now he was going to be forced to accept a child that was not his to save face. He was twenty-five years older than his wife. He hadn't been able to get her with child. Now to his shame, the prince who didn't even remember his Cassie restored his honor.

Lord Stowell was standing farther away from the King. He watched the eye game between Bolwin and Carrington. He was sure that they knew each other, but the way Carrington turned his head it was as if he was guilty of something. Lord Henry Stowell decided he would keep an eye on the two of them. He wasn't privy to the information the King had. If he knew that Sean suspected something, he would have reported what he witnessed. He and the King grew up together. Family always looked out for one another even if the other was King. He did not like what he saw. If Carrington was making outside deals with Candea, he would report it.

Sean and Thomas pulled apart. The Duke moved up closer to them and waited.

"Duke Bolwin," the King began, "we need time to look at your proposal, and we will meet with Lord Hightower this afternoon. As you know, if we do this, it will not take effect until the present contract expires."

"Yes, Highness, that was the main reason for our early visit to give you time. We will await your decision. We have been ordered to stay as long as you deemed it necessary. I am at your service."

"Duke, you and your companions will be my guest tonight at the evening meal, I will see you then." Sean thought the interview was over but Bolwin asked him a further question.

"Your Highness, may I beg a favor from you?"

"Yes of course you can," Sean answered him.

"I have a person traveling with us who feels indebted to me. I would like to bring this person to your table. I helped save my friend's life and my friend is trying to repay me."

"Who is your guest?"

"Well, Your Highness, I am not at liberty to say in public. My friend's life was at stake once, so I try to be extra careful."

Thomas intervened, "Is this person a risk to my brother's well being and safety?"

"Oh no, Your Highness, not to anyone here. In my friend's country there was a civil war, it was not safe there any longer. I will explain further when we arrive if you will allow it."

"That is acceptable to us. It seems that I am allowing many things this day," the King finished.

Bolwin and his party bowed and backed a way a little, then turned to leave. As they were leaving, two of them had smiles on their faces. Bolwin looked around for Carrington but the sniffling weasel was gone. Lord Stowell didn't miss a thing.

Court was dismissed for the day. Sean and Thomas went to Lord Hightower's office to find Lord Hamilton already there. The proposal was discussed slightly. Everyone knew that King Sardin didn't care about his people. All he wanted was money. His peasants were the poorest in the region they were heavily taxed; all who could leave Candea did. They migrated to all the neighboring kingdoms. There were so many people coming to Fastonia they had to limit the number who were allowed to migrate there. Sean tried his best to keep his villages and towns from being overcrowded. If more people came, their low crime rate could increase.

The King decided he would wait and see how patient Bolwin could be. He was not known for his patience. Time would tell and soon Sean thought.

Thomas ran into Bolwin in the King's gallery. The duke was admiring Sean's collection of weapons, both present and past. There were battle-axes, big and small, a collection of swords from around the world. The King was able to have a sampling of the finest Toledo blades and daggers that money could buy. The blades and daggers were engraved with beautiful drawings. The prize piece of the collection was a special ceremonial sword belonging to a Templar Knight from the Crusades. There were shields of every size, shape and design. On the opposite wall were expensive Persian rugs and paintings. One look at the gallery and you knew that this was a very rich king. Duke Bolwin had to stop himself from drooling.

Thomas watched him as his greedy eyes took in all the treasures. One could almost see him calculate how much each piece was worth.

"Do you like my brother's collection Duke?" Thomas asked as he walked up to him.

"Yes, Prince Thomas, it appears to be priceless," was his answer. The duke turned toward Thomas and bowed, "Your Highness, if you were King, would you collect such things?"

The question caught Thomas by surprise. He answered him that he did not know what he would collect if anything. Then the duke asked him a strange question.

"Prince, if you could, would you be King?"

Thomas looked him directly in the eyes. "What man hasn't thought about being a king. I would be lying if I said otherwise. But here in this kingdom, my brother Sean is the rightful ruler."

The duke replied, "I hear that only eighteen months separate the two of you. That's not much for a man who would be king." With that said, he backed a few steps away, turned and left. Thomas was speechless and staring at his back.

The prince turned on his kneels trying to digest what the duke said to him. He hurriedly caught up with him and asked him what was he trying to imply?

Bowing to Thomas he said, "Your Highness, it is well known in certain circles that you wish to be king. I am not trying to imply that you wish your brother harm; but that you could put Fastonia's immense wealth to better use than this collection of weapons."

"Duke, you tread on dangerous ground now; if we weren't in the King's Gallery, I would run you through as if you were a wild boar. But the King would be upset if blood splattered on his Persian rugs. I would take this as a warning if I were you." Thomas' reply was very soft spoken and controlled. That should have made the duke pause instead of further inflaming him, but it didn't.

Instead Bolwin unwisely said, "Then, young prince, if I were you I'd watch my friends."

Almost before Bolwin closed his mouth, Thomas' sword was at his throat, barely nicking the pale flesh with the point of his blade. "Consider yourself lucky this day that there is pressing business that I must attend to. If there was not, I would be wiping your blood from my blade unto your shirt."

With this said, Thomas sheathed his sword, as he walked away. "I'm sure we will have another chance to finish this conversation."

The duke stared after him wondering if the prince could be used in one of his plans if only temporary, until he was of no further use. Maybe, he should just be killed outright instead of holding him for a supposed ransom. Both brothers were going to die, in what order still had not been figured out yet.

After Thomas left Bolwin he wondered who could have spread that tale. Could it have been an associate? He only partially opened up to his friends. He tried to never let his guard down, because of rumors like this one. He was never serious when he said that he wanted to be King. He didn't think he was, but if Sean died without issue, he would be King. They had been getting alone so much better due in part to this crisis. His brother always tried to be friends with him, but the problem was within himself. He was jealous of Sean. There he had admitted it, this was a first. He never realized it before, but he was. Sean had been groomed to be King all his life. He would not step down for anything. He was the rightful heir.

As Thomas walked to the military compound to check on Sir Benjamin, he realized he did not want to be King. He just wanted it because it was Sean's right. He did not want all that responsibility, paperwork and meetings. If he were King, when would he have time to visit all his lady friends? That was enough for him. Nothing could interfere with his pleasure.

It would be best for Sean to remain King. He doesn't seem to mind all the work. I must speak with my comrades though, someone was talking out of turn and it must stop now.

Thomas walked into Sir Benjamin's room to look in on him. He was asleep again, but the physician said that was good. He was regaining his strength little at a time, but he must rest. Prince Thomas thought again about his conversation with Duke Bolwin. He wondered if a group of malcontents wanted to try and use him to remove his brother. It must be that group of northern lords that wanted more land. The only way more land could be gained would be through a war with Candea or Mayfair.

That was absurd. Sean was a good king even better than his father. He had foresight and wisdom where his father was more military minded. Old King Phillip expanded their borders to their present boundaries. Sean strengthened all borders; no land holding had been lost under his rule. Castles had been built along their borders with all kingdoms, even friendly ones. Their coastline defense had been strengthened also. There were more warships now and more in the planning stages. No one dared to encroach onto their territory.

The only wars Fastonia had in the last eighteen years were on the sea with pirates. Thomas had to find out what was really going on. He wondered if Bolwin was trying to conquer their kingdom by making Sean wonder about him. That would separate them and could throw the kingdom into a civil war. That must not happen; for then, they really would be easy pickings.

BOOK TWO
CHAPTER FIVE

The dining hall was overflowing with guest for the King's hospitality was well known. All nobles that could come did come. This was the place to be if one had daughters of marriageable age for there were plenty of eligible young men. There would be dancing afterwards and all the young women who aimed high; were trying to dance with either the King or the prince. These two brothers were the most eligible bachelors in the kingdom.

The King and prince walked into the room and a hush fell over the assembled company as they all bowed or curtsied at the same time. Sean's taking his seat was the sign for everyone to be seated. The King's favorite music was being played softly from the balcony in the dining hall. Conversations restarted as the servers made their way to the tables.

Lady Deborah commented to her friend, "Look, I told you the King is interested in me. Did you not see him smile in my direction?"

Lady Elizabeth wanted to say no, but instead she said, "Are you sure you can capture his heart? He has never been in love or so it is believed."

"I'm sure I can. Look at me, I'm beautiful. If you were a man, wouldn't you want me?"

Lady Elizabeth choked on her original answer and required some water. She thought to herself that if she were a man, she would run as fast as possible.

As Sean and Thomas were seated, he noticed that Bolwin's place was empty. The King turned towards Lord Ainsley and inquired about the duke's absence.

"Charles, is the duke ill? I have never known him to be late for anything?"

"No, Your Highness, last I heard, he was on the dock looking for one of Candea's ships."

Sean kicked Thomas under the table. The prince started paying attention to their conversation; he was watching Lady Mary Hadley quite closely. Her brother, Earl Patrick was an acquaintance of Sean's.

Mmm, he thought, *she sure seems to have grown up since I last saw her…"* he looked toward Sean as casually as possible. He didn't have to kick him so hard.

The King asked, "Charles, is there anything that I can do to help?"

"Thank you, Highness, I'm sure the duke has everything under control by now."

Charles didn't know that he had given them a small clue. No Candean ship was expected in port. The dock master kept excellent records. Their next ship was not expected for another four weeks. This missing ship's hold was empty. They did not pick up goods in Fastonia. They brought them there to be loaded into their wagons. The only thing that was bought from Fastonia was supplies for a voyage. The ships were always loaded to the brim when they made port.

The questioning of the ship's captain proved fruitless. He didn't know anything. Sean slowly shifted his eyes to Lord Beaumont, but he lowered his head to hide the lie in his eyes.

Once the meal started, Bolwin walked into the dining hall followed by a slight figure with bowed head. She was wearing a beautifully simple rose-colored gown with a matching scarf covering her hair. The scarf was held in place by a circlet of dark pink tea roses. As they approach the King's table, everyone had stopped talking and was staring openly at them. Bolwin bowed low to the king while the woman curtsied. He made his apologies for being late.

"Your Highness, please forgive my lateness. I was in a meeting and had to go and get my guest."

Sean's heart skipped a beat. He waved him off. He must see this woman's face clearly. "Who do we have here?" the King asked.

That was the question that was going through most of the assembled guests' minds, especially the men. She looked to be a shapely woman from what he could see of her figure.

"Your Highness, I would like to introduce the Lady Me'na, daughter of the late King of Marrak," Bolwin supplied.

Me'na curtsied again to Sean. As she rose up, she looked into his eyes and he was instantly awestruck with her beauty. She smiled sweetly at him. She did not know that she could be a pawn used to over throw his kingdom.

"Please, Lady Me'na, sit here next to me."

The King called over an attendant to move her place settings to his left. Prince Thomas was sitting directly across from her. Duke Bolwin was forgotten as he found his own seat at the table.

"Lady Me'na, this is my brother, Prince Thomas," was the reluctant introduction.

Thomas got up and went around the table to her. "Lady, it is my pleasure. Welcome to our country," he replied as he lifted up her hand to kiss her palm. Sean rolled his eyes upward as Thomas made a fool of himself.

"Thank you, Prince Thomas. I feel very fortunate to be here," was the soft reply.

Everyone in the hall was watching the exchange until Sean fixed them with a royal stare.

Thomas took his seat across form her and made Me'na uncomfortable with his stare. She thought, *My God, the King is the most magnetic man I have ever met. I feel as if I'm being pulled to him and I have no self- control. He is so handsome with those green eyes and those ridiculously long lashes. Heart, please slow down. Hands, do not betray me and tremble.*

Sean started to talk to her, but she was so mesmerized by his lips that she was not sure she heard him. "My apologizes, Your Highness, could you say again, the splendor of your palace has taken my breath away."

That was the best Me'na could do. She couldn't say that watching your lips form words intoxicated her, could she?

Thomas was watching the byplay across from him. He didn't want Sean to get her.

While Me'na was apologizing, the King thought, *Those eyes, they are the color of amber. I could easily get lost in their depths. Such a perfect oval face, skin the color of pale gold with hair a dark brown, a naturally perfect contrast.*

Duke Bolwin eagerly watched what he knew would happen. Her uniqueness would at first intrigue any man, but he saved her for the King. She was going to be a means to an end, maybe the catalyst the he needed to separate the brothers. Bolwin did not tell the King that he had made her a virtual slave. Her brother gave her to him to kill, but he soon found a better use for her: to lure King Winslow into a trap.

Sean had never seen a woman like her before. He was physically keeping himself from kissing those cherry-colored lips. He asked her if she was a Nubian. There were many Nubians in his country, but none looked as she did.

"Your Highness, I am almost a pure-blooded Nubian. My mother was half Nubian. She died delivering me."

"I am sorry to remind you of that. Tell me about your country. I have heard of it," he said.

"Father brought my brother and I to many small countries. He started out as a mercenary when he was a young man. He was in control of the last country in which we lived most of my life. He claimed himself King of Marrak for the last twelve years. I am not sure where exactly I was born but I can never go back to Marrak." She lowered her voice. Sean did not mind leaning closer to her so he could hear.

"Micah, my brother, overthrew our father. He was killed in the civil war that occurred. After everything was over, the order was given for me to be executed by the insurgents who supported him. I was taken away before that could happen."

"You are safe here with us. I'll not have you harmed," Sean reassured her.

At this point in the conversation, Duke Bolwin interjected quietly, "I found her fighting for her life in an alley behind the palace, and we rescued her. Then she was brought to Candea. King Sardin does not have a grand palace such as this one, Highness, or have many visiting diplomats or princes from other kingdoms as you do. It was thought that maybe she could find something here in Fastonia that is exciting and fun for one so young. That is if you would grant her asylum here."

All the while, the duke was speaking in a low voice. Everyone was trying to hear what was being said. Sean looked up to the balcony and signaled for the musicians to continue playing. The sound would drown out their conversation.

The duke continued. "I was going to speak with you privately about my plans on the morrow. She is a princess born and must be treated as such," he finished.

"Agreed, all proprieties will be afforded her," Sean answered Bolwin but was looking at Me'na.

Thomas was trying to find something to say, anything at all. It was the first time in his life that he was tongue-tied. Sean didn't seem to be having that problem.

The King turned his full attention to her, forgetting the rest of his guests. The men at the table fully understood why. This was a unique woman, very beautiful. To look at her made them feel as if they were on fire and wanted to burn. He could be excused for this for they wanted to be in his place.

Bolwin tried hard to drink his wine without choking. He was ecstatic. It seemed that both brothers would vie for her attention. That was good. If brothers wouldn't fight for one reason, they would fight over the love of the same woman. That was a given, at least to his way of thinking. It was bad enough that the little beggar wouldn't let him come near her without trying to claw out his eyes. She had better be good tonight or he would give her precious virginity to his men.

This is good, this is very good, he thought.

Duke Bolwin did not want Thomas to talk to Me'na tonight. He wanted Sean to be fully enamored of her. He turned toward the prince and started a conversation, asking questions that he already knew the answers to. He got Charles involved in the talk. He knew Thomas respected Charles. If he could get the conversation around to horses, Charles would never shut up. He loved horses they were his passion. Now that he had all the men talking about which horse made the best warhorse. The king had time to be captivated by Me'na, he thought. Bolwin looked over at Martin and smirked.

Lord Henry Stowell was in attendance at the King's table tonight. He merely watched who looked at whom. His wife Cynthia tried talking to him but to no avail. She gave up and engaged Princess Edwina in conversation. Henry was sure an undercurrent was at work here. He would just sit and silently watch his cousin's back.

The King continued to talk to Me'na in low tones, asking her questions about likes, dislikes and anything he could think of. He wanted to continue listening to her voice. She was feeling the same way about him. Me'na was very nervous. She had never met anyone like Sean before. He actually listened to her, really listened and asked the appropriate questions. This was the first time in her life she felt drawn to a man. If she didn't know better, she'd say that she was falling in love. But, she had no idea what love was like, having never experienced man-woman love before.

The King on the other hand, knew what he was feeling because he had not felt like this before. He'd had feelings before, but they were shallow. All it took was one little fault on the woman's part and he was ready to discard her. But now, he wanted to protect this woman, love this woman. He had only known her for the last hour and a half, but it felt like a lifetime. Somehow, he knew this was real. He had to find out if she was feeling any of the emotions that he felt. But how could he find out what he needed to know?

Then it came to him, he would end the meal and go into the ballroom to start the dancing. If he could but hold her in his arms and feel her heartbeat, he would have his answer. The King stood up and declared that the meal had come to an end and it was time to enjoy the remainder of the evening dancing.

Finally, Thomas thought. *Maybe I will be able to dance with her since Sean has appointed himself her personal guide.*

As the King led the crowd into the ballroom, he made sure that Me'na's hand was on his arm. He planned on dancing with her exclusively, no matter how hard Thomas would try to worm his way in. The orchestra began to play the King's favorite song. He swept Me'na literally off her feet.

She felt so bubbly and alive for the first time in years. Duke Bolwin had kept her a virtual slave to him for some months. She prayed an escape for her could be found here in Fastonia.

Sean on the other hand was not thinking about anything. He had his answer. Her heart was beating so fast, if it had wings, she would fly away. The King had in no way felt this clumsy with a woman before. He was known for being detached. He didn't want rumors to start about him with different women especially since everyone in the region knew that his counselors were looking for a wife for him. He wanted to have a serious relationship, but he was also afraid to lose his heart. He had seen how some women trampled over men's hearts when they felt their catch was securely in their nets. Now within a couple of hours, all that had changed. He couldn't wait to have a relationship with her.

Neither Sean nor Me'na realized that they were still the only couple dancing in the middle of the room. Everyone else was watching. They looked like cupid had made them for each other. All assembled, could feel the aura that surrounded them. Lady Deborah in particular.

Prince Thomas was trying to get away from Lady Constance when he realized that the best way to get close to Me'na was to dance with someone else. He escorted Constance onto the floor. Once he was dancing, everyone took it as a signal to dance.

Thomas danced with Constance only a short time as the song was ending. He missed his chance to dance close to Sean. As the song ended, Sean held Me'na as tightly as he could without raising eyebrows. He waited for the next song to begin. Thomas escorted Lady Constance back to her group of friends. He turned around to see Sean start to dance with Me'na again.

No, no, he thought, *I've got to get to them.*

He rushed onto the dance floor, tapped his brother on the shoulder, and asked for a dance. Thomas was the only one that would even think to tap the King. Sean narrowed his eyes at him and asked Me'na if she minded.

"I would be happy to dance with you, Prince Thomas," she replied a little breathless.

The King asked Lady Mary for a dance so that he could be close to Me'na and Thomas.

The prince looked at Me'na with the happiest look that he could muster and said, "I have a feeling that you are going to be the most popular lady here tonight." She blushed at his comment. "I wanted to dance with you before all the other suitors came."

"Prince Thomas, do you really think that other men will want to dance with me? I'm just a country girl," she said.

At that, Thomas laughed a little too loudly. He did that for Sean's benefit. With any other woman, he would have thought that she was fishing for compliments, but not her. She appeared to genuinely not realize how beautiful she was.

Amazing, simply amazing, Thomas thought.

"Yes, Princess, they will come to you, eagerly awaiting their turn."

"You do not have to call me princess. It is not necessary. Lady is fine with me," she told him.

"Whatever you wish. I will comply." Thomas smiled.

For the next several hours, only a few other men got a chance to dance with Me'na. Sean and Thomas would not allow anyone else the opportunity. All around the room, the ladies noticed how taken with the newcomer both Winslow brothers were. There was much whispering and gawking at the exhibit before them. Never had anyone seen the King so taken with one woman as he was with her. Prince Thomas was always taken with someone, at least once a week, but this was different. Both brothers were after the same woman, not only the Winslows, but also their beaus.

Finally, as the evening came to a close, Sean and Me'na were dancing together when she complained of being overheated. They were dancing close to the balcony.

"Your Highness, would you escort me outside onto the balcony? I feel as if I cannot breath."

"Certainly, forgive me for not thinking of this sooner. Let's go at once."

He had wanted so much to ask her to go on the balcony earlier, but he didn't want to pressure her, didn't want to ruin anything. The palace servants opened the double doors for the pair to step out into the night.

The guests were leaving through the main entrance and couldn't wait to get outside and talk about the King and the newcomer. Duke Bolwin watched them go through the doors. He was feeling very pleased with himself tonight. The King had barely left her side all evening. Now that he had dangled her in front of his nose, he would let them grow close before he tried anything. King Sardin had given him several plans to use, if one didn't work, there was always Carrington. That alone should work, at least it would allow him to capture the prince and spread rumors or kill him.

He wanted the King to think that his brother was trying to overthrow him and cause a civil war. Once the war started, he would gain control with all the confusion that it would cause. If he gained control of Winslow Town, it was only a matter of time before the rest of the country came around. The ship out in the harbor was not allowed to dock. It didn't matter. It was a decoy anyway. His men were coming aboard another ship bound for Fastonia from faraway Timbre. They would be here on the last night of the moon's final quarter. *Only a few more days* he thought.

The duke started laughing to himself as several onlookers hunched their shoulders and looked at each other.

Out on the balcony, it was a very different setting. The King had a chair brought out for Me'na to sit upon and catch her breath. She stood up and declared that she was fine now. She told him that she had to get back to Bolwin. She said she didn't want to make him upset any further.

"Why should his being upset matter to you, my dear?" he asked.

"I am beholding to him." She spoke so quietly he had to bend closer to hear her. "He says that I owe him because my brother threw me away. I must repay my debt to him then he will release me. He has fed and clothed me. These are things that cannot be repaid easily. I will work for him until he is paid."

Sean's face turned red with his fury. He could not believe that the duke with all his egotism would make a princess repay him with physical labor. It was unheard of.

"My Lady, you will stay here under my protection. You have nothing more to fear or repay. I will see to it that your debt is repaid to him." Sean just couldn't believe it. What kind of a monster was Bolwin anyway? But, this sounded just like that vile little man.

Me'na placed her hand on his sleeve. "Your Highness, if you do that, then I will owe you. I will be forever repaying someone." She hung her head in despair. Sean picked up both of her hands and held them in his warm grasp. He kissed her hands so tenderly that Me'na's eyes watered with unshed tears at his kindness. There was a lump in her throat that she could not swallow.

"Me'na, I will grant you asylum here in Fastonia. That way you are not beholden to anyone. With asylum comes food, clothing, and a suite in the palace. It is yours for the taking,"

Sean looked so earnest, she started to cry. Me'na curtsied to her new liege, took his hand and pressed it to her face. Sean's whole demeanor changed. He began to tremble at the feel of her skin on his. The tears on his hand humbled him. He hurriedly helped her to rise up. He wasn't sure how much more he could stand this night. He was head over heels in love with this unpretentious woman.

As she stood up, Sean opened his arms; she went into them as if she had been doing it her whole life. She relaxed in his embrace and turned her face up to his. His mouth came down on hers gently; as if the others that he had kissed before was only a rehearsal for her.

This was her first kiss and she didn't know what to do next. So, she stood there and leaned into him ever so slightly; which made him hold her closer and her moan. Abruptly, she pulled away from the kiss. Me'na didn't know what to make of these new emotions rushing through her, they scared her a bit.

"I'm sorry, I didn't mean to force you into anything that you are not ready for Me'na," Sean apologized.

"No, Your Highness, you didn't. I am an unschooled woman in the art of male, female relationships. I never had a mother to teach me the things that I should know. I am the one that's sorry, I'm sure my kiss was as a child's, you must be disappointed," she said.

Sean's heart leapt for joy. He thought that he reviled her, but that was not the case. "No, not in the least. It was gentle kiss, completely from the heart. I enjoyed it. I could not tell that this was your first kiss." Me'na blushed profusely and Sean laughed out loud when he thought how he sounded. "I'm sorry, my lady, I didn't mean to embarrass you. It seems that I cannot get my words out correctly when I am near you."

When he spoke, the laughter was gone from his eyes to be replaced with affection. He picked up both of her hands and held them in his. Me'na first looked down to their hands then into his eyes; what she saw there gave her hope. Her heart was already a casualty in this age-old battle between men and women. She gave it readily to this man, whom seemed able to touch the far reaches of her soul.

If this is love, I must be careful lest I lose myself, she thought.

Thomas stood outside of the doors listening. He thought that it was time to break up the cozy little drama being played out on the balcony. They were getting too close.

"Brother, I was looking for you and here you are keeping our guest all to yourself, for shame," Thomas said as he walked through the balcony doors. He could tell he startled both of them; they looked guilty, as if they had been caught doing something forbidden. Me'na gave a nervous little laugh, but Sean wasn't fooled. He knew that his brother was interested in her. As soon as he got her settled, he would have a talk with Thomas.

Me'na curtsied to Thomas as he approached her. She thought that he was handsome also, but Prince Thomas appeared to be dangerous. She knew that she would not be safe with him. Me'na knew he wouldn't hurt her physically, but she felt that he would trample her heart if given the chance. She had seen the look that was in his eyes before, too often in the last several months. It felt as if he could see through her clothing. He unsettled her.

Ah, but the King was a different matter altogether. He made her yearn for things that she did not yet understand, but was eager to learn. Sean made her feel warm and feminine, as if she was born to be his. How could this be? She had just met him that very evening.

Too many new feelings and emotions to sort through. I need to sleep on all the goodness that came out of tonight. The day started badly as they all did when in Duke Bolwin's company, but oh, what an evening it turned out to be. Me'na smiled at her secret thoughts.

Both brothers noticed and smiled with her. She faced Thomas and looked him directly in his eyes, her soft gaze mesmerized him. No woman had ever looked at him like that before. Mostly the women who were with him wanted to marry him for his title. That was why he treated them as he did. They didn't want him for his sake, nor did they want to get to know him. Everyone wanted something from him, but not this woman. He wanted to give all he had to her. She needed to be taken care of.

"Lady Me'na, no need to bow to me. You are the same as I," he told her. "I am a prince and you a princess. Please relax.

"Thank you, Prince Thomas, I will try to remember. I may be a princess, but we never lived as you do. This palace is spectacular. Father never stayed in one place long enough to build a palace like this. For a long time, we lived on the run, fighting insurgents and living off father's readiness to sell his sword arm if necessary. He made his fortune and kingdom that way," she finished.

"Tomorrow I can show you around the palace if you like?" Thomas said.

Sean intervened. "I offered our guest asylum here in Fastonia and she is going to accept it. I have the day planned out. She must get settled in her new home first."

The King turned his attention away from Thomas and back to the vision before him. "Lady Hathaway will act as your companion and guide. She is our mother's aunt. She will see to it that clothes are made for you and your suite is decorated according to your taste. Whatever you need, please feel free to come to me at any time, my lady," the King offered her. "Duke Bolwin will be sent word that you are under my protection. He too is in the palace." All of a sudden, Sean asked her, "Where have you been staying?"

She told them that the duke had provided a wagon for her comfort with several of his men standing guard. They were astounded. Neither liked Bolwin, but they thought at least he had her in a room at the nearest inn.

"That settles it madam, you are staying here under my protection alone. I will not abide any disagreement on your part. You must be protected," the King in Sean told her. He looked at Thomas to see if he caught his meaning. He did. Thomas just shrugged his shoulders and smiled that infuriating smile of his. The one that said loud and clear, "So what."

Sean walked into the opening of the balcony and called for a page. Two pages came to him. He told them to have the housekeeper prepare the suite on the east side of the palace. That was the one nearest him. It was empty. It was as close as he dared.

He looked at his brother. Thomas nodded his head in his direction. The nod said, "So this is how it's going to be. All's fair in love and war." The line in the sand had been drawn.

The King instructed the older page, James, to deliver a message to Duke Bolwin. He ordered pen and paper and wrote a short note to the duke. He was informed of Lady Me'na's new residence and whose protection she was under. If he had any questions, he would see him in the morning.

Sean placed Me'na's hand on his arm and looked at Thomas. "I am escorting our newest citizen to her rooms. I will see you in the morning."

Thomas thought, *You bet you will.*

Me'na turned towards the prince and bid him a good night. He reached for her free hand and kissed it as he bid her likewise. A smug Sean smiled over her head at Thomas.

BOOK TWO
CHAPTER SIX

The King rose early the next morning. He didn't need to be shaken today. He was on top of the world. He was in love for the first time in his life. Sean was standing on the balcony off his bedchamber when Lord Henry Stowell came in to wake him.

Sean turned around when he heard footsteps. "Henry, how are you this morning?"

"I am fine, sire, thank you for asking. Are you ready to eat or would you prefer a bath first?" Henry asked him.

"Henry come here."

Lord Stowell walked out onto the balcony. The sun was coming up in the east.

"Have you ever seen a more beautiful sunrise?" the King asked him.

Henry smiled at him and said, "I don't think so, Sean. This one is special."

When they were alone, Henry often called his cousin by his given name. They were only days apart with Henry being the elder.

Sean said to him, "Yes, she is special. How did you know I meant her?" was the puzzled question.

"Well, don't forget, I'm married and felt the same way every time I looked in Cynthia's direction."

"Do you still feel that way about her? This is not going to disappear is it?"

"No cousin, I don't think it will. She looked at you the same way all evening. She looked sick." Henry dodged a playful slap on the shoulder from Sean.

The King asked all of his gentlemen to break their fast with him that morning. He was in such a good mood that he wanted to share it. The order was given for the meal to be served in the small dining hall that was sometimes used for family meals or small intimate gatherings.

As the men waited for the extra food to be cooked and brought to the table; they all fed off of the king's good mood. Sean pulled one of the pages aside and gave him a missive that he wrote the night before to his aunt, Lady Hathaway. He instructed her to have tons of clothing made for Me'na with all the little necessaries that woman liked to go with them. He wanted her to have everything that his aunt knew women liked, spare no expense in this. He told her that Me'na was very important to him and to keep Thomas away from her until he could get there in a few hours.

The servers brought out plenty of meats, jams, and bread, eggs and the special little biscuits that the King loved so much. There were sweet rolls—Thomas' favorite—along with plenty of tea and ale. Sean knew that the scent of the sweet rolls would bring Thomas out of his room searching for the smell.

A seat for him was already prepared when he arrived. All the men started to laugh when he appeared still tucking his shirt and walking with his boots in his hands. Thomas' love for sweet rolls was well known.

"Well, wasn't anyone going to send for me?" he asked.

That sent the King and his companions into laughter again. He rolled his eyes upward and dived into the rolls like a schoolboy.

After breakfast, Thomas went to the military compound to check on Sir Benjamin who was up and asking to get up so that he could go back to his post. The physician fed him some chicken broth and weak tea for his stomach. That seemed to revitalize him even more.

"Your Highness, thank you for visiting me. I am told that you and the King have been here several times to see me."

"Yes we have, Sir Benjamin. I also bring word from your brother. He is worried about you. I promised him that I would personally look after you. He is on sensitive business for the King and cannot come to you yet. Do you remember what happened?"

"All I remember, Highness, is being jumped from above, then surrounded. I killed two of them, ran them through I did."

"Exactly where were you when this happened? We checked with Captain Lovett and he said that you were supposed to be several miles from where we think you were attacked."

"Highness, I patrolled my usual territory, but since Sir Robert was ill and I didn't have any one to talk to I kind of wandered off my path," he became excited.

"Take your time, Sir Benjamin. Don't make yourself ill trying to tell me everything today. I can come back later if necessary," Thomas said.

"Thank you, Highness, but I am fine. I rode along the mountain range on our border with Candea. That is not anyone's usual territory. We patrol that area periodically so as not to have a set schedule. But I was closer to the southern garrison so I thought that it would be safe for one knight to be out that way. I knew that I shouldn't have gone out alone, but there were no extra knights to ride with me and I will not shirk my duties."

As he spoke about his duties, he sat up straighter in bed. His brother Lord Geoffrey was a good friend of the prince, he didn't want to embarrass him. "The plan was to stop in the garrison to eat the evening meal and stay the night then head out the next morning."

The prince interrupted him at this point. "How long does it take you and Sir Robert to patrol your assigned path?"

Sir Benjamin tried to straighten up in the bed. "Highness, usually it takes about two days to complete our assignment. We ride the far southern border along the jetties and part of the mountain range. Nothing ever happens there, it's too peaceful for me."

When he said that, Thomas remembered how he felt when he was doing boring work that he thought was better suited for old men. "Yes, we always assign our younger knights to the south. It's to learn patience."

Sir Benjamin had to smile at that. "Yes, sir, I guess I was about five miles from the southern castle when I was attacked, from above and around. Besides killing two of them, I didn't remember anything else until I awoke yesterday, sire."

"Uh, the area that you patrol has a shallow port, a ship cannot dock in the jetties but a long boat can. Did you see any evidence of boats that had been drugged ashore?"

"No, Your Highness. I had just started to patrol in that area."

"Where is Sir Robert?" Thomas turned and asked the physician.

"Highness, he is still unconscious. Sir Robert has been running a fever for the last several days. It looks like he might have been poisoned. He became ill after his evening meal four days ago. He was scheduled for duty the following morning."

Thomas was deep in thought, this was just too much of a coincidence; it was as if someone was trying to prevent the patrolling of the far south and the west mountain range.

"Mmm, I must speak with Captain Lovett. I'll have him send three different senior knight patrols in three different directions on the southwestern border and coast. Sir Benjamin, rest and get well. Do what the physician tells you to do." With that, Thomas was off in search of Captain Lovett.

By this time, Sean had finished morning court and was off to check on Me'na. He walked into the outer receiving room, waiting to be announced. His aunt came out to get him."Your Highness, I think she is a lovely young woman," she gushed.

Sean smiled and his eyes shone. There were bolts of material and seamstresses going back and forth quickly, bowing when they saw the King standing there. Many had never seen him up close and they were impressed with his good looks.

One of the apprentices ran to get Me'na. She came out and made a very graceful curtsey to him and bide him a good morning. "Oh, Your Highness, thank you so very much. There is so much. I am overwhelmed with your generosity."

"My pleasure. Whatever you need, my dear. I just came to make sure that you were getting alone with my aunt."

Me'na was drawn to him as she was last evening. It was not a dream, and everything she felt was real. She didn't realize she walked very close to him and just stood there with a silly smile on her face. Lady Hathaway shooed everyone out of the room and back to work.

"My dear King, I am most grateful to you for taking me into your palace. I do not have the words to thank you properly. Could you join me for a light noon meal? It is about that time, sire."

"Yes, Me'na. Let's have our meal in the gardens. Come, I will arrange it. Aunt, do you need Lady Me'na now?"

"No, Your Highness, we will not need her for a couple of hours. You two young people go and enjoy yourselves." They were hurried out the door and into the hall before either one of them knew it.

The servants brought out a small table and chairs and placed them in a shady spot in the garden. Sweet smelling flowers and busy little humming birds surrounded them. Sean pulled her chair out and seated her to his left. He had his chair placed close to her, but not too close to raise eyebrows. He wanted to protect her reputation at all costs. They began their meal with enthusiasm. Love usually makes one eat.

"Me'na, when you are settled here in your new home; I would like to talk to you about your future."

Sean placed his large hand on top of her smaller one. She blushed at him.

She didn't trust herself to speak. She knew that she loved him at first sight. It was all she thought about in the night. With the King placing his hand on top of hers, she felt that he must have some feelings for her, Me'na could only hope. She was aware that she had only known him for twenty-four hours, but it felt like a lifetime. She wanted to spend the rest of her life with him and bear him many children. This was new for her. She never wanted to be a mother before. Nothing that happened to her in her past life made her want to share the pain with anyone, let alone children. King Sean had changed so much for her in such a short time. She couldn't keep the smile off of her face or the bounce out of her walk. Me'na was in love, full blown.

Sean looked in her eyes to try to see if she felt the same way about him that he felt about her. Her amber-colored eyes were smiling so bright that the warmth from them enveloped him. He picked up her hand and kissed her palm. As he kissed her, a tingle went up her spine. She shook faintly and placed the hand that held hers on the side of her face. He lost control then. The King stood up and pulled her in his arms. He kissed her softly at first, then ardently.

This time, Me'na was going to do a better job at kissing. She pressed her lips against his, felt him sweetly suck her lower lip till her mouth opened slightly. He causally slipped his tongue in her mouth just a little. He didn't want to frighten her with his passion. But to his surprise, she responded in kind. Sean felt her lips form a smile and he pulled back to take a look at her. She had a very satisfied look on her face, and he had to laugh.

"Oh so now you are trying to show me up." He continued to smile.

"Oh no, Your Highness, just trying to do a better job so that you do not grow bored, that's all." She continued to look smug.

"It's Sean, when we are alone, please call me Sean. I yearn to hear my name fall from your lips.

She said, "Sean."

Hearing her say his name with her slight accent made his heart race. Sean wanted her to be his wife. He hadn't planned to ask her anything today. But the way she said his name gave him the courage to tell her how he felt. Some people would think it was too soon to ask her, but he always knew he'd fall in love the moment his bride walked into his realm.

"Please, Me'na, sit down, I want to speak with you about something near to my heart."

When she heard him say; "near to my heart" her own heart soared with hope. She sat down but felt so nervous, she thought that she would cry.

Sean pulled his chair closer to her so only she would hear what he had to say. His personal household squad was standing a small distance away from them with their backs turned so as not to intrude. They were virtually surrounded. He held her hands again, took a deep breath and began.

"I know that we only met last evening, but I feel as if I have known you my entire life. From the first moment that I laid eyes on you, I had to know you, and to love you." Me'na was smiling while tears slowly trailed down her face. Sean continued. "I find that I do not want to go through the remainder of my days without you at my side. I know that this seems fast, it is fast, but I love you with all of my being."

His saying he loved her made her cry harder. Sean understood that about some women. Some of them cried when very happy. She did look happy. He reached for a napkin to wipe her tears away. As he was wiping her tears, she passionately grabbed his hand, kissed it, and wouldn't let it go. He didn't try to remove his hand. It was now wet with her tears, seared with her kisses.

"What I am trying to say is, I want you to get to know me and consider spending the rest of your life as my wife. You may not like being married to a monarch so I want you to be sure. Often my time is not my own."

Me'na placed her fingers against his lips to quiet him. "Sean, I love you so much that if I died tomorrow, I will feel as if we loved a lifetime. I do not need time to think, I did all my thinking last night when I couldn't sleep because images of you filled my heart. I would marry you anytime you chose. I love you."

He looked at her closely, very closely; she was smiling and crying at the same time. Could this be what the bards sang about? Could this be true love? If it wasn't, this was a pretty good imitation of something that he had never felt before. Sean had started thinking the only love he would ever have was his brother's love, and that was bumpy at best. He felt grateful, thankful to Bolwin for bringing her into his life. He didn't think that he would ever hear himself say that.

"Are you sure, my darling, sure that you want to share me with my kingdom? It could be a thankless job for you," he said.

"I consider any time that we get to spend together, as time well spent. Do not worry about me, my love. I will be fine as long as you love me." With that said she leaned over to him and gave him the best kiss that she could muster.

In Duke Bolwin's room, he and Beaumont whispered about their plans. The duke told him that everything was going accordingly to plan with that little wretch Me'na. The King seemed captivated by her, so much in fact, that he sent a note to him removing her worthless person from his tender care. Bolwin told him that their ship had come in off the southern coast and within about forty-eight hours, they should be in control.

The ship was anchored a long way out to sea. The men would be ready to come ashore on the night of the last quarter of the moon. They would come ashore in long boats and position themselves in a cave about one mile from the palace grounds. Bolwin would give a signal and the men would move into the trees that surrounded the palace rear walls. After that, the King would be sent a note telling him that the prince was captured and he must come to negotiate his release. Once Sean was out of the palace, his men would come over the wall and secure the castle. The King would have taken the majority of his knights with him to get Thomas. He would be surrounded on all sides with Candea's infantry. If it happened as quickly as it was planned, the King would not have time to summon his large army. They could take the city for the price of a few lives, Fastonian lives. As long as Carrington did his part, all would go accordingly.

BOOK TWO
CHAPTER SEVEN

All that day and well into the evening, Sean and Me'na walked around the palace looking so happy that the entire castle was a very happy place to be. Me'na stayed in her suite with Lady Hathaway all day hurriedly trying to finish one of the gowns for the evening meal. The King had planned on announcing their impending nuptials to his nobles. He had almost forgotten the crisis that was going on until Thomas came in to report to him.

"Sean, it seems as if someone is trying to keep us from patrolling the jetties. As you know, ships cannot drop anchor there but long boats can. Sir Benjamin was attacked close to there, and Sir Robert was poisoned to prevent their patrol."

Sean looked at him as if he hadn't heard correctly. "You mean someone actually tried to kill one of our knights right under our nose?"

"Yes, brother, that's right. I sent several seasoned knights out to look for clues that younger men could miss. They should return by nightfall."

"Thomas, when they come in, I want to be there to get their report first hand."

"As you wish, Sean." Thomas turned to leave but Sean stopped him. "Thomas, I need to talk to you."

They were in the official throne room. "Come, brother, let's walk in the garden." Both men walked through the palace to the garden. Once there, Sean turned to him and started talking.

"I have asked Lady Me'na to become my wife, and she accepted."
Thomas was not prepared for this. He thought that Sean was going to tell him

anything but not this, he wasn't ready to hear this.

"What? Sean, you only just met her last evening. How could you ask her to marry you so fast?"

"I loved her the moment I first saw her, she felt the same way."

Thomas asked him, "Is it just lust? How can you be sure that it is love? You have never been in love before."

"That is how I know. I have no desire to rush and bed her as if the feelings were going to disappear. We can wait until our wedding night. Don't misunderstand, I want to bed her, very badly, but I will restrain myself. Tommy, I know that you were interested in her too, but I loved her first."

Thomas walked to the closest bench and sat down. He looked at his elder brother with wonder. The look he saw on Sean's face was happiness. He had never seen his brother look like that before.

He really must be in love. She is a beautiful woman, well brought up and a princess. Just what he needed to satisfy his counselors as if Sean cared to satisfy them, he contemplated.

Sean had sat down beside him. He really was sincere in wanting his brother's blessing. "Well, Sean, are you sure that she loves you?"

"Yes."

"Then if you are sure and she is also, I give you both my blessings. You know if I could have had just a little time with her, I'd be marrying her instead of you. I am the better looking Winslow you know."

Sean grabbed his brother and hugged him. "I know that what you felt for her was more than your usual interest. She is someone special and she has need of a strong man. You could not help yourself. But I do thank you for bowing out gracefully and not trying to make her choose. It would only cause her more pain. She has had enough of that to last a lifetime. I will announce our wedding to the nobles at the evening meal. Please stand with us and show your support."

"Sean, you know that I will support you in whatever you do, whether it's a marriage or an orgy. I'm just that kind of supportive brother."

"I don't know if I should hug you or choke you, but I do know that I love you."

Thomas bowed low to his brother, backed away a little and left Sean in the garden. He called over his shoulder, "I will see you at supper."

At the evening meal Sean, Me'na, Thomas, Aunt Amanda, and their cousin Henry stood together as the King announced his impending wedding in four weeks' time. After the King finished speaking, Thomas stepped forth, raised his goblet, and made a toast.

"To my elder brother and Princess Me'na, may they have a long and fulfilling life filled with many children."

The assembled crowd stood and raised their goblets and drank deeply, especially Lady Deborah. She couldn't believe what she had heard. Is he mad?

Why doesn't he just lay with her and get it over with? He didn't have to marry her, did he? He felt no such compunction with me. She looked over to Lady Elizabeth and could almost swear she was gloating.

The witch! What did she know about anything? Her with an old man for a husband. Just who does this little beggar think she is anyway? Lady Deborah was so incensed that she had to step outside for a moment.

While she stepped outside, Duke Bolwin was so beside himself that he almost fell out of his chair. This was better than originally planned. He would kill the King then rape his wife before his eyes. If Sean were still alive after the rape, he would make him watch as he plunged his dagger into her heart. She would think twice before biting him again. He would see to it with her last dying breath.

Charles leaned over and asked him, "Where did you find her again and why did you hide her from me? Is she someone that you were trying to sweeten the deal with? Just in case the King said no to the decrease?"

"Charles, I told you all about her. Don't get jealous on me now," Bolwin countered.

Charles looked at him and shrugged his shoulders. Lord Beaumont had a smile on his face that didn't reach his eyes. Richard promised him that he could have the girl before she died.

Lord Henry Stowell, Duke of Newberry was sitting next to Thomas. He watched Bolwin's face. He thought that maybe it was time that he spoke with his cousin. Something was going on and Lord Carrington pleaded a headache to escape tonight's meal. That man never missed a meal no matter what. He came when his leg was broken. They had to arrange a special place for him. So, this was completely out of character for him. *I will speak with the King in the morning.*

After the meal, everyone came to congratulate the happy couple. Thomas for the first time felt what it was to have come close to having the one woman he could love. He really felt he could love her. He had never lost a woman to any man. This was a new experience for him. He was going to be as gracious as possible if it killed him. It probably would.

After the dancing, Sean escorted Me'na to her suite. "Sean, I don't want to go to my suite. I don't want to leave you alone tonight."

"It's only for a short time, my love. We will be married soon. It takes time to plan and arrange a royal wedding you know."

Inwardly, Sean was pleading with her to go into her room. He didn't know if he could bear being alone with her in his chamber. With Sean, being in love for the first time, he wanted to satisfy the growing hunger he felt. This new hunger was one he didn't think could be satisfied easily. It would take a lifetime.

"All right, Me'na. Come. We can sit on the balcony and talk all night if that's what you want, love," he decided. "I am a very demanding lover as you will find out soon, I have my limits and I will reach them quickly if we are alone too long. Promise me when I say it is time for you to go, you will go."

He looked at her with those green eyes. They were making promises that his lips denied.

Me'na looked at him as earnestly as she could. "I will go when you say it is time. I do not want to distress you, my love."

The King led her to his suite of rooms. Two knights stood there and opened the door to the outer chamber. All of his companions were there except Lord Carrington. He told them that they were dismissed for the night and he would see them in the morning. As they were leaving, Henry asked if he could speak with him.

"Sire, I need to speak with you at length in the morning. Something is afoot with the Candeans and Lord Carrington. I can't say exactly what it is, but there is something."

Sean was concerned because Henry was no worrier. If he said that he suspected something, Sean believed him. "Cousin, I can speak with you in the morning unless it is a dire emergency. If it is, we can talk now."

Henry nodded his head that he thought it could wait until morning.

Me'na had walked out of his chamber and onto the balcony. She wanted him to be able to conduct his duties with her around.

"Thomas and I, along with Lords Hightower and Hamilton, believe that there is something amiss here. We do not know what it is, but it is there. Wake me at the usual time we will include you in the meeting, then you can tell all what you suspect. Be careful, Henry. Don't let on that you are watching them. I mean it, cousin. I know how you can get carried away when on a secret mission. I don't want to lose you." Sean put his hand on Henry's shoulder.

Henry asked, "What about your betrothed wife? Do you think that she knows anything?"

"No, she is consumed with getting enough dresses made and staying away from the duke. She hates him. He made her his virtual slave because he claimed to have saved her life. She is fine, I am sure of it."

Henry bowed. Upon rising he said, "I am very happy for you. I can see the love she bears for you in her eyes and smile. She will make a good wife. Good night, sire." With that, Lord Stowell left the King alone with Me'na.

Sean walked to the balcony to join her there. When she heard him, she turned around with a smile on her face and reached out to grab his hand. She held unto his hand while she talked to him about what she wanted for their future.

"Sean, I want to have many children for you. I also want a son that looks just like the father and is kind as he is. All of our children must have your green eyes. They are so beautiful." She felt as if she could not stop talking. She had so much to tell him.

The King looked at her talking excitedly about their children to come. She wanted to give him so much that she was keyed up and overly excited. Sean placed his hands on her shoulders and kissed her to quite her stream of words. That did the trick. Me'na immediately melted in his arms as she surrendered to him.

Sean felt such overwhelming love for her that he had to get her as close as possible to his heart. He thought he was crushing her. He adjusted his grip and loosened his hold on her. She mistook the movement and hoped that he was not trying to break free. All of a sudden, Me'na became the aggressor. She did not want their kiss to end. She crushed him to her. She wanted him to feel all the love that was inside of her.

Sean slowly brought their kiss to an end. He was close to reaching the point of no return, she must go. He hugged her and placed his chin on top of her head. She listened to his heartbeat slow down. When his heartbeat became normal again, she looked up at him but his eyes were closed. Me'na placed her head back on his chest until he was ready to release her. She didn't care how long he held her.

The thoughts going through his mind were a jumble. He wanted very much to show her how much he loved her. He knew if he wanted to, she would capitulate. But he wanted a perfect wedding night for her and he would not allow his nature to ruin that.

Me'na pushed back a little and put both of her hands on the side of his face. She brought his mouth down to hers, and tenderly kissed him. She didn't push anything for she could feel that Sean was close to what he called the point of no return.

After the short kiss she said, "My love, oh how I love you. I could stand here the remainder of the evening, but I won't. Please escort me to my room. If you are the demanding lover that you claim, I will need my rest."

The King smiled at that. "Me'na, there is a secret passage between our rooms. If there is any trouble in the night, please use it to come to me. There could be trouble in the coming days, my love. I have assigned several of my most trusted knights to guard you at all times. Come, let's walk to your rooms and I will show you."

They walked to the main entrance and two knights were on guard there, then two more in the inner sitting room. The King introduced them to her as Sir Tristan and Sir Douglas. Both knights bowed to their King and his lady. They went in her sitting room and there were two more knights standing before the bedchamber, Sir Jamie and Sir Howard. The King introduced her to these men also.

Sean told her, "The knights guarding you tonight, will introduce you to their replacements in the morning. There will be a total of eight knights assigned to you until this trouble has passed. They must be introduced to you so that you will know them." He placed his hands on her shoulders and turned her to face him. "If any man comes to guard you and you don't know him, run and come to Thomas or me whomever you see first."

They had stepped into her chamber and he sat her down. "I believe that Duke Bolwin has a plan of some sort and he may try to hurt you that is why you have guards. After the trouble is gone, you will be as free around here as possible. I could not bear it if something happened to you."

She looked at him with grave concern. "Sean, is the trouble because of me? Have I done something?"

He reassured her that it had nothing to do with her that he only wanted to keep her safe. She was the most valuable person in the world to him. She must be kept safe.

"No, my love, we have been watching him even before he arrived in Winslow Town. He should not be here. I can't say any more at this time."

"Sean, show me the secret passage to your room."

She followed him to her wardrobe closet. Once inside he pressed a panel in the back and a dark passage stood before her.

"Me'na, this leads to me only, I know that it is dark, but that is what I want if you have to hide or escape. If the trouble gets bad, hide in here, I will look for you here first." He placed his arm around her waist and hugged her to him tightly.

"Only Thomas, Lord Hightower, and Lord Hamilton know this exists. And one other person, my cousin Lord Henry Stowell knows also. I will introduce you to him tomorrow. If any of these men come for you, it's OK to go with them." She was afraid now but tried not to show it.

"Sean, look at me. Are you sure that this is not because of me? If I have caused you, any trouble after all the kindness that you have shown me, I'll leave. I could not bear it if you were injured."

She was close to crying. Me'na thought that she had gotten so close to happiness and now to have this happen. What should she do? Sean looked at her. He understood how she felt and tried to hold her closer if it was possible to be any closer. He just didn't like the resigned look of her eyes. She thought that him loving her was going to hurt him in some way. She appeared to be looking for an escape route, Me'na at that moment looked like a hunted animal.

She put on a false smile and said to him. "Good night, love. I'll go to bed now and rest."

He didn't like the way she said it. Sean didn't believe her. She wanted him to leave so that when he awoke in the morning, she would be gone. He picked her up and sat down in a chair with her on his lap.

"Why are you lying to me? You plan on running away, don't you?"

Me'na buried her head in his shoulder and cried her heart out. She cried for all the lost dreams that would never be realized, and all the unborn children that would not be. In her heart of hearts, her Sean was being stolen away from her. He was slowly fading.

They sat like that until she cried herself to sleep. Sean didn't know what to do. He was afraid if he left her alone she would run and he'd never see her again. That must not happen. He placed her in her bed and went to the door. He told Sir Jamie to go to his aunt's room and ask her to come. It took some time for Lady Hathaway to get a robe on and come to Me'na's room. Once there Sean explained what was going on briefly and told her that Me'na blamed herself. He was afraid if he left her alone, she would leave.

Before he could say another word, his aunt told him she would stay with her until morning. The King had a lounger brought into the room for his aunt to rest on. After she was settled, he went to find Captain Lovett. The captain was ordered to place soldiers under Me'na's balcony. There was already several standing watch in the rear of the palace; but the King wanted three under her balcony alone and they were to be changed out every two hours. He wanted no one falling asleep on the job. Heads would roll if they did.

Satisfied that Me'na wouldn't disappear on him, Sean finally retired for the evening. Visions of his beloved's tear-streaked face haunted his sleep.

BOOK TWO
CHAPTER EIGHT

Before breakfast the next morning, Sean went to check on Me'na and his aunt. Lady Hathaway was still asleep in the lounger when he entered the inner room to be announced. Me'na was coming out of her bed chamber when he walked in.

"Not still trying to run away from me, are you?" he asked her.

She bowed her head. "No, Your Highness. I was going to make an appointment to see you. I wanted to apologize for my cowardly behavior last evening. I am sorry. As your wife I must show more courage and strength."

"Come with me, love."

He walked her out onto her balcony. There they stood arm and arm looking at the busy comings and going of the citizens of Winslow Town.

"Me'na, you do not have to make an appointment to see me. You are my betrothed. That gives you passage to see me whenever you want to."

"Hold me, Sean. Tight," she said.

He complied with her request. They stood with arms wrapped around each other for some time.

"Love, I have a meeting to go to this morning. Please have breakfast with my aunt. After you have eaten, I want you and Lady Hathaway to walk around the palace. You need to get to know your new home. Once you have made some friends here, you will be required to pick some of the high-ranking noble women as your ladies in waiting. Submit their names to me and we will go over your list together."

Me'na started to object, but he held up his hand. "I do not want you to pick some of these women who wanted me to marry them. They would try to make your life miserable. My lady aunt will point out the troublemakers to you. I will not have a jealous woman trying to make you pay because I didn't love her. I want you happy and fulfilled." He looked for understanding in her eyes. He had an overwhelming need to protect her. "I am not going to try and pick your friends."

"Thank you, dear husband. I know how some people can be. I appreciate you looking out for my happiness." Me'na stood on tiptoe and planted a kiss on his lips.

"That's good morning. I will always greet you this way no matter what time of day or night." She was happy again. Sean left her to have his working breakfast meeting.

Henry joined the men at their meeting on Duke Bolwin. He told them what he had seen and how Carrington missed last evening's meal. The man was greedy he always ate. He was filled in on the happenings and suspicions that they had. All agreed that what ever was going to happen; would probably happen tonight.

After everyone had finished eating, Sean decided to send for Duke Bolwin and force his hand. He was not going to sit there and let his enemy attack when they were ready. It was thought that if their hand was forced; if would catch them off guard and unprepared. So, the duke was on his way to the throne room instead of the public room where the King usually held morning court. As Duke Bolwin and company entered the chamber, he noticed that the prince was there and so were all of the King's gentlemen including Lord Carrington.

Lord Henry Stowell had placed himself across from Carrington so he could watch him without being obvious. The three men approached the throne and bowed low to the King and prince.

"Good morning, Your Majesty, we came as quickly as we could," the duke began.

"Thank you for being so prompt. I do appreciate it. Let me get down to the matter at hand so that there is no misunderstanding."

While the duke was in the throne room talking to the King, his men were being put under house arrest. Fastonia's soldiers were walking around town looking for Candean soldiers that were not in the barracks. Within the hour, all of the known soldiers were locked up. The only ones not locked up were the ones that they couldn't find and the unknown soldiers that had yet to come ashore. They would come ashore when darkness fell.

The King was sitting with his long frame causally draped upon his chair. He had to restrain his impulses; he wanted to squeeze the duke's neck until his eyes bulged out. He managed to sustain his composure.

"Duke Bolwin, at this time, I cannot lower the tribute that your country pays Fastonia. King Sardin will have to find another way to improve the lives of his people. The fifteen percent per ship that is paid leaves your kingdom with substantial revenues to make improvements. But if this does not meet with your expectations, then I am sorry. The tribute will remain the same or you can always dock all of your ships in Saint John instead of here."

Sean knew that the port of Saint John's harbor that was deep enough for ships was small. The majority of their coastline was the same as Fastonia's southern coast. The only difference being, Fastonia's jetties were only about three miles long, where over half of Saint John's coast was the jetty. Sean sat there watching the duke's face first contort with rage, then simmer. He was visibly trying to get his self under control. Lord Ainsley stepped closer to the duke and placed a warning hand on his arm. He knew him well. After what seemed to be hours of silence, the duke finally spoke.

"Your Majesty, I regret that you did not see this our way. Is there anything that I can do to change your mind?"

"No, there is not. You may go the interview is over."

Sean was rude on purpose. He was trying to provoke the duke into some sort of action. Duke Bolwin's first thoughts came out of his mouth in a torrent.

"Just who do you think you are talking to, King Winslow? I am not some insignificant subject of yours that you can talk down to…"

Before the words were out of his mouth, Thomas jumped down from his chair, pulled his sword out and had it pressing against Bolwin's throat.

"I told you that you would give me another chance to finish our conversation. I am going to run you through right here and now. Get down on your knees and beg my brother's forgiveness. NOW!"

When the duke first raised his voice to the King his personal detail rushed the Candeans and surrounded them. By the time that they got there, which was only seconds later; Thomas had already jumped down. Duke Bolwin was now on his knees to Sean. The King was not surprised that Thomas had his sword pricking Bolwin's throat. Blood was slowly trickling down his neck.

Thomas turned toward his brother and asked; "Do I kill him now or would you like the pleasure?"

Sean let out a sarcastically uncharacteristic laugh. This was a side of him that few saw. Only Thomas, their cousin Henry, Lord Hightower and Lord Hamilton knew existed. Bolwin threatened everything that he held dear. Now that he had Me'na, he would tolerate danger no longer or play this game of cat and mouse. He had to admit to himself that he was enjoying this game that they played. The warrior in him wanted someone to fight; but his kingdom was peaceful and therefore dull. Having a wife and maybe a family soon changed that. He wanted the dullness back.

Duke Bolwin spoke. "I am sorry that I spoke out of turn, Your Highness. King Sardin said not to come back unless I had a new contract from you. I did not know what else to do. I am desperate, Your Majesty, please reconsider." He said all of this with Thomas' sword still at his throat.

"Thomas, do not kill him yet. I have a message for King Sardin."

Thomas sighed and slowly removed his blade from the duke's throat. He really wanted to kill him. He moved away a bit but kept his blade on him. As the prince removed the blade, Bolwin stood up. The King also stood. The duke didn't realize just how tall and menacing he could be. All the years that he had been negotiating with him, he never took him seriously.

The unsure young king that he once was existed no longer. But now, this full-grown King who looked down to him was another matter all together. He was actually started to become frightened. Sean walked down the steps to him and stopped about a foot from his face. He was at least six inches taller.

"Duke Bolwin, I will forgive your outburst. Your King has made your position very perilous today. Do not take forgiveness as a sign of weakness. I would just as soon allow the prince to run you through as to look at you." Sean used his height to appear menacing.

"Take this message back to your King. When the current contract expires in six months. We will consider whether or not Candea will be able to continue using our ports. Do not come here, we will meet with your King's envoys at the border next time. I never want to see your face in my kingdom again. Is that clear?"

"Yes, Your Majesty it is. Will we be allowed to go back to the rooms that we have here in the palace. It is too late in the day to start out for Candea now," the duke begged. Sean looked at the knights surrounding them.

"Escort our guest back to their rooms. They are allowed to come and go as they please. Duke, use the time I have given you to get your things and your men together. I want you gone by dawn."

With that, Sean turned his back and walked to the throne. The King reclined in his seat when he reached it and crossed his left leg over his right knee. He gave the appearance of being very bored, which was how he wanted to seem. Thomas stood there, waved his sword at Martin Beaumont and bowed to him. Beaumont nodded his head. It was a silent challenge.

Lord Charles Ainsley didn't know what to make of the situation. Everything had gotten out of hand so fast. There was no time for him to think before Richard opened his mouth. He must speak with the King. He turned toward Sean before he left.

"May I say something, Highness?"

The King nodded his head. The knights made the others keep walking. Bolwin wanted to hear what was said but couldn't.

"Sire, I have known you since we were young men. You were always a monarch that I respected and admired. I am so sorry that things reached this point so fast. If any of this could have been prevented, I would have done something." Charles walked closer to the throne carefully. He wanted to make a personal appeal to Sean.

"I do not want to leave your fair land this way. I fear that if I return with the duke, I will not be allowed to come back. If possible, do not forbid me from coming. If you remember, I was born in Fastonia near the border. This is my homeland. Things are pretty bad in Candea for anyone from here, even me, that's part of the reason that I came. The duke did not want me to come this time. King Sardin has had me under surveillance as a possible spy as he has had others from here."

What he said made Thomas and Sean look at each other. They were remembering what Lord de Walt said.

"Charles, come closer," the King instructed him. Lord Carrington had already left the room when Thomas placed his sword at the duke's throat. "Gentlemen, you may go and find your pleasure, I will expect to see you all back in about three hours. All but you, Henry. I have need of you." Henry bowed.

"Yes, sire, at your pleasure."

Once all the remaining men had drawn close to the throne Charles finished what he was saying. "I wanted to come home, back to Fastonia. Sire, if you remember Ainsley family history, the only reason that I was brought to Candea, as a young boy was to manage my mother's lands. There was no male heir to inherit the Earldom so old King Augustus gave it to me. Since that time a male relation was found in Saint John, he is a distant cousin of my mother's.

He will inherit in another two months when he is twenty-one and I will be left without lands." Charles paused to catch his breath.

"There is a small earldom here that was my deceased elder brother's. The one here is not as large as the Candean grant. I believe it is the property of the crown now."

Sean looked to Lord Hightower who nodded yes. It was being kept in trust for him, it had long been forgotten.

"Charles, do you want to lay claim to this land?" the King asked him.

Charles fell down to his knees. He was very grateful that Lord Hightower remembered the earldom. If he hadn't remembered, then it would be much harder to establish his claim on it.

"Yes, Your Highness, if possible I would. I am not a traitor to Fastonia. If I go back, I don't know what I would do. A man without land is no man at all."

"Charles, you must swear fealty to me here and now. Otherwise, you will have to leave."

"King Sean Phillip Matthew Winslow, I do swear to honor and protect this kingdom. To not bear false witness against it to another. I pledge my life in defense of the crown."

"You may rise, Charles Ainsley, Earl of..." Sean looked to Lord Hightower for the name of the earldom, he mouthed Montral. "Earl of Montral. Welcome home."

Charles rose up he was noticeably moved. He was so happy to leave Candea he didn't know what to say at the moment. Thomas went to him and shook his hand; Sean stepped down and embraced him.

"Charles, I will have your things moved to another room until I give you leave to claim your earldom properly. You are to have nothing to do with the duke or Lord Beaumont while they are here. I need you to tell us everything that you know. When will the attack start?" All eyes were on Lord Ainsley.

"Attack, what attack?" he asked.

"The one that will happen tonight," the King told him.

"I know nothing about an attack, sire. Who is attacking us and why?"

Sean looked at Thomas who nodded his head. "Duke Bolwin is going to attack us tonight. We have collected intelligence that points to this being the night. Whatever you can tell us will be helpful." Charles looked thoughtful for a bit.

"Oh, that's why he brought her here."

"Brought who here, Charles?" the King asked.

"Princess Me'na. Duke Bolwin would answer none of my questions about who she was or why he brought her. She hates him from what I could see. He made her into his slave. She had to feed him and wash his feet on this journey."

"Is she a party to this?" was Sean's almost inaudible question. Thomas could see pain on his brother's face and hear it in his voice.

"No, sire, she wouldn't let him get within two feet of her without trying to claw his eyes out. She was restrained for the journey here. He kept her in a wagon. Her hands were tied with cloth so as to not make any marks, but her feet were in chains. You should be able to see the bruises on her ankles, I saw them."

Sean was so relieved he didn't realize he had been holding his breath. Thomas thought she would never know how close he came to cutting her beautiful throat if she was a party to all this. Henry walked to Sean and placed his hand on his shoulder.

Charles continued. "I asked the duke why he brought her and he evaded the question. Then I asked if he brought her to sweeten the deal in case you said no. I thought he wanted to distract you and break your concentration with such a beautiful woman. He merely accused me of being jealous. I saw him look over to Martin and wink his eye."

Thomas added, "Well, she did distract him."

That broke the tension. Everyone enjoyed a good laugh at the King's expense who had the decency to blush a little.

"Well," Sean started, "Henry, would you please get Charles a room on the same side of the palace as yours. Place guards at his door to keep Beaumont and Bolwin out. I want this to appear to be house arrest to them. This is to protect you Charles as long as they are here. You are not a prisoner, you are home." Charles bowed low to his King.

"Thank you, Your Majesty, you do not know how long I have wanted this, thank you again." He backed up a little then followed Henry out into the hallway.

Thomas left to go on his rounds. At the military compound, Lord Chaney was waiting for him. He stood up immediately when Thomas entered the room.

"Highness, good day. I have come to give my report personally."

"Please be seated, William," the prince told him. Thomas nodded his head at him to begin.

"Highness, I have sent several members of my ghost squad across the border with Candea. They all report no more troop movement. At this stage in the proceedings, I would have to agree with them that an attack would not come from the border. They have only untrained farmers there. We believe troops at the borders are a diversion. We further believe that the attack will come from the southern region. We have only a garrison there and inexperienced men patrolling the area. We have received word from our feathered message carriers that the ghost squad assassins are in place in King Sardin's castle. We have only to send word either way."

"Good, good, William. This is excellent. You must be tired. Did you ride all night?" he asked him.

"Yes, Highness, that's my job as your captain."

"Go into the palace and give your information to the King then seek your bed. You will need your rest for tonight. Before you go, send a carrier to Lord Statton. Have him send half of the knights back here quickly. He is to remain with the rest of our infantry. Tell the King that I go to speak with Lord Geoffrey Blackmon out in the harbor. I'll be back directly."

Lord Chaney bowed and left. Thomas placed his feet on top of the table and sighed. He contemplated killing Me'na, even though he thought he loved her. He couldn't stand the thought that she was to be Sean's wife. He rather see her dead instead of with another. Thomas thought he really should feel bad at wanting her dead instead of with Sean, but he didn't. Having never been denied a woman, this was a new experience and he didn't like it. If he killed her, he would have raped her first. He had to get a taste of that woman no matter what. The next couple of weeks should prove interesting. He did love her. He thought she would never consent to be his mistress so, he would have had to marry her. Marry her he would if he had half a chance. He still wanted her even knowing that she loved his brother.

He thought, *If I can get her alone and force my attentions on her she would choose me over Sean. I just know it. She was never given a fair chance to sample my kisses. I've been told that my kisses make women forget their names*. He had to laugh at himself.

Mmm, Me'na, Me'na. As soon as I get back from the dock, it's me and you. You don't know what I have in store for you. I want your amber eyes to look at me the way that you look at my brother. You won't tell Sean. You'd be afraid to cause trouble between us brothers, Ha.

Thomas took his feet off of his table and stood up. He straightened his jerkin and prepared to leave for the dock with a self-satisfied smile. As he was walking out the door, Lord Carrington rushed to him.

"Highness, please, you must come with me. I happened upon a couple of Candea's soldiers in the tavern off of the waterfront. They were well into their cups and talking about fighting and killing Fastonians tonight. I thought that I had best come and get you. Come please before they leave."

Thomas hurried behind Lord Carrington, not really watching where they were going. He didn't think to ask him what he was doing in this part of town. It wasn't his usual hangout. As they walked into the alley, the hair on the back of Thomas' neck started to rise up. He placed his hand on his sword hilt and cautiously followed Carrington into a ragged building.

All of a sudden, Carrington disappeared and four men were upon him. He pulled his sword out and shouted his war cry. He started slashing and swinging his sword at every sound he heard. He must have sunk his blade into someone because he heard a body fall then another. Then everything went black as Carrington came from behind him and hit him on the head with his blade, Thomas crumpled to the floor.

He awoke with a terrible headache and a dirty rag stuffed into his mouth. His hands and feet were tied and he was laying on a floor with a blanket thrown over him. He started to struggle against his bonds but it only made them tighter. He decided to lie there and listen for voices. As he was lying on the floor, he tried to remember what had happened.

I remember following Carrington down an alley and into a building. Somebody hit me on the head with something. No one knows where I am. They think I have gone to the docks to speak with Geoffrey.

Thomas heard voices coming into the room where he was. Suddenly the blanket was removed and he was picked up by his arm and dragged to a chair. Duke Bolwin stood before him.

"Well, well now isn't this a surprise, Martin? Not so confident without your sword, are you, Prince? Martin, remove that rag from his mouth for a moment. So, you're going to run me through uh? When as soon as your brother gets here?"

The duke slapped Thomas hard across the mouth twice. A trickle of blood drained down the side. He strained against his bonds. Martin cuffed him on the back of his head. Thomas slumped forward.

"Martin, don't knock him out. Throw some water on him." Martin picked up a bucket of slimy water and threw it on Thomas. He raised his head and looked Bolwin dead in the eyes.

"What do you want, little man?" the prince asked him. Bolwin stood there looking at a drenched, tied to a chair Thomas and he was still a bit frightened.

"What, are you still scared of me, little man? My hands are tied, I can't get them around your throat. Wetting your pants, are you?"

Thomas laughed out loud. They didn't want anyone to hear him. Martin balled his hand into a fist and hit the prince on the side of his head. He kicked his chair so that Thomas fell down then kicked him in the stomach.

"That's enough. We don't want him to die yet. Sit him up again."

Martin picked Thomas and his chair up and settled him till he sat straight up. He then stood looking at him with his fist balled up, ready to strike him again.

"Prince, we are going to take this kingdom away from you and your brother tonight. You are going to help me do that."

Thomas shouted at him, "Like hell I will! Do you expect me to betray my brother you, scum?"

"You will, or you will die here and now. That is your choice. You and your brother thought you were smart this morning, insulting me as if I were a nobody. It does not matter whether you help, you will die regardless." Bolwin crossed his arms against his chest.

"I'll leave you alone for a while to think about your future as fodder for the hogs. Martin, secure him tightly again and throw him in that corner. Put that blanket back over him. Make sure his big mouth is closed."

Martin hit him in the mouth then stuffed the rag back in and tied it closed. Both walked out into the sunshine leaving an unconscious Thomas alone on a dirt floor.

BOOK TWO
CHAPTER NINE

Me'na and Lady Hathaway walked for what seemed like hours around the palace and didn't see the same thing twice. She was shown the formal and family drawing rooms. The private dining hall that Sean and Thomas had eaten their noon meals in when they were children. Their mother, Queen Maryanne always found time to sit and talk to her boys at least once a day. It was their favorite time of the day.

There was an informal dining hall where the King often ate with his gentlemen for the morning and sometimes the noon meal. It this room it was usually men only. He used the formal dining hall for the evening meal when the nobles made their appearances. There were two different ballrooms, one that was used after the meals and then there was the very formal one that was only used for weddings and royal occasions. Sometimes there were visiting kings and princes from neighboring kingdoms that the Winslow's entertained.

On the floor where the King resided. There was space for a nursery. It was waiting for his and Me'na's children. Me'na had already been given the Queen's suite; she didn't know it until Lady Hathaway told her. It contained a large number of rooms. There was space for her ladies in waiting to congregate in the daytime. There was a small extra bedroom for whichever lady was on duty that night. Her personal guards had their room to rest and take meals in. She had a receiving room that guest would wait in to talk to her. It was more than she had ever had. To top everything off there was one special room that would contain nothing but clothes, shoes, hats and whatever accessories she had.

Amazing, simple amazing, she thought.

Earlier that morning the King had sent over a necklace for her to wear at the evening meal along with several rings. Me'na thought that she must be the luckiest of women and told his aunt so.

"Lady Hathaway, the King wishes to have you help me pick out my ladies in waiting since I do not know anyone here. He wants me to show him my list so that he can weed out the troublemakers. Do you think that is a good idea?"

"Well, Sean is just being a man, he can't help himself. I will point out prospects for you tonight, and then we will interview them and present our list to my nephew."

"I thank you so much for helping me get my clothes together, showing me around and most of all being like a mother to me. I never knew my own mother, so there is a lot that you can teach me if you are willing?" Me'na looked at her with such hope and admiration in her eyes that Lady Hathaway could not say no to her.

"I will do my best and fill in for your mother. Where do we start first?" Me'na was a little embarrassed at her next question, but she asked it anyway.

"Let's sit on this bench. Can you tell me what to expect on my wedding night. I do not know anything. Sean was the first man that I have ever wanted to kiss and did kiss. I am ignorant of these things."

She had tears in her eyes when she finished. She was so afraid of not being what he wanted her to be that she forgot to be who she was. That's all that Sean wanted from her. Lady Hathaway took her hands, raised her chin up, and began to talk to her as a mother would.

The King was back in the public receiving hall after the noon hour. There were only a few more cases that he needed to hear. He was wondering where Thomas was; he hadn't seen him since that morning. He should have concluded his business with Geoffrey by now.

After the last case was dismissed, the King called for Lord Carrington to come forth. He was nowhere to be found. He planned on cleaning house today. He would be rid of all questionable subjects now. He sent his knights in search of him around the palace but they could not locate him. Sean requested that the Earl of Dovenmire, Lord Robert go in search of him. He was told to take whom ever else he thought that he needed.

He asked the Duke of Richmore, Lord Connor to accompany him. They left the palace along with their squires to search the town. They finally remembered that Lord Carrington had a bad habit of gambling, so they went to his favorite gaming house, which also doubled as a gentlemen's club. The squires were left outside with the horses. There they found him drowning his sorrows in a mug of ale. Both men sat down at the table with him. Lord Carrington raised his head up when they sat down. He started mumbling incoherently about wanting to get out of the plan but someone wouldn't let him.

"Neil, sit up. What are you talking about? The King is looking for you. What did you do?" asked Lord Connor.

He was crying and drooling all at the same time. He was a stinking mess. Earl Robert was not so gentle with him, he did not like him or trust him. He had been acting very jumpy and nervous lately. He shook him hard.

"Neil, you are a peer of the realm. Act like it. Straighten yourself up, man. Oh, what's the use," he said. Earl Robert let his head hit the table. Connor looked at him and shook his head.

"Neil what did you do? Maybe we can help you if you tell us?"

"Nobody can help me. They are going to kill the prince and it's his fault entirely."

"Who is going to kill the prince, and whose fault is it?" Connor asked him. Carrington kept on talking as if he had not heard him.

"He got my Cassie with child. What was I to do? I couldn't kill him." Both men looked at each other and then around the room to see if anyone heard.

"Con, we had better get him a room upstairs."

Robert went to get a room, while Connor tried to lift up Carrington. Both men were able to carry him up the stairs to a room in the back. They took off some of his clothes and his boots then pulled covers up to his chin.

"We had better get back to the King. He has already asked about the prince. Let's go."

They walked down the stairs and out of the door to their horses. The men along with their squires galloped quickly back to the palace. In the clubroom at the last table in the corner sat Martin Beaumont. He had been watching the proceedings with mild interest. He was there to tie up any loose ends.

As soon as he was certain that on one was watching the stairs, he walked up them and checked all the rooms until he found the right one. Carrington was lying on his back drunkenly snoring. Martin walked over to him and placed his large hands around his throat. He did not remove his hands until all the life had left Carrington's body. He left out of a window onto the street.

Lords Connor and Robert raced back to the palace as fast as they could. They jumped off of their horses leaving them for the squires to attend to. Both men were in their mid thirties and were in great physical condition, they ran at breakneck speed through the palace to reach the King. They were told that he was in the garden with Sir Jonathon Hightower, Earl Patrick Hadley, Sir Adam Downing and Lord Hamilton.

As soon as they reached the entrance to the garden, they slowed down. They calmed themselves and walked smartly into the area where laughter was coming from. The King was speaking.

"Adam, you are still walking around like a love-sick cow. How long has it been since you last seen Lady Mary Beth, maybe ten minutes?"

There was more laughter at the expense of Sir Adam who was experiencing his first bout of love. At the sound of the footsteps coming quickly toward them, the men looked up with smiles on their faces. The smiles were replaced with concern when they looked upon the faces confronting them. Lord Connor and Lord Robert kneeled down to Sean.

"Highness, there may be trouble brewing with Prince Thomas."

"Stand up, Connor, Rob. Tell me what this is about."

They complied and told the King exactly what they were told by Lord Carrington. Everyone's face had paled, as the tale was unfolded, everyone except the King's whose face was livid with rage.

"Are you sure about these details?" he asked them.

"Yes, Highness, we are," answered Rob.

"We placed him in a room at the Boars Club. He was passed out drunk."

Sean stood and immediately called the nearest palace sentry to him. "Go and get Captain Lovett, bring him here immediately. I will be in the throne room awaiting him."

An angry Sean marched into the palace and directly to his throne. He sent Sir Adam in search of Lord Hightower and sent Sir Jonathan in search of his other gentlemen. He wanted everyone accounted for.

"Lord Hamilton, would you be so kind as to check on my betrothed. Make sure that she is fine and report back to me."

Lord Hamilton bowed with the dignity of an elder statesman and went about his task. Lord Hightower was soon located he was on his way. The rest of the King's gentlemen were filing in. They were all there and very concerned when they looked upon the King's countenance. Sean waited silently until Captain Lovett rushed in and kneeled to his King.

"Captain Lovett, rise, when was the last time you saw the prince?"

The captain came to his feet and remembered that he had not seen the prince since the previous day. "Your Majesty, I have not seen the prince since yesterday."

"It appears he may be missing, I have been looking for him since this morning after we broke our fast. I want you to send a detachment to the Boars Club and bring, drag or whatever you have to do to get Lord Carrington here immediately. Then I want you to head up a troop and try to locate my brother." Sean sat as straight as an arrow. His face was calm but his hands gripped the arms of his chair.

"On second thought, I want half of your men with you and the other half with Lord Chaney who is in the palace. You two start at different sections of the town. Daniel, go in search of Lord Chaney and bring him to Captain Lovett. He was in the weapons room of Prince Thomas' military compound."

Sean stood, to all who knew him well, you could tell he had himself physically under control. His mental state was another thing. He started pacing while he was waiting for Lord Hightower. His men had always seen a happy go lucky king, never this serious one. When Lord Hightower arrived, he was filled in on what was going on. Sean thought it best to fill in his gentlemen and Captain Lovett on all details.

As soon as Lord William Chaney arrived, he and Captain Lovett left to go and find the prince. Sean sent Sir Timothy Walls when he arrived to the docks to speak with Lord Geoffrey Blackmon. The last time anyone had seen Thomas he was on his way to the docks. Sean told his companions to remain with him until he needed to do something, any thing. He had no idea what he might have to do. In the meantime, Lord Hamilton had arrived back and was ready to give the king his news.

"Your Highness, the Lady Me'na is on her balcony. I told her to expect you. I knew you would want to talk to her. I hope I did not overstep, sire."

Sean got out of his chair and stepped down. "No, that is why you are a long time trusted friend. You know what I want before I do. Thank you." Sean placed a hand on his shoulder. The King turned to his men who were at odds on what to do next. "Please retire to my chamber and ready my mail, I will be there directly. Everyone get your mail on first and await me there."

Sean turned to go to Me'na's suite and his men all went to their suites to dress for war. Squires were sent to ready horses after their masters were readied. Within the hour, all the men were waiting for the King in his chamber. Lord Robert sent the King's squires, Sir Adam Hamilton and Sir Jonathan Hightower to the stable to ready the King's warhorse. Some of the men were out in the garden, the smaller one off of the King's chamber practicing their swings. They felt that they needed to loosen up.

Sean walked into Me'na's room unannounced. She turned around immediately for she felt his presence. She was all smiles when he arrived. Sean tried to hide his feelings from her. He went to her and pulled her into his arms. He put his face in her hair and inhaled deeply. She knew something was not right with him, even though he hadn't said anything, she knew.

"Come, love, sit and tell me ails you?" she asked him.

Sean looked at her and marveled at the calming effect that she was having on him. Oh, how he loved her, he loved her as if they had been together for years instead of days. He braced himself as they sat, he didn't want her to be afraid.

"I think Thomas may have been kidnaped. We are looking for him now."

Me'na looked at him and wondered at his strength. If Sean were the one missing, she would go mad.

"Who do you think could have done this? Have you checked on the location of Duke Bolwin? He is a vile man, capable of anything."

Sean thought for a moment and remembered that the duke had not been seen since that morning."No, sweet. My mind is so filled with worry that I did not think of him. All I wanted to do was make sure you are safe before I did anything else."

"Sean, he is capable of many things that you do not know. I was kept a virtual slave to him. I did not want to tell you, I was afraid that if I caused trouble, my spear of happiness would evaporate, I know it's silly to think that, but when you have been treated as badly as I, you would understand."

Her eyes watered with tears and Sean scooped her up into his arms. He kissed her on her forehead and squeezed her tightly. She looked up at him."I am better now, you have seen to it. I am not afraid anymore. Is there anything that I can do to help you?"

"No, my love, there is nothing. I want you to stay in the palace and remain safe. I have to find my brother. He may be a bother sometime, but he's my problem. Do not leave from here, please don't try and help. I must go now but I'll be back as soon as I have something to report to you. The evening gathering has been suspended. Take your meal in your room for my sake."

Sean stood and pulled her up with him. She put her arms around his neck and kissed him passionately. This time he was on the receiving end. It was a good feeling to have her grab him around the neck and kiss him. After the kiss, Me'na looked up at him and smiled a devilish smile at him.

"What's that look for?" he asked her.

"How was it? I really applied myself this time."

He was amazed by her ability to make him forget his problem, even if it was only momentarily. He grabbed her to him and held her tightly. "You are really good for me, you know that? The kiss was the best that I have ever had."

She always knew what to say to ease him.

The compliment meant a lot to her. She wanted to be the best wife that she could be for him. After all, she came with nothing except the clothes on her back, literally. There was already talk in the palace about the swiftness of the King to get married. She paid attention to who said what, for they would not be allowed in her inner circle.

As Sean prepared to leave, he looked at her again and felt a chill up his spine. He thought, *No, not her, not her. Please not her. I can't lose her, first father, maybe Thomas...*

He hung his flaxen head. Me'na rushed to him.

"My love, what is wrong, please tell me."

Sean just sort of stood there looking through her. She placed her hands on the side of his face and looked into those green eyes that she loved so much. She saw hollowness and deep pain that she feared she'd be unable to ease for him.

"Nothing, my sweet. I'm just worried, that's all. Do not worry. You just be safe. I had best go. My men are waiting for me." With that, Sean turned and left.

The room had suddenly gone cold to her. Her arms had goose bumps and she rubbed them to herself. *There must be something that I can do. I know that evil duke better than most.*

She sat down and wrote a note to her beloved in case she didn't make it back safely. Me'na poured all her love for him in the note and placed it on her bed. She looked back at the paper and thought she could never write down all of her feelings for him. They were immeasurable. She put her old clothes back on and looked over the balcony. The guards were still standing beneath it, if she was quiet she might be able to leave unnoticed. It wasn't that long of a way down. She had climbed further down than that when she attempted to escape her brother.

I can do it, she thought.

Me'na went to the door to see if her guards were still there and they were. She quietly closed the door.

I think the duke is on the third floor. It is just as easy to climb up as it is to climb down.

Me'na used her belt to tie her dress between her legs so she could climb up. Once she started, it wasn't so bad as long as she didn't look down. She soon reached the third floor of the palace. Now it was only a matter of finding which room was the duke's. Me'na soon found the duke's room and she was in luck, for he was there. She quietly listened.

"Martin, did you leave a guard on the prince? We don't need him getting away."

"Yes, Richard I did. Stop pestering me about it, I told you I did," was Martin's sharp reply.

"And what about Carrington, did you kill him also?" Richard asked.

"If you ask me one more time, I will kill you as well and cut my losses. I'll tell King Winslow that you planned everything and forced me to do it."

Martin didn't like being quizzed this way. Richard acted as if he had to be led by the nose. "You just remember you said that I can have the girl."

"Don't worry, I don't want her skinny butt, she's all legs anyway."

"You have not seen what I have, but that's fine with me, I don't like sharing."

Me'na felt her skin crawl as they spoke about her. She knew it was her they spoke of. Martin always stared at her.

"Martin, it's time to go back to Thomas. We must leave here before we are arrested."

She watched them as they left the duke's room and later emerged from another room farther away. They climbed out of the window and down the trellis. Me'na climbed down and snuck around the palace to wait for them. The part of the palace that the duke was housed in was in the old quarter; it was close to the front of the bailey. He was housed in the worse section. Darkness was starting to fall and she wasn't sure she'd be able to find her way back, but she would try. She flattened her body against the wall and followed them out of the palace grounds.

They went a long way from the castle down a winding alley. They came upon a ragged cottage that was leaning to one side. A soldier was standing in front of the door. He moved to one side as they approached. Bolwin told him to join the other soldiers in the barracks. Both went inside and lit a candle. Thomas had squirmed around enough to move the blanket off of him. He peered up at them as they brought the candle close to his face.

"Well, what say you? Do you like your accommodations? I admit, it's not the palace but," he shrugged his shoulders. Martin dragged Thomas up into a sitting position and untied his mouth.

"Let me go," he screamed at them. "My brother will kill you when me finds me. I'll kill you."

Martin kicked him in the stomach. "Shut up. No one can hear you. I am tired of listening to you," Martin told him.

Me'na couldn't believe her luck she had actually found him. All she had to do was to wait for them to leave and free the Prince. She waited in the shadows.

Duke Bolwin cut a lock of Thomas' hair and took his rings off his fingers. He chose the prince ring and put it with his hair in a piece of cloth. These he put in his pocket to give to the King. He had Martin put the rag back in Thomas' mouth, then they turned to leave. Bolwin turned back to Thomas.

"Do you know how easy it was to find someone who would betray you? All we had to do was to find a man with a young wife and that was that. Carrington's wife Cassandra was your lover, wasn't she?" He didn't wait for acknowledgment. "Did you know that she carries your child?" Thomas managed to keep his face from betraying his thoughts. "No, didn't think so. He was eager to have you killed but he didn't have the guts to do it himself. When approached by one of my agents, he readily complied. He wanted to back out, but a deal is a deal. We had to kill him, as we will kill you and your brother."

Thomas struggled against his bonds. Martin stood behind him and put his hands on his shoulders, effectively pushing him down.

"Martin will first rape his little betrothed before his eyes then squeeze the life out of her. Won't that be a high time?"

He was laughing, Martin started laughing, and then they walked out into the night, leaving the prince alone.

Me'na was devastated. She didn't care about herself, but she would not like Sean die. No matter if she died in the process, she would not let him die.

The Candean soldiers that were coming up the southern coast from Timbre had arrived in Fastonia. The last quarter of the moon proved to be very dark, that was good for the Candeans. They were able to row their boats pass the sentries on duty in the fortress. It was too dark for them to see much. They came ashore about a mile away from the fortress. The boats were dragged ashore and stashed inland. The soldiers made their way through the dense trees to the road that had been cleared for them during last month dark phase of the moon.

They could not light any torches for they could be seen at the southern fortress. The captains had walked the path several times to be sure that no mistakes were made. The duke's men were holding their families' hostage in Candea they had no choice. No one wanted to do this, they would have preferred to avoid this duty; but their choices were limited.

So, off they went to find the caves that they would hide in. Weapons were already there waiting on them, they just had to get there without too much noise. Soon the caves were located and the men sat and waited for the signal. The duke was going to shot a flaming arrow into the sky and they would start toward the palace.

Me'na crept into the cottage and felt her way to Thomas. She was very careful, it was dark. She didn't want him to kick her thinking that she was the enemy.

"Prince Thomas. It's me, Me'na. Speak so that I can find you."

Thomas heard her and started groaning against his bonds. Me'na soon found him and tried to untie his mouth.

"I followed the duke here and waited for him to leave. The King is very worried about you. He has men looking all over town. I've seen some, at least I was not sure whose soldiers they were. I decided to keep quiet in-case they were the duke's." She was able to get the rag out of his mouth.

"Me'na, do you have a knife with you to cut my bonds?"

"No, Prince, I could not find one when I left, I will try to untie you. Do you want me to go back to the palace and get the King?"

"No, they may catch you, keep trying. Why did you come to help me?"

"I could not stand to watch my beloved eyes look so sorrowful and not do anything to help him. I know that he will be displeased with me; but I can weather the storm. I'd rather that than to see those eyes look bottomless again. Besides, I know just what the duke is capable of. He is worse than what you think, Prince."

"Quiet, Me'na. Did you hear something? Sounds like someone may be out there." Me'na was silent as she worked on Thomas' bonds. Suddenly, the door opened and in walked the soldier.

The King was in his chamber getting dressed. He stood with his legs and arms apart. His gentlemen were putting his armor on him. Sean carried a knife in both boots plus a Toledo dagger up his gauntlet. He preferred to wear just a breastplate so that he could put his two special shorter swords on his back, but his men feared for him. The armor wouldn't permit the swords in the middle of his back. His sword was strapped on his left side. He wanted his ax on his horse along with the broad sword on the other side of the animal. His shield was placed on his horse and everything was in readiness.

As they were walking out of the palace, Duke Bolwin and Lord Beaumont approached them. The King had men looking for those two but they were unable to find them. As soon as they were spotted, Sean's men lunged for them.

"Your Highness, you need to call off your dogs or you will never see your brother alive again."

"Where is he, you vile beast? How do I know that you have him?" was Sean's tight response.

"Names. Why do you call me names? King Winslow, you brought this upon yourself when you refused my request for a decrease. King Sardin was most specific when he said not to come back without the agreement."

The King's men kept their swords drawn.

"I cannot go home, so I have nothing to lose. This is what happens when you ignore me."

"Do you have proof that you have the prince? How do I know that he is not with a friend?" Sean asked him.

Duke Bolwin reached into his pocket and pulled out the cloth that held the prince's hair and ring. He gave these things to Sean's squire Sir Adam who stepped forward for the object. Sir Adam gave them to the King. Sean opened it and found his brother's prince's ring and a lock of Thomas' black hair. He stepped toward the pair very slowly.

"If you have injured my brother in any way you will die tonight. We will not wait for your surprise attack tonight."

The duke's face showed his shock at this knowledge. He tried to cover it but not quickly enough.

"Ah, you see we know a few things also. Lord Carrington was found dead today. The barkeep remember seeing a large man going up the stairs. He saw you out of the corner of his eye, Lord Beaumont."

Martin just stood there balling up his fist as if he would hit the King. Lord Colin Firth and Lord Connor Ramsey pushed up to him with swords drawn, waiting for him to make a move.

"Don't split him open yet, men, I need to know a few things first." Both men backed away a little, not much. Swords were still drawn. Sean walked up to Bolwin and put his hand around his throat. "I could kill you and it would not disturb me. Tell me what I want to know now. We may spare you. Don't tell me and you are going to die here and now. Make your choice."

He was choking him tighter and tighter. Sean's men were smiling grimly at the duke. They wanted the king to kill him now. Duke Bolwin raised up his hand.

"Please stop so I can talk. I will bring your brother out into the open square in the center of the town. You can retrieve him there in about one hour. Do not follow me or you will never find him, Your Highness."

"Go now and get him, or so help me I'll peel the skin off of your worthless bones and feed you to the dogs, alive."

Duke Bolwin and Martin Beaumont swiftly walked away into the night. Sean ordered Lord Chaney and Captain Lovett to get the troops together and meet them in the square. The King told Lord Hamilton to send word to the ghost squad to kill King Sardin. He would end this now. They were to hold the city if they could; reinforcements would be sent immediately from the border to assist them.

Sir Timothy Walls was sent to tell Lord Geoffrey Blackmon to bring the ships into the dock. He was to send the men from the ships to the town square and to come with them. Sir Benjamin Blackmon and Sir Robert Temple came out of the infirmary with their breastplate on, ready for battle. The physician released them an hour ago so they could help the King. The knights from the border would arrive at any time now. They were all on horse and it was just a matter of getting there. The infantry was to stay at the border and watch for movements. No one thought about long boats coming ashore on the jetties. That was too dangerous and foolhardy.

The Duke and Beaumont were on their way to the cottage when they saw Thomas and Me'na try to slip out of the door. The soldier that was supposed to be with his unit came back. He discovered that his unit was locked up. Not wanting to be locked up himself, he came back to guard the cottage. Me'na managed to hit him on the head with the chair that was in the room. She got his sword and cut Thomas' bonds, they saw the duke at the same time that he saw them. Thomas started to run and shouted for Me'na to hurry but her dress caught on a rock and down she fell. Thomas saw her fall, stopped, but did not go back for her. He left her to the duke's tender ministrations. Martin

Beaumont grabbed her by the arm and dragged her into the cottage.

"This is even better than having the prince. We have the King's intended bride. Tie her hands, Martin. We'll use her instead; the king will never get over her death."

"You said that I could have her before we killed her and I want her."

Me'na spit at him and he viciously slapped her across the face splitting her lip. She wouldn't cry she would not give them the satisfaction of her tears. She resigned herself to die with dignity, as Sean would have. She loved him enough to save his brother and give her life in return if that's what it took.

She didn't wonder why Thomas didn't try to come back and get her. What did it matter anyway? She had loved Sean for a lifetime. It felt that way even it was only a few days. She would carry their moment in time to her grave. It was better than what she thought life originally had in store for her. She knew it couldn't get any better unless she could actually marry him. Life made her into a fatalist. She was coming out of it due to that green-eyed King whom she loved with all her spirit.

I do not want my death to make him not try to love again. He has much to offer.

As Me'na had all these dark thoughts, she never once thought that she could be saved. She figured that she had been saved already when she fell in love with Sean.

Duke Bolwin told Martin to go outside and shoot the flaming arrow. His soldiers in the caves saw it and started the march to the palace. It was only about a mile away.

Earl Robert Langston and Earl Hadley saw the flaming arrow in the night sky. They went straight away to the king who was conferring with his commanders.

"Sire, we saw a signal of some kind, a flaming arrow was seen in the sky. It must be a signal for the Candeans." Sean turned to Captain Lovett who was on his way out. "Captain, send some men to check out this possible sign. Rob, from which direction did it appear?" the King asked him.

"It appeared to have been shot into the southwestern sky sire. The woods behind the palace are thick; a small infantry squad could be coming through there."

Captain Lovett was on it before the King could issue the order. Sean knew that his soldiers were well trained and the best in the world. They would find out if anyone was back there. After this, he planned to send woodsmen into the forest to thin it out a bit. He would give the extra wood to the peasants for fire. Even at a time like this, he was still thinking about his people, amazing he smiled to himself.

"Sire, might I inquire the reason for the smile? We could all use some levity about now" Connor asked him.

"Con, I was thinking about having those woods thinned out after this is over with the extra wood being given to the people. My mind is always on my people I cannot help it. Even with my brother's life on the line, I still remember my duty to the people of Fastonia." The King just shook his head. All started to speak at once.

"Sire, you are the best king any of us remember Fastonia having. King Phillip was a good king also, but with you, it seems to be second nature. I mean you do it without trying, ruling that is." That lengthy statement was about the most that anyone remember Earl Patrick Hadley saying at one time. It was how they all felt.

The Candean soldiers were coming out of the caves and into the woods behind the palace grounds. The grounds were extensive; they stretched several miles in either direction. Captain Lovett and his men were well armed and ready. He emptied nearly all of the men out of the northern garrison that was located in Winslow Town.

They marched steadily toward their prey not knowing how many men were out there. Geoffrey Blackmon and his sailors were making their way to the town square. William Chaney had all the necessary weapons from the armory brought to the square for the men. These sailors were seasoned veterans. They hadn't had a fight in weeks and this was right up their alley.

As the Fastonians were preparing for a possible battle, the Candeans were trying to break out of the barracks. They could not understand why they were locked up. Their captain thought that the duke must have offended the King and that he was in trouble. No one really wanted to go to his aide, but they did want to know what was going on.

By the time that Captain Lovett found the army he was looking for they were almost at the palace. They clashed immediately. It was very dark however there was some light. The fighting was intense and some of the Candeans went around the fight, they were going to try and reach the palace.

As this was going on, Sean sent word to Me'na to ensure her safety. Sir Tristan knocked on her door to inquire if she was all right, but she never answered. He called Sir Jamie to go with him into her room. It was dark and they had to bring a candle. She was nowhere to be found they searched everywhere. No one wanted to go to the King with the news that she was missing.

Sir Tristan walked up to the King who was standing outside of the palace walls with his household detail giving orders to his men. Tristan kneeled down on one knee to Sean and bowed his head.

"Sir Tristan, why have you left my betrothed wife alone?" the King asked him. Tristan stood and looked his King in the eye.

"Sire, we looked everywhere we could and she was not to be found. She did not leave through the doors, we never left our post. The balcony doors were open, but we couldn't find a trace of her, Your Highness."

Sean looked at him as if he had grown two heads. "What do you mean, she is not in her room? I left her in your charge. Speak, man, speak!" The King was losing his renowned control. He felt helpless and angry all at one time. He wanted to strangle Tristan and anyone else he could lay his hands on.

He turned around and rushed to Me'na's rooms. His gentlemen ran behind him, trying to keep him from doing anything rash. Sir Douglas and Sir Howard were still at their assigned stations. He rushed into her rooms. "Me'na, Me'na, where are you?" he shouted.

Sean ran through her whole suite looking for some trace of her. On her bed, he found a note. The King looked at it but couldn't make himself pick it up. Henry stepped forward, picked up the note, placed it in Sean's hand and led him to a chair to sit by the candlelight. His cousin ushered the men out of the room so Sean could read the note in private. He just stared at it for a couple of minutes unable to comprehend that she was gone. Finally, he was able to read what she wrote.

My Dearest Love:

I want you to know that my life changed when I met you. You made me want to wake up in the morning and not go to sleep in the night. Visions of you are constantly in my head and heart. I think I have loved you all my life. You have completed me and made me whole. I am going to try to find Thomas for you. I know the duke better than most and have seen what he is capable of. He is an evil man and would kill your brother just to have something to do. My dearest love, I want you to know that my life changed when I met you. You have given everything to me, and I have nothing to give in return. Freeing the prince will be my gift to you. I am going to make it back to you with the prince in tow.

I am not trying to die. But I am leaving this note for you in case things do not go as planned. Please do not be angry with me. I do this out of the great love that I bear for you. You are the best thing that ever happened to me in my life. If I don't make it out alive to you, I will be waiting for you on the other side with my arms open wide.

I love you with all my heart and soul. We will find each other again and renew our love.

All my love, your Me'na.

Sean's eyes watered. He felt something was going to happen at their last meeting. He let the paper fall to the floor and stared with unseeing eyes into the darkness. Henry walked in the room. They had to get to the town square.

"Sean, what did she say?"

Sean looked at him with a tortured heart and could not respond. He had to repeat his question to him. Henry bent down and picked up the letter. He folded it and stuck it in his shirt. Sean looked at him with hollow eyes.

"She is going to try and free Thomas. She believes she has nothing of value to give. So she will try to free him. She speaks of material things not of herself, which is the most precious gift that she has. Me'na is all I want and desire." Tears streamed down Sean's face, he felt she was going to die. He of course was going to move heaven and hell to make sure that didn't happen.

He wiped at his face and stood up to his full height with shoulders thrown back. "Come, Henry, we have a duke to kill."

Duke Bolwin and Martin tied Me'na's hands behind her back and walked with her to the square. As they approached it, a large force could be seen waiting for them.

Suddenly, the clash of steel was heard coming from the palace grounds. The King was approaching the square when he heard the commotion. His household guard immediately surrounded him along with his companions. His guard numbered about one hundred fifty men tonight; any one of them would give their life for him.

They were sitting on their horses when the duke appeared. He had Me'na hid with Lord Beaumont behind a building. The King's men were engaged slightly, but the sailors bore the brunt of the fighting. The Candeans were coming around the palace with Fastonians chasing them. They were trying to reach the King's back. The sailors engaged them with relish.

Coming at breakneck speed down the road were the knights from the border. They could hear the battle rage and pushed their mounts harder. They jumped into the fray along with the Candeans who managed to break out of the barracks. They had no weapons and the fight was not going the Candeans way. Their captain managed to get some swords and handed them out to his men. Sean directed the fighting from his vantage point. He kept trying to move around so he could fight but his men pressed ever closer to him.

The duke hollered out to Sean. "Your Highness, I do not have your brother anymore but I have someone better."

He stretched out his hand and Beaumont walked up dragging a struggling Me'na. Most of the fighting had ceased when the duke started to holler to the King and the men turned to listen.

All this time, Thomas was trying to make his way to the palace. He had been in a cottage that was on the edge of town and Winslow was a large city. He could not find a horse to borrow. It took some time to get there. He heard the battle rage and quickened his pace, hoping that he could get there in time. He didn't want Me'na to die. Sean would never get over it. Thomas had finally realized that Sean loved her more than he wanted her. She freed him out of the great love that she bore his brother.

Sean saw Me'na. He started moving toward her. She shook her head to him and appeared to be saying I'm sorry. His men moved in closer to him, trying to block his path. He got off his horse.

"Well, King, it looks like I am holding the upper hand this time. Should I slit her throat, maybe tie her to two horses and pull her apart? What shall it be? What kind of death should an almost queen get?"

All of the men couldn't believe what they were hearing. No man brought a woman into battle that was cowardly and unworthy of a soldier. The Candeans didn't know what they were fighting for, but this wasn't it. Most of them dropped their swords or sheathed them. They would not be part of murdering a defenseless woman. All eyes were on the duke and the King.

"Let her go. Fight me like a man of honor. Do you have any honor Bolwin, or does my wife have more honor than you?" the King shouted.

The Candeans and Fastonians couldn't believe that the woman the duke held captive was the King's bride. They had heard of the fairy tale romance between the two and didn't want to see it end this way.

The duke had his arm around her neck while Beaumont held an arrow pointed at the King. Charles had heard the fighting and came outside to help his new king.

As he approached Sean, he started to talk to Bolwin. "Richard, don't do this, it is not necessary. Why kill her, she means nothing to you."

"Hello, traitor, are they treating you well?" he shouted to Charles.

"Richard, you know that I was born in Fastonia, I am simply coming home. Is that why you are holding her?" Charles asked him.

"This has nothing to do with you, Ainsley. It has to do with me being king after Winslow is dead." He looked at Sean.

"A life for a life, sire. What shall it be?"

Sean started walking forward again. His men were rushing to stop him. Connor and Henry had already dismounted their horses and rushed to hold him back.

"Let me go, now! Do you hear me?" he raged.

"Yes, Sean I hear you but I cannot let you pass. You are our King," Henry calmly answered him. He didn't feel calm. This was the worse he'd ever felt in his entire life. He knew how much Sean loved her. Sean looked at them with such agony in his eyes.

"But that is my Queen, I cannot let her die. I must go to her."

"No, sire, we cannot let you pass," Henry answered him.

All of his gentlemen surrounded him and tried their best to support Henry. As he was the King's cousin, most of the disagreeable task fell to him if Thomas was not around. He shouldered the responsibility well. He could weather the coming storm. Sean looked at Me'na with sad eyes.

She smiled to him and shouted. "It is all right, my love. He can do nothing to my heart."

"Shut up, before I cut your tongue out," Bolwin told her. He turned and gave her a vicious backhanded slap. She fell to the ground.

"No!" the King shouted.

This time his men were pulling him back physically. They never realized how strong he was; four of them were trying to contain him. He was dragging them with him until Charles threw himself in front.

"No, sire, that's what he wants you to do."

As they were trying to handle the king, Bolwin told Beaumont to shoot the arrow at them. Charles turned around and saw it coming; he pushed Sean out of the way. The arrow caught Charles in the shoulder. Beaumont readied another arrow. Thomas was almost to the King; he was coming through the crowd.

"Winslow, watch as I slit her worthless throat," Bolwin shouted.

The duke pulled her neck backward. She was trying to pull away from him, but his grip was too tight.

Thomas was within a few feet of Sean, shouting his name. Me'na tried elbowing the duke but Beaumont hit her in the stomach. If the duke hadn't been holding her head back, she would have fallen.

Sean saw her get hit again and became enraged. He was dragging Connor who had one arm with Henry restraining the other. Robert and Patrick braced themselves in front of him, pushing back.

Sean looked in Thomas' direction when he heard his name. He kept trying to get to Me'na. He saw Bolwin place his dagger at her throat. Thomas seemly came from out of nowhere and dived at his brother. As Sean was falling, Beaumont let lose his arrow. He saw Me'na's throat cut, and Bolwin letting her body fall to the ground.

"NOOO!" he screamed.

BOOK ONE
CHAPTER TWO

Sean woke up in a cold sweat screaming, "Nooo!"

It was the same no that he had been screaming in his dream. He got up and sat on the side of his bed. He placed his elbow on his legs, and held his head in his hands.

"It was more real this time than it ever has been. I wonder if I'm going to meet this woman soon. The dream was somehow different this time. He looked at the clock and saw that it was only one a.m. Sean lay back down in his bed but he did not get back to sleep.

The morning dawned bright and sunny as the alarm clock on the side of the bed went off. Sean looked at it and hit the snooze button. It was seven a.m.

Fifteen more minutes please.

He didn't go back to sleep, he remembered his dream very vividly. Usually, he only remembered bits and pieces, but this time, he awoke with full memory. Was she real?

He had been having the dreams about her since he was twenty or so. He remembered they started after he was knocked unconscious on the football field during a game against Texas A & M. Thomas was on the opposing side. He had run onto the field to see what had happened to him. Thomas' face was the first one he saw when he awoke. The football was still in his hands, he didn't drop it. That was the first and last game that he didn't play the whole time.

After that incident, he started having the dreams. His doctor thought that maybe they were a result of the blow to the head and would stop eventually. They didn't, they only became more real to him and frequent. After a while, he started to play a game with himself. He would try to make himself daydream the dreams in an effort to control them. That didn't work either. Finally, he just gave up and accepted them as part of his life. Only within the last two years did he start seeing a psychiatrist. The doctor told him that he might have lived recent lives. Yes, the doctor said lives. Sean thought that was preposterous for a long time. But now, maybe there was something to it.

After a nice hot shower and doing his toiletries, Sean prepared to shave. He was growing a low beard and mustache they were coming in nicely. He grew it because he had a beard in the dream. Maybe that would help Me'na recognize him, if she was looking. He was convinced that she had to be dreaming about him also and was just as tormented.

He was so tired. The only bright spot today was that after this he had two days in a row off. Thomas asked him to work the first half of his shift because he had urgent business, he didn't say what her name was. Sean finished dressing and went into the kitchen for some toast and coffee. The coffee was ready and he really needed it. Today was going to be a long day. He looked out the kitchen window for his newspaper and it was not where it should be again.

"Boy, that kid, one day he'll surprise me with it being where I want it."

He went to the front door, got the morning paper, and laid it on the table. Sean put two slices of bread in the toaster and poured the coffee, he took it black. The phone rang and he had to look for it before he could answer it. It was on top of the refrigerator, how it got there was beyond him. As he picked up the phone Sean got his favorite strawberry jam out of the frig.

He held the phone on his shoulder while he got his toast. "Hello" he answered. It was his brother on the other end.

"Sean, you didn't forget you promised to work four hours for me this afternoon, did you?" Thomas asked.

"Good morning to you too, Thomas. How are you?"

"I'm sorry. Good morning, brother, and how are you this fine day?" Sean had to laugh at the lack of sincerity in Thomas' voice.

"No, I did not forget, you won't let me," Sean told him.

Thomas laughed with him. "I really appreciate this, Sean, I owe you big time. At least, you have two days off in a role."

"You still owe me from the last time. When are you going to pay your debts?"

Thomas said, "Tell you what, since you are off Saturday and Sunday, I will work all day Monday for you. How about that for pay back?"

"I'll believe it when I see my name scratched off the duty roster and your name replacing mine when you come in. Deal?"

"Deal," Thomas agreed.

"OK, I'll see you later. My toast is getting cold."

"Bye, Sean, and thank you again," Thomas hung up.

"Yes, three days off." He did the little hump sign with his arm and sat down to breakfast.

As Sean drove to work, his attitude took on a more positive note. He hadn't had three days off since, well, never. This was the first time in a long time he would actually be able to do some of the things that he wanted to do. He wasn't sure what, but he'd wear himself out trying to find out. There was plenty for him to do in the city. He loved living in Houston. He didn't even mind the traffic. It was a big change from the traffic in Beaumont.

As a native Texan, he felt the most beautiful women in the country lived within its borders. He thought about dedicating his off time to finding one of those beauties. Maybe drive over to Galveston or one of the other beaches. Yes, he was going to enjoy himself as never before. Sean pulled into his parking spot whistling, got his bag off the seat and briskly walked into the hospital. He spoke to one and all that he happened to pass in the hall on his way to his locker. A few other doctors were in the locker room when he got there. Everyone seemed to be half asleep.

Sean reported to emergency to begin his long day that didn't seem as long anymore. It was a regular day, few emergencies in the morning with it picking up in the afternoon. Everyone kept asking him why he was so happy. His only answer was, "I have three days off in a row."

He and a couple of his friends went to lunch in the cafeteria, it was extremely busy; but he didn't seem to mind much today. Dr. Kristoff Sanderson who was one of his closest friends couldn't believe Thomas was actually going to repay a favor. That was unheard of, he told Sean to beware and not believe it until he signed the duty roster.

"Kris, if he betrays me this time, I will never do a favor for him again, I mean it."

"I hope so, Sean. He tries to use you because you are more dependable than he is. He is used to you always telling him to forget it."

"Not this time, I really need to be off. I'm burnt out after too many weeks without much time off."

Kristoff just shook his head. He knew Thomas was not trustworthy. If he broke his word to Sean this time, he would have a talk with him. He didn't care that they were brothers. He was more of a brother to Sean than Thomas was.

Kristoff stood up and went to get more coffee and sweet rolls for himself and Sean. When he sat down, Sean noticed that Kristoff's hair was braided differently again.

"Kris, who braided your hair this time, another new victim?" Sean asked.

"Say, why does she have to be a victim, man?" a smiling Kris asked.

"You know why. You're always looking for a girlfriend who can braid. I've never known you to date anyone that couldn't."

"Aw, man, do you know what they are charging these days to do this? Call me prejudice, I only date braiders."

"Do you think I can get…what's her name?"

Kristoff answered, "Nicole."

'Do you think I can get Nicole to do something with my hair?" Sean tossed his hair back and Kris almost fell out of his chair laughing.

"No, I think the effect would be totally lost on you. Anyway, I'm not introducing you to her yet."

"Why? I only bite once." Sean tried to look serious but couldn't.

"Man, I know, that's the problem. You lose interest fast, but the women always need just one more nibble. What's with you anyway? How do you do it?"

"Elusive charm," was the simple answer.

Kristoff became serious. "Sean, why can't you settle with one woman for any length of time?"

"I don't know. I feel as if I'm waiting for someone from my past to reappear in my life. I have no idea who," he admitted.

"Well, if it's meant to be, it will be," Kris said.

"Yea, you know, I've always believed, a guy only had to know a woman for ten minutes before he knew if she was marriage material. I just haven't met a woman that can last over ten minutes." He smiled. "I'm ready to marry. I just don't have any prospects yet. Maybe the mystery woman from my past will reappear." He shrugged his shoulders. "Who knows?"

Kristoff shrugged his shoulders also. This wasn't the first time Sean had spoken of a mystery woman coming back to him. Maybe he was right. Kris hoped he was. Sean needed a good woman. They moved on to the topic of football which was more interesting.

After lunch, they were very busy. There were accident victims being brought in every hour. Elderly people suffering from the Texas heat. A couple of shooting victims and a host of other problems filled his day. Thomas even came by early as a sign of good faith to Sean and signed the roster for Monday. He almost became a patient himself when his brother kept his word. Thomas was full of surprises and a couple of other things not worth mentioning.

Sean's official shift had ended and he was sitting in the cafeteria at the beginning of Thomas'. Things had slowed down a bit and he was going to relax for a while. He was thinking about joining his friend in private practice. Jim had asked him months ago to join him. He said that the money was good. You had weekends and holidays off. He could actually have a life. That way, he would be able to do what he went to medical school to specialize in, surgery. He was a brain surgeon by trade and a very good one. He had just about made up his mind to buy into the practice, when he was paged back to emergency.

Sean walked over to the house phone. "This is Dr. Sean Williams. I'm on my way."

After jogging into the emergency room to find his patient, the nurse pointed him to room number three. The first-year resident handed him a chart and brought him up to speed. It was a head injury, his specialty. He didn't look at the patient's name out of habit. He always wanted to see the medical part first, before looking to the name. As he walked into the room, he looked at the name on the chart. It said, Me'na Collins.

"Me'na," he said out loud and dropped the chart.

The resident, Lucas picked up the chart and held it out to him.

"Doctor?" he asked.

Sean rushed to the bed and looked down at her. She was unconscious. The nurse was wiping blood from her face looking for facial injuries, and there weren't any, just blood. Sean gingerly touched the back of her head, it was wet with blood. She moaned a low sound that was very familiar to him. He'd heard it before. The staff was watching him. He was only faintly aware that they were there.

Lucas asked him the question that everyone wanted asked, "Do you know her, Dr. Williams?"

"Yes, a very long time ago I knew her," he quietly said.

Nurse Cooper and Nurse Canton looked at each other in a knowing way but said nothing. Sean turned to Dr. Lucas Grant and asked him if x-rays had already been taken.

"Yes, they are coming up on the computer now."

The hospital used the new digital imaging system. X-rays were on the screen, it did away with the need for film.

Sean picked up her hand and felt her pulse. It wasn't strong but it wasn't weak either. He squeezed her hand gently and placed it back on the side of the bed.

Me'na opened her eyes and looked at him. "Sean, is that you?" Before he could answer, she had passed out again.

Oh my God, he thought. *She is real and she knows me too. Get a grip, Sean. You are her doctor first. Save her. Then get the answers to your questions.*

He opened her eyelids and looked at her eyes, and then he listened to her heart and whatever else he could think of. Nurse Cooper had to call to him twice after she finally got the images for him. Sean walked to the screen and studied the images very closely. He would need to operate, but he couldn't do it. He was personally involved.

Sean turned around and said, "Nurse Cooper, please page Dr. Kristoff Sanderson, stat."

The pressure to her brain was going to have to be relieved very soon before complications set in. Sean was not going to take any risks with Me'na's well being. She would not die, not as long as he was around.

"Nurse Canton, have her prepped for surgery, Dr. Grant call ahead and have a room prepared."

As Me'na was wheeled out of the room and into the elevator, Dr. Sanderson came in.

"What do you need, Sean?"

Sean brought him to the x-rays and they talked about what needed to be done. Kristoff asked him what he needed him for.

"Kris, I am personally involved with the patient, I'm too close to do this. I need you, my friend."

He asked, "Is it a family member?"

"No, it's a woman from my…" he couldn't finish. How could he say from my dreams? Who would believe him?

"No need to say anything more, my friend. There is always a woman from somewhere. Let's go up and scrub."

After both doctors scrubbed up, they went into the operating room. Kristoff was curious as to what this woman looked like. He walked to her side and discovered that she was very lovely and he smiled to himself.

Well, she is a looker. How did he let that get away? he thought.

Dr Sanderson was one of the hospital's most competent surgeons after Sean. Sean was their premier showpiece. He was used to attract other doctors and benefactors. He had been with them since he finished his residency and they did not want to let him go.

Dr. Sanderson started the operation with Sean assisting him. Everything was by the textbook. Sean had to emotionally detach himself from what he was doing. Half of the time, he kept trying to tear his eyes away from her face. It was a face that was well known to him. He knew the oval shape quite well. Her coloring was the same golden as in his dreams with the same hair a shade darker. He couldn't recall if her eyes were amber colored. He'd just looked at them, but in his present state of mind, he didn't remember. Sean was sure that they were. Everything else fit with what he remembered. He was amazed that he could function as well as he did. He was hardly breathing.

The surgery was over. Me'na survived and so did Sean. She was wheeled to recovery. The next forty-eight hours would be critical.

Dr. Sanderson wrote his orders for Me'na's care, he and Sean went to the cafeteria for coffee and conversation. After they were seated, Kris asked Sean if he would tell him about her, if he could.

"Kris, at this point in time, I can't say much; my emotions are a jumble. She was the last person I expected to see, but the one I needed to see the most. Does that make any sense to you?" he asked.

"Yes, it does if you are still in love with her. Are you?" Kris asked him.

"I have always been in love with her, only her. Her face has haunted me throughout all my relationships. No one else measures up. She is like a dream to me." He didn't elaborate that she was a dream. How could he? "She would give whatever it took to secure my happiness." Sean remembered his dream from last night. Me'na gave her life so that he could have his brother back.

"What happened, Sean? She sounds like the perfect woman to me."

"I don't know. It's complicated." That was as good an answer as he could give. "I do know this, Kris. I will not let her get away this time without a fight. She is precious to me. She holds my future in her hands."

Sean knew he could not live a full life until this past life was examined closely. He knew it in his heart that Me'na was his future and his past. It seemed that she knew it too, she recognized him on the spot.

"I know the nurses call me Dr. Freeze, that's not a very flattering name to be known as. I dated a few of them but none of the relationships went anywhere at all. They tried I tried, but all the relationships just left me wanting. I mean no one could meet the standards she placed on my heart." Kris was nodding his head while listening to Sean. "I dream of her at night. I dreamed about her last night. Then she shows up here. God must be trying to tell me something."

"Well, Sean, this woman and you are connected. Neither of you will be at peace until this is sorted out, one way or the other. You both must confront the past issues and the present one at hand. Do not let anything dissuade you this time; it may be your last chance." Sean was thinking the same thing. Kris said, "You are off work, but I know you aren't going anywhere until you see her again. C'mon, let's go and see how our patient is doing."

The doctors walked into the recovery room together, Kris read her chart while Sean looked in her face. She was so still, barely breathing. He picked up her hand and rubbed the top of it. Kris walked over to him and handed Sean her chart. He didn't want to let her hand go. He made him hold the chart while he read it. She was doing great, better than expected.

Sean finally smiled. Kris walked over to the charge nurse, Amanda Hathaway, and gave her orders for the night. He wanted Me'na moved to a private room first thing in the morning.

"Sean, she is doing great, I'm having her moved to a private room in the morning. I'm going home now, but call me if you need me. The time does not matter, OK?"

"OK, man. Thanks for everything, especially the listening part. I'm going to stay here for a while. I will call you in the morning to check on her progress. See ya," Sean looked at him with clearer eyes than he'd had all evening.

He sat on the side of Me'na's bed, just holding her hand for about thirty minutes. He looked up and saw the hospital gossips standing in front of the window. He nodded his head to nurse Hathaway who looked, then walked to the blinds and closed them. The nurses outside were offended that they had been caught gawking.

"Who do you think she is? A former girlfriend maybe?" one asked.

"It would seem so. It looks as if he's still carrying a torch for her."

"She must be the one that wounded his heart. I knew there had to be a reason that he didn't date much. He's so good looking. What a waste." They walked away, wanting to know more.

Me'na was coming out from under the anesthesia slightly. The surgery had been over for the last two hours and Sean still sat holding her hand. Occasionally he would check her brow.

Mostly he was going over his dream from last night in his mind. He now knew he remembered the last dream so vividly because the fates were sending Me'na into his life. He had several dreams about her, but throughout all the dreams she always died. Either with him holding her in his arms or with him trying to get to her. Sean was convinced that this time, she was sent to him so that she could live. He would do whatever he had to do to make sure of it. She moaned a little, her moan was so familiar to his ears, too familiar.

Nurse Hathaway stood. "Dr. Williams, I need to leave for a few minutes. Are you going to be here a while longer?" she asked.

He looked over his shoulder to her, "Yes, Amanda. Do whatever you need to do. I'll be here for some time." She nodded her head and left them alone.

Sean stood and placed his lips on hers very lightly. He wanted to see if she would have any reaction to him. He was certainly having reactions to her. As he gently kissed her, she parted her lips and tried to kiss him back. He was encouraged, and felt her smile against his mouth. He moved back slightly and looked at her with tenderness.

"Is this my Sean?" she asked him.

"Yes, Me'na, it's me. Do you know me?"

She opened her eyes wider and looked into his. "I would know those green eyes anywhere. I've painted and dreamed of them enough," she told him.

He grabbed her hand and kissed it, then continued to hold it. Me'na started to drift off again, but this time it was a natural sleep, her body was exhausted, it needed rest. Sean placed her hand down and put his head on her bed. There were tears in his eyes, it was real, everything was real. They had really lived and loved each other before.

He thought, *My God, what am I to do now? We need to talk and compare what she has dreamed with my dreams. Thank you, God, for this chance again.*

Nurse Hathaway nosily came back into the room. She didn't want to disturb them, but she needed to get back. They had to work out all the problems this time, this was their last chance.

He got up and went to her. "Amanda, I'm going home now. Ms. Collins will probably sleep through the night. Call me when she is brought to her room and give me the room number. I'm off for the next several days but I'll be back to see her in the morning."

"As you wish, Dr. Williams. Any special orders for her?"

"No, technically she is Dr. Sanderson's patient. I'm consulting with him, and she's my friend." Amanda looked deeply into his eyes as if she was trying to tell him something without saying it.

"Go home, Dr. Williams, I'll call you with the room number. Your friend is in good hands, I'll care for her personally."

"Thank you. Good night, Amanda." He turned toward the door then looked at Me'na again. She looked peaceful. It was all right to leave.

Sean walked down the hall to the elevator. His mind was full of so many thoughts and emotions. When he arrived in the locker room, he gathered his things to take a hot shower before he left. The hot water felt like a massage, it was just what the doctor ordered.

He finished his shower, wrapped a towel around his bottom and padded into the dressing room. He dried himself off and dressed in his street clothes, got his bag and went to his car. After he had buckled himself in he paused, he didn't know if he'd be able to sleep tonight. His mind was fertile ground. He was going into uncharted territory. His dreams and reality were crashing in together. He started his Jaguar, slowly pulled out of the parking garage and headed home. He had a lot to think about tonight. Her lips were as soft as he remembered them. He had to shake himself; he never kissed her in the present before. But the feeling the kiss invoked in him was real. He loved this woman, could it work? He would try to do what ever it took to make it happen.

BOOK ONE
CHAPTER THREE

Sean didn't go to sleep that night until it was almost morning. When he awoke he was as fresh as if he had slept all night. He lay in bed with his arms behind his head looking upward but at nothing in particular. He hadn't arrived at any solution to his current situation. He had to speak with Me'na again. That talk would help him save their future.

He arose this morning with a sense of urgency as he went to take a shower and shave. While the water was getting hot, Sean went into his closet to pick out something to wear. He decided to dress in all black. His mother had always told him that with his hair and eyes, black was his color. He was very meticulous in his appearance today. Sean was putting his best foot forward this morning.

Last night he ordered two dozen yellow roses to be delivered to her room, they should be there when he arrived. He stood back in the mirror and was pleased with what he saw on the outside. On the inside, he was a quivering mass of jello. He was too wired up to eat. Just coffee. He'd get something later.

The drive to the hospital seemed to take longer today for some reason. Sean did not want to see Thomas yet. He wasn't scheduled to come in until eleven this morning. His brother would be asking him why was he here when he had three days off. He would do his best to keep Thomas out of his business this time. He would not allow his brother to ruin this relationship.

"Good morning, Dr. Williams."

He smiled a greeting and kept walking to the elevator. In the elevator, Deborah Chaney who was always trying to get a date cornered him.

"Sean, you are looking nice this morning. Got time to take a break with me later?" she asked him.

"No, Deborah, I'm off today. I'm visiting a friend."

Thankfully the elevator reached the sixth floor where Me'na was before more conversation was necessary. "See you in a few days," Sean told her as he was getting off.

He took a right turn off the elevator to room six sixteen. He stood before the door and took a deep breath before knocking.

"Come in."

His angel was reclining on a pillow with her face turned toward the door. "I thought you were a dream, but you're real," Me'na touched her lips and smiled at him.

He walked into the room and quickly to the side of her bed. Sean took her hand, brought it to his lips, and placed a feather light kiss upon her skin. Me'na felt chill bumps go up her arm when his lips made contact with her. He didn't let her hand go neither did she try to remove it. Sean made space on her bed and asked if it would be all right to sit on the side. He had to get as close as possible to her. She automatically understood and said yes.

"Your name is Sean, right?" she confirmed with him. She didn't ask him, she felt that she already knew it to be so.

"Yes, and you're Me'na?" she nodded her head slightly, but frowned when her head began to hurt a little. "You must be careful. We had to relieve the pressure on your brain last night. Your head may hurt for a little while."

He got up to check her chart. He liked what he read and she was going to be fine. Sean sat back down on the bed and reached for the hand that was already on its way to him.

"You are a doctor?"

"Yes, but I couldn't operate on you last evening. When I saw your face I knew I was too emotionally involved. I cannot explain it to you." He looked into those amber colored eyes that he remembered so well.

"You don't have to. I understand. I remember you also. I know I have not met you before, but I have come to realize I have known you my entire existence."

She reached up with her other hand and rubbed his face. The comforting touch made him press his face in her hand. She cupped his face and tried to bring his lips down to her. Sean bent down and placed his lips on hers. He first kissed her bottom lip, as he did in the past. She parted her lips and he was lost. The kiss lasted for some time until Sean remembered she was still a patient and must take it easy. He pulled back reluctantly, she smiled.

"I'm not going anywhere, we have time."

In order to bring himself under control, Sean asked her if she liked her flowers.

"Yes, the yellow rose and the gardenia are my favorite, but then you knew that, didn't you?" she asked him.

"I did, but I didn't know if I knew it or remembered it. This is all so very confusing. Me'na we need to talk as soon as you are released from here. I'll talk with Dr. Sanderson and see what his plans are for you."

"Sean, I would prefer that you be my doctor. I trust you to take care of me."

As she said that, he remembered the last dream he had a couple of nights ago. He didn't do such a good job taking care of her then, she died for him.

"If you insist, Me'na, I'll take care of you, very good care."

He'd gotten up and was pacing around the room. Me'na put her hand out for him to grab it. Sean took the offered hand and held it tightly.

"Are you tired, if you are, I can leave and come back later?" he asked.

"Don't you dare go anywhere on me, Sean Williams." After she said his last name her eyes widened at the surprise of her knowledge. "I don't know how I knew your last name. Magic?" she asked teasingly.

He smiled and said, "It has to be. Can you talk for a little while? I just need to clear a few cobwebs."

She remembered not to nod her head and said, "Yes I can."

"Exactly how do you remember me?"

"Well, I'm an artist. I have painted your face for a long time. I can't remember when I first saw you in my head, but I think I was around seventeen or eighteen. I just started painting one day and when I finished, there you were. I have sketches of you in charcoals, watercolors, and oils." Me'na paused and looked thoughtful. "You know I think the first time I painted your face was when we moved from Austin to Houston. Are you originally from here?" she asked.

"No, I'm from Beaumont, about seventy miles or so east of here."

"I know Beaumont," she said. "I have cousins there. I've even visited there in the summer sometime." Both were silent as they realized how close to each other they had always been, this was amazing.

"Me'na, it's time that you took a nap, you're beginning to tire. I'll not be the cause of your recovery taking a long time. No arguments," he said as she started to disagree.

"Come here, Sean, if I take a short nap, do you promise to be here when

I wake up?"

"Yes, I will be right here," he said as he walked toward her. "Your lunch tray should be here in about ninety minutes." She made a face at that. Sean had to smile at her. "You have to eat. You must regain your strength. Do you remember how you got here?" he asked her.

Me'na's face changed a little. "Yes, I was hit by a car on purpose."

"On purpose? Me'na, are you sure?"

"I'm sure. I have been stalked for several months now. It's been reported to the police but they don't know who he is."

Sean gingerly pulled her into his arms. "No one will hurt you again. I will not leave you alone when you get out of the hospital. You will move in with me or I move in with you, but you will be protected, I swear it." He held her tightly, kissed her brow and placed her back on the bed. "Now you go to sleep. Everything will be taken care of."

Me'na closed her eyes and went to sleep. This was the safest she had felt in weeks. Her Sean was here everything would be fine.

BOOK ONE
CHAPTER FOUR

Sean waited until she had fallen asleep before he left her room. He went down to admitting to find out if she had insurance. The clerk told him that so far, they didn't have any information on her.

"I want you to call me," he gave her his card, "if there is any problems with her bill. Put my name down as guarantor. I'll take care of everything she needs."

"Yes, Doctor. I'll take care of that now." Sean left the office and headed to the cafeteria to get a tray to take to Me'na's room.

"Sean, man, come here," Thomas called out to him. "What are you doing here? Aren't you off?"

"Yea, you know I am, I'm visiting a sick friend. I was just getting me something to take back upstairs."

"Who's sick? Anyone I know?"

"No, you don't know 'em." Sean tried his best to not say woman or female or anything gender related to his brother. "Well, Tommy, I need to get back, I'll talk to you later."

With that said, Sean escaped as fast as he could. Thomas walked to his table thinking that Sean was trying really hard to not tell him who it was.

It has to be a woman, he thought, *I'll ask around and see if anyone knows anything*. He sat down deep in thought. *This will be interesting. He should have just come out and told me her name. Now I will have to snoop around for the information*. Thomas had a smile on his face as he contemplated all the nagging he was going to give Sean.

As Sean walked back in her room, Me'na was awake. She felt his presence leave her room. She woke up shortly after he left. She wanted to pout, but when she spied his tray, how could she begrudge him a meal? She couldn't and quickly replaced the pout with a brilliant smile that made her eyes sparkle.

"Hey, I tried to get back as quickly as I could. I didn't want you to think that I had left," he explained.

"No, it's alright, you have to eat too."

Her tray was arriving as soon as he placed his on a table. Sean took the tray from nurse Boykins and served Me'na. He brought her bed up enough for her to eat and placed his tray on the side of hers. She removed the lid to find broth, jello, milk, and crackers. Me'na looked over to his tray and asked him if he wanted to trade meals.

"No, Me'na. Eat, this is good for you. I'll help you eat." Sean picked up the spoon and blew on the soup to cool it off for her. "C'mon, be a big girl, open wide."

She opened her mouth and clamped down on the spoon he held. She wouldn't let go. Sean started to laugh at her and before they knew it, both were laughing heartily.

"Thank you, Sean, but I can finish. You are so kind to me. I was only trying to lighten the atmosphere. You seemed so doctorish for a moment."

"Well, I am a doctor now. I just want you to get well as soon as possible."

"I will, my love," she said.

Sean remembered his dream. Me'na called him my love there too.

"What's wrong, did I say something to upset you? If I did, I'm sorry," she apologized.

The look on his face changed with remembrance for a moment. "No, it's nothing you said. You have called me my love before in my dreams."

"Is that how you know me? I wanted to ask when the time was right."

Me'na looked at him with so much love in her eyes, he was humbled with the knowledge that no one had ever looked at him that way before.

"Well, I guess it's right now. I don't know where to begin." Their lunch was forgotten for a time, and then he said, "Me'na, I'll make a deal with you, drink this soup down, and I'll tell you." She quickly picked up her bowl and drained it, placed it down and waited. Sean really didn't know where to begin first. There was so much to tell.

"Come, sit beside me."

He began. "I have dreamed of you for a long time. The first time that I remember dreaming was after a head injury playing college football. I was knocked unconscious and the dreams started about a month later. I've had them ever since." She listened intently. "In my most recent dream, this by the way was the night before you had your accident. You and I were going to get married. The time and place appeared to be early sixteenth or seventeenth century in a kingdom named Fastonia." He had her rapt attention.

"I was a king and you were a foreign princess that needed asylum. I don't know if a country by that name ever existed or if only in my dreams. But we were there along with my brother Thomas and dozens of others. The man who brought you to my kingdom was trying to gain control of the country by starting a war."

She asked him, "Was our love a great love?"

"Yes, the kind of love they write songs about." He grabbed her hand again.

"Do we marry, Sean?" she asked him.

That was one question that he was trying to avoid. He got off the bed and walked to the window. As he started to speak again, there was a knock on the door. Sean went to see who was there. Thomas. He looked toward her and told her he'd be outside the door for a minute.

"Thomas, what do you want? Awfully proud of yourself, aren't you?"

Why are you hiding this woman from me, Sean? I was just curious, that's all."

"I am *not* hiding anyone from you. This has nothing to do with you," Sean ground out.

"If that's the case, can I meet her?"

"C'mon, you will not give me any peace until you do, but be brief. She's had a head injury." Sean rolled his eyes at his brother and walked into Me'na's room first.

"Me'na, I want you to meet my brother Thomas." She looked at him, reached for Sean's hand and smiled at Thomas.

"Thomas, this is Me'na," Sean looked into her eyes for understanding. "This is my girlfriend."

"Well, I didn't know you had a girlfriend." Thomas walked up to her and gently shook her other hand. "Why have you two been so secret?"

Me'na squeezed Sean's hand. "No secret. Your brother has been very busy working and I've been out of town on business, that's all." Me'na laid her best smile on Thomas and he felt it.

He thought, *Wow! She is some woman! Where did he meet her?*

"How long has this been going on, Sean?"

Me'na interrupted Sean before he could speak. She felt the tension between the brothers and wanted to relieve it. "So many questions, Thomas.

Why is that?" Now Thomas was on the spot and she felt Sean relax.

"Just wondering, that's all. My big brother is a very private person. I just never knew how private he was until now."

"Come on, Thomas, she has to get some rest I'll see you out." Sean led him out of the room.

Thomas turned to her and said, "It's was a pleasure meeting you. Hope to see you again soon."

"Bye, Thomas."

As soon as they were outside her door, Thomas pulled Sean further down the hall. "Man, she is beautiful. Have you known her for a long time?" he asked.

"Yes, I have. It feels like my whole life." Sean regretted saying that to his brother almost as soon as the words left his mouth.

Thomas looked at him then said, "You are in love with her. You got it bad. Does she feel the same way?"

"I would say so, nosey."

Thomas laughed at being called nosey, because he knew he was. "Sean, what is it about Me'na that attracted you to her? What could have melted that cool veneer of yours?"

Thomas was just dying to know. Sean was very laid back. He never got excited or animated about anything. It would have to be something very big for his elder brother to bat an eye. This woman had to be very special.

As Sean started to answer him, he had a silly smile on is face. "I love her warm golden skin, her brown eyes, her wit, and her dark brown hair, I ..." his brother cut him off.

"Alright already, I get the point. She kinda favors your high school girlfriend Tammie. Don't you think?" he asked.

"No, I don't think. Just because they are both black women doesn't mean I was looking for her replacement. Me'na is completely different from any other woman I have known. I've always known her."

Sean walked a few steps further down the hall and leaned against the wall. "Why the twenty questions? Are you trying to make sure my social life is equal opportunity?"

"No, brother. I'm the equal opportunity lover. No one is turned away with a signed application."

"The only reason that is is because you go through women so fast. We'll have to start importing them just for you." They both started laughing, realizing how dumb their conversation had become.

"Thomas, just be happy for me, that's all I ask of you. Please?"

Thomas put his arms around him and gave him a bear hug. Sean wouldn't have been more surprised if he'd won the lottery.

"I am. I am. Take good care of her. Looking at her, I can tell that plenty of men are always chasing her. Are you ready for that? You know whenever someone is happy, that's when others try to break them up. Be on your guard."

Thomas slapped him on the arm and left to go back to his patients. As he left, he thought, *Yea, you had better watch out* for *me. I plan on having a taste of that.* He smiled to himself.

Sean was not fooled though. He knew his brother. He would be on the lookout for Thomas.

As he prepared to go back inside Me'na's room, his best friend Kristoff was coming down the hall. He spoke with him about Me'na. He was on his way to see her before he left for the day. Sean stopped him before he could go in.

"I read her chart. Everything looks OK. Is there anything else to be concerned about?" Sean changed into his doctor persona.

"No, I think we'll be able to release her in a day or two. I want her to stay one more day for observation. Do you agree, Sean?"

"Yes. I just wanted an objective opinion. I don't trust myself where she's concerned. I would be over protective."

Kris shook his head in understanding. "Do you know you are the talk of the hospital? Everyone wants to know what she means to you. Last time we spoke you couldn't say much then. Can you speak of her to me now?" Kristoff wanted to know if this was the mystery women from his past they were talking about yesterday.

"She means the world to me. It's as if we haven't missed a step, just picked up where we left off."

Sean hoped that wasn't true. He said what he thought he could even to his best friend. "I love her more than anything; I will not lose her again. I feel at peace when I'm with her."

Kris said, "As your personal physician, that's love if I ever heard it before. My previous diagnosis still stands. "

Sean confided, "I fell in love at first sight. It was the same for both of us. The feelings have not lessened, only intensified with time." Of that, he was sure of.

"Well, let's go in and examine this paragon."

They went into her room but she had gone to sleep. Dr. Sanderson opened her eyes to check them. Me'na looked at him startled, but when she saw Sean on the side of him, she was relieved. She'd been dreaming about the accident, for a moment she thought it was Richard Bains.

She believed he was her stalker. The police didn't have anything on him. He had fired her a year before the stalking started. She loved her job at On Demand Advertising. She was in charge of the art department. He had asked her out several times but she kept refusing him.

She told him she did not date coworkers; it would complicate things. But she had dated a coworker after that. He confronted her and it wasn't long after that, that he started picking on her department. He was one of many vice presidents employed by the company. He embarrassed her and shortly after that, she was fired for unimaginative work.

Sean introduced Kris to his girl. "Me'na, this is Dr. Sanderson. He operated on you last night."

"Hi, Me'na, how are you feeling today?" he asked.

"I'm fine, Doctor. When can I go home?" She was anxious to be alone with Sean.

"If you continue to improve tomorrow, maybe later that evening I'll release you. We'll see," was his answer. "I'll leave you two alone, but I'll be back tomorrow afternoon to check on you."

"Thank you, Doctor."

After Dr. Sanderson left, Me'na moved over so Sean could sit beside her.

"Sit, love, beside me."

"Me'na, thank you for going alone with me when I told Thomas that you were my girlfriend. He's a pest."

"I feel I am, Sean, even though we only just met. Don't you feel that way too?" she asked, tilting her face up to him.

Sean looked down into her eyes and could not help himself. Me'na wrapped her arms around him as tight as she could. She didn't want to let him go. Her tight grip was just the thing he needed most. Sean held her gingerly, he was aware of her injuries. But with the pressure she was putting on his lips, he soon forgot about that. He placed his hand on her hip; she tried to press her body next to his. It was awkward at best. Me'na uttered a low moan and Sean gave up pretending. He needed her desperately. He would consume her if he could.

Several minutes went by. Someone had to remember where they were. The doctor in Sean rose to the occasion. He slowly pulled back, rubbing her back as he laid her down on her bed.

She put her hands on each side of his face and rubbed his beard. "I like this beard. You look so sexy with it."

"I grew it for you. I always had it in my dreams." He smiled at her.

"Did you? Will you tell more about the dreams? We were interrupted before."

"I'll tell you but first I'm concerned about your safety. Do you have any idea who is responsible for stalking you?" Sean was going to protect her, even if it cost him his life in the process.

"Well, I think that it's my former boss. I didn't want to date him and I think he waited a year to find something to fire me on. He started harassing my department about small things at first, then it escalated as time went by. It appears he waited long enough so the blame wouldn't be placed on him."

"What's his name, Me'na?"

"Richard Bains."

As she said his name, the first name Richard, rang a bell in his mind. He couldn't put his finger on it at the time.

He must be in my dream somewhere, I just don't remember him.

He tried to school his face so as not to upset her.

"Do you know him, Sean?" she asked.

"The name is familiar. I have to think on it for a while. It'll come to me. Don't worry." She looked at him so trusting. It was a humbling experience for him.

"I don't know what to do about him. I'm afraid that he will kill me soon. I hate to admit it, but I'm scared to death." There were tears in her eyes as she admitted it.

He held her to him trying to soothe her. "I'll care for you. I'm bringing you to my house when you are released. We'll hire security around the clock. You will not be left alone at any time. Your Sean's here. Ssh."

He held her until she went to sleep again, which she needed. Her body was very tired. Sean laid her down on her bed, fixed her covers around her shoulders and pulled his cell phone out. He called information for a number to a security service. He ordered security upgrade for his house and a personal bodyguard for her when he wasn't around. The bodyguard would be there in an hour to sit at her door. Sean wrote her a note and placed it where she would see it as soon as she woke up. He was going to talk to the head of his department and ask for a personal leave of absence. Me'na would be his primary interest for the time being.

When Sean arrived back at her room the bodyguard had arrived. He was told to wait for Sean outside the door if no one answered his knock.

"I'm Sean Williams, and you are?" he asked.

"Dr. Williams, my name is Henry Stewart. Here are my references and employment history."

Sean looked them over very carefully. He told Henry that an unknown person was stalking the woman he would be protecting. He was also told that she was very precious to him and he wanted nothing further to happen.

"Let me see if she has awakened, and I'll introduce you to her." Sean peeked in the door, but she was still sleeping. He got a chair from out of the room for him to sit.

"May I call you Henry?" Sean asked him.

"Yes, sir."

"Will you be working alone or will you be relieved?"

"No, sir, I will work alone. But if extra help is needed, call this number." He gave him the security office's business card. "If we are going somewhere that is very public, I recommend that you get an extra man to help me."

Sean looked at him. "Thank you. We will. I'm going inside before she wakes up." He went into the room and sat on her bedside to watch her sleep. He sat there for about fifteen minutes before she woke up.

"I'm sorry for dozing off like that. I couldn't help it." she smiled at him.

"Don't worry about that. You should sleep and I should not be here monopolizing all your recovery time."

"Are you leaving me?"

"Only for a short time. I hired a security company to update the wiring of my house against intruders. I need to be there to supervise their work and find out how everything works. There is a guard at your door. He will only let in hospital staff with a badge that matches their face. You will not be alone. I am here with you now."

She reached for his hand and felt the strength in him. She was safe for now.

"I'll introduce the guard to you." Sean went to the door and asked him to come in.

"Me'na, this is Henry Stewart. He will protect you when I'm not around."

They shook hands and he promised her he would help protect her. After Henry went back to his post, Sean prepared to leave.

"Sean, I know we just met, and I'm putting a lot on your shoulders. This is my problem though. You are going to a lot of trouble for a virtual stranger." He started to say something but she raised her hand. "You don't owe me anything. Just because I've painted your face, and have seen you in my mind's eye all my adult life, it doesn't mean I'm your responsibility, Sean. You don't have to do anything."

Sean had so much he wanted to say, he couldn't get it out. He simply moved things off of her bed so that he could pick her up and sit her on his lap.

"Now listen to me. We have a connection. You can't deny that." She nodded. "You love me even though you don't know me. Am I right or not?"

"You're right, Sean."

"I love you also, I have waited for you my entire life. You are not going to get away this easy. You, Me'na Collins, are going to let me take care of you. I will not give you a chance to deny me. When you are released tomorrow, you're coming home with me. No arguments. I am not going to force you into a relationship with me until we figure this thing out. I couldn't live with myself if I allowed something to happen to you."

"Are you always this demanding, babe?" she asked.

"You have no idea." He wagged his brows at her. He asked her, "Are we set now?"

"Yes, we are in total agreement, Sean."

"Good, now if you don't kind, may I have a kiss so I can settle my heart down?"

"One of my kisses will never settle you down. They have the opposite effect," she teasingly said.

"I don't care what effect they have, but I must have another before I go."

She eagerly complied with the request. Me'na seared his lips with the hottest kiss he'd ever remembered having. She was going to make sure he wouldn't forget to come back, not since she had just found him.

BOOK ONE
CHAPTER FIVE

Sean went home to make sure that all of the security details that he needed were in place. The men showed up and were very thorough in their work. Everything was done as he had specified.

After they left, he drove to his favorite furniture store to buy a bedroom set he thought Me'na would like. Everything in his home was masculine, not fit for a woman. He would rather she share his bed. It was big enough for the two of them, but he didn't want to press his luck.

He bought a beautiful four-poster bed with an optional canopy attached to it. The canopy was a little different he had the movers put it on the ceiling. It draped down as an umbrella on all four sides. The effect was a cascading waterfall of ivory gauze that she would be able to see through. His Me'na was ultra feminine, he knew she would like it.

He bought her a dresser, étagère, nightstand, mirrors, the whole nine yards. He wasn't sure what she would like, so he almost bought everything he saw. It had to be delivered immediately or he'd go elsewhere. It was delivered within three hours.

Before he could go back to Me'na, he had to stop and buy some much needed groceries.

Once everything was in place, he went back to the hospital. Before he reached the hospital, he stopped at Newman's and bought her a comforter and accessories to finish off her room. He thought she might like a dusky rose color. Sean had been gone about five hours and he worried about her.

Upon entering the hospital Nurse Cooper stopped him to inquire about his patient. "She's doing very well. Thank you for asking."

"Dr. Williams, could I ask you a question about her?" Sean stood there and nodded his head.

She asked, "Is she a relative of you and your brother, if I'm not being too personal?"

"Janie, she is my girlfriend if that's what you want to know."

Janie appeared offended. "Yes, thank you, Doctor."

Sean walked on to Me'na's room.

Henry was out front, watching everyone that got close. No one got within five feet of him unless he gave them the once over.

"Henry, why don't you take a break since I'm here now? Do you have a cell so I can call you when I leave?"

"Yes, here's my card." He took a card out of his wallet and gave it to Sean.

"I've been thinking that you can't be expected to sit all day and all night, that's unfair and it's tiring. Call your agency and have someone sent over to spell you around midnight."

"Are you sure, Dr. Williams?" Henry asked.

"Yes, if you're tired you can't do a very good job. This will be a one-time thing. She may be released from here tomorrow. So, I'll call you about ten tonight, that's when I'll leave and go home. But see if your boss can have someone over here before I leave so that I can meet him," Sean said.

"You're the boss." Henry called the agency and requested an additional man to come about nine forty-five.

Sean walked into the room. Me'na was up and standing at the window. She didn't turn around. She felt his aura move into the room. Without turning she held out her hand.

"Love, I've missed you."

Sean walked to her as quickly as he could and took her hand. "I made sure that the house is ready for you and I had to do a little shopping, there was no food."

She laughed. "The perfect bachelor's house. No food, but I'd bet there was beer and a pizza box in the frig."

"How'd you know that?" he asked. She laughed harder at him, he joined her. "Well, you know men," he added.

"Yes, I know you."

"Yes, you do," he told her. "Let's sit on the sofa for a minute." Me'na shook her head no. "Why not Me'na?"

She faced him and draped her arms around his neck. "Because I want to feel you against me first."

Sean's eyes softened. He hugged her to him and placed his head on the side of hers. He was careful with the bandage.

She asked him, "Did y'all cut my hair off? I'd better not have a shiny bald spot on my head." Me'na exaggerated her Texas accent.

"OK, Tex, your hair is fine. We only cut out a very small spot."

She said, "Hm, a small spot to a man is not seen the same by women." She patted her head.

He removed her hand. "Stop, baby, you might move some of that fake hair I personally planted before it's had time to take root." He wisely moved out of her grasp. She started to go after him, but she moved too fast and got dizzy. Sean got to her quickly and led her back to the couch.

"I'm sorry. This is my fault, I shouldn't have been teasing you." Me'na used the opportunity to hit him anyway. She was silently laughing at him, she had tricked him.

"Did you trick me? I'll be darned. The love of my life used her injury to fool me. Tsk, tsk, tsk. A very bad girl," he told her.

She looked at him. "What did you say?"

Sean looked surprised. "Uh, you tricked me?"

"No, silly, you called me the love of your life."

He answered, "Oh that."

"Yes that. Do you mean that, babe?" Me'na asked.

"Yes, I do. I didn't realize I said it until you called me on it. But it's the truth I love you totally. No reservations on my part. What about you?"

She smiled the special smile that was becoming known to him as the smile she reserved for him only. It was slow in developing and sexy when finished.

"I feel we have always loved each other. We kind of well, fell into place as if we were seeing one another before the accident," she said.

"You didn't answer my question, Me'na."

She knew what he wanted to hear her say. She wouldn't torment him any longer. "I love you, have always loved only you. I don't know how or when I started to love you, but I do. I was not whole until you came into my life. Does that answer your question?"

He had a great big grin on his face and said, "Yes, I guess it does. Stand up, baby."

She stood up as he opened his arms to her. Me'na fit just right. Her head came to his chin. Sean raised her chin with his thumb and started to kiss her. She relaxed against him and gave him everything he desired of her. Me'na didn't hold back and neither did Sean.

"Excuse me, Sean. I can come back to visit later if you're busy."

Both turned their heads at the sound of Thomas' voice. Sean looked upward for the strength not to throttle his brother. He didn't release his hold on Me'na.

"Yes, Thomas," he asked.

"I just wanted to see how Me'na was doing, that's all. If you're too busy, I can come back later."

Me'na loosed her hold on Sean. "No, Thomas, we have time to sit and talk with you, right, love?" She looked up at Sean. Me'na turned around in his arms so that her back was against his chest. Sean wrapped his arms around her.

"Yeah, sit down, Thomas, rest yourself." Sean hoped he sounded as displeased as he was.

Me'na and Sean sat on the sofa while Thomas sat on the chair across from them. He thought, *She called him love, l-o-v-e. Aw man, she must be under the influence of her meds. This may be harder than I thought.*

He looked at Me'na, none of his thoughts showed on his face. "Well, how's the star patient feeling today. You know you are the talk of the hospital."

"Why would that be, Thomas?"

"Sean is very private, you know that," she nodded her head. "The nurses around here had their hearts broken when you showed up. Sean had been very standoffish toward them. Now they know why" Thomas chuckled.

Sean told his brother, "If you had this wonderful woman at your side, would you look?"

"No, I wouldn't. Me'na, you have to know how beautiful you are. You're simply breathtaking," Thomas complimented her.

"Thank you, I appreciate that seeing as how my head has a bandage on it and your brother cut a lock of my hair out."

"It's only a small lock. It will grow back," he consoled her. Thomas got up to see for himself. "You mind?"

"No, go ahead see for yourself."

Thomas looked at her head and tried to look farther down until he ran into Sean's eyes. He shrugged his shoulders at him. "It's small. You should recover the hair in no time. Don't worry." He sat back down. "Well, since I feel like I'm intruding on you two, and I have rounds to make anyway, I'll leave. May I visit you again before you leave the hospital?"

"Sure, why not? Thank you for coming, Thomas, I really mean it." Thomas stood up, kissed her on her cheek, and turned to leave.

"Me'na, I'll be right back. I have to speak to Thomas." The brothers stepped outside the room, past Henry and into the hall.

"What was that all about, Thomas?"

"What do you mean? I can't visit your sick girlfriend?"

"You're up to something, I can smell it. You might as well tell me now, I'll find out what it is anyway."

"OK Sean, here it is. I think she may be too much woman for you. Are you sure you can handle a hot little number like that?"

By the time Thomas was finished speaking; Sean had him by the collar and up against the wall. They stared at each other for a moment. Henry watched in case Sean needed him.

"You, little brother, had better watch your manners when around my woman. I'll not tolerate any of your usual shenanigans. We are not twenty and eighteen any more." Sean still held him by his collar. Henry got up to shield them from prying eyes.

"Let me go, Sean, I'm not trying to steal her from you. I'm just checking, trying to look out for you."

Sean let him go, but he didn't move away. "I don't need checking. You had better check yourself first before it's too late." Sean turned around and went back in Me'na's room.

Damn, there is more to this than meets the eye. I'm just the man to find out what's going on.

Thomas with his indomitable streak went his way down the hall trying to figure this out.

BOOK ONE
CHAPTER SIX

On the way to Sean's home, they stopped at Me'na's townhouse to pick up some clothes. They went in while Henry looked to see if anyone was watching them. He was standing on the side of the building partially hidden by bushes. He could not be seen from the street.

A black Lexus slowed down in front of the building and pulled over to the curb across the street. The windows were tinted but the driver rolled his window down a bit to stare at Me'na's home. He stopped his car and Henry tried to make his way over there to approach him and write down his license plate number. He went behind Me'na's townhouse and then he walked casually down the sidewalk.

Henry looked at the plate and wrote down the number, he placed it in his pocket. As he walked up to the car, the driver looked in his side mirror and saw him coming. He made the mistake of staring too long in the mirror; that afforded Henry a chance to see what he looked like. Henry was also a licensed private detective. He had a photographic memory when it came to faces. The man inside the car turned the ignition on and sped away as Me'na and Sean were coming outside. Henry jogged across the street to them. They were standing there wondering what had happened.

"Doc, I think that might have been our stalker. I got a good look at him and wrote down his plate number. I'll call this in. We'll be able to find out who it is."

He pulled out his cell and called his office. He walked away from them as Sean helped Me'na in the car. She was trembling. Sean locked her door and placed her bags in his trunk.

He walked over to Henry. "How soon will we know anything?" They started walking back to the car.

"I'll give them about twenty minutes or so. They will call back as soon as they find out anything."

Both got in the car. Sean reached over to grab Me'na's hand to show he was there. She looked over to him and gave him a weak smile.

"I'll be alright. I have two strong men to protect me." She looked out of the window while Sean and Henry made eye contact in the rear view mirror.

Sean's home was only about an hour's drive away, Me'na lived closer to downtown. Sean asked Henry if he could recognize the driver if he saw him again, he said he would be able to.

Me'na turned around to Henry. "I can draw, Henry, and if you can describe him to me we'll see what he looks like."

"OK, Ms. Collins, we can do that."

"Henry, call me Me'na please. You make me feel like an old woman," she said to him.

"OK, Me'na," and he smiled for the first time.

Sean looked in the rear mirror at him. "And I'm Sean."

Henry's smile reached his eyes. When he smiled he didn't look so forbidding anymore. He told Me'na he had to be serious. Her life could depend on it.

They arrived at his home and he opened the garage door. They pulled into his garage and parked alongside his black Jaguar. He popped the trunk and Henry went to get the bags. Me'na was opening her door by the time Sean came on her side.

"Allow me the pleasure of opening your door. You twenty-first century women, too independent," he said, shaking his head. She just giggled at him as she took the offered hand he held out.

"Henry, the door is open, put those bags in the middle room. Go through the kitchen, dining room and turn to your left, the bedroom is on the left; I left the door open."

Me'na whispered to Sean, "I thought for appearances sake, I wanted it to appear as if I had been here before. I don't want Henry to think we're weirdos."

"We are, you know."

They both laughed at what life had given them in already knowing each other.

After she was settled in, she asked Henry to describe the man that he saw to her. As he was describing the face he saw to her, the image on the pad was familiar to Sean. It looked like the duke in his dreams. If he were stalking her, there would be trouble.

When she finished, she told Sean and Henry that this was her former boss, Richard Bains. Henry received the call he was waiting for, Me'na was correct. The car belonged to Bains.

"Baby, give me that policeman's card that's handling your case. I'm going to call him and have him come over."

Sean called Detective Hamilton. He said he would be right over.

Henry was given the room across from her with Sean right next to her. Sean told Henry to make himself at home. He told him there was plenty of food in the cabinets. At this Me'na covered her mouth to keep from laughing at him. He just smiled at her. Whatever he needed was at his disposal. All he had to do was to tell him and he'd get whatever else was needed.

As Henry settled in, Sean showed Me'na to her room.

"Oh my God, this is beautiful, Sean. Oh thank you so much. I know you went to a lot of trouble for me, but I promise, you won't regret it."

Sean beamed at her pleasure with the room, it was what he thought she would like. Me'na walked around everything, touching and rubbing all the furniture. She especially liked the canopy over the bed.

"Sean, come here, this is my favorite out of everything. This ivory canopy. I dreamed of having one like this when I was in college." She threw herself into his arms and planted a big kiss on him. He thought he was going to like having a girlfriend around; there were plenty of fringe benefits.

Me'na looked at him smiling. "Yes, I am your girlfriend."

"How did you know what I was thinking?"

"I think it was that leer in your eyes that gave you away."

"Baby, I didn't mean to leer at you. I told you that I would give us both time to figure this out."

Me'na hung her head giggling at him. "I was teasing you, I have my work cut out. Give me a little time and you'll be more relaxed before you know it." She reached up to place her hand on the side of his face. "I promise no more teasing until you loosen up."

"I'm just worried about you. I don't want anyone to hurt you. I can't lose you again," he confessed.

When he said again she looked into his eyes, but he lowered his head to kiss her. She thought something must have happened to her in one of his dreams. She didn't want to distress him, so she was going to forget it this time. If he said it again, she would need an answer.

Sean asked her to take a nap until dinnertime and he would cook for them. She didn't realize how tired she was until she lay down. Sean waited in her room as she changed clothes. He tucked her in and gave her a kiss on the forehead. By the time he closed the door, Me'na was asleep.

He went to the kitchen to look in his many cookbooks to find something to cook for the three of them. He considered himself a gourmet cook. He made his living that way all through college until his residency years. Once he found his recipes, Thomas knocked on the kitchen door. It was normally not locked, but because of the stalker, nothing would be left open.

"Say, bro, got time to shot some hoops with me?" Thomas walked in and went straight to the frig for something to drink.

"No, not today, Tommy. Me'na is sleeping and I promised her a gourmet meal."

"She's here with you?" Thomas asked as he sat down at the breakfast table.

Sean looked at him. "Yes, she's staying here with me for a while. And before you ask, Mr. I Need To Know Everything, she is being stalked and I'm trying to keep her safe."

Thomas was astounded. "Is that how she got in the hospital?"

"Yes, her stalker tried to kill her. I've hired a bodyguard for her and had the security on the house upgraded. So you'll have to knock from now on, no doors can be left unlocked."

Thomas nodded his head in agreement. "I understand. Will you be safe? A stalker is unstable, and he could hurt you too."

"Well, we should be fine. You saw Henry at the hospital. He will be living here too. Sometimes we might have more than one guard, especially when we go out. But I can take care of myself."

"Not against a bullet you can't, Sean. I don't want you getting hurt either. You know it's just you and me in Houston since Mom and Dad died, plus cousins down the interstate. But you are my brother, whether you like it or not, you're stuck with me." They grinned at each other.

"Tommy, I've taken a short leave of absence from work, I need to be where my heart is. If something were to happen to her again, I'd die." He really meant it. He couldn't go on living without her.

Thomas reached out to Sean. "You really love her, don't you?"

"With every part of me that's warm. More each day," he admitted.

"Will you two marry soon?" Thomas wasn't sure he wanted to share his brother with anyone.

"We have a lot of things to talk about. This incident made me comprehend exactly how much she means to me. Me'na is my everything. Without her, life is meaningless."

Thomas sat back to digest what Sean said. "Wow, bro, I'm sure she feels the same way about you. When she looks at you, her eyes glow. Well, she glows all over being as lovely as she is."

"Yeah, she is beautiful." Sean did the unexpected and invited Thomas to dinner with them. "I want you to get to know her. She has a great sense of humor. Will you stay?"

"Sure, I'll stay. She will probably be my sister-in-law in the near future."

Sean started cooking while Thomas went into the den and talked to Henry about being a bodyguard. By the time that the dinner was ready, Sean wondered where the police was. He didn't have much longer to wait.

Officer Hamilton was standing outside the front door preparing to ring the doorbell. He looked at the large house, and wondered what type of security Sean had. Henry answered the door and showed the detective in. Everyone was introduced and the detective was told that Me'na was resting. Sean informed him she had just been released from the hospital.

Henry gave Detective Hamilton the picture that was drawn of Bains. He told him that the car parked outside of her home belonged to him.

"Dr. Williams, I paid a visit to Mr. Bains before I came here. He told me that it was just a coincidence he was in the neighborhood. I didn't believe him. We'll keep an eye on him." He turned to Henry, "Are you her bodyguard?"

"Yes, I am," Henry answered him.

"That was a wise move, Dr. Williams. Stalkers are unpredictable, and we never know when they'll show up." He stood to leave. "Don't leave her alone at any time. One of you should always be available."

Sean walked him to the door and thanked him for coming. Me'na had awakened and came into the room with them.

She went to Sean. "Baby, was that the police?" He put his arms around her when she sat beside him.

"Yes, that was Detective Hamilton. He visited Bains, but he lied and said it was a coincidence. The detective didn't believe him." She looked over to Thomas and spoke to him.

"Well, as long as I'm here with you, I'm safe." Sean just hugged her tightly to himself. Thomas watched all this with interest. He was looking for a way into Me'na's life.

Everyone ate dinner without incidence, which was rare for any meal that included Thomas. For once Thomas behaved himself and was subdued. His brother and Me'na looked too cozy with one another for him. He wanted her so bad that he had to squirm in his seat. But how could he get her away from Sean without having to fight him. He figured there had to be a way. He'd keep looking for it. Me'na got up to take her plate into the kitchen and Thomas followed her on a pretext of helping.

Once alone, he asked her, "Do you really love my brother or is this just for my benefit?"

"Why would we put on a show for you?" she asked him.

"I feel a connection between the two of us. Don't deny it."

Me'na looked at him. She didn't want to believe she heard him correctly. "There is no connection with you, Thomas. What you feel is pure lust, nothing more."

Thomas moved in for the kill. He grabbed her by the arms and tried to pull her against his chest. Me'na pushed back as hard as she could and tried to slap him. Thomas caught her hand and licked the palm.

"You pig, leave me alone! Don't make me tell Sean about this."

Thomas decided to lie to her. "He would never believe you. I'd tell him that you brushed your breast against my arm and I was only trying to move out of the way."

Thomas knew Sean would believe her. He always came on to his brother's women. Obviously, she thought he was telling the truth.

"Don't let this happen again or I will tell him," she threatened him.

Sean yelled out, "Hey, what's keeping you two!"

Me'na came out of the kitchen with her cheeks pink and Thomas was smirking.

"Here I am, babe. I'm going to my room for a while." She kissed Sean and left.

Henry got up from the table and went back into the den. He knew something had happened in the kitchen. Dr. Williams' brother had trouble written all over him.

"What did you do to her in there, Tommy?"

"Why is it always me? She may have done something to your brother." Thomas tried to defend himself.

Sean said, "Because I know you, you like to meddle and flirt where you don't belong. If you offended her, you will not be welcome in my home any longer."

Thomas stood. "You'd put me, your brother out if she said I offended her?"

Sean stood also. "Yes, I would. You will not ruin this relationship for me. I've learned my lesson and learned it well. I'm ready to cut my losses now if she says the word."

Thomas threw his hands up in the air. "Tell her I'm sorry for whatever it is I am supposed to have done this time. It's time I go home while we are still speaking." He left and closed the door behind him.

BOOK ONE
CHAPTER SEVEN

Everything had been proceeding well. Me'na's recovery was nearly complete. She felt fine and wanted to go out to dinner. Sean agreed, Henry called his agency and asked for another man to accompany them out.

The two of them had been getting alone as if they were always together. Sean asked her what she did for a living and she told him she now worked freelance for several major companies.

One very prominent company had been trying to hire her to head up their art department; she really liked The Ramsey Corp, she was seriously considering it. Connor Ramsey, a self-made man, headed it. He knew talent when he saw it. He had to have her.

"Me'na, why don't you take this job? Would you like working for him?"

"Yes, I would, but I might have to travel sometime. Now that you are in my life, I don't want to go away even for short periods of time. I'd miss you."

Sean kissed her. "Don't worry, baby, I'm not going anywhere. We have time. Remember, you said that to me and it's still true. Take the job only if you really like it. I'm here to stay."

"Would you like to meet him before I decide, Sean?"

He held both her hands. "Yes, I would like that. Set it up once you're ready to go back to work. Me'na you know, you don't have to work, we're together now. I'm prepared to take care of you for the rest of your life, I love you." Sean kissed the hands he held. He meant every word he said to her. She smiled and hugged him. As he turned to get dressed he said, "Hurry and get ready. We leave in an hour."

Sean closed her door and made his way to his room. He had not had one of his dreams since she arrived, he was sure there was some significance to that. If he had another dream to tell him or warn him of something, he welcomed it now. The last dream brought Me'na to him when she was in danger. Maybe the next dream would help to solve the puzzle.

Henry and the extra man helping him Tristan Guillory rode in a car behind them. They wanted to be able to chase Bains down if he showed up without endangering Me'na. They had reservations for seven thirty at Club Capricorn. Most people had to wait at least a month to get a reservation, but Sean had grown up with the owner, Robert Langston. He always had an open invitation.

Me'na had never been to Club Capricorn before, so Sean enjoyed showing her a good time. She had on a beautiful off the shoulders red dress with a jagged slit on the left side. This was the first time she had an occasion to wear her dress. When she saw it at a boutique while in New York, she had to have it. She was only five feet three inches tall, but with her red stilettos on, she was about five six.

Henry and Tristan sat at the table next to them. A very popular local band was the entertainment that night. Me'na and Sean danced the night away. The food was the best the city had to offer; they had a great head chef that was world renown. The owner Robert Langston heard Sean was there that night and came out to say hello to him.

As he approached, Sean saw him. He stood up and shook Robert's hands.

"Sit down, Rob. I want you to meet my girl. Me'na, this is Robert my very good friend from Beaumont. Rob, this is Me'na, my girlfriend."

Me'na reached her hand across the table to him. "Hi, Rob. Any friend of Sean's is a friend of mine," she said.

"Ah, mi Cherie, how are you? How did Sean manage to get a very classy lady like you to be seen in public with him?"

"All right, Rob, trying to show me up, huh?" Sean smiled at him.

Rob gave a very continental shrug of his shoulders. "I was always the one with the most charm, you know that. Me'na, this guy is Mr. Serious, I hope you can loosen him up a bit," Rob said to her. She giggled at the two of them.

"Well, Robert, I'm trying to, but it's hard work."

Sean looked toward her. "Not you too, I'm besieged on all sides. Help."

She loved this side of him, but then again, she loved all sides of him.

Robert soon left them to finish the evening with promises to come and visit soon. A waiter came to the table and told Sean that he had a phone call and to follow him.

"That's strange. No one knows that I'm here." He looked covertly toward Henry before he left the table. "Baby, I'll be right back. Henry and Tristan are beside you, remember?" She nodded her head. "Don't look toward them just in case we're being watched. I'll be right back. This seems fishy."

He kissed her cheek and followed the waiter. Me'na sat and waited. Sean hadn't been gone fifteen seconds when Bains approached her table and sat down. Me'na waved her finger at Henry on the side of the table. She wanted to find out what he wanted first.

"I did not ask you to sit down, so get up and leave before Sean gets back," she told him.

"Well, well, so the kitten has claws. Is that your new boyfriend or, are you being kept by him because he has a wife?" he asked.

"My private life is none of your business. Say what you came to say and leave."

"Fair enough. You're known for your fairness, aren't you?" He was thinking about her dating another guy at work when she told him that she didn't date coworkers. He reached for her arm. She moved it in just enough time. "If I can't have you, he will not have you either." Henry was standing behind him now, listening. "I'll see you dead before you have another man."

Henry put his hand on his shoulder. Tristan walked around to Me'na. Sean was on his way back to the table when he saw Henry pull Bains away.

"Let me go, you big ape!" Bains was shouting.

Sean rushed to the table. Henry released him but told him that he was a witness to his threat. The police would be visiting him very soon. Bains tried to run out of the club before Sean got to him.

Sean grabbed him by the collar. "You! I know you." Sean balled his fist and hit Bains in the mouth. He went sprawling onto the floor. The maître d' came quickly to Sean.

"This man is stalking my lady. Call the police." The maitre d' rushed to the phone to call, but Bains had run out of the club by that time.

The police came to question them. Me'na, Henry, and Tristan made a statement. They promised that the information would be forwarded to Detective Hamilton. Sean gathered Me'na and their things and took her home. She kept up a steady stream of conversation so as not to think about anything.

Sean held her hand tight within his warm one. He understood what she was feeling. He rubbed his hand against her cheek her skin was so soft. She reached for the hand and kissed it. No woman before had ever kissed Sean's hand. It gave him ideas best left for another time and place. He pulled into his driveway and Detective Hamilton was waiting for them. Henry and Tristan pulled in behind them.

"Come in, Detective. It's good to have you here so quickly."

Everyone went into the house through the garage. Henry and Tristan locked up the garage door and kitchen. Sean showed the detective into the den. Hamilton asked what happened. Both bodyguards told him what they saw and overheard.

"Now that I have a witness, maybe I can finally get this man off the streets for good."

He took the drawing of Bains and said the first step would be to get a restraining order against him tomorrow. The detective recorded their statements and asked them to come to the station tomorrow to sign them and issue a complaint against Bains.

"Is that all that we can do to him?" Sean asked.

"No, but this is the way to legally start everything that Ms. Collins needs to do."

A shot rang out. Someone had shot into the house. The detective told them to turn off the lights and get down. He got his gun and went outside. By the time he got there, the car was getting away. Sean held Me'na as close to him as he could, she was crying. The detective came back inside and told Henry to turn the lights back on.

"He got away, but I saw part of the license plate number. I need to call this in now." He stepped away from them and called the police station.

Sean pulled Me'na up off the floor and held her in his arms on the sofa. She laid her head on him and quietly pulled herself together as he slowly rocked them.

"Dr. Williams, a squad car will be here to sit in front of the house and we will have a patrol car driving around the neighborhood. I'll catch him don't you worry, ma'am. I have to go back to the station, but I'll be around tomorrow."

Tristan saw him to the door. Henry called him over to talk. As they huddled together, Sean prepared to take Me'na to her room. Henry stopped him.

"Sean, one of us is going to stay up all night in the front part of the house and the other in the back. I put in a call to the agency to send over two fresh guys for the morning shift. Tristan and I will sleep while they are here. This way, we'll protect the inside while the cops are outside. Does this meet with your approval?"

"Yes, Henry, whatever you think is necessary. I'm going to take Me'na to her room."

They walked down the hall to her room, both were very quiet. At the door, she asked him to come in and talk. They sat on the love seat in her room.

"Sean, in your dreams do I die?"

"Me'na, how could you ask me a thing like that? Especially after what just happened, your nerves are unsettled." Her question unsettled his nerves more than anything.

"No, love, do I die? I need to know," she pleaded with him.

"It's only a dream, Me'na, it's not real life. It doesn't mean anything." Sean was trying to avoid the subject. He didn't want to tell her.

"By the way you're acting, I probably died. That's OK. It really is, Sean." He was shaking his head no. She laid her head on his chest. "If I died, that was the past. This is the here and now. We can learn from what went wrong the first time." She tried to calm him now.

Sean didn't have the heart to tell her that she always died. He was never able to save her. He was determined that this time he would prevail.

"Baby, do you believe we have lived before?" he asked her.

"I think something must have happened, I haven't been able to figure it out yet. Either we lived before or the fates are trying to correct a mistake before it happens in real life." She moved as close as she could to him. Sean gladly pulled her inside his embrace; they could almost feel each other's heart beating.

"I never believed in past lives before, but this could make a believer out of me. Will you stay with me tonight. I don't want to be alone," she said.

He sat there for a moment without speaking. Could he trust himself in the same room with her lying down? He wasn't sure he could. He said, "I don't think I should. I'm right next door to you. Me'na, you're still not one hundred percent recovered."

"Sean, I need you in here with me tonight, please," she begged him.

"Me'na, you still need to take it easy. Do you realize I want to make love to you right now? I mean at this very moment in time? I have a hard time remembering you need to recover. When I look at you, all I see is the woman

I love. The woman I need to make my own in every sense of the word." She made a sad face that he couldn't resist.

Damn, he thought, *if I wasn't a doctor I could forget her condition a lot easier.*

"OK, I'll bring the chaise in here and put it next to your bed; I'm not making any promises about behaving myself." She squeezed him tight and kissed him her thanks.

"I'll sleep in my granny gown. It will put out any fires you have."

"I doubt that, but you can try, baby."

Sean knew he would get little sleep. He would lie there watching her all night. He was a regular full-bloodied American male. She was trying him to the point that he'd not been tried before. But the time was not now. They had enough on their plate. He was sane enough to remember that. Things done when emotions were running high were most oft, regretted later. He would wait until their lives were normal.

Me'na was true to her word, she had a flowered high-necked gown on that couldn't tempt a satyr, but Sean was no satyr. He loved her deeply. It didn't matter what she wore. He wanted her more than he had ever wanted any woman before.

They turned off the light and talked through the night. Both learned or had their memory refreshed about each other. It was so weird, but there was something bigger than the both of them at work here. If she were any other woman, he would not be laying in the chaise. Me'na didn't ask him to, she didn't need to. It was the right thing to do now.

They finally went to sleep close to three in the morning. Sean had to give her something for her headache. It would also help her to sleep for about eight hours. Finally, as he dozed off, he started dreaming about Fastonia again.

BOOK THREE
CHAPTER ONE

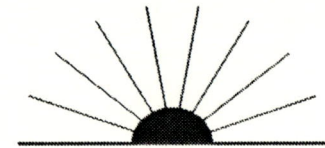

"Darn, this is my favorite dress," Me'na bent down to untangle the heel of her shoe from the lace on the bottom of her dress. There was a small hole in the lace. *This would be hard to repair,* she thought.

"Come, Me'na, our carriage is waiting," Richard Boleyn called to her.

"I'm coming. Give me a moment."

She couldn't say what she was thinking, even though she disliked him, she needed to keep this job. She had enough problems with him. She didn't want to add to them. As she walked to get into the second carriage, he called out for her to join him.

Great, just great. Now I'll have to fight him off all the way to the inn. Why didn't his friends ride with him? Someone up there must hate me, she thought, looking upward.

Me'na had no desire to sit next to Richard. He was a predator. She was not going to be his next victim.

The remainder of their party rode in the accompanying carriage. The ambassador, his assistant Martin Bauman, and the special trade negotiator Charles Ainns accompanied her. She didn't want to make this trip.

The ambassador had an ulterior motive. The plan was to get her away from home. He didn't desire her to have anyone to run to. This way she was all alone and at his mercy. He would have her as his mistress before he double-crossed her. The ambassador had a side deal going on that she knew nothing about.

Me'na sat looking out of the window at the busy dock. This was really a very important kingdom to her country. The best goods came from here, and all ships docked here either for supplies or to trade. She saw many ships waiting for a slot to drop anchor. Her ship had to wait two days for a place and they were expected to see the King that very evening. She'd heard he was very good looking and single. A girl like herself didn't stand a chance of attracting him.

Maybe I'll get a chance to dance with him at the ball if I walk past him, enough times he's bound to notice me.

She found out the hard way that when men of power noticed her. They only wanted to make her their mistress. She would be no one's mistress, not even the King's. Well, maybe she'd think about if it was the King, she smiled to herself.

They traveled through the busy streets of Winslow the capital city. Me'na saw merchants on the streets hawking their wares. She had never seen so many shops or people before. There were all kinds of shops. There were dressmakers, boot and shoe craftsmen, and watchmakers. There was even a small café right there outside an establishment.

"Oh my, I would love living here, it looks so exciting," she said to no one in particular.

To her he said, "Sit back, Me'na, and stop gawking. You're acting like a country girl." He had ruined her high spirits once again. "Don't sit and pout. Appear to have class if you don't mind. I don't want you embarrassing me tonight."

She looked over at him and rolled her eyes. He tried to pat her hand, but she removed it as if his touch was poison, to her it was. They arrived at the palace about thirty minutes later. She didn't speak to him again.

As they were getting out of the carriage, Martin Bauman told the drivers to bring their luggage to the Golden Swan Inn. Adam, Boleyn's manservant would see that they acquired three rooms; Me'na was to have her own. As they walked inside the palace, they were met at the entrance. Boleyn registered with the secretary and waited to be announced to the King.

He turned around to her. "Me'na, wait for us here. There is no need for you to meet his highness at this time. You will be there for the official talks with him and at the dinner gala."

"As you wish." Mockingly she curtsied to him.

Charles Ainns smiled at her. He also thought Richard was pompous. Me'na wondered around the room looking at all the people from different parts of the world. They were all here for the same thing or so she thought; to be granted the right to trade with Fastonia. As she walked through the public rooms of the palace, she found herself in the palace museum. It was so quiet and peaceful here she thought she would admire all the pieces presented. She walked toward the portraits at the end of the gallery to look upon the faces of the King's ancestors. While standing there quietly someone appeared beside her.

"I think I'm better looking than the picture, don't you?"

She turned to see who was disturbing her concentration and the man beside her looked just like the painting of the prince she was looking at. Her eyes widen, she dropped into a curtsey immediately.

Prince Thomas bent down to help her up. "Please, rise and tell me your name."

She stood up as straight as she could, shoulders thrown back and introduced herself. "My name is Me'na Collins, Your Highness. I'm with the group from Timbre. We're here to open trade negotiations."

"Well, Me'na, you never answered my question. Don't you think I look better in person?" Thomas was gently teasing. She realized that he was trying to put her at ease and she smiled at him. "My lady, you are gorgeous, but I assume you've been told that many times before."

"Thank you, Your Highness, and I have been told that a couple of times."

"I can see that you are an imp. I shall have to be very careful with what I say. Come, walk with me and I'll personally show you the gallery and answer any questions you may have."

Me'na took the offered arm and they walked around the gallery with Thomas explaining who the people were and any interesting tidbit he thought she might like to hear. He asked, "Will you be coming to the dinner and the ball tonight?"

"Yes, Your Highness. I'll be accompanied by the ambassador and his assistant. We also have Charles Ainns with us as trade negotiator. I understand that he is originally from Fastonia."

Thomas stopped and wondered if this was the same Charles Ainns that he and the King grew up with. Richard Boleyn sent his assistant in search of her. As he approached, the prince asked her if that was the ambassador coming their way.

"No, Prince, that's the assistant though I don't know what he assists at. I came on the journey as a scribe to pay for my passage. I know it is a man's job, but I was desperate. I'm to stay at the hotel except for tonight."

Bauman approached them and bowed to the prince, "Excuse me, Your Highness, but I've come to fetch Mistress Collins. Our interview is over for now and we must retire to the inn."

"She'll be along in a minute." Thomas dismissed him without further thought.

Me'na turned toward Thomas and curtsied to him. "Thank you for the tour, Your Highness, but I must go now."

He stopped her before she could back away to leave. "Will you dance with me tonight?"

She bowed her head. She then looked at him and answered, "It would be an honor to dance with you, Your Highness."

Thomas looked so handsome as he smiled to her and said, "Until then."

They parted ways with Thomas singing softly. He was quite proud of himself. Before his upcoming marriage, he planned to find himself a mistress to spend his time with. He had to marry but he didn't have to be faithful. It wasn't a love match. It was political. This piece of feminine fluff he just met would fill the vacant spot of mistress, of that, he was sure.

Walking back to her party, Me'na thought about meeting the prince. *He is very handsome and cultured, but he couldn't be anything else. I wonder if the King is as attractive as his brother? Hmm, tonight is shaping up to be a turning point on this trip. With luck maybe I can stay here and work. I'll ask the prince if he knows of anything that I might be able to do here. Maybe he knows of a noble family with need of a high-born governess.*

By the time she reached the carriage, nothing could spoil her good mood. "What kept you, girl?" Boleyn asked her.

"I was speaking with Prince Thomas when Martin found me. He is a wonderful man."

"You didn't say anything to him, did you?" Richard asked.

She looked at him mystified. "What do you mean by that? He spoke to me about his family. I was in the museum when we ran into each. He's a very nice man." He just looked at her and turned his head to look out of the window.

BOOK THREE
CHAPTER TWO

Me'na dressed with utmost care that night, she would be introduced to the King, and she wanted to make a good impression. She was wearing a pale pink gown with pink that was a shade darker in the ruffles. The bodice was tight and pushed her breast upward. She had managed to have an even paler shade of pink covering her breast, which would have otherwise been exposed.

She didn't need a corset. Her waist was the hand span of a grown man. Me'na, as most women of influence was a slave to fashion. The corset was one thing she had refused to wear. She didn't need it anyway. The back of her dress had the smaller bustle that was now in vogue. She also wore a small pink hat with tiny flowers sewn on that she placed on her head with a jaunty tilt. She thought it looked dashing. The shoes of course were pink with the same flowers on the top.

She looked in the mirror and tried to pinch her cheeks for color. Her skin was a golden hue. She couldn't pinch herself hard enough without bruising. *Well*, she thought, *at lease my lips are red on their own.* It was a good consolation.

A knock sounded on her door then a voice shouted out that it was time to leave. Picking up her bag, she prepared to leave and enjoy herself.

The inn was a short ride to the palace. It just took them a while waiting in a very long line of carriages to disembark. Once on the inside of the palace they were shown to their seats at the table. There were so many people there of different nationalities, Me'na knew this night would be one to remember.

She hoped to make contacts here. It seemed as if each day he grew another pair of hands that were always trying to find their way under her clothes. The price of passage to Fastonia just had to be worth all the problems she was having. She only agreed to translate Martin's scribble into something legible, not be his paramour. The ambassador promised to find a worthy family with small children.

She had no family to protect her from him and she was afraid that he would ruin her if she kept refusing him. She was the last surviving member of her family. They were once a powerful family that had fallen into hard times. Her brother had lost everything he inherited gambling. He even lost her dowry. She had nothing to bring to a marriage.

Once everyone was seated, the King and prince walked into the dining hall. An awed hush fell upon the room for the King was magnificent. He nodded his head and everyone was seated. The servers started bringing in the food. The food was so plentiful that she didn't know where to begin.

As she was taking a small bite of pheasant breast, she felt she was being watched. It didn't feel sinister, though it did make her heart beat faster. She wasn't sure if she should raise her head and try to see who was looking at her, or continue eating.

She thought, *Why not? I am looking for employment here*. With that thought, she raised her head and looked around; when her eyes came upon the King, she stopped. *Oh my Lord, he's watching me,* she thought, *what should I do? You silly goose, just smile your sweetest smile on him, see what happens.*

Me'na smiled at the King. He in turn smiled back and raised his goblet in salute to her. She demurely lowered her head and peeked upward. She could see the King softly laughed at her peeking.

Sean called a servant over to him. "Jamie, you see that lovely woman down there in pink? Ask her to join me at my table. Bring her place settings here, be discreet."

"Yes, Your Majesty, right away."

He left to do as he was bid. Thomas looked at his brother to see who he was referring to the servant about. When his eyes settled on Me'na he thought, *No, no, no. She's mine, I saw her first.*

He turned to Sean. "Sean, that is the woman I told you about today. I have plans for her with me."

"Thomas, why don't we let the lady decide? You after all will soon be a married man. You'll have a wife and soon there will be children. I think your hands will be full enough with all that."

As Me'na got up to follow the servant, several heads turned to see where she was going. When she was placed on the King's immediate left, the whispers started. Richard Boleyn watched her sit by the king and thought this change of events just might be advantageous to his cause. He would still have her after the king was through with her. King Winslo was not known as a ladies man, but he had left quite a few women with broken hearts.

Boleyn accepted an offer from a Barbary Coast pirate who wanted to buy Me'na and sell her. He had an order from a caliph who wanted such a woman as her to add to his harem. It didn't matter to him that she was from a once powerful family. There were no slaves in his country. He needed to make some money and make it fast. This was as good a way as any. He smiled a sinister smile to himself.

As Me'na sat down, she thanked the King for inviting her. "It is my pleasure. Tell me, what is your name?"

"Your Highness, I am Lady Me'na Collins." She smiled demurely at him. Not to be outdone, Thomas greeted her also.

"Thank you for joining us, Me'na. You will add cheer to this table."

"Thank you, Prince Thomas."

Sean looked at his brother and knew what he was trying to do. He was trying to make it appear as if he had asked his brother to invite her. He did not witness the episode before her coming to the table.

Sean and Me'na talked the entire time they were eating. Thomas sat there staring at them. From Thomas' view point, they were behaving as if they shared a secret. A secret, which was not going to be shared with him. He was ready to go into the ballroom and dance with her if he could catch Sean slipping. The dinner was prolonged because the King was deeply involved with his new guest.

Sean happened to glance in Thomas' direction and saw him staring at Me'na as if she were a feast. He picked up a strawberry off his plate and fed it to her. Thomas started to cough. It made him sick.

"Are you all right, prince?' Me'na asked.

"I am fine. It was something I saw that caused me discomfort," he replied.

Sean smiled in his brother's direction. "He'll be fine. Thomas is a hardy fellow."

Me'na giggled and laughed at his jokes all night. She was very receptive to anything he did. They got alone like old friends who had a history together and were now reunited. Me'na was already infatuated with the King. She hoped it didn't show. Men of power and influence had tried to seduce her before. She'd have to be careful. She had never been this totally taken with a man's charms as she was with the King.

The King was totally spellbound with her. He wanted her at his table because she was beautiful. Now he wanted to keep her there because she had beauty and brains. A rare combination indeed, but he didn't like women who only thought about fashions and shopping. He wanted someone who could converse with him on the intellectual level, then change gears, and tell him a joke. So far, his idea woman was still a dream, until now.

"Tell me, Lady Me'na, what are your plans after the trade summit is over?" he inquired.

"I was hoping I could find employment as a governess here in your lovely kingdom."

"Let me think on it for a while. I may have something for you," the King replied.

The something that Sean was thinking about was himself. He wanted this woman as he had wanted no other in a very long time. His brother would not get her from him.

Thomas was trying to come up with a plan to get her away from Sean. He was only marrying because the marriage would help the kingdom, he didn't want to.

The meal had come to an end and the King escorted Me'na into the ballroom with Thomas following behind them. Sean and Me'na started the dancing off. He whirled her around the ballroom, while Thomas seethed with annoyance. The prince asked Lady Constance to dance with him. The rest of the guest took to the floor also.

What started out for Sean as a dalliance, turned into something more serious. He thought he must find a way to keep her in Fastonia. He did not want her to leave. The King was not one to believe in love at first sight, but he was fast becoming a believer.

"Me'na, would you consider staying in Fastonia whether you found employment or not?" he asked her.

"Your Highness, I need to be able to support myself. My brother lost all of the family's money gambling. I would be destitute without something to do," she admitted.

They had been dancing for about an hour when Sean asked her to go out onto the balcony with him. Once on the balcony, he pulled her in his arms and kissed her with all the passion he felt. She responded in kind for a moment, and then pushed back.

"Your Highness, please, we're moving too fast. You must slow down."

In her mind, slowing down was the last thing she wanted to do. She didn't want Sean to think she was forward or anything. She would have to be herself, even if it meant losing a chance to be with him. Me'na was not going to let him sweet talk her away to his bed tonight. That's what men with power did with women that were not marriage material, but her resolve was weakening.

He captivated Me'na. He was so tall and broad of shoulder. His green eyes were the jewels that topped off an already gorgeous package. It didn't get any better than this. Me'na did have a weakness for green eyes though.

He asked her, "Please stay, I'll make sure you do not want for anything, you have my word."

Me'na thought very carefully and closed her eyes. *I'll kiss him one more time. If my toes curl up, then I'll stay.*

Reaching up, she placed her hand on the side of his face and lowered his head to her lips. She closed her eyes and kissed him with everything she felt. Sean pulled her tightly against his chest, she felt so good to him. He made up his mind that he wouldn't let her go, no matter what it took. When they finally broke contact, Me'na's heart was beating very fast. This was not her first kiss, but it should have been. She didn't have many kisses to compare with his, but the ones she had, didn't come close. The King hugged her to him; he almost knocked her hat off trying to get her as close as possible. *Well that's it,* she thought. *Not only did my toes curl but I just lost my heart to him.*

"Me'na, what say you, what will it take to keep you here? What must I do?"

"Your Highness," she started, "I will be no man's mistress, I'm not that kind of woman. I'll only stay if you think this could turn into something more, something beautiful."

"Let's have a seat." They sat down on the bench.

"I do not want you for a mistress. I would not dishonor you that way," he said to her.

"But, Highness, you couldn't marry me because I'm not of royal blood. Noble blood, yes, but not royal." This was hard for her to say. "You do not know me well enough to plant thoughts of a possible marriage. That's cruel." She didn't want him to see how taken with him she was.

"I can do whatever I want to do. I am the King after all. Look at me, what do you feel when you look upon me? Please be honest, it is important." Sean lost sight of his original intentions toward her. He was looking for a new bed partner not a wife. He spoke from his heart. His brain didn't know what was going to be said until his heart opened his mouth.

Me'na hoped that maybe he felt the same thing she felt. Ever since, she felt him stare at her; her heart would not stop pounding. She looked down at her hands in her lap. Sean picked them up and kissed them. He turned her hands over, while looking her directly in her eyes he kissed the palm. Me'na's breath caught in her throat. He held onto them, he hoped that maybe it would help her say what he wanted to hear. The kiss he placed in her palm helped his case.

"Well, Your Highness," she began, "I have never been in love before. I do not know what it feels like to love a man. I know that from the moment, I first saw you. I have not been able to catch my breath. I can feel you here," she pointed to her heart. "My heart is fluttering, if it had wings. I would be soaring right now. I can't describe it any better than that."

Sean was happy to hear her confession. He felt the same way. He didn't realize it until he heard her out. After spending the evening with her, his feelings went beyond the present.

"Me'na, I have never believed in love at first sight, lust yes, but not love. I had begun to think there was no one out there for me. I was ready to settle down with a woman because I need heirs, not for companionship, just heirs." Sean let her hands go and wrapped his arm around her.

"But when I first laid my eyes on you at dinner, I knew that I would have to get to know you. I too have not been able to catch my breath. This is a strange thing for me also. I did not want to fall in love. I thought it would make me weak, less of a man." He hugged her tighter and kissed her forehead.

"I have seen men led around by their noses following their women. I vowed that would not happen to me. But here I am, pouring my heart out to a virtual stranger, a beautiful stranger; but a stranger nonetheless. I wouldn't have had it any other way. I hope this answers the question that you had in your eyes."

Me'na felt a warm flush steal across her entire being. This had to be love, what else could cause her emotions to ramble like this?

"Yes, it does, Your Highness," she said.

"Please call me, Sean. I would like to hear you say it. Your Highness seems so cold and unfeeling."

She smiled, looked down and softly said, "Sean."

"Ah that's better," he said. "Are you afraid? You still look unsure."

"Your Highness," she said. He gave her a stern look. "I mean, Sean." He smiled with pleasure.

She studied his beautiful eyes carefully before she started to speak. "I am afraid a little. This is all very new to me." Me'na was still leery about being dependent upon a man that was not her husband. She let out a nervous giggle.

"I feel acceptance and an odd sense of feeling like we met before, but I know that's impossible. I also see a sparkle of mischief in your eyes. I will be on my guard for that though." He laughed at her last statement for he did have a great sense of humor.

She asked him, "Tell me, Sean, what would a king want from someone like me? I don't have anything to give but myself."

"I want everything I see and everything I can feel." For extra emphasis, he hugged her tighter. "I also want the passion I detected a moment before. I see a woman who will demand a great deal of care and commitment on my part, because she is worth it.

"My question to you still is: will you stay here with me?"

Me'na put her arms around his neck. "Yes, Sean, I will stay. I will let whatever is happening to the both of us grow into whatever it is meant to be. But I will have one problem, after the trade summit is over. I will have no place to stay."

"You will stay here in the palace with me. We have plenty of rooms for you to choose from," he told her.

But Me'na was justly concerned. What if things didn't work out the way she wanted them to, what then? He could see that something else was troubling her. He knew what it was.

"Me'na, I can see you are worried that things may not work out between us. Never fear, I would not abandon you. If you ever decide you wanted to leave I would give you enough funds to get settled wherever you wanted to go, you have my word. Things will work out, of this, I am certain. Please, take this chance at love with me. You will not regret it."

She looked thoughtful for a second.

"OK Sean. Let's see what happens with this new found love affair we have. It is love, don't you think?"

He pulled her up with him as he stood; he knew she needed more said than he did. After all, she was a foreigner in his kingdom and she didn't have any friends or family to back her up.

He took the first plunge. "Me'na, I know I care for you, but I do not mind if you need further convincing. I will do my best to prove to you that you are not making a mistake." That was just what she needed to hear from him.

"Thank you, Sean, I feel better now. Can I trouble you for a kiss?" For her answer, he just pulled her into his arms and kissed her as if he was starving, in a way, he was; he needed to feel her love inside him, needed to feel it in his bones.

BOOK THREE
CHAPTER THREE

The King was in such a good mood that morning that he infected his gentlemen with his enthusiasm. Everyone was smiling or telling jokes, no one knew exactly why the king felt so good. They had an inkling that it had to do with the woman he spent last evening with, to the exclusion of everyone else. No one was going to broach the subject unless he brought it up first. He finally did.

"Connor, would you do me a favor?" Connor cut his laughter short, "Yes, sire, anything. What can I do for you?"

"I need you to go to the Golden Swan and ask Lady Collins if she would join me for breakfast. She is traveling with the ambassador from Timbre."

Connor responded, "Right away, sire." He left to go and fetch Me'na and the remaining men decided it was time to tease the King.

Lord Robert started first. "Sire, do you mean to say we won't be eating with you this morning?"

Before Sean could respond, Lord Patrick said, "My heart will be broken if I cannot sup with you. I'll just kill myself."

He took an imagined knife and stabbed himself in the heart. Everyone roared with laughter including Sean. Their king was the type of man that his men felt comfortable being at their ease with. They joked with him often on nonsensical subjects, he enjoyed a good ribbing.

"Patrick, if I had the choice of looking at your face across the table or hers, you lose. You are just not my type."

Everyone laughed with the king at Patrick. At that moment, Prince Thomas walked into the room and asked Sean if he could speak with him. The gentlemen left the King and his brother alone.

"What's on your mind, Thomas?"

"Sean, you know what's on my mind. It's Lady Collins. I met her first that should count for something," Thomas replied.

"Brother, it usually does count, but this time it's different. You know I've never tried to talk to women that you were interested in. We have always respected each other's domain for lack of a better word." She does something to me I cannot explain it." Sean walked to the window and stood looking at the morning. "She has already carved a place in my heart, maybe I am falling in love. It's about time."

Sean looked at Thomas for understanding, he had bowed out for Thomas before. It was his turn now. Thomas walked around the inner chamber with his hands in his pockets. He was deep in thought, Sean walked to him and together they stepped out onto the balcony.

"I know what you're saying, Sean, but she does something for me also. I want her, I need her."

"But you are getting married within the next two months. She has already told me she would be no man's mistress. Not even mine."

Thomas turned to look his brother in the eyes. "You mean to tell me it has already gone that far for you?" Sean nodded his head yes.

"Why, Sean, you don't have to marry her, just seduce her. You're the King, women have succumbed to your charms before, she eventually will also. I wasn't going to marry her, just put her up in a cottage close to the palace and visit her like we do with mistresses."

"That is not enough for me, Thomas. I want to grow old with her and have little girls that look just like her. I want my daughters to have that golden skin and that long mahogany hair. That's why having her as a mistress isn't enough for me."

"Sean, you can still have all that with her. You just don't have to marry. Men in our position have dozens of mistresses. It is accepted as a way of life. You have had several mistresses at one time. Our father had a mistress, but he still loved mother."

"He may have loved mother, but she cried to me one time about how father had broken her heart with his women. She couldn't stand it but tried to make a good showing since she was his Queen."

Thomas was astounded at this revelation, he never knew this about his mother. She was closer to Sean than him. He and his father were cut from the same cloth.

"Well, I guess you have a point then. What will you tell your ministers about marrying someone not from one of the royal houses?"

Sean leaned on the top of the balcony and said, "To hell with them, I will marry who I choose to marry. I am the King, the absolute ruler. I do not share power with the ministers nor do I need anyone's approval for what I do."

Thomas nodded his head. In Fastonia, the King was still the supreme ruler unlike some monarchs in other kingdoms.

"Thomas, I do not know if she would marry me. I haven't asked her yet. We are going to take things slowly for a moment, but my mind is already made up. She will be my Queen. It's just a matter of time."

Thomas clapped him on the back. "Well, big brother, I hope it works out for you. I will bow out gracefully for you. I hope she is worth it."

"Thank you, Tommy. I know she is. Your support means a lot to me."

The brothers walked back into the chamber. Thomas left to go about his day.

Me'na had awakened in a splendid mood nothing could ruin her day. She got out of bed and went to the window to look at the sunshine. It looked like even the birds were singing just for her. Her spirits were so high. The only thing that could ruin it would be for last evening to have been a dream. She pulled on the bell cord and waited for a maid to come to her room. Once the maid appeared, she asked for a bath.

Me'na wanted to be at her best today. They were meeting with the King and his ministers. She would be waiting in one of the alcoves for Martin to bring in his notes for her to transcribe. Women weren't allowed to hold positions of employment unless they were a seamstress or a governess. Today the price of passage was steep for she would be unable to see Sean. Anyway, she picked out her best business attire. It was a burgundy colored dress. The maid came back with two boys dragging a tub and other boys bringing in pails of hot water. She put a few drops of her favorite scent, gardenia into the hot water. The room was immediately filled with its scent. Next, the cold water was brought in, she put her finger in the water and it felt just right. Me'na thanked the boys and gave each a coin. She pinned her hair on top of her head, and stepped into the water.

"Ah, this feels so good." She sighed.

She leaned all the way in the tub, rested her head on the slope, and closed her eyes. She lay there for a while.

There was a knock on her door. Boleyn didn't wait for her to answer the door. He found it was unlocked and walked right in. He had watched the coming and going of the servants and knew she was indisposed.

Me'na looked at him. "Get out! I did not say for you to come in here." She reached for the nearest towel to cover her. "Did you hear what I said to you? Get out! Right now I mean it."

He walked into the room closed the door and sat down in the nearest chair. "Well, maybe you do, maybe you don't. Your door was open. I thought you were expecting me." He knew she wasn't. This gave him an advantage he thought.

"Me'na, you have something that I want and you're going to give it to me. Whether you give it to me now or later does not change the fact that you will be giving it to me."

"Giving what to you, what is it?" she shouted at him.

"You will give yourself to me, darling, didn't you know that?"

"I will give you nothing, now get out! I will start screaming if you don't."

He told her calmly, "I'm not going anywhere, and no one would believe you. Look at you. It would appear to anyone that you are preparing yourself for me."

Me'na starting screaming and shouting at him. He got up to silence her when the door burst open. Lord Connor came into the room and went straight to Boleyn. He wore a ceremonial sword, as did most nobles. He pulled his sword out and placed it at Boleyn's throat.

"What goes on here? Why are you in this room? Speak," Connor told him.

"Well, she invited me in, then got mad at me. What was I do?" Boleyn claimed.

Connor looked to Me'na. "He's lying, I did not ask him in. I forgot to lock my door after the tub was brought in and he just walked in. That's the truth, I swear it."

Connor looked at Boleyn and said, "Gentlemen do not just walk into ladies rooms without being asked. Women do not scream at them to get out, I could hear her down stairs. She did not sound like she didn't mean it." Connor lowered his sword, "I suggest that you leave now while you still have breath in your body. This lady is under the King's protection."

Sean hadn't told him that, but it made Boleyn leave with undue haste. Connor backed toward the door and said to her, "Lady Collins, King Winslo sent me to ask if you would join him at breakfast this morning."

She was delighted, "Yes, I can be ready in a few minutes."

Connor doubted that, he didn't know any woman who could get ready in a few minutes. "I'll be waiting for you outside your door. No one will enter. You have my word."

"Thank you, my lord." He went outside to wait and Me'na jumped out of the tub and hurriedly dried off. She put on her dress and started to comb her hair. She arranged it in the current style and placed her bonnet on her head. Me'na looked in the mirror. She was pleased with what she saw, grabbed her bag and went to the door. Connor was truly surprised to see her so quickly; if the king didn't want her, he'd take her. Any woman who could get ready that fast had his attention.

Upon arriving at the palace, Connor took her to the private room the King has meals in sometimes, he asked her to wait. She looked at the table setting everything was gold. There was one yellow rose in a vase in the middle of the table. Me'na picked it up and sniffed the aroma of the rose. As she was putting the rose back in the vase, Sean walked in.

"Good morning, Your Highness." She curtsied to him.

"Good morn to you also, I thought you were going to call me Sean. What's with this, Your Highness?" he asked her.

She blushed, "I'm sorry, I forgot. Sean."

"Much better, come let me seat you."

He moved toward her and she felt the heat of his presence; she was overcome with longing. She didn't have a clue what she was longing for, but it was there and it was palpable. As she sat down, Me'na waved her hand at her face a little; her breath was gone. She could not breathe again.

Sean asked her, "Are you hot? I'll open one of the windows for you."

"Thank you. I don't know what came over me all of a sudden." She looked down at her plate. Her face had reddened a bit.

The servants knocked and entered the room to serve the King and his guest. Sean had a big appetite. He had steak, eggs, bread and some type of hot cereal. Me'na had some eggs, a piece of bread and a small serving of the steak. On the table before them were biscuits, sausage, sweet rolls and tea. The servants left them alone and Sean asked if there was anything else she might like.

"Oh no, this is more than enough, I don't want to over eat. You might not like me any more if I became fat."

Sean pretended to think about it. "No, I guess you're right. I don't think you could fit into that lovely dress you wore last night." He smiled at her. The humor broke the tension that was in the room; Me'na was still upset with Boleyn and didn't want it to ruin her time with Sean. He could tell something was not right.

He placed his hand on hers and asked, "What is it, my dear? Have I done something to offend you? Tell me what it is and I will make it right."

She responded instantly, "Oh no, Sean, it is not you. It could never be you. The ambassador upset me again, but that is not new. He is a hard man to work under, very demanding, that's all. Never you."

He smiled at her. He was determined to speak with Connor and see if he knew anything about this.

"Well, when you get to know me, you're find I am demanding also, in a different way." The change in his voice made her blush. She lowered her head and peeked up at him through her lashes. "You look so adorable when you do that. I could just kiss you," he told her.

Me'na decided to try and make him uncomfortable. "What are you waiting for, Sean? I'm here within reach."

Instead of making him uncomfortable, he quickly reached out to her and brought her around the table to him. Sean turned his chair slightly and pulled her onto his lap. Once she was seated, he began an assault upon her senses. Me'na felt overcome by passion, she felt as if her body was on fire. She tried to return his kisses as best she could. Her body was pressing itself against Sean. She had lost control, Me'na responded purely by instinct.

Sean realized she was not experienced by the quickness of her arousal, he took more control, he would bring her along slowly. He gradually ended their kiss, squeezing her to him and kissing her all over her face. *She would make a fine wife,* he thought, *full of fire and passion*. Just what he wanted.

"Why did you stop, Sean? It was so wonderful. I could kiss you all day." She tried to start again. He could only take so much, without bedding her.

"I stopped, kitten, because you are not experienced in the ways of men and women. That is as it should be. I can only take so much of your kisses before I will require more. Do you understand what I mean?" he asked her. Sean looked into her amber-colored eyes and pleaded for understanding. Finally understanding dawned in her eyes, her cheeks colored and she rested her head against his shoulder.

"I am so sorry, I didn't mean to cause you any discomfort. I'll try to behave from now on."

Sean raised her chin with his thumb. "I don't want you to behave. I like you as you are. If we keep going like this, you will have no choice but to become my wife. I find that I cannot part with you, not even for a moment."

She smiled at his words. What if he really meant them? Time would tell.

He as a King was not within her reach. He would have to marry someone that was royalty. Her eyes took on a shadow that he didn't understand.

"Kitten, what is it? Tell me so I can fix it."

"You speak of marriage, but you cannot marry someone like me. I bring nothing to your country, not military alliance, not anything financial. This is but a dream that you weave."

Sean tightened his hold on her. "I am the absolute ruler of Fastonia, I need no military alliances. I have more than enough. My kingdom is very rich. We need no money, but I do need you."

As he spoke to her, she was beginning to have some hope. She knew that she loved him; she didn't want him to regret his decision.

"Are you sure you want me, no regrets?" she asked him.

"No regrets," Sean responded. He kissed her very tenderly and tried to keep their passion under control, but it was hard. Me'na kissed his ear lobe giving him shivers. She laughed seductively. Now she had a little control. "Me'na, I didn't mean to talk to you about marriage this morning; I was saving that for a special dinner I had planned. But things got out of hand pretty fast. I could not help myself."

"Sean, don't announce our marriage to anyone yet." He looked at her puzzled. She thought he was misunderstanding her because of the hurt look that appeared in his eyes. "I don't want the ambassador to try and use that against you in the negotiations. Can you speak with him today or early tomorrow and finish the deal? I want the whole world to know how much I love you." Me'na started kissing his ear lobe again and then his neck as she spoke. She was enjoying this new found sensuality of hers.

She continued. "I know the initial meeting is over so maybe we can rush him a little." Me'na reached and grabbed his hand; she rubbed her thumb against his palm. "I don't want him to think that he can use me against you, he would use whatever leverage he thought he had."

His beautiful green eyes cleared with understanding. "As you wish, but just until this is over, I must tell my brother. I will see if I can rush him."

"OK," she agreed. Me'na got off Sean's lap and finished her meal with gusto.

He watched her eat. "I don't know if I can afford to feed you now. I had better reconsider," he joked with her.

"You do and I'll not kiss you anymore."

"Please, never that." They had a good time playing with each other. The meal passed with the both of them holding hands and thinking about the future.

BOOK THREE
CHAPTER FOUR

Before the King began holding afternoon court, he called Connor over to him to talk. “Sire, I was going to speak with you after court today. I found a situation that I handled but you should be made aware of.”

“Go on, Con, tell me,” he said.

“Highness, as I was going up the stairs at the Golden Swan, I could hear a woman screaming. I ran to find out what was going on and the sound was coming out of Lady Collins’ room. I naturally burst into the room to find the ambassador from Timbre inside her room.” Sean’s face began to darken with rage.

“She was shouting at him to leave. She was not happy at all with him. She was in the bathtub and had forgotten to lock her door. He apparently just walked in on her and refused to leave. I threw him out. I then stood guard while she dressed.”

Sean couldn’t believe his ears. “Con, what was his excuse for being in her room?”

“He said she invited him in but I didn’t believe him. She didn’t sound like she was pleased or just having a lover’s spat. While I was standing outside her door, Lord Ainns came out to see what was going on. When I told him, he wasn’t surprised. He said the ambassador had been trying to corner her for some time now. She didn’t want anything to do with him.”

Sean nodded his head the whole time and seething on the inside. “Con, can I trust you to keep this secret?” the King asked him.

“Keep what secret, sire? I just asked you if you enjoyed your meal,” a faithful Connor said.

"Thank you, my friend, I knew I could count on you."

Connor bowed, and left the King to seek his own breakfast.

Sean sat on the throne thinking about what he would or wouldn't do. "There must be a way I can show my displeasure with the ambassador's conduct as a gentleman." *Hmm*, he thought, *I will find a way*.

The King called for the doors to be opened and for court to begin. All the various representatives from nations around the world came forward. They submitted their offers to the king's secretary days before. Sean and his ministers went over all the offers to decide which ones were best for Fastonia. Usually, all offers were accepted unless the country participated in slavery. Sean was dead set against the idea of slavery. No man had the right to make one group of people slaves. Some of his principal exporters were black and several of his major military alliances were with the African nations.

The proposition from Timbre was still on his desk. He would see them tomorrow. He was a fair man. He would not allow his distaste for Ambassador Boleyn to overrule his judgment. He just didn't want to see the man until then. He might challenge him to a duel or an old-fashioned fistfight. It had been a long time since anyone fought him, not since before he was King. Only his brother would fight him, for anyone else to even try would be considered treason. Once court was over for the day, he'd ask Robert Langston to practice fencing with him. He was one of the best the court had to offer; this would give the king an outlet for his anger.

Thomas came in to sit with him during this session of court. There were many offers proposed that day. Some large and some small, they were appropriate for the size of the country they represented. Sean wanted different nationalities to have use of Fastonia's ports. He liked the goods brought into his kingdom. It gave his people a chance to see how other people lived and the products they had to offer.

Many of the sailors who docked in Fastonia often stayed and married a local woman. The population was a mix of the world's races as was his ministers. His was a busy port, not crime free, but very low crime rate. A man felt safe to bring his family in the port area. Sometimes, the best vegetables to buy were to had right off the ship before they were taken to the marketplace.

As court was winding down, the King's men were filing in one by one surrounding the throne in a semicircle. His best friend Kristoff was reclining on the steps on the dais along with his cousin Henry, Duke of Lindsey. Colin, Lord Firth and Lord Langston were his fencing partners; they kept him on his toes. Lord Connor was his confidant whenever Kristoff was not around. He was also a good friend whom Sean trusted implicitly. The Earl of Penmark, Lord Patrick and the Earl of Dunmore, Lord Morley were his hunting and riding buddies along with his brother. They could ride for hours without complaining.

Sean called an end to court, he was ready to relax and maybe go for a ride. He saw the Ambassador of Timbre in court along with his assistant Martin Bauman. Me'na was not with them. Sean sent one of the pages to bring the ambassador to him. As Boleyn walked up the King, Sean felt distaste, but he kept it off his face.

Boleyn bowed to him. "You requested to see me, Your Highness."

"Yes, I did. Thank you for coming. I will meet with you and your negotiator tomorrow morning."

"Thank you, Your Majesty. We will be here early to await your pleasure," he answered.

"Where is Lady Collins? I do not see her."

"I have her doing some paperwork for me back at the inn. She will be here with us tomorrow, sire. If you prefer, I can do without her services if you do not want a woman present."

Sean looked at him and knew he was trying to use Me'na as bait. He knew the King was interested in her. Everyone did after all the attention he paid her.

"I want her present tomorrow and I want you and your entire staff as my special guest tonight. You are to sit at my table with the prince and myself. As soon as Lady Collins is finished with her work, would you be so kind as to send her to the palace later today? I would like to speak with her."

"Yes, Highness, I will send her here as soon as we get back to the inn. Thank you." With that he left to go and get Me'na.

Me'na was drowning in paperwork. The ambassador had given her more work than necessary. Martin Bauman didn't do anything but hold the door open for Boleyn. He certainly didn't help her with any work. All of this copying was making her fingers cramp. The King would not be seeing any of this. Boleyn was just trying to even the score with her for having him thrown out of her room earlier. She was tougher than he thought. It would take more than this to break her. Besides, she had a big secret he knew nothing about.

Me'na hugged herself with the knowledge that Sean was in love with her; soon, she would be his Queen. Nothing he did mattered anymore, She was beyond him. Me'na didn't realize she was just staring off into space with a smile on her face. She sat like that for several minutes, just thinking about being Sean's wife. Her thoughts were interrupted when someone knocked on her door.

"Who is there?"

"Me'na, it's me, the ambassador. Let me in please." He was trying to be nice to her, which wasn't in his nature.

"What do you want?"

"Me'na, just let me in, I have a message for you from the King."

That got her up. She opened the door a crack.

"Yes?"

"May I come in, please?" She moved back a mite for him to come in. "What is your message?" she wanted to know.

"Well, the King wants you to come to the palace as soon as you are through with your work. But you can go now seeing as how you've worked so hard. Me'na, I want to apologize for this morning, I was out of line and I'm sorry."

"Are you really, Ambassador? Is this a trick of some kind?" she asked. She knew he didn't do anything for anyone for nothing. There must be a catch somewhere. Was he trying to throw her off her guard?

"Ambassador, if I leave, who will finish my work? Martin?"

"Don't worry about it, my dear, everything will be fine. You just run along now, have a good time." He turned around and left out of her room.

Me'na hurriedly tidied herself up. She put on a very pretty dress that accentuated her coloring. She wore her favorite scent, gardenia. To her it was the most beautiful flower and the sweetest smelling one. She hoped Sean noticed, for she was running out of lovely gowns and didn't want to appear in the same one twice. She knew she was bringing so little to him. He would be disappointed when he saw that she only owned ten dresses and seven hats. Her wardrobe would cost him a pretty price. He would have to buy her shoes, gloves, jewelry, undergarments and Lord knew what else. Walking to the carriage, she started to lose her happy feeling.

She would be a burden to him, with her being so poor. She had no land, no title, no nothing. What did he want with someone like her anyway? Maybe this marriage idea wasn't a good thing after all, her eyes filled with tears. She would be doing all the receiving and Sean all the giving. His nobles wouldn't like that, they'd hate her and she wouldn't blame them.

Me'na cried to herself all the way to the palace. She didn't know how she was going to tell the King that she wouldn't be seeing him anymore. It was breaking her heart to even think about not looking into his eyes every night when she went to sleep. He had become such a part of her thoughts and dreams that she didn't know where one began and the other left off. And this was from just several days of knowing him, what would she do without him now? Tears started going down her face again. She was so close to having it all. Within her heart, Sean had already taken a large portion for himself, this he did without her being aware when it happened. Maybe she should just go back to Timbre with the ambassador and find new work. There wasn't much a woman could do in the nineteenth century, especially a woman of noble blood. Things were expected of her that she could no longer do or afford to do.

By the time she reached the palace, Me'na had worked herself into a state. She sadly wiped the tears away from her face and resigned herself to the fact that she wasn't right for him. She absently gave her hand to the driver and walked to the entrance. The attendant there was expecting her and delivered her to the king's own personal sitting room to await him. She wiped her face again and tried to talk herself into feeling cheerful, for Sean's sake. She didn't have long to wait.

Sean walked in and his presence surrounded her. It was as if he was everywhere at the same time. She stood there with her face to the window and her back to him. Sean approached her and placed his arms around her shoulders and under her neck. He bent his head to kiss her ear lobe, Me'na shivered all over. He hugged her tighter in response. *How can I leave this man? He is everything to me*. She leaned her head back on his chest and placed her hand on his arms.

I love you so much already. I am losing myself in you. If I don't break it off now, I'll never be able to leave. Me'na turned in his arms with a smile on her face. "Kiss me, my beloved, and kiss me as if there is no tomorrow."

Her bottom lip trembled so he kissed that first. They wrapped their arms around each other and held on tight, for this was going to be her goodbye kiss if she had the courage to leave. As she kissed him, she started to cry in his arms.

"What's this? Tell me so I can fix it," he begged her. Me'na looked for her courage, but it was slowly going away. She could not leave him, that made her cry all the harder. "No, baby, what is it? Come, sit down. Tell me what is going on. Has the ambassador done anything else to you?"

"How do you know about that?"

"The Duke of Richmore told me everything that happened. You were not to blame for any of it. Come, let me wipe your tears away. Tell me what troubles you."

She blurted out, "If you marry me, I will be a burden to you. I have nothing to offer, you will be forever giving to me. The nobles will hate and resent me." Poor Me'na, her shoulders drooped even more. "I don't even have a lot of clothes. I will need a large wardrobe as your wife, and it will be expensive. You cannot pay for everything. I should come to you with a dowry but I come to you as what you see here; just a woman in love with a man."

Me'na hung her head in despair. Sean couldn't believe what he had just heard her say. Was she thinking about leaving him because she had no clothes? He wanted to laugh at her for being silly, but he knew this was important to her as a woman. He was not going to let her leave if this was her only reason; no way would he allow that. He thought long and hard before he opened his mouth; he did not want to minimize her concerns. She had a point. Some of his nobles were petty enough to hold this against her. He looked grim for a moment, if they did, they would find themselves suddenly landless or worse, exiled. He would tolerate no one trying to make her existence difficult, no one.

"Me'na, look at me, please. I love you, and you love me, right?" She nodded her head yes. "That is all that matters to me, our love. My brother's bride comes to him with not much more than you do. They marry for reasons far different than ours. We are a love match; I will not lose you because you come to me with a few dresses."

She corrected him, "Ten dresses and seven hats."

"OK." He laughed. "Ten dresses and seven hats. I wouldn't mind if you had no dresses at all, including what you have on now."

She turned all shades of pink. "Stop that now," but she had to laugh at him.

"See, you're smiling now. We will be fine, I promise you. If you came to me with a hundred dresses, I would still have to buy you more. What Queen is seen in the same dress within a month, that would be the ruination of us all," he teased. She was feeling better now.

"As your husband, I will want to buy you things, jewelry, clothes, a horse and anything else you want. Sometimes, I will be tied up all day and you would be alone. But I'll give you your own carriage and horses plus escorts to ride around town; then there will be your ladies in waiting for company." Sean took both of her hands in his and kissed them.

"Besides, I plan on keeping you busy having my daughters. They must look just like you."

Me'na added, "And have your green eyes. You know, Sean I have a thing for green eyes." She took her hands out of his and brought his face close to hers; Me'na looked deeply into those eyes she loved so much. "I love you very much. I hope that I don't disappoint you or embarrass you in anyway. After all, I am virtually a stranger."

"But," he answered, "a stranger that has my heart in the palm of her hands." They stood together and Sean kissed her with all the love he had stored inside his heart. He had waited a lifetime for her and they would not be parted.

BOOK THREE
CHAPTER FIVE

The next few days passed in a wonderful bliss for Sean and Me'na. They were so wrapped up in each other the King had to be reminded of his negotiations and treaty talks that were still going on. Thomas filled in for him sometime, but Sean had the final word on everything, he had to come down from his cloud.

The King was in what he called his conference room with his minister of finance Lord Hightower, and his defense minister Lord Hamilton. Their assistants and secretaries accompanied them. The prince, in his official position as Caretaker of the Candean Province, was there to make sure the necessary roads were started. Candea had been annexed into Fastonia a little over two hundred years ago.

After the war was over, the King decided to make the reigning prince its caretaker. Candea was a hotbed for radicals under the last king that ruled, King Sardin. Once improvements were made in that country, the people settled down to get back to the business of living. King Sardin was not a good king. His people were over taxed and under nourished. No one in that country wanted to be known as Candeans, they considered themselves Fastonians. They prospered under Fastonian rule. The common man turned into the authorities all the troublemakers that were in hiding. Duke Richard Bolwin and Earl Martin Beaumont never made it back to Candea after the war. Their land was confiscated by the crown and divided into small farms among their townspeople.

The first King Sean who spelled his last name slightly different than the present King; relieved the people of taxes for two years. They had to show that improvements were being made, or be held accountable. The war was a good thing for the people. It helped to wash away the evil of King Sardin's regime.

Going over all of the different proposals, Sean wanted to be with Me'na. He couldn't keep his mind on his work. Thomas had to nudge him, "Sean, what's wrong with you?"

"Nothing, my mind was elsewhere. Forgive me. Where were we?"

"We were discussing the new road to be built to my Province's main city. I want to get started on it soon; the present road is beyond repair. We lose a lot of time bringing goods to the city because the bogs hamper us. Will I get the materials that you promised?"

Sean looked over to his brother. "Yes, brother, all will be done as promised. When do you think we can get started?"

"Well, I want to start before the rainy season, so I'll say within the month?"

"That will be fine. Let the engineer know your plans so he can hire the men we need." Thomas merely nodded his head.

Lord Hamilton asked the King, "Sire, what about this contract with Timbre? I think what they suggest is fair."

At the mention of Timbre, Sean's whole exterior changed. He tensed up immediately. He remembered what the ambassador had tried with Me'na. Sometimes it was hard being King. He had to remember to place his personal feelings outside his decisions. That was the hardest thing about it that he had to do. Everything else came natural to him. He was a born leader. People followed his lead automatically even when he was a young boy. There was just something about him, he was regal without trying.

The King decided to approve all of the proposals presented to him that day. He was tired and needed some relaxation. "Gentlemen, this will be all for the day." Both ministers rose from their seats, bowed to the King, and left the room. Sean stopped his brother from going.

"Thomas, will you fence with me for a little while. I have a lot of pent up energy that has to be released or I'll go crazy."

"Why is that, brother? What are you not getting?" Thomas asked but he already knew what the answer was.

"Thomas, if you have something to say, just say it."

Thomas knew that Sean didn't want to hear what he had to say. He would say it anyway. "I have stepped back as you asked me to do in regard to Lady Collins. As much as I have wanted to get to know her, I have left her alone. How can you be sure other men have left her alone?"

"What are you insinuating about her? Why must you try to ruin her good name because I fell in love with her? You always do this when you don't get your way. You know what? I'm sick of it." Sean walked up to Thomas and stared at him.

"What, do you want to fight me now because I was merely curious about her? Why are you defensive if there is nothing to what I'm saying?" he asked.

"Spit it out, Thomas, you are just dying to tell me something, go ahead, do it."

"Well, I didn't want to be the one to tell you, but since I'm your brother," at this Sean rolled his eyes upward. "I have heard that Lady Collins is the ambassador's paramour that Connor had to break up a lover's spat."

"Whom did you hear this from?" Sean demanded.

"Why I overheard Martin Bauman tell this to Kristoff. Of course, Kristoff didn't believe him. He actually challenged him to a duel, which Bauman accepted."

"Since you didn't hear this from Connor, it is safe to assume the ambassador is trying to ruin her reputation. I already knew about this. Con told me as soon as it happened. Just to set the gossip straight, Thomas, Boleyn walked into her room uninvited, Con heard her screaming at him to leave all the way downstairs. He ran up the stairs to her aide and threw him out." Sean had started pacing around the room. "Charles Ainns confirmed the ambassador has been harassing her for the entire voyage to Fastonia. She has not and will not give him the time of day. I hope this will satisfy your curiosity about her character."

They both stood looking at each other, waiting to see who would budge. Henry, Duke of Lindsey their cousin, took the decision out of their hands. He hurriedly came into the room to tell Sean that Kristoff was preparing to duel with Martin Bauman in the inner garden.

"What? He knows how I feel about duels. I know why he's doing this. C'mon, let's get out there," Sean told them.

All three men hurried through the palace to the inner garden. The inner garden was hidden away from view of everyone, nobody would see them fight. Sean knew that was why Kristoff chose that location. People started to follow them outside but the Prince stopped them, this was not a public affair.

By the time they reached the garden, rapiers were heard clanking. From the speed of the swords, Sean knew Kristoff was making Bauman work hard.

Kristoff didn't lose his temper often. It took a great deal to make him angry. But once he became angry and if he was fighting, he was deadly. Sean wanted to get to him as quickly as possible to prevent him from killing Bauman. He knew his friend wouldn't want blood on his hands once the rage had passed.

As they arrived, the King's gentlemen had surrounded the fighters. Sean did not want to break Kristoff's concentration and be responsible for him getting injured. The King told Lord Robert and Lord Morley to start walking behind Bauman with their swords drawn but not pointed at anyone. This would prevent Bauman from lunging at Kristoff when he saw his King. Sean then walked behind them to stand where Kristoff could see him and clear his head. The red haze cleared slowly from Kristoff's eyes when he saw Sean, he lowered his rapier. Robert and Morley then pointed their swords at Bauman until he lowered his blade. Sean looked at him and told him to go, Robert and Morley escorted him back into the main body of the palace.

"OK, everyone, go back to whatever you were doing. It is almost the dinner hour and it is a special dinner." Sean wanted to be alone with Kristoff.

Everyone left except Thomas. Kristoff stood there looking at Sean but not really seeing him. Sean walked up to him, put his hand on his shoulder, and led him to a bench to sit. Thomas sat on the other side of him. He waited for Sean to begin. Sean didn't have a chance, for Kristoff started to apologize to him.

"Your Highness, I am sorry for a lack in judgment, I had to do this. Please do not ask why, just know I had to defend someone's honor that could not defend herself."

He squared his shoulders and was prepared to accept whatever the King dealt out to him. Thomas looked over at Sean and smiled, then patted Kristoff on the back for support.

"Kristoff, I will abide by your wishes and not inquire about this episode; but please next time instead of dueling, come to me for I need the practice."

Thomas laughed and Kristoff grinned at him, he was relieved Sean would not question him. He was protecting the honor of the woman that his King and best friend loved. He would do anything for Sean and he knew that.

"Kris, since you have so much pent up energy, would you like to fence? But please put the practice point back on your sword, I don't want to end up with holes in my new jacket."

The three of them left the garden together; Sean and Kristoff were off to the practice room, while Thomas forgot his pettiness and went to find his engineer.

Bauman went back to the Golden Swan to report to Boleyn about what had taken place. He was not supposed to get involved in a duel. His mission was to spread filth about Me'na to the court. The ambassador did not want the King to get involved with her anymore. He figured if Sean thought she was attractive, he'd let her sit in on the sensitive issues and bat her eyes or some other feminine ploy women used. It was obvious he had little regard for Me'na and women in general. They were only good for having babies and advancing a man's place in life. Other than that, they were useless.

"Richard, I didn't get a chance to tell my story but to one man. It was just my luck that he turned out to be the King's best friend."

"You fool, who was this man?" Richard lashed out at him.

"Lord Kristoff, he's the Duke of Traveton. I didn't know who he was until it was too late and he had challenged me to a duel. The King broke it up before any blood was spilled."

Richard thought for a moment. "Kristoff, that name is familiar, I believe he is the holder of the Golden Blade, Fastonia's fencing champion. You were lucky; he should have stuck you in your stupid head for all your bumbling. Now, you cannot accompany me to the banquet and I will be all alone with Charles Ainns, you know how he despises me. Lady Collins," this he said with much distaste, "has already informed me she is the special guest of the King and will not be seated with me."

"Richard, what about One-Eyed Bill? He wanted to see her again before he made his final payment. What are you going to do about that?"

"Shut up. You're asking too many questions. I need time to think." Richard walked to the window and stared out. "She's still in her room right now getting dressed. Bill is in the tavern down stairs waiting to look at her." He walked back and forth figuring out a solution to his dilemma.

"He's going to have to be satisfied with taking a quick look at her. Go down there and have him sit close to the stairs. I'll pretend to stop and look for something and hold her up. I told her I would escort her to the carriage. She can't go down there alone. It's not safe for a woman. Go now, quickly." Bauman left to do his master's bidding.

It was almost time for them to leave. The ambassador finished dressing and primped in the mirror like a peacock.

Me'na was near tears in her room. Her beloved sent her several dresses to choose from along with a maid to do her hair. His aunt Amanda told him she was probably nervous and needed help to dress. She personally picked out some of her own daughter's never before worn gowns for Me'na to choose from. She picked out a lovely lavender dress with a short train of lace and gardenias, her favorite flower. She had just a little bit of her fragrance left to wear, Sean loved it so much. She'd have to ask his wonderful Aunt Amanda where she could get more. Sean promised her she would have pin money to buy whatever she needed and wanted. Me'na didn't want to show her ignorance and ask exactly what was considered pin money for a Queen. She'd ask his aunt, who was a great old lady. She accepted Me'na into the family without question. Thomas on the other hand, begrudgingly accepted her. He still wanted to have her for his own mistress. No one but the immediate family knew about Sean and Me'na. He was going to announce it tonight to his countrymen.

Richard knocked on her door lightly. He was doing his best to appear nice. "Me'na, are you ready, my lady?" That stuck in his throat.

Me'na stopped looking in the mirror and stared at herself. That couldn't be the ambassador. He sounds human.

"Who's there?" she asked.

"Me'na, it's me the ambassador, I've come to escort you to our carriage. Are you ready? Take your time if you're not done."

Me'na came to the door and was absolutely beautiful, the most beautiful woman that he had ever seen. He bowed to her out of respect before he could stop himself. He couldn't help it. She closed the door behind her and accepted his arm. She did look wonderful with her lavender hat perched on her head. The hat had a short lavender veil with small gardenias intertwined with lace trailing on the back of the hat. She looked and felt great. She was in love with the most wonderful and generous man the world had to offer. Nothing could go wrong now, but just in case, she crossed her fingers for good luck.

As they were walking to the stairs, the ambassador moved in front of her to lead her down. When they had descended the stairs, Richard started patting his pants looking for something.

"Me'na, stand right here for a moment. I forgot something upstairs."

He turned around and went back up the stairs; he hid on the side of the wall to listen. Everything went quiet when the men saw her standing there looking like a fairy princess. She was aware that every eye in the place was on her, *Please hurry.*

While she stood there, One-Eyed Bill walked up to her and offered his assistance to her.

"No thank you. I'm waiting on the ambassador, he should be right along."

He kind of walked around her as if appraising her value, which he was. He tipped his hat to her and sat down.

Richard came bounding down the stairs and looked first to Bill who nodded his head, he could see moneybags in his future. "Come, Me'na, I have found my watch. I'm sorry to have kept you waiting."

He spread his arms in a very gallant gesture and followed her out to the carriage. Once seated in the carriage, he asked her if anyone bothered her while he was gone.

"One man came up to me and asked if he could help, but I told him no and he easily went away."

"Good, my dear, I'm glad you are still safe. By the time that we return, the public room will be closed and we can go to our rooms in peace."

The remainder of the ride was silent, each thinking their private thoughts. Richard was thinking about the small fortune he would make. There would still be enough money left over to spend freely. He would pay his creditors off first, and then he would treat his mistress to a trinket or two.

For Me'na it was an entirely different scenario. She was in love for the first time in her life, and he was a king. Every young woman dreamed about marrying a prince, but to get the king instead, Oh, but life was sweet right now. She was smiling to herself it was hard not too. As they arrived at the palace, they had to wait in a long line of carriages. There were so many people there, more than she had seen in one place in her whole life. As her carriage pulled up, a footman opened the door and helped the ambassador out first, and then she tried to make a graceful exist from the carriage. Me'na remembered to gather her train in her hand as she got down. The footman made sure that she didn't fall or trip.

As they walked into the palace, Lord Connor, Duke of Richmore and Lord Kristoff, Duke of Traveton were waiting to escort her to her very special place. With two of the handsomest men of the court as her escort, heads turned as the trio passed them. Me'na was so nervous, she had to keep her mind's eye fixed on Sean, if she didn't she might trip and fall.

Everything was so bright and beautiful in the palace, the Winslos were known for the pageantry in which they did things. Everyone was either standing and talking or finding their place at the table. All eyes were on the beautiful young woman taking a place at the King's table. Kristoff and Connor each sat on one side of her. They talked quietly to her trying to calm her. They were joined by the Earl of Penmark, Lord Patrick; the Earl of Landover, Lord

Morley; the Earl of Dunmore, Lord Colin and the Earl of Dovenmire, Lord Robert. Thomas' best friend, the Duke of Fanshire Lord William was already there. Their wives accompanied those that were married. The King's cousin Lord Henry, Duke of Lindsey was going to be a late arrival; a place was saved for him next to the Prince.

The King and prince were announced, all stood as they made their way to the table. Me'na felt her heart flutter when she looked at Sean. He was so handsome in his black jacket. As the brothers sat down the guest were seated.

Sean spoke, "Good evening to all."

The entire hall replied with one voice, "Good evening, Your Majesty."

That was the cue for the servers to begin bringing in the enormous amount of food that would be consumed that night.

The servers brought in the imported roasted corn that was served in five-inch wedges and a corn pudding was also made from it. Corn was the new favorite among the nobility. They consumed it by the barrels. All sorts of beans were served that the King also imported from the tropical islands. The seafood was brought in on hugh trays that had to be wheeled in by the male servers. There were shrimp cooked just until they turned pink with their tails in the air. Lobsters were the favorite of the King, so there were plenty of them along with the prince's favorite oysters. The different types of fish were abundant, as were the clams, eels and calamari. There were those who did not care for the seafood; for them there was roast duck, venison, beef, pork and roasted swan. The chef was famous for his stuffed squab, which was Henry's favorite.

The baker served many different types and shapes of bread. He even had one made in the shape of a heart. He heard that the King was falling in love with Lady Collins. This special bread was placed directly in front of her. She blushed profusely, for also in the center of the heart, he placed some of the popular strawberries that were one of the newest imports into Fastonia. Sean reached over and squeezed her hand.

Everyone was talking at the same time, mostly they were wondering at the status of Lady Collins. Down toward the end of the table sat a man that neither Sean nor Thomas had seen before. His face was chiseled, no beard or mustache, his cream coloring made his mahogany hair look darker. It lay in curls in the nape of his neck. He stared toward them most of the night, not intimidating, mostly as someone interested in what he was a part of tonight. Sean looked him in the eye once but he merely raised his goblet to him and lowered his head.

"Thomas, do you know that chap at the end of the table with the brown hair, the one that has been looking this way most of the night?"

"What side of the table, Sean?"

"He's sitting next to Sir Adam Hamilton. See him?"

"Yes, I see him now. No, I do not know him. I don't think I've ever seen him before tonight."

"If he keeps staring this way, I will have him brought here." Sean did not want any danger coming to Me'na, he didn't know this man, and therefore he could be a threat.

Lady Mary Beth was trying to find out from her dinner companion who Me'na was. She had been in the country when Me'na arrived. Lady Cassandra, wife of Lord Carrington was more than happy to fill her in.

"Well, she arrived several days ago with the Ambassador of Timbre as his cousin, who knows if that is true. But anyway, the King and the prince have both been vying for her attention. It appears the King is winning that battle. She is seen in his company more and more each day."

Lady Mary Beth's eyes couldn't have been more wide opened. The King chased no one, not even her. "Come on, Cassie, tell me more," she said.

"I heard, mind you, from a reliable source that there is more to this picture than meets the eye."

"What could be more delicious that this?" she wondered.

"The King is fabulous. He is so good looking. I love that blond hair. Every time it falls in his face, I want to reach over and move it," Mary Beth confessed.

"You and every other woman of the court. I don't know, but I think he has fallen in love with her."

Mary Beth's face was crestfallen. She thought she made the perfect wife for Sean. She was not alone in that opinion, most of the women felt that way about him. He's was just so, adorable. He had just enough of a dangerous sparkle in his eye to make him look rakish. Their conversation was overheard by several of the men sitting near them. Sir Timothy and Sir Jonathan started to laugh at the women's conversation. They thought what they over heard was just stupid.

"What's so funny young, Timothy?" Lady Mary Beth asked him.

"Begging your pardon, madam?" he started.

"I am not a madam. Do I look that old to you?" Lady Mary Beth said.

"No, my lady, I am sorry, I meant no disrespect to you. We just thought your conversation was frivolous. We were just having fun. I am deeply sorry," he finished. He and Sir Jonathan turned the other way but their shoulders were shaking still.

Most of the diners had finished all the main dish courses, the servers then brought in the desserts. There was some of the other new-imported fruit, the orange. It was already peeled and placed in small dishes. The strawberries and the native blackberry were also in small bowls with thick cream poured over the top. Me'na enjoyed the apple dumplings. She thought they were cute little packages. Sean's favorite the fig was everywhere on the table. Also, there were cakes and various puddings and pies. Sean and Me'na were served some champagne that had cut strawberries in the glasses. He requested this especially for them. The palace's winery was very extensive, so there was something for everyone.

For the most part Thomas sat and stewed in his seat the entire meal, he was not happy. He was looking at Me'na. In his mind, he saw her leaning against him with her head on his shoulder. She looked up at him with adoring eyes. She should have been his woman, not Sean's. This was not fair and he would do something about it, he just didn't know what at the present time. He was becoming slightly inebriated. Sean looked over at him.

"Thomas, are you alright? Your face is becoming flushed."

"I'm fine, I fear that I've had too much too drink. I'll go and walk out on the balcony, that'll clear my head." He pushed back in his chair and looked over at Me'na. "If you will excuse me, my lady, I need to get a bit of fresh air."

Saying that to her he bowed and left the gathering to go outside, his best friend, Lord William Chaney, went with him. Thomas had so much dignity and class, no one but Sean and William knew his condition.

Lord Henry made it to the dinner soon after it started. He had taken his seat next to Prince Thomas. He sat eating his food and only raised his head to nod at Sean that he had completed his mission.

Once Thomas and William reached the balcony, he finally let go all of the emotion that he'd been holding in all dinner. "Will, what should I do? I want her. I must have her," he implored.

Will leaned against the balcony and looked down for a long time before answering him. "Thomas, she is your brother's lady, and from all the indications, she will be his wife. I think on this one that you should back away. Why don't you and I go on a hunting or fishing trip? Anything to get you away from here. She is becoming an obsession with you." He turned toward Thomas and waited for his reaction.

"I know, I know. He has already asked her to be his wife. He said he fell in love with her the first time he saw her."

"Didn't you tell me your brother has always said he would fall in love at first sight with his bride to be? This appears to be providence, Thomas. You can't fight the fates. This is bigger than the both of you."

"I know what you are saying is true, but I met her first. I am not used to being denied access to a woman I desire. I need to go Candea anyway and make sure the road from here is being done properly, I just can't go. Would you go for me, Will?"

"You could order me to go, and I would go, but I know that the both of us should go before your obsession becomes overwhelming." As William spoke to him, he put his arm on his shoulder to soften what he side to Thomas a bit.

"I don't know. What you say is true, but it will be hard for me to give her up," the prince confessed.

Trying to make Thomas smile Will said to him, "Look at it this way, she is too short, she only comes up to your shoulder. What are you going to do with a short woman anyway?" He smiled.

Thomas smiled in return. "She's short alright, but that little package has a waistline no bigger than a hand span." They laughed together and went inside the ballroom to await the others.

Henry had gotten up and handed Sean a package under the table that he placed in his pocket. The King called an end to the meal and invited everyone into the ballroom for an announcement. He escorted Me'na inside the brightly lit room where the stringed orchestra was playing softly in the background. He looked toward Thomas and beckoned for him to join him. His aunt Amanda stood at his side along with Henry, Thomas stood on the other side next to Me'na. William just shook his head at his friend. He could see that he was headed for trouble. When everyone was in place, the King started speaking to them.

"I want to announce to everyone that I have asked Lady Me'na Collins to be my wife and she has accepted."

The King's men started the applause off loudly as men do. The rest of the court joined them. There was much whispering and many shocked faces in the ballroom. The court formed lines according to rank to wish the couple congratulations and best wishes. Some of these well wishers didn't sound as if they meant it, but Sean didn't seem to mind, he was on top of the world. No one wanted the King to think they disagreed with his decision, he was known for not accepting their disapproval on his personal life well. He would rule and rule fair and wise, but his personal life was his own, they knew and understood that. They acted accordingly. No one wanted the king upset with him or her.

By the time Me'na thought her smile would fall off, Cameron Bishop walked up to her to congratulate them. He kissed her hand very sweetly and shook the king's hand firmly. He made eye contact with Sean; he was trying to say something without saying it. Sean immediately recognized him as the fellow that looked their way most of the night.

"Sir, may I have your name please?" the King asked him.

"Yes, Your Highness. My name is Cameron Bishop. I am a visitor to your country."

"Who brought you to the dinner? A cousin maybe?"

"Yes, sire a cousin." With that he casually walked off to stand alone propped up in a corner with some other men.

Sean watched him and decided that he would keep his eye on him, you never knew about people these days.

After all the hand shaking and well wishing was over, Sean and Me'na led the way onto the floor for a solo dance. He whirled her around the floor in the latest dance craze that actually had men and women dancing close together. Their bodies touched ever so slightly, just enough to tempt the saints. Not many people danced that way at first, but if the king thought it was alright, then who were they to question it.

After their dance, the crowd gave them a roaring applause. Sean soon relinquished Me'na so that she could dance with each of his gentlemen. By the time she got to Lord Patrick, she was so over heated and thirsty, she felt she might faint.

Sean went to reclaim her, he took a close look at her face, "Let's go out to the balcony my love before you faint." She grabbed hold of his arm and let him lead her out. Once out there she took a big breathe of fresh air and smiled at him.

"I didn't realize I needed that until now. Thank you for looking out for me, my love," she said.

Sean had given her a seat to sit upon. He reached into his pocket and kneeled down in front of her. He gave her a small box with a bright red bow. She started smiling like a little girl when he placed it in her hands.

"Oh, Sean, what is it?"

He laughed at her, "You must open it beloved, I'll not spoil the surprise."

She quickly untied the red silk bow that she placed in her pocket. Opening the box, she discovered a golden locket that was heavy in her hand. She opened it and found a picture of her Sean in it with a lock of his hair. She burst into tears immediately.

"What's this, Me'na? Have I not pleased you? If it is not to your liking, I will purchase you a new one. This one belonged to my mother. My father gave it to her the night he asked her father for her hand."

She threw herself at Sean so hard that he almost toppled over. Her arms went around his neck and she was covering his face with kisses and tears. He managed to stand them both up without falling and returned her kisses. They slowed down a little to catch their breath.

"I take it that you like the locket then?" For his answer, she started kissing him and crying again.

Me'na stopped, looked into his eyes and said, "I love you more than I thought possible to love anyone in my life. You have made an empty life full again, I could not live without you now." She was smiling through her tears. Sean reached inside his jacket to get a handkerchief to wipe her face.

"It appears to me that it is going to be a very wet existence being married to you. I guess I can survive, I must accept the good with the bad I suppose," he teased her.

"Oh you, I guess so." They laughed together then became very quiet, which led to a very romantic kiss.

Outside the door stood Cameron Bishop, keeping watch over them. None would get pass him.

BOOK THREE
CHAPTER SIX

Thomas curiously looked toward the balcony double doors that Sean and Me'na passed through some time ago. He wanted to intrude on them but he didn't move. That new fellow Cameron Bishop stood there as if protecting them from something or someone. Thomas thought he looked a lot like one of William Chaney's ancestor's portrait that he seen before. He favored the original Lord Chaney that lived about two hundred years ago. That lord and the earlier Prince Thomas whom he was named for were best friends. *Hm, providence again, or maybe a lovechild's lineage of the former William Chaney*, he thought. He would ask Will to take a look at the chap.

The doors opened and Sean and Me'na stepped back into the room. They made their way to the refreshment table for something cool to drink. This night, Sean didn't sit on his throne and brood as usual. He was the life of the party. His close friends noticed the change in him and thought Me'na brought out the best in him, they told him so. Laughingly he agreed heartily with them to her embarrassment.

Thomas came over to her and asked for a dance. She looked toward Sean who nodded his head but kept watch over them. The dance started out nice but it didn't stay that way for long. He soon was trying to dance her into a corner, where one of the alcoves was. She wouldn't go in with him. Sean watched them from across the room. He wanted to see how far his brother would go before he embarrassed himself. Me'na was pushing him back ever so slightly but strongly; so as not to attract attention to her plight.

She thought her future brother-in-law was drunk and didn't remember who she was. *He would not try to take advantage of his brother's fiancée* she thought. It was obvious she didn't really know Thomas.

Strolling along ever so casually was Cameron Bishop, his left hand in his pocket. Sean watched him as he intentionally bumped into Thomas. This was getting more interesting by the moment. He watched so that maybe he could learn who this man really was. He had asked around, no one knew him.

"Excuse me, Your Highness, my lady. How clumsy of me. Are you two alright? Here Lady Collins, let me help you to steady yourself. Prince, are you well?"

Thomas looked at him with as much venom as he could muster being as drunk as he was. Will was also watching from across the room and made his way to Thomas to help Cameron. He could tell Cameron was really protecting Me'na. He looked really familiar to him. Once he arrived on the scene, he gave Me'na's care over to Cameron and walked Thomas to his suite. Cameron gave her his arm and escorted her back to Sean.

"Thank you, sir, for your gallantry. I appreciate your timely escort back to my beloved."

"Don't mention it, my lady." He bowed at the waist to her. He looked toward the King and bowed to him.

"Thank you, Cameron Bishop, or is it Lord Bishop?"

"Cameron is fine with me," he answered.

"My thanks to you then, sir."

"My pleasure, Your Highness." With that said he bowed again and disappeared in the crowd.

"Sean, is he a friend of yours?"

"I've never seen him before tonight, but it seems like at least this night he was my friend."

Sean grabbed hold of her hand and together they walked through the crowds and mingled with the guest. He wanted her to make friends, so she would not be lonely when he wasn't around. Some of the married women genuinely wanted to be her friend. They were very supportive of her marriage to the king. Even if you didn't want her to marry the King, you'd best get on her good side now. It looked like she might have a lot of influence with him. No one wanted to be on her bad side, if you were on the Queen's bad side, wouldn't your husband soon be on the King's bad side also?

They figured she seemed to be a nice person, really in love with their king. You could tell by looking at the way her eyes followed him around the room when they were apart. They would spot one another and then walk toward each other. Sean left her alone with the wives of some of his gentlemen, these people was as close to him as anyone could be. She brought out the human side of the King, he was thought of as being high over them, which he was, but now he seemed more approachable. Sean didn't want to be more approachable or so he thought before meeting Me'na. She changed everything about him.

The ball was winding down and some of the guests were starting to leave. *At last*, Sean thought, *now I can have Me'na all to myself.*

He took her walking to his rooms before the guests were gone. Upon entering the inner sitting room, Connor, Kristoff and Colin were already on duty.

They stood when he approached with Me'na, "Me'na" he said, "go in, kitten, I will be there in a minute." She nodded her head.

"Your Highness, do you want us to retire for the evening?" Kristoff asked him.

Sean smiled at them. "No, I do not, for after Me'na leaves me I will really need the support that men can give me. Find your pleasure for the next couple of hours then return. I should be tied into many knots by then."

They laughed together then left the King to find their own sport. Sean walked back into the room to find Me'na staring at his gigantic bed with an awed expression on her face.

"Will I sleep in this huge bed with you, or do you visit me? I don't know how this is going to work."

"Come." He led her into an adjoining chamber with a winding passage that led into another sitting room. The sitting room opened into a smaller room that finally led them into the bedroom. It had a huge bed also, but the rest of the furniture was very feminine in appearance.

"This is your suite of rooms, both rooms are interconnecting, but only you or I will use this passage. Everyone else must go through the regular entrance."

"Oh, Sean, this is so beautiful. This was arranged just for me?" she asked.

"Yes, I had the carpenters bring in some of the furniture from storage, and then they will build whatever else you need or replace what you don't like. You may do whatever you like with this room."

She grabbed his hand and went over the entire room with him touching and commenting on every piece. Finally, she let his hand go and whirled herself around the center of the room. She was the happiest that she had ever been. It showed. Sean was seated on the edge of the bed watching her enjoy her room with all the gusto possible. Me'na once again launched her body at him, but this time she did knock him on his back. He fell flat on the bed. She kissed him everywhere possible on his face and neck.

"You are the best husband that a woman could want. I am very lucky and blessed that you love me, aren't I?" she asked him impishly.

"Yes, you are, for I love you more each day if that is possible."

He grabbed her behind the head and lowered her lips for a real kiss. Sean was a strong man and he had a good hold on her. She couldn't move if she wanted to, which she didn't. As the kiss deepened, Me'na was soon out of control again. Sean rolled her over and continued his assault. Time lost all meaning for her. This was new territory that was never ventured into previously. Alarms started going off in Sean's head, they kept ringing until he regained a measure of control. Me'na didn't understand what was happening but he did. He raised his head and looked down at her closed eyes, she started smiling.

"What are you smiling about, imp?" he asked her.

"Had you going there, didn't I? I will make a fine royal wife. You will never have to look for love in another's arms while I still have breath in my body."

He turned serious. "I would not do that to you. My father had mistresses my whole life, everyone knew about them including my mother. She suffered because of it. I will not cause you pain that way. I will honor you as my wife, friend, lover and the mother of my children."

As he spoke, he moved and pulled her up into a sitting position. "I love you too much for that." She kissed his hand and the tears started again. "Here, keep this kerchief, you need it more than me." He kissed her happy tears away.

While Sean was enjoying the privileges of having a fiancée, Thomas was brooding in his room. William had left him long ago to find his own room within the palace. He lay upon his bed envying his brother's luck at finding a true love. Thomas didn't want to find a true love so to speak, he just wanted right now's true love. With him it changed monthly.

He had never been denied his wants before. Usually the women just capitulated to his will because he was the prince. That only made him want Me'na more, he didn't think she would be an easy conquest. Thomas thought she would provide him with a challenge; it just wasn't fun to him any longer. The women gave themselves to him with little pretense as to what the payoff could be. Most saw themselves as future princesses or if Sean had no children, Queens. Thomas had no desire to be King. Candea caused him enough headaches that he didn't want any more responsibilities. Sean could have the kingship he didn't want any part of it. He only wanted a part of Sean's woman.

Thomas sat up in his bed and threw his legs over the side, he was still fully dressed, and it was still early. Lady Constance was to be this night's tryst but he was in such a foul mood that when she knocked on his door he told her to go away.

He put his head in his hands moaning his imagined plight. Thomas didn't know why he just couldn't let Sean and Me'na alone. *I wonder if her skin is as satiny smooth as it looks. I just want to touch her and rub her. Is that too much to ask for? Her waist, so small, ahhh*! He screamed in his room. Immediately the closest sentry ran to his room knocking on the door asking if he was alright.

"I'm fine. I'm fine. Just a little hung over soldier. Go back to your post."

He heard the sentry turn and leave his door; Thomas let his body fall back against the bed. His arms were over his sky blue eyes while his head was near to bursting. Those eyes of his gave him a cold appearance but nothing could be further from the truth. His hair was coal black and hung about his forehead and ears in large uncontrollable curls. He was constantly moving his hair out of his face, or a lady friend would accommodate him. Thomas was shrewd, he knew woman always wanted to feel his curls and straighten his hair; it gave him boyish charm when he wanted to appear that way. They loved him; women young and old flocked to him.

He and Sean had a great sense of humor. The palace was usually a happy place to be unless the brothers were quarreling. They didn't argue much anymore, Sean told him to grow up and stop acting like a little brother, be a man. Women had spoiled Thomas, or maybe Thomas spoiled himself. Whoever did the spoiling; it was now too late to change him.

He and Sean were not usually attracted to the same type of lady. Sean liked his women to be small of stature, little waist, and not with overly large breasts, but ample. He liked his women to be able to think for themselves and not have to pester him about what to do all the time. He wanted a wife that loved making love. He was a demanding man, and some things were not open for compromise. Some of his friends had horror stories to tell about the bedroom that had kept him single until Me'na. Basically, Sean wanted an equal partner in all things.

But, Thomas liked his ladies taller and with long legs. He didn't want them to think for themselves too much. He would tell them what to think and what their opinion should be when asked. He wanted a brood mare and lover all mixed in one. Now that can't be too much to ask for.

His way of thinking about women had started his last argument with Sean. They were discussing what made a woman a good wife. Sean told him that he wanted a partner to share his life and throne with. He wanted a woman's gentle touch on some of the more sensitive matters that he had to deal with. The king was rather brisk at times when he shouldn't be. He wanted a wife who would sit on her throne with him and maybe reach over and squeeze his hand if he was being overly intolerant and smile her special smile at him. That way he would know that maybe he should soften the blow a bit instead of just coming out with a no.

Thomas on the other hand, told Sean that he wanted someone to have his babies, host his parties and run his household. Sean couldn't believe what he heard his brother say and told him so. Thomas then told him that he was weak toward women and should have his nose wiped by their old nursemaid. Sean told him to shut up or he would shut him up. Connor, Kristoff, Colin and Patrick all ran in the room when they heard Sean raise his voice. They knew what the King would and could do to his brother. They must be separated before blood could be drawn.

Colin went in search of William, who then led Thomas out of the room; they went riding in the hills behind the palace. Kristoff and Connor brought the king out into the inner garden to fence. They gave him a good workout with Colin and Patrick trading places with them when someone tired.

After that disagreement, the brothers apologized to each other and promised to never argue like children again and they hadn't, it had been three years since then. Me'na was the type of woman that Sean liked. It was probably why the king didn't believe his brother really wanted her. Thomas got up and walked outside to his balcony to think on this problem and on what he should do about it.

The mysterious Cameron Bishop went back to his room at the Blue Fish Inn. He stared at the Golden Swan that was directly across the road from him. He wasn't sure which room Me'na was in. He searched through his bureau drawers to make sure his pistol was still there. When he placed his hand on it, he took it out to make sure it was loaded. Satisfied it was as it should be, he stuck it under his pillow in case he had need of it. He had traveled very far to be here tonight and was beginning to tire. He took his boots off and stretched his long frame out upon the bed. With his arms behind his head, he closed his eyes and thought about Me'na.

He had made a deathbed promise to protect her and he would with his very life if it came to that. Cameron was not above killing if he had to. He had done it several times before and would gladly do it again to protect her, even if it meant killing a prince. He hoped it wouldn't come to that, but he was very familiar with the type of egotistical man that Thomas was. The Timbren Ambassador was also on his watch list along with One-Eyed Bill and Martin Bauman. He knew Richard Boleyn had a disgusting operation going on with Bill. The ambassador often had women stolen and sold into the slave trade to whore houses around the world. He would make sure Me'na was not their next victim. Cameron allowed himself to fall into a light sleep, he would not be far away should Me'na have need of him.

BOOK THREE
CHAPTER SEVEN

Richard Boleyn sat in his room waiting for Me'na to return to the inn. She informed him that she would no longer need his protection or his help in gaining employment. This change of events would not stop the ambassador from selling her to One-Eyed Bill. All it did was accelerate his plans for her. Tonight he would have her in the biblical sense then he would tie her up until Bill could be found and have her put on his ship. He would have to come up with a good enough story for the king to believe him about her disappearance. It wouldn't be easy but it never was, that was part of the thrill he experienced whenever he changed someone's life. So like the spider, he waited for her to return on this her last night.

Sean and Me'na were still laughing and talking about what they both wanted for the future.

She told him, "Beloved, I want many children fathered by you, at least ten."

"Ten children, Me'na, you would grow fat fast and I would have to put you in the fat queen's castle," he teased her.

"Oh, so there's a fat queen's castle, eh? What about a fat king's castle?" she asked him.

"Fat kings look distinguished, while fat queens look fat." The King was laughing so hard that when Me'na attacked him it was easy for her to push him down on the floor.

"Fat, I can't believe you said fat." She began to tickle him. Sean didn't know just how ticklish he was until her fingers started in on him. He had to raise his hands in surrender before she would stop.

"Oh, Sean, don't make me leave you tonight, I want to stay in the palace with you. Please."

Me'na sat on his stomach as she asked this question of him. He looked at her. She was pleading her case so earnestly he could not refuse her. Sean just didn't trust himself around her. He was afraid that things might get out of hand and she would resent him for it.

"Me'na, I want you to stay. It's just that I love you so much that I do not want to dishonor you. You are very hard for me to resist as you well know."

"You are hard for me to resist also, beloved, but I trust us to wait for the right time. I will not fail you."

She bent down and drew his lips into a kiss. Sean liked it when she took control. He never felt that way before about anyone. He rolled her over onto the plush rug on the floor.

"Baby, we will marry tomorrow if that is agreeable with you, I can wait no longer to make you mine."

He looked down into her eyes and there were tears shining in them. She reached up and pulled his head down, with her lips close to his ear she whispered.

"Yes, it is most agreeable with me, my husband."

She then proceeded to place kisses on his ear lobe, which drove him wild with desire. They were both lost in this newfound eroticism of hers. Me'na didn't realize she could drive him to distraction with simple well placed kisses. For the first time in her life, she felt the full power of what it meant to be a woman.

Finally, the red haze of passion started to fade with the realization that on the morrow she would be his. Sean helped her to get up off the floor; they seated themselves on her chaise.

"Kitten, what time can you be ready to marry me?"

"I can be ready at about eleven in the morning. It will take me some time to find an appropriate dress. I can't just marry the King of Fastonia in any old thing."

Sean had his arms around her as they reclined on the chaise. He could think of what he wanted her to wed him in, nothing; but that might not be looked upon as suitable by her.

"Well, whatever you want to wear will be fine with me. So, if you can't find anything you like, the wedding will be a private affair. Not many people will see us anyway. Only my men and they do not talk about my personal matters. They will witness the marriage so that it is legal and binding. I'll not lose you to anything or anyone." He squeezed her firmly to reassure her of his faithfulness to their love.

"Sean, I must go back to the inn to get my things, I have nothing to sleep in tonight."

"Well, do without. I do." Me'na looked at him with large rounded eyes.

"You mean that you sleep naked."

"Yes, I do, you will have to get used to it, I cannot tolerate clothes when I sleep, I have to be free."

"You're free alright." She started giggling. "Sean, I must go for my things tonight. There are some very special keepsakes that I have there."

"Me'na, must it be tonight? It's getting late," he told her.

"You can send some soldiers with me. They will protect me," she reasoned.

"I can go with you too."

"No, Sean. You're the King. If you come the innkeeper will wake his family and then everyone would be awake. No one will sleep. You just can't walk into a place like that. Baby, be reasonable," she pleaded.

Something inside him was screaming, *No, don't let her go without you. It could be her undoing.* Sean was a logical man and he couldn't find the logic in his sense of foreboding. He would send guards with her she should be fine. Me'na did have a point about his waking up the entire inn. The last time he had gone into a place like that, it was late at night and everyone had to get up. Nobody believed the King was there until they saw him for themselves.

Sean stood and went to the door; he called the nearest sentry to him. The King gave him orders to have a carriage and five members of his honor guard waiting outside for his bride. He then turned around. Me'na was ready to go, the sooner she left, the sooner she could get back. Sean looked at her and his heart told him to keep her with him, no matter how hard she argued. He started to open his mouth to tell her he didn't want her to leave, when she placed her arms around his neck and kissed him again. Her kiss wiped out everything he had been thinking about, the only thing that remained was his passion for her. Once the kiss was over, he walked her outside.

Five soldiers were waiting for Me'na outside the palace with a carriage for her to ride in. Sean walked her down to the buggy and placed her inside. he gave her a kiss and told her to hurry back to him.

"I will, my love, I'll not be away from you longer than I must." She smiled at him.

The King walked over to the captain. "Sir Tristan, guard and protect her at all times. Do not let harm come to her, there will be hell to pay if she's harmed in any way. Am I making myself clear?"

Captain Tristan stood straighter. "I will guard her with my life, Your Highness, if it comes to that."

Sean nodded his head to the captain; he had made his point clear to him. If Me'na didn't come back, then nobody had better come back either. Sir Tristan got on his horse and led them to the inn.

"I'll be right back, Highness," Me'na shouted back to him. She leaned out of the window and threw him a kiss. He stuck his left hand into the air to catch it.

Sean waved his hand to her. As the carriage pulled off, he felt a chill go through his body. He shook his shoulders and the sense of foreboding returned. He stood there watching the carriage until he couldn't see it anymore. Terror started to run through his heart, he almost started running after the buggy to stop them. He'd never had a feeling like this before, he actually felt afraid and helpless for the first time in his life. He stood there for a long time, just looking at nothing in particular. Connor walked to him and placed his hand on the King's shoulder.

"Is anything wrong, sire?" he asked.

"I don't know, Con. I have a terrible feeling that something bad is going to happen. I don't know what it is, I just can't shake it."

"Come. Let's go back into the palace and talk. Kristoff and I were looking for you to gamble a little. But, we can talk until she returns unless you want to follow her."

Sean seriously thought about following her. His head told him he was being foolish, but his heart said go after her. Me'na was protected she was not alone. Sir Tristan was one of the best fighters that he had. He would take care of her no matter what.

As a king, he had to be logical. His heart could not over rule his head, though, there were times that he had let it. He wished this were one of those times now. He turned toward the door and saw Kristoff standing there with a sad look on his face. Sean walked up the steps to reenter the rear of the palace, his feet dragged on the ground. All of a sudden, he felt very ancient, as if he had lived through this before. He shook his head as if to clear the thoughts and went inside the palace.

As Me'na and the soldiers arrived at the Golden Swan, Cameron Bishop was looking out of his window from across the street. He saw her get down to go inside the inn with Sir Tristan following her and banging on the door.

The innkeeper had been asleep and was walking to the door very slowly. He opened the door a crack and Tristan pushed it all the way open. When the innkeeper saw one of the king's men there, he opened the door and was very cordial, more cordial than he would have been otherwise.

"Come in. Come in, my lady, and good sir. Let me get you some candles to light the way." He handed them a couple of candles and sat down until they told him what else they might need.

Me'na turned to Sir Tristan. "Captain, I'll go upstairs and get a few things. It should not take me but several minutes."

"My lady, the King told me to protect you with my life, and I swore that I would. I cannot let you go upstairs alone."

"Nonsense, Captain, I'll be fine. Everyone's asleep. I'll be right back." She turned and ran up the stairs as fast as her dress would allow her.

Unbeknownst to either of them, the ambassador was waiting in her room. One-Eyed Bill was in the ambassador's room waiting to take her away this very night. Bauman would stand in front of her door once she went in.

Me'na turned her key in the lock and stepped inside the room, she placed her candle on the table. As soon as she walked away from the candle, Boleyn jumped her from the back. Across the street, Cameron could see the light from the candle was not moving, he assumed she had put in on a table or mantle, he waited.

Before Me'na could scream out, Boleyn stuffed a rag in her mouth and grabbed her arms. He wrestled her down on the bed and hit her to knock her out. He then tied her legs to the bedpost and was trying to finish tying her arms when she started waking up. She tried to sit up but by that time, he had finished tying one arm and hurriedly seated himself on her to keep her still.

"You awoke too soon, I haven't finished with your arms yet, but it doesn't matter; I WILL have my way now, Your Highness," he drooled.

She shook her head back and forth, she tried to buck her body to unseat him but he was too heavy. Boleyn stretched his body out on top of her as best he could and tried to nuzzle her ear. She almost knocked him over. He could not dirty the place that her beloved Sean had kissed earlier. She was screaming behind the rag that was now tied to her mouth. Boleyn slapped her repeatedly until he could see the imprint of his hand mar her cheek. He didn't want to damage the merchandise that could make his profit decline. He held her free arm and began to rip at the bodice on her dress, tearing it off. She was left with only her shift showing. He then proceeded to try to pry his hand into the remaining pieces of her dress and to rip it away.

Me'na was terrified now, Sir Tristan was down stairs waiting for her and she couldn't scream to call him to her aide. She started to cry. Large teardrops ran down the side of her face. She didn't know what to do. She might try to lull him into thinking she had given up fighting and lay still. On the bedside table there sat the water pitcher within reach of her free arm.

She thought, *Lie still. Let him start to think he had won, and then hit him with the pitcher*. Me'na stilled all movements and just lay there.

He told her, "It's about time that you realize there is nothing you can do to stop me. You might as well enjoy it, I will. As he looked down to raise her shift up, Me'na quickly reached over to grab the pitcher and hit him over the head. He crumpled like a rag doll.

Downstairs Sir Tristan was starting to get worried, she was taking longer than he thought was necessary. She had been up there about fifteen minutes now.

He told the innkeeper, "I'm going upstairs to see if I can hurry her along. May I have a candle?" he asked.

The innkeeper gave him the candle and Tristan started up the stairs. As he entered the stairwell, Me'na had managed to untie her other hand and push the ambassador to the floor. She took the rag out of her mouth and started to scream. She was untying her legs and screaming as loud as she could. Tristan heard her and ran the rest of the way up the stairs. Bauman who was holding a pistol, aimed it at him as soon as he topped the stairs, a shot rang out and hit him in the shoulder. Me'na heard the shot and tried to get out of the room through the window. She was terrified.

Cameron also heard the shot. He pulled on his boots and started running down the stairs. The soldiers outside burst through the door and scared the innkeeper, he pointed at the stairs. Sir Jamie, Sir Howard, Sir Douglas and Sir Benjamin ran the rest of the way. At the top of the stairs Sir Jamie had to jump down immediately as another shot rang out. Sir Benjamin pulled his pistol out and shot Bauman in the chest, he fell forward dead. Howard ran on down the hall looking for Me'na's room, he found it and crashed the door open. He hurriedly looked about the room but Me'na was nowhere to be found. He saw an open window and went to it. Boleyn grabbed him by the leg and tried to stab him when he fell. Luckily, for Howard, Boleyn was as inaccurate with his assassination attempt as he was in trying to rape Me'na. Howard fought him off and proceeded to beat him. Douglass ran in and helped him to subdue Boleyn. Jamie brought Tristan into the room and laid him on the bed. He tried to stop the bleeding.

By this time, Cameron had run into the Golden Swan Inn and found that there was nothing for him to do. He left out with his pistol in his hand searching for Me'na. He'd thought he'd seen a glimpse of something white, like a woman's undergarment outside the window, but whatever it was had disappeared into the darkness. It was not safe for a young woman to be out at this time of the night, and especially one that was not dressed. He searched the alley behind the Swan Inn but she was not there. Cameron stuck his pistol into his pants and proceeded to search each and every open space looking for her. He would not find her.

One-Eyed Bill heard all the commotion and decided that the best thing he could do was not to leave via the door but to try the window. As he was raising the window, he saw Me'na run into the shadows. He tried to hurry and get out of the window before she vanished into the night. He had to find her before Bishop did, he must leave the country as fast as possible. Cameron Bishop would kill him if he could, he was afraid of that man. Bill could say one thing, he wasn't a coward. But when it came to Bishop, if you weren't afraid of him, you were too stupid to live anyway. He was a proficient killer he had never been beaten. He was lethal, a lethal killing machine. Bill did not want to tangle with him again. The last time he was lucky to get away with his life. Bishop must have had a weak moment. He didn't have many of those, of that he was sure. As he crawled down the roof, he jumped down to the ground and scampered into the darkness.

BOOK THREE
CHAPTER EIGHT

Thomas finally stopped feeling sorry for himself and fell into a drunken slumber. He slept for about an hour and awoke with a terrible headache. He rang for his manservant to go down to the kitchen and make his special tea that always managed to help ease the pain. Trevor brought the hot tea to him and inquired if there was anything else that he might need.

"Yes, have my horse saddled. I have some making up to do."

"Right away, Your Highness." He turned to do the prince's bidding.

Trevor was used to the prince leaving at all hours of the night. When one had a lot of women to keep happy, sometimes sleep must be sacrificed. It was a small price to pay in the long run.

Thomas went outside to the stable and waited for Magic his horse to be brought out. As soon as his horse was readied, he galloped away into the night. He rode for about fifteen minutes when he thought that he heard someone softly crying. He slowed the horse and listened very closely. *Yes, there it is again*. He rode between the buildings listening for the sound.

"Hello? Is anyone hurt? This is Prince Thomas. I can help you," he called. "Hello? I won't hurt you. Come out please I want to help."

He was shocked to see Me'na stumble from behind the building looking all tattered and bruised. Thomas jumped down from Magic and ran to her.

"Me'na, what happened to you? How did you come to be here?"

She put her arms around him and started to cry. Thomas picked her up and placed her on his horse; he got on behind her and started back to the palace. He thought why should he bring her back to Sean, if he was so careless with her in the first place. *I'll take her to the cottage, I have plenty of women clothes there*, he reasoned.

Me'na thought she was safe at last. She could not be more wrong. She couldn't tell where he was bringing her. She had gotten lost trying to run away from Boleyn. When he stopped in front of a tall stately townhouse, she started looking around at her surroundings.

"Thomas, this is not the palace. Where have you brought me?"

"This is my private home. I use this house when I want to have small intimate parties. I thought that you might want to rest and clean up a bit before I brought you back to Sean. The way you look now would worry him to death."

"Yes, I do look dreadful. Thank you for your concern," she told him.

The prince rang the gatekeeper's bell. The old man got up to see who was disturbing his sleep this late at night.

"Prince Thomas, how good it is to see you again. Let me open the gate a bit." The gate opened onto a beautifully tree lined drive that went right up to the main house. Me'na could see the detail in the gardening even at night with the light of the full moon.

"This is where I come when your husband-to-be drives me insane. It's small, but it serves its purpose."

He got off the horse and assisted her down. She was still a little shaky on her feet. He led her into the house and lit some candles.

"Me'na, first tell me, what were you doing out at night?" She sat in the offered chair,

"Sean and I decided to get married tomorrow, well it's today now. I needed to get a few things from my room and I had need of them for the morning." When she said they were going to marry today, Thomas thought that he had died, he was so shocked.

"I can see you are surprised by the change in plans. I love your brother too much to be parted from him any longer. I want to be his wife as soon as I can." Her eyes were glowing when she talked about Sean. Thomas was envious of his brother again.

"He wanted to come with me, but I wouldn't let him. So he sent five soldiers with me. The only problem was that the ambassador was waiting in my room for me. He knocked me out and tied me to the bed."

She started shivering from the coolness in the house. Thomas walked over to a closet and picked out a shawl for her shoulders. He was absolutely stunned by her revelation.

"I still had one free hand, so when he was over me I reached for the water pitcher and hit him in the head."

He interrupted her. "Where were the soldiers?"

"Four of them were outside and Sir Tristan was waiting for me downstairs. Well, as I was untying myself I started screaming for help, and then I heard a shot rang out and someone fall. I was afraid, so I climbed out of the window and thought I would find the soldiers there, but they had run into the inn."

"My God, what did you do next?" a captivated prince asked.

"I tried to stay in the shadows but someone was following me, I didn't know who it was so I hid. Then you found me." He reached over and grabbed her hands in his they were ice cold.

"Come upstairs with me and I'll get you something to put on. You can't go to my brother with only your shift on."

Thomas brought her to a bedroom that had belonged to the former lady of the house. It was fabulous. He started looking through all the dresses that were hanging up in the wardrobe and came across a robe. He gave her the robe to cover herself. Her body was even more curvaceous than he first believed. Most women just tried to look thin which was unappealing to him, but this was the jackpot of jackpots. No way was he going to let Sean have her first. At this point it didn't matter what he had to do to get her. He was not above imprisoning her within this room. The worse Sean would do to him might be to make him stay in Candea. He could handle that for a while. She was worth it.

"Me'na, I'm going to go downstairs and get some water for you to wash your face and hands. I'll be right back."

"Thank you, Thomas."

While Thomas fine-tuned his plan, Sean was pacing back and forth waiting for Me'na. All of his gentlemen were up now. It must have been about midnight when Sir Benjamin arrived back with a wounded Tristan. As soon as the King saw them, he ran over to find out what disaster had occurred. Tristan was bloody and unsteady on his feet; he refused to lie down until he had given his report to the King.

"Your Highness," he started. Sean's heart was beating very fast and he knew that something very bad happened to Me'na. "Your Highness, I waited downstairs for Lady Collins, she had been in her room for about fifteen minutes when I decided to go and try to hurry her along." He swayed a little bit on his feet.

"Midway up the stairs I heard her screaming, I started running the remainder of the way then I was shot. I don't remember much after that. Benjamin will have to finish for me."

"Sit him down first," the King ordered Sir Benjamin. He sat Tristan down in the nearest chair and finished the story.

"Sire, by the time we heard the shot outside, we ran in the inn and up the stairs. I shot and killed Martin Bauman."

Sean turned around and violently knocked over the nearest table and chair. He never showed his rage; he was always slow to anger. Thomas was the hothead. Everyone was still and hardly breathing. Sean walked with his fists balled up behind his head. Kristoff looked at Connor who hunched his shoulders. They were the King's closest friends, and they hadn't seen him angry like this in a long time. Not since his last argument with his brother.

"Finish, Benjamin."

"We went into Lady Collins room and she wasn't there. Her window was open and we thought that she had gone through it when the shooting started. Howard was the first in the room and he found Ambassador Boleyn on the floor. He fought the ambassador and was nearly stabbed. Douglas helped subdue Boleyn. I left Jamie, Douglas and Howard to look for Lady Collins, Your Highness. We have Boleyn tied up in Lady Collins' room with the innkeeper watching him."

Sean turned around and said to no one in particular. "Saddle my horse, we are all riding to the Golden Swan right now!" The King went to his suite and changed into his riding garb.

He had his ceremonial sword on his left side and his pistol in the middle of his back. He pulled on his riding boots and quickly walked to the stables. His horse, Sultan was almost saddled when he arrived. His men were mounted and waiting for orders.

"Sire," Kristoff called to him, "I hope that I have not overstepped, but I have called for a squad of one hundred men to meet us at the inn."

Sean turned in his saddle, looked at Kristoff and nodded his head. Kristoff had overstepped, but it was allowed. He and Connor could do things the others would have first asked permission for. They knew what Sean needed and when he needed it. He trusted them implicitly with his very life.

They were off into the night with only the full moon to give them light. They rode hard, it was not far away but they were in a hurry. The soldiers caught up with them and all arrived at the same time. By now the entire street was awake and wondering what was going on? People were looking out of their windows when the soldiers appeared. The King got off his horse and looked around, he was the tallest there; it was easy to spot the blond hair shining in the moonlight. People started pointing him out to each other.

He called Captain Downing over to him, "Captain, have your men start looking for my wife, have them ask questions of everyone. If someone acts as if they don't want to cooperate, make them."

Sean briskly walked into the inn. He went up the stairs looking for the ambassador. When he found the busted door, he turned into the room. The innkeeper sat in a chair with the pistol provided him pointed at Boleyn.

Sean looked toward him and said, "You may leave now, good man."

The innkeeper bowed and backed out the room. He ran downstairs to tell his wife that the King was upstairs. She must make some tea if he asks for anything. Sean walked close to Boleyn and slapped him twice across the mouth. In the room with him were his two friends who would guard his rear.

"Well, ambassador, what have you done with my lady?" Sean waited impatiently for an answer.

Boleyn looked up at him and the King appeared even larger to him. He was very afraid. He had no courage when it came to confrontations with other men that he didn't start. He didn't answer Sean fast enough. The King reached down, pulled him off the bed, and slung him against the wall. He went to pick him up again and threw him against the wall one more time.

"Please, Your Highness, give me a chance to speak."

"Speak." Sean stood over him like an avenging angel ready to strike fear into him.

"Your Lady attacked me and I was just protecting myself. That's all, I swear to you."

"You liar! You tried to attack her. My men heard her screaming for help. Where is she? Tell me or so help me I will kill you with my bare hands."

He started pleading for his life. "I don't know where she is. There is this man who wanted me to kidnap her so that he could sell her as a slave in the east. He was threatening my life; I did not have a choice."

Sean walked over to him and put his foot on his throat, "Where is this man that you speak of?" He removed the foot so Boleyn could talk.

"I don't know right this minute. He was in my room. He goes by the name of One-Eyed Bill. He has a patch over his right eye. His ship is in the harbor waiting for him."

"What is the name of this ship liar?" the king demanded.

"It's the, let me see; I remember now. It's the *Blue Gin*."

Kristoff said, “Sire, I’m on it.”

He turned and went downstairs to get some of the soldiers to follow him to the port. Sean picked him up off the floor and collared him against the wall. The King looked into his beady black eyes without flinching.

“You will be imprisoned and executed if anything befalls her. This is a promise I make to you with Connor as my witness.”

Boleyn looked to where Connor stood with his arms folded across his chest. He had a smirk on his face. Sean carried him by his collar out of the room, when he reached the end of the hall. He threw Boleyn down the stairs. He went screaming all the way down. The King and Connor stepped over him; Connor called one of the soldiers who was in the inn.

“Soldier, pick up this piece of filth and deliver him to the prison. Keep him there. Tell the prison master to keep him in irons until further notice from the King. Take a couple of men with you then report back to your commander.”

“Yes, your lordship, right away, sir.” James proceeded to pick Boleyn up and deliver him to the prison.

Sean sat down in the chair offered to him by the innkeeper. The innkeeper’s wife brought over hot tea for him to drink. She almost burned herself trying to curtsy and set the cup down.

“Thank you, my good lady. I appreciate the tea. Innkeeper, do you have something a little stronger to lace this with.”

“Yes, Your Majesty, I have just the thing. It’s a new import called vodka.” He hurried to the table to pour some in the tea, but Connor told him to leave the bottle.

“Yes, your lordship.”

Sean looked at Connor. “Con, would you be so good as to see if Captain Downing is out there? Ask him to come in if he is.

“Yes, sire.”

Connor went to the street and spotted Captain Adam Downing coming back to the inn. “Captain, come inside. The King wants you.”

Sean addressed his men. “Take a seat gentlemen. Try this vodka. It’s good and it doesn’t have a smell.” His men sat down and pulled the tables together. The innkeeper brought glasses for everyone.

“What is your name, sir?” Sean asked the innkeeper.

“It’s Edward, Your Highness,” he replied.

“Do you have writing tools here?”

“Yes, sire, I’ll go get them.” He brought Sean paper and ink. He then proceeded to write instructions on the paper for his secretary.

"Edward, send your bill to me at the palace for the damage done to your door upstairs and for this bottle of alcohol. Send it to my attention and I will send someone over to pay you on the morrow."

"Thank you, Your Highness. May I ask a question, sire?" The King nodded his head.

"Sire, who is this young lady who has disappeared?"

"She is to be my wife. We will marry tomorrow morning at eleven," he stated.

"I will pray that nothing befalls her, sire." Edward backed away, he had a sad expression on his face.

"Thank you, Edward." Adam stood before the King to make his report.

"Your Highness, we have searched the entire neighborhood, she is nowhere to be found. We did a house-by-house search. No one has seen anything."

"Keep looking, Adam. She has to be here somewhere."

"Yes, Highness."

Cameron Bishop tried to come inside but the King's men were denying him entrance. "What's going on there?" Connor asked.

"There is a man here who wants to help, your lordship." Sean told Connor to see who it was.

"Your Highness, it's the man from the dinner, a Mr. Bishop."

"Let him in, Con."

Cameron walked to the King's table.

"Sit down, Mr. Bishop. Tell me what you have seen."

Cameron was about the same height as Sean, they were equal in size.

"Thank you, Your Highness. My room is across the street from here. When I heard the shot, I looked through my window and thought I saw someone climbing out of her window at least it appeared to be her. I only caught a glimpse of something white trailing in the air like a shift. If it was her, she jumped safely to the ground."

Sean's face tightened considerably, his hands were clasped together. While Cameron was telling his story, he balled his left hand into a fist and rubbed it with the other hand.

"Right after she went out of the window, I saw a man go around the corner of the building. He had a patch over his right eye and looked like a pirate to me. Since I had not gone to sleep and was still dressed, I put my boots back on, grabbed my pistol and ran out the door to try and catch him. By the time I made it to the alley, he was gone and so was your lady."

Sean stared into his eyes with much intent, a lesser man would have tried to hurry and finish his story to get out of the king's view. But Cameron was not a timid man. He had the heart of a warrior. He was an ancient soul.

"I further searched everywhere for them but couldn't find her." Sean was leaning forward and was hopeful that maybe Me'na had found a place to hide. "I found one man who said he had seen a woman matching her description being picked up by a man on a black horse. He said that the horse had white stockings and a curly tail." Cameron finished his story, Sean sat back in his chair to let this new information sink in.

"Edward, if it is agreeable, my men and I will wait here for word from the Duke of Traveton. It should not be much longer."

Sean looked toward the innkeeper waiting on his assent, it didn't matter if he agreed or not. He couldn't make them leave even if he wanted to.

"Please, Your Highness, my family and I will do whatever it takes to help you in this matter. Stay as long as you need to." Edward was actually happy that they would remain here a while longer. It would be good for business the next day.

Sean looked over at Cameron and asked him where was he from. "Your Highness, I'm from northern Timbre; the same area your future wife is originally from."

Cameron watched the King closely. This was a man whom he could like and trust. The King looked you straight in the eye without flinching or turning his head. He would make a fine husband for Me'na he thought.

"Did you know my lady when she lived there, sir?" Sean asked him.

"I knew her family quite well. Her father was an honorable man who died before his time. Your betrothed is younger than I, she would not remember me."

The entire time Cameron spoke, Sean wondered what his part in this whole affair was. He seemed to be an honorable man who had seen the ugly side of life and was jaded. Sean had a gut feeling he could trust this man. If he really was someone from Me'na's former life, mayhap, he could be talked into staying in Fastonia. Sean wanted her to have someone that she could feel a connection with. He didn't want her to feel foreign and out of place. While they were sizing each other up, Kristoff returned to the inn. He walked directly to the king's table and waited for Sean to tell him to be seated. They were always formal when in public, no matter how good a friend he was to the King. There were just some things that could not be forgotten.

"Sit, Kristoff. Tell me what you found." The King noticed the grim set of

Kristoff's mouth.

Kristoff took a deep breath then began. "Well, sire, we found the ship in the harbor. It was anchored in slip seven. Once we boarded, the first officer led us on a search of the ship. The captain was not aboard her. The officer, a Mr. Hale, was not aware that he had left. He did confirm that sometimes they indulged in the slave trade for the houses of pleasure in several ports of call."

Sean sat back in his chair and leaned his head on the rear of the seat. He closed his eyes and exhaled a tortured breath. Kristoff stopped momentarily to give his friend time to adjust to this information.

"He told me when I convinced him he had no other choice. They were waiting to pick up a special woman of color that the caliph of Berman had ordered. It seems this One-Eyed Bill has several operatives in all the ports he drops anchor in. He spied Lady Collins on a visit to Saint John about six months ago. He then described her to the caliph." Kristoff did not want to go on; he knew how he'd take news like this.

"He wanted to wet his appetite for her. He accomplished this then received his order to acquire her. The ambassador has worked for him for years, so when Bill told him about her; Boleyn went about trying to find her."

Sean balled up his left fist again and used his right hand to rub it. Cameron watched Sean as Kristoff unraveled some of this puzzle. He looked like a man about to explode.

"It was pure chance that Lady Collins was looking for work when the ambassador happened to cross her path or so Lady Collins thought. Her brother Micah had ruined the family's good name and lost all respect and money he inherited. It was also rumored that their father Lord James had been poisoned, they do not know by whom though. Lady Collins and her brother have different mothers; the ambassador had investigated the Collins family and found that there was a third child."

Sean sat up. He had removed all emotions from his face.

"This lovechild, who was a son, was claimed by Lord James. He is the same age as her brother Micah. The elder Lord Collins made public that he was going to change his will and make this illegitimate son his heir." The King took a drink of only the vodka this time. He didn't need anything to cut it with.

Kristoff continued with his tale. "He died before he could do so. The ambassador investigated all the women he sold to Bill. He wanted to make sure there was no family who would make a big fuss when they disappeared. This, Your Highness, is recorded in a book that I took from the ship."

Kristoff produced the book and handed it over to Sean. Cameron didn't know what was in that book, but he hoped his name was not there. He didn't want anyone to know too much about him until he was ready. He sat back and remained unruffled. He was a man used to playing with a loaded hand. Kristoff got up, bent low to Sean's ear, and whispered.

"Sean, I talked to several men who say she was picked up by a man on an expensive black horse with white stockings and a long curly tail."

He sat back down, he knew of one man that rode a horse like that: Prince Thomas. Since Cameron was sitting at the table, he overheard what Kristoff said. From the look on the King's face, he surmised that the owner of that horse must be someone close to the King, like his brother perhaps.

BOOK THREE
CHAPTER NINE

Thomas had food prepared for Me'na to eat. The entire time she was eating, she kept asking Thomas to send for Sean. He finally left the room pretending to send word to the palace. Instead, he went into his study and removed several books until he located the small bottle of sleeping medication he had gotten from the palace physician. He told him he had trouble sleeping most nights and just needed something temporarily to help him rest. Thomas actually wanted the medicine so that after he had been married at least a year, he would rid himself of an unwanted spouse. He could give Me'na just enough in her tea to knock her out so that he could have his way with her.

If necessary, he would imprison her in her room until she came to him willingly, then he would tell Sean she had chosen him. He went to the tray that held both teacups; into hers, he poured a small enough amount that he hoped would not kill her. Thomas walked up the stairs to the bedroom that was going to become their love haven. He would convince her that she wanted to sleep with him but was embarrassed about not waiting until they were married.

It was all worked out in his mind. After she drank the tea, he would tell her Sean was on the way to get her. Set her mind at ease about the wait, and then he would sit and watch her pass out. Just in case anyone saw them come here, he could always lock her in the secret room behind the wall. Sean knew about this house but not the secret room. It would work out just fine there was nothing to worry about; he could win over any woman with his charming smile. Thomas knew he was very handsome, his light blue eyes against his midnight black hair was devastating. He could talk the pants off of anything alive; Me'na should prove to be no different. She was only a woman. He walked up the remaining stairs and knocked on the door. This would be the last time he knocked on the door of his woman's room he thought.

"Come in, Prince Thomas," she called out. Thomas opened the door and smiled at her with all the charm he had.

"Well, I brought us some tea to drink while we wait for my brother." He placed the tray on the bureau and brought her the tainted cup of brew.

"Thank you, I really appreciate your being so nice to me and not fussing at me."

"What do you mean, my dear, about not fussing at you?" he inquired.

"Well, the King wanted to go with me but I talked him out of it. I told him if he went to a small inn, it would cause a stir. A king just can't go walking down the road, as if he were an ordinary citizen. Everyone would come outside and you never know there could be a person that wished him ill. If he was hurt because of me, I would just die." She lowered her head a moment then raised it, Thomas could see the tears in her eyes, she couldn't bear it if something happened to her Sean.

"Do you have any idea how much I love your brother?" she asked Thomas.

He merely shook his head and took a sip of his tea. "Please drink your tea, my dear, before it grows cold." He sounded so concerned, but he figured if it became cold, she might not drink it.

Me'na picked up her cup and drank it straight down. "My, I didn't realize how thirsty I was until now. Is there more, prince?"

"Please call me Thomas, after all we are almost family; and yes, there is more if you want it."

Me'na got up and went to the tray that held the teapot and poured more for her. After she sat down again she started talking about her love for Sean.

"I love your brother so much I have forgotten where I end and he begins. It's like he is the missing piece to my existence. I was not complete until I laid my eyes on him at dinner. I felt someone was watching me eat." As she remembered, she began to smile and her eyes misted again. It was such a loved induced smile that Thomas felt like he was intruding on her memory. She went on. "I looked around the room to see who was looking at me and when I saw Sean looking, I smiled at him. He smiled back and raised his goblet in a salute; I thought I would faint because he smiled back."

Thomas thought, *How quaint.*

"Well, anyway, I fell in love with him when he smiled at me. That's all it took and he has had my heart ever since."

She sat there with a silly grin on her face; Thomas resisted the urge to wipe the smile off with one of his kisses. He wanted to see her face contorted with passion; he knew she had to be a sensual woman by the way she was shaped. He could bide his time, she was the meal and he the spider spinning a web. Me'na started to feel tired and sleepy. She yawned.

"Ohh, I'm so sleepy. Do you mind if I take a little nap until my beloved gets here?" she asked him.

"Go ahead and rest. When he arrives I'll send him up to your room."

Thomas stood up and straightened his jacket. Me'na stood and walked him to the door. As she closed the door, she leaned against it and hugged herself with the memory of Sean still fresh in her mind.

Thomas went to his bedroom and decided to take a bath. He wanted to be fresh when he claimed his prize.

Me'na took off the borrowed robe and climbed beneath the covers for a quick nap. Before she could go to sleep, she had to get up and write something. Images of her beloved were filling her heart so that she had to write him a love letter before she could seek her rest. She found what she was looking for in the bureau drawer. With paper and pen in hand, she sat down at the writing desk to write a love letter.

My dearest Sean,

There aren't enough words in the world for me to express the love that I feel for you. It is so much that I am near bursting. I had to write how I feel about you before this passage of time elapsed. Each day my love for you grows larger, sweeter and consuming. I cannot wait until I am your wife and waking up to your face each morning. I love the way your hair falls in your eyes and you impatiently brush it aside. I could not live without you; if I tried to, it would be like living without a heart and soul. You are so precious to me; every move you make is remembered. I was asleep until you awoke me. This is the way you make me feel all the time. So, the times when we are apart, I have so much love to carry with me that I am never alone anymore. You have secured your place in my heart and soul for eternity.

All my love,

Me'na.

Me'na finished her letter, folded it and sealed it with a kiss. She sat there for a minute or two thinking about how blessed she was to find her soul mate when all she had been looking for was a job. Well, she did find one sort of. Being a wife, mother and Queen were going to keep her busy from now on. She didn't mind, actually she couldn't wait for it to begin. She placed her letter on the bureau next to the mirror and went to get in the bed. Her eyes closed almost immediately and she was sound asleep.

The King knew of one person who owed an expensive black horse with white stockings and curly tail, his brother. He sat and hoped Thomas had found her and brought her back to the palace.

"Connor, Kristoff and Patrick, get the men ready to go back to the palace. Thomas rides a horse like that, as we all know; maybe he found her and brought her back. She could be waiting for me now."

In Sean's heart of hearts, he didn't believe what he said. He had a terrible feeling he would never see her alive again. Yet, he had to hold out for some type of hope, no matter how small it was, he needed something to hold onto.

Cameron looked at him and saw a man who didn't believe what he said. His eyes were vacant and sad."Your Highness, may I help you find Lady Collins tonight? I am very resourceful and I have my ways of getting to the heart of the matter."

Sean knew Cameron was on his side. He didn't know how he knew, he just did. "You may come with us. May I call you by your first name?" Sean asked him.

"Of course you can, Your Highness. Please call me Cameron."

"Well, Cameron, come with me."

Everyone stood and followed the King out the door. Outside the soldiers were mounted and waiting on further orders. With the King leading them, they set a quick pace back to the palace. All the way back Sean kept remembering how he felt before she left. He had had such a feeling of dread, if anything happened to her, it was his fault. He should not have let her go alone.

By the time, they reached the palace it was almost dawn. They rode into the stable area and the stable boy ran out to get his horse. Sean dismounted.

He turned to his men and the soldiers.

"Captain Downing, you may relieve your men and let them seek their rest. If I have need of further soldiers, we will require some fresh men."

"Thank you, sire. I will await your command." Captain Downing turned to his soldiers and dismissed them from duty for now.

Sean spoke to his gentlemen. "Please remain here. I may need to ride out again."

He turned away and walked toward the open door of the palace. Kristoff leaned toward Connor. "I sure hope she's here and the prince does not have her. I'm going in the stable and check for his horse." He rode into the stable and dismounted, he looked in the stall that housed the prince's horse and found it to be empty. "Damn! What is he up to?"

Connor and Cameron followed him in when he didn't return. "Kristoff, is the horse here?" Connor called out.

Kristoff walked toward them holding his horse's reins in his hands. He shook his head no. Cameron closed his eyes and swore to his self. He knew that Thomas was not trustworthy. The prince always looked at Me'na lustfully every chance he got.

Cameron looked toward Connor. "Your lordship, does the prince have another residence in town?"

"Yes, he does. He has a private home that he uses to entertain his friends in. His closest friend is the Duke of Fanshire, Lord William, who is sitting on his horse outside the stable with the rest of the king's men." He turned and left the stable and went back to wait for the King with the others.

Sean walked quickly toward Me'na's room, hoping and praying she was there asleep. As he arrived at her door he stopped and gathered his failing courage and went inside. The candles had gone out but there were still embers in the fireplace.

"Me'na, are you here? Please, kitten, where are you?"

Sean lit a candle and went to check out all of the rooms that made up her suite. Nothing, and no one had been in here for hours. He walked toward her bed and saw that it had not been slept in all night. Where was she? He didn't want to face the truth that Thomas must have her. Sean turned around and left Me'na's rooms.

He rejoined his men out in the courtyard. The King jumped on his horse and just rode off without a word to anyone. They scrambled to catch up to him; all feared the worse.

William knew in his heart that Thomas had her. He just couldn't resist what he was told he couldn't have. His friend was spoiled and wanted what he wanted now. He didn't believe he couldn't have everything he wanted; he used his royalty to the utmost, Thomas was selfish. William rode out with a heavy heart; he feared the king would kill his brother this day.

As Cameron rode, he knew if Sean didn't kill Thomas he would. If Thomas was guilty, which he believed him to be, he would pay for hurting Me'na. His face was grim and his eyes were dead. He had no compunction whatsoever about killing the prince. He knew Sean might not be able to kill his brother, but he could without batting an eye twice.

The prince's townhouse was on the other side of town, so it would take about forty-five minutes to get there. Sean rode hard as the sun was trying to come up in the eastern sky. It was so beautiful as it started its rise that morning. Such beauty was wasted on the men who rode with the King. All looked tired and broken hearted.

Connor remembered how the prince was trying to get next to Me'na every time he saw her. *Please, God, don't let him have her hidden in his house. It will destroy the King*, he thought.

Henry knew Thomas had to have her. They all grew up together; Thomas wanted what everyone else had. What he had was never enough he always wanted more.

Robert, Colin, and Morley didn't know the prince as well as the others so they were not having the same black thoughts that everyone else had. They actually hoped the prince had her and was waiting until morning to bring her to the palace. The only thing they couldn't figure out was why he didn't send word.

Patrick had been to the gentlemen clubs with the prince many times in the past. He knew if Thomas had her she was not safe and was probably no longer a virgin by now. He prayed the prince would not betray his brother this way.

Kristoff and Connor rode a few paces behind Sean; they looked at each other with renewed determination. They were going to do whatever it took to keep the king from murdering his brother. He would not be able to live with himself if he had to kill him, it would forever change him. No one wanted Sean to change; he was a good and strong king. Very fair and wise, much wiser than someone thirty-four would normally be. He was born with an old soul.

Sean didn't do much thinking as he rode toward his brother's house. He knew what he would do if Thomas betrayed him, he would skin him alive. Me'na was such an innocent lady; she did not know the power she possessed over men. She didn't know her slightest smile was intoxicating to them. She was a natural seductress without trying, which was the best kind. She lit up a room when she entered it, if anything happened to her, the light in Sean's life would be snuffed out forever. On they rode.

Thomas crept back into Me'na's room. He quietly closed the door and stood watching her sleep. She was so beautiful, so tempting. This was all her fault, he couldn't help himself. She had no right to look the way she did. It was sinful and he wasn't responsible, that made him feel better about what he was preparing to do. He raised the covers off of her body and salivated.

My God, why should Sean have her all to himself, it was not fair. He was the king and now he had the best looking woman in the kingdom.

As he climbed onto the bed, he moved her over a bit. She just moaned and called out to Sean. That just made him mad, didn't she know who she was about to service. He was much better than his brother she should be honored. Thomas lay on the side of her and started to touch her. She started to moan a little bit and move some. He bent his head to kiss her cherry red lips. In her sleep, she thought he was Sean.

"Mmm, Sean," she mumbled. Me'na opened her eyes and stared into the face of Thomas.

She started pushing him back, but he was much stronger than she was. He kept trying to kiss her and she sealed her lips closed. Me'na started to buck him away from her. He grabbed both her hands and held them over her head.

"No, baby, you are now mine. Sean is not coming for you. I told him that you wanted to be with me instead."

"Let me go, Thomas! Get off of me! Sean would not believe that. He knows I love him."

She kept moving her head from side to side trying to avoid his kisses. Thomas had jammed his knee between her legs to part them. With his free hand, he tried to raise her shift up. As he got a tiny peek at her curvaceous body, he momentarily paused in his assault to admire his prize. It gave her the chance she was looking for.

Suddenly, Me'na had the strength of a man. She threw Thomas to the floor and tried to escape him. She jumped over his body on the floor and ran for the door, it was locked and the key was in Thomas' possession. He rose up and caught her by the ankle. She fell flat on the rug. Thomas dragged her to him and sat on her stomach. She was kicking her legs at him and twisting her body. He hit her on the chin to silence her. She passed out. He stood up and deposited her on the bed. Thomas was out of control now. He suffered from uncontrollable lust. It was akin to blood lust on the battlefield. He was all over her at once.

Suddenly, he heard shouting. Someone was in the house calling his name.

Oh my God, he thought..*That's Sean!*

He got off of her and put his robe back on. He walked out of the room with all the dignity he could muster. Thomas locked her in. He looked like a wild man. He tried to run his fingers through his hair to bring his curls under some semblance of order.

He leaned over the banister and called out, "Sean, is that you screaming in my house?"

"Where is she, Thomas? I know she is here. If you have harmed her, I will kill you."

"Harmed who? What are you talking about? I am here alone," he lied.

Sean ran up the stairs and came toward him fast. "You are a liar. Your gatekeeper's wife said you had a young woman on your horse that looked like she needed aid. She said Me'na looked as if she had been in a fight, which she had been. Now where is she? For the last time you had better tell me."

"Alright, Sean, here it is. Me'na left you for me. She wanted to tell you herself but I told her I would do it."

Me'na regained consciousness and ran to the door when she heard Sean's voice. She tried to open it but found it locked. She started calling out to Sean. He went to the door of the room she was locked in and called her name.

"Me'na, are you in there?"

"Yes, beloved, get me out! The door is locked from the outside," she called to him.

Thomas came upon Sean's back and tried to hit him over the head with a candlestick holder. Sean heard him coming so he was able to move a little out of the way. Thomas managed to hit him on the shoulder; both brothers were of equal size so the hit from Thomas was powerful. Sean went down and landed on one knee. He quickly turned and rose up swinging at Thomas. He caught him under the chin and sent him flying down the hall.

While the Winslos were fighting each other, the King's men had surrounded the house. Kristoff and Connor were trying to catch up to Sean to stop them from killing each other. Sean jumped on top of Thomas while he was down and started beating him all about the face and head. Connor reached them first and tried to pull Sean off of Thomas. The King pushed Connor away so hard he fell against the hall table and hit his head. He was all right, but his head hurt something terrible. Kristoff seeing how Connor had faired decided to try another method.

He wanted to make this a personal plea. "Sean, Sean, stop what you're doing before you kill him! He is still your brother." Kristoff's words slowly began to sink in. Thomas had passed out long ago from the punches.

Me'na was trying to find a way out of the room she didn't want the brothers to fight because of her. She couldn't break the door down, so she went to the window and raised it. She saw Sean's faithful retinue outside. She gathered her shift between her legs and prepared to climb down. Me'na looked to see if she could make it, she thought she could. All she knew was that she had to get to her beloved as quickly as possible.

As she was climbing from the third floor, Henry spied her on the second floor roof. "Look, there's Lady Collins trying to climb down!"

They rode to her window, Henry jumped off his horse to go and get her. The rest of the men jumped down, ready to assist.

Out in the hall, Sean had regained his senses. He got up off of his brother and kicked him in the ribs. Thomas merely moaned.

"Kristoff, check to make sure Connor is all right."

Kristoff helped Connor to get up, he was fine. Sean then proceeded to kick the door down and ran into the room.

"Me'na, Me'na, where are you!" she heard him and tried to go back up the roof.

"Sean, I'm out here. Come get me!" she shouted.

He ran to the window and saw how precarious her perch was. His heart was in his hands. The roof tile she was trying to hold onto was loosening. He didn't think she could make it back up. He saw Henry trying to get to her before she fell. Sean stepped out onto the roof to help her up. He leaned down and reached his hand out to her. She touched his fingers and tried to give him her hand. She was scared she would bring him down with her. Cameron was standing directly below them, waiting. Sean grabbed her hand and was trying to pull her up but she lost her footing on the tiles. Henry was almost there, but the tiles were giving him a difficult time also. He completely lost his footing and fell to the ground. At most, he may have broken his leg by the way he landed.

Me'na felt she was falling. She looked up to Sean. "Beloved, I love you, be not afraid." Saying that, her hand completely slipped through his and she fell to the ground and landed on her back.

Sean screamed, "ME'NA!" and tried to jump off the roof to her, but Kristoff and Connor caught him just in time.

Cameron screamed and ran to her broken body. He picked up her head and cradled it in his lap. He took his jacket off and covered her body with it. He rocked back and forth holding her; tears were streaming down his face. Sean managed to run out of the house and reach them in record time. Kristoff and Connor followed him. Connor saw the letter on the bureau addressed to Sean and put it in his pocket.

The King saw how Cameron reacted to what happened to Me'na and didn't knock him out of the way. He nodded to Kristoff who helped Cameron up. Sean took his place holding her. His face was already wet with tears when he reached them; he held her close to him and kissed her face over and over. He cried the worst cry of all; he sobbed uncontrollably. It was like an ancient death cry, heart wrenching and gut tearing. All the men gathered around, there was not a dry eye in the group.

As Sean settled down a little, Connor gave him the letter from Me'na that he had found. "I cannot read it, Con, please, read it to me."

As Connor started to read the letter to the King, eyes misted over again. There was such an out pouring of love, honor, and trust that the men felt privileged the King allowed them to hear it. As Connor finished reading the letter, he folded it and placed it in Sean's pocket. The King got up holding his precious bundle. He asked Cameron to hold her while he got on his horse. Once he was seated, he reached down for her and placed her close to his heart.

They prepared to ride back to the palace. Kristoff grabbed the King's horse's reins and led Sean away. They were solemn as they went back to the palace, for the King was in mourning.

BOOK ONE
CHAPTER EIGHT

Sean woke up with a start. His face was soaked with tears. He looked over to Me'na to make sure she was just sleeping and not dead. He listened to her heartbeat and she woke up. Me'na saw he had been crying and reached up and grabbed him to her. He cried his heart out, she held and rocked him and kept him safe.

Sean stood facing the hot water in the shower. He wanted it to wash away his pain, but couldn't. He carried a great sadness inside his heart. There was no escaping it. Me'na would want answers now, but he didn't have the courage to tell her. He stepped away from the water to grab his shampoo bottle and his eyes watered again. Sean lathered his hair and tried to find the words to tell her the truth about his dreams. There was no way out of it this time. He scratched his scalp so hard he unintentionally made his head hurt.

"Self-mutilation won't get you out of this one, stand tall. You've always been a straight shooter. She's deserves the truth." He had stayed in the shower for a long time; too long, he was starting to wrinkle.

"Sean, please come out," Me'na stood outside the shower door talking to him. "We need to talk. Come, my love, it is OK. I'm going to step into the bedroom so you can get out of the shower."

He turned the water off and grabbed his towel, which he wrapped around his hips. He reached for the medium sized towel to dry his hair, he rubbed his head angrily. After wiping at his chest he opened the door and stepped out.

Me'na stepped into the bathroom and gazed appreciatively at Sean until he blushed.

"Well, I see I can make you turn red. That's good information for me to keep in my Rolodex. Here, let me dry your back. You're going to have to sit on this stool so I can reach you all over."

Sean obediently sat down on the stool she pulled from under the counter. Me'na started drying his back, his neck, and his arms thoroughly. He watched her in the mirror. She saw him but pretended not to notice. She knew he was upset and it had something to do with his dreams, she'd bet her last dollar she'd died in it again.

Looking her in the face through the mirror, he reached for her hand. Sean turned the stool around and pulled her into his lap. Me'na settled herself, rested her head against him, and waited for him to speak. He hugged her tightly and began to talk.

"Me'na, you deserve to know every time I dream about us, you always die. I can never get to you in enough time to save you. The last couple of dreams I've had both ended with you dying because other people were always trying to come between us." He stopped and raised her chin to look her in the eyes. "You understand that I couldn't save you either time?" he asked her.

"Yes, I understand what you are saying, Sean. So the past two times I died, right?" He nodded his head yes. "Then this is the third time, and you know what they say: third times a charm." She smiled at him.

"Me'na, be serious. This is not a laughing matter. This time it is real. I'll not lose you ever again. Look me in the eyes and understand I will do what ever is needed to protect you."

She looked at him and studied his beautiful green eyes. They were so intense; she knew he was deadly serious. Me'na kissed him lightly upon the lips.

"Sean, I died in the last two dreams right." She didn't wait for him to answer. "Can you remember what went wrong so we do not repeat those mistakes?"

"Yes."

She started to tell him her theory. "I think we have been given this chance to correct a wrong. Each time we were denied the culmination of our love." She looked to him and he nodded his head.

"So we have been granted this last chance to get it right. God must want us together or he wouldn't have brought you to me in my time of need. That's the way that I see it," she finished and hoped he would see it the same way.

He was thoughtful for a moment, and then his facial expression changed to one of hope.

"I had hoped I would dream again, so that I would know our next step. In the dreams, a man named Richard is always the cause of our unhappiness. I believe if we can outwit him this time, we will win. I feel the same way as you about our third chance. So when you appeared to me in the flesh, I had hoped this time I would make it work for us."

Sean held her tighter if that was possible. "But, baby, my brother is also in the picture as a troublemaker. We will have to prevail over him also to survive."

Me'na told him about the other night when Thomas tried to kiss her.

"I will never keep a secret from you about him again, but he told me you would not believe me and think that I made it up."

Sean was thunderstruck. He would believe anybody over his brother, Thomas always lied to get his way.

"Me'na, I do not believe anything that comes out of his mouth. He has always tried to hit on my girlfriends. Thomas wants everything I have. He's always been that way."

Sean stood Me'na up on the floor and went into his closet to find something to wear. He selected his gray slacks, and the coordinating shirt.

Me'na stepped back into the bedroom to give him some privacy. She wanted to stay and look at his splendid frame, but now was not the time. There was much to do and talk about. She had no intention on dying. No way was she going to leave her Sean to all those nurses that gave her the evil eye when they thought she wasn't looking. No, No.

She sat on the bed and waited while he combed his hair and gathered his thoughts. The Sean that walked out of the bathroom was not the same Sean that entered it. He now could make sense of what it was he must do. He was very analytical and methodical in his thinking. Those were traits that served him well as a surgeon. But as a lover, boyfriend or potential husband, he would have to change gears and use his heart more. Each time Me'na died, he'd felt something was going to happen. This time if he got that feeling again, he would listen to it. No way would he allow her to get in trouble without him being right by her side every step of the way.

They walked hand in hand out of his room to the kitchen. There were two different guards there. Their shift would be ending soon then Henry and Tristan would take over.

Me'na turned toward Sean. "I'm going to cook you breakfast. Don't look surprised! I can cook," she told him. "You sit and read the paper or something. Want some coffee while you wait, babe?"

"Yes, ma'am, I sure do."

He got up and showed her where the coffee was kept before she shooed him out of the kitchen. Sean walked outside and found the paper. This time it was where it was supposed to be. Of course, it was the last place he looked.

In no time flat, Me'na had the kitchen smelling good. She brought Sean his coffee, black along with a small glass of OJ. As he read his paper, everything seemed so domestic. He hoped when Bains was put away for good this scene would be permanent. The only change he would make would be that they were both in the kitchen cooking together and having a good time at it. She had a great sense of humor and was a wonderful person from what he remembered from the dreams and what he could see. He wanted to make her his wife; he loved her already, truly, deeply and completely. That would not change. He would broach the subject with her today.

Me'na walked to the table carrying a plate full of waffles, another one had ham, bacon and mini steaks. She placed them in front of him. She went back to get the eggs and brought out one platter of scrambled eggs and another one had eggs easy over and sunny side up. She knew Sean liked his over easy, he didn't say so, but she just felt it. By that time, the guards going off duty had wondered into the breakfast area and were getting hungry. Me'na invited them to sit and eat. She cooked enough for everyone to join them.

"Sit, gentlemen. I cooked extra for you to eat too."

She didn't have to tell them twice. Howard and Jamie sat down, got a plate and didn't say a word until they were finished. By the time they finished, Tristan and Henry wondered in the kitchen. They took up the guard positions while their relief ate breakfast. Sean had a large appetite and he was afraid Me'na would spoil him with all this good food. He would not let that happen, at least not now.

In the dreams, she was trying to protect him or do something for him that got her killed. Not this time, not until Thomas was taken care of and Bains in jail or dead, dead would be better. When everyone had finished eating, Howard and Jamie volunteered to clean up before they left. They would be back later that night until Bains was behind bars.

Sean took Me'na by the hand and led her up to the third floor of the house. He brought her to his conservatory. It sat along the entire length of the rear of the house; it was about fifteen to twenty feet wide at both ends. There were all sorts of plants, exotic flowers and local favorites there. Me'na was a plant enthusiast also. She prided herself on her green thumb and ability to make anything grow from seed. They wondered amongst the flowers and greenery for a while before Me'na asked him what he wanted to talk about. Sean looked at her and smiled at the connection they had; it was amazing. They were so there with each other, it felt good to be in her space.

"Let's sit down here in the middle of the tulips," he replied. Sean had comfortable patio furniture up here; there was even the soothing sound of a waterfall in the mist of the flowers. "Me'na, tell me how you know you love me."

There was such a need for validation in his eyes and the timber of his voice that she would bear her soul to him easily without fear of rejection. Me'na turned toward him and sat with legs crossed under her thighs on her seat.

"I have always known I love you as I've said before. I do not know why and I do not care. It's enough for me to know that I do, without fear or reservation. Sean, the first time I saw your face in my head, I painted it from memory." Me'na reached over and picked up his hand. "When I finished it, I said to the painting that his name would be Sean. I don't know why. That's just the name that came to me. I would imagine the type of person you would be, and how you would cherish me, you know girl stuff. But as time went on, I was looking for you in every man I dated. They all came up lacking your qualities, the real ones and the imagined ones. Now that I have gotten to know you, I find the ones I imagined are real. Does that make any sense to you?" she asked. He grinned and nodded his head; she was saying all the right things.

"I just know that I can't lose you." She bowed her head and said, "I don't want to go home, I want to stay here with you. I want to be with you always."

Sean lifted her face, leaned toward her and kissed her slowly, and thoroughly. Me'na melted, whenever he touched her, she was jello. When he withdrew, he began to speak.

"I want that too. Don't leave me and go home. We have history together that other couples don't have. We've known each other at least for two different lifetimes. There was danger to our survival as a couple that we won't let happen again. We know the people who do not want us together and this time we will prevail." Me'na smiled at him as he kissed her hand.

"We know the danger and I will listen to my heart instead of my head where you are concerned. Each time before, my heart warned me. I didn't listen, I had to be logical. I have learned that love is not logical, it rarely makes sense.

It is emotional, intuitive and instinctive. There is little place for logic in a romance. I want you for my wife. Tell me if there is anything else you desire from me, baby, and it's yours."

"You are my future. Without you, there can be no fulfillment. You offer me so much love and passion I'm humbled by the shear magnitude of it. It is there in everything you do and I have claimed it. Yes, I will become your wife and partner in life." She smiled and her eyes were tearing at the love that surrounded her.

Sean stood and grabbed her hand to stand her up. She reached up and rubbed the sides of his face. He lowered his lips to her and took possession of his prize.

After the kiss, he told her, "Let's go down to the courthouse right now and get our marriage license. No more unsure moves, I know what I want and what you want. Let's go."

Me'na hugged him tightly and walked with him down the stairs. Tristan and Henry piled in the other car and followed them to the courthouse. Once there, they filled out the paperwork, paid the fee and was told they would have to wait three days before they could marry. Sean told her the waiting period gave them enough time to buy a ring and get all her stuff moved into his house. They would not say anything to Thomas until after it was over, because he was one of the troublemakers.

Sean bought Me'na the largest diamond the store had to offer. The set came with the engagement ring, her band and his diamond band. Me'na hoped he would want to wear a band. She didn't have to ask him he told the sales person up front they wanted a bride and groom set. That made her so happy that she gave him a big squeeze around his waist. He looked at her with surprise; he would be proud to wear his wedding band, he wanted to be married to her.

After the ring shopping was done, they went to a small café downtown to eat lunch. Henry came into the café with them and Tristan stood outside the entrance watching for Bains.

After Me'na was seated, Sean pulled Henry aside to tell him to be on the lookout for his brother also. Henry nodded his head, he understood. He knew that something had happened in the kitchen the other night with Thomas.

"I'm going to go and tell Tristan to be on the lookout for him as well Sean." Henry stepped outside the café to inform Tristan. They stood there talking strategy for a moment.

Tristan asked him, "What type of car does he drive?"

"This Dr. Williams drives a red Beamer."

Tristan just nodded OK. Henry walked back in and took a seat in the corner away from Sean and Me'na. He didn't want anything to happen to her again, they were such a nice couple. They just wanted to love each other and be left alone. He would do his best to make sure nothing else happened.

Sean ordered his usual steak, corn, mash potatoes and rolls. Me'na asked him if he ever ate anything different.

"Sometimes I eat chicken or barbeque ribs, maybe with a salad. I can barbeque pretty good," he bragged.

"Braggart," she admonished. "I want to cook you one of my favorite Creole dishes. Do you like seafood and okra?" she asked him.

"Don't tell me you can cook Creole foods?" she nodded yes. "Will you cook it tonight, pretty please, baby?"

She enjoyed watching him act like a little boy. It made him all the more handsome if that was possible.

"We must stop at the seafood market and go to the grocery store before we go home. Home that sounded nice, didn't it?" She looked over at him.

Sean reached for her hand and kissed it. "Yes. It sounds right."

They finished eating with no encounters with Bains or Thomas. That was a good sign. Sean told Henry where they were going just in case they got separated in traffic.

At the seafood market, Me'na bought about two dozen Texas blue crabs and two pounds of large Gulf Coast shrimp. Sean told her he already had the other ingredients she needed except the okra. The grocery store would be the next stop to buy some frozen okra. The two cooks debated the pros and cons of buying it frozen, in the end, Me'na won out. She promised to show Sean how to cook this dish.

As they pulled onto the street leading to Sean's house, the police were outside waiting for them. Detective Hamilton was walking around the house rechecking the alarm system. Me'na stopped laughing at Sean's joke when she saw them, her heart started beating faster. He put his arm around her as best he could while driving the remaining block to the house.

"Don't worry, kitten, we have more help than we ever had before. It will be fine."

Me'na reached over and squeezed his thigh. "I hope so. I really am afraid."

Sean pulled into the drive and drove the car into the garage followed by Henry and Tristan. He helped Me'na out of the car while Henry walked over to the detective to see if anything had happened. Tristan walked around the house looking at all windows and making sure no one had been hiding outside.

After he made sure Me'na was inside. Sean detained Detective Hamilton for a moment.

"Detective, do you have anything new to report to us?"

The detective pulled his note pad out of his pocket and flipped through the pages. "Yes, Dr Williams, I'm afraid so."

Sean stopped him from speaking he called Henry and Tristan over so they could hear.

"We went to Bains' house last night after the incidents of yesterday. He wasn't there but I had a search warrant with me so we entered. He has a room in the very back of his house that is devoted to Ms. Collins. He has snapped pictures of her everywhere in the city. He even had one with you in it, Dr. Williams."

Sean looked surprised. "With me, when?"

"Yeah, y'all were coming out of the hospital and getting into your car. There was even a picture with your license plates enlarged."

Sean's face took on a grim look. Detective Hamilton understood how he felt, but he couldn't have him running around like a vigilante, he was going to have to make Sean stay out of it.

"Doctor, now I don't want you trying to do my job for me. I can handle Bains when we find him. An unmarked car has been parked outside his home, but he hasn't showed up yet. We don't know where he is at this time."

Sean blew his temper; he couldn't hold it in any longer. "Tell me something, how are you going to keep him from killing her if you can't find him? Answer me that, OK?"

"Settle down, Doc. I understand that as a man you want to take care of your lady. But sometimes we men have to ask for help, even though we don't like to."

Sean was ready for him. "Who do you think these two guys are? Interior decorators? I'll tell you who they are. They are professional bodyguards I have asked for help. I'm doing my part. You just do yours."

Sean was so angry he thought he would explode. He took off walking down the sidewalk swinging his arms; Tristan ran to catch up to him. Henry stayed and talked further with the detective. He was trying to make sure that everything that could be done was being done. He didn't like the feel of this, it made him uneasy.

Tristan had calmed Sean down enough so that he was in better shape to see Me'na.

"Me'na," Sean said. "She's in the house alone, I'd better get back." He walked back to the house and tried to lighten his mood. He would tell her the truth, but he didn't want to look so grim.

Detective Hamilton left and the men went into the house; Me'na watched them through the window. She could tell that her Sean was trying to put forth a good front. He had promised she would be kept in the loop.

As Sean walked into the kitchen, Me'na flew into his arms. She was worried he could tell; but she was trying to appear unconcerned. He told her everything the police had to say, nothing was held back. It was agreed she would never be alone, period.

Trying to lighten the mood, Me'na asked Sean if he would help as promised or just eat like a caveman. "Well, I forgot my club at the cleaners, so I guess I'll have to help cook."

This was the first time his smile didn't touch his eyes, they were sad. Me'na showed him how to clean crabs he could already clean shrimp. She placed them in the refrigerator and showed him how to brown the okra and not break it up while getting rid of the slime. He'd never seen it done the way she did it. She used oil and didn't place the top on the pot, which kept it from steaming. She showed him how to put just a little water in the pot to keep it from burning and before you knew it, he'd done it. Sean was very proud of himself; he was after all a fine cook in his own right. Me'na showed him all of her secrets with the tomatoes, garlic, onions, Accent, and just a touch of hot sauce. When it was almost done, she had him put the crabs and shrimp in.

"Sean, do you have any sausage in the freezer?"

"Yeah, I order that sausage that's made in Beaumont. All of a sudden I can't remember the name. I think it starts with the letter …"

"Never mind, I found it. This is the best." Sean agreed with her wholeheartedly.

She sliced the sausage up and placed it in the pot. Everything smelled good. The rice was done. She'd started cooking that and some cornbread when they were outside. After he washed his hands again, he turned to her and pulled her in his arms.

"I never would have guessed you were Creole. Nothing in my dreams led me to that. Maybe this is something different that can help us change things, anything different is a plus."

Me'na kissed his nose. "I'm one hundred percent first generation Texas born Creole. Here's how we Creoles finish cooking." Me'na grabbed his head, pulled it down to her lips, and kissed him nonstop. She pulled back, "How's that for seasoning?" she teased him. For her answer, he grabbed her again and kissed her just as fiercely. Dinner was forgotten for a while.

BOOK ONE
CHAPTER NINE

The night passed uneventful until the phone started ringing. When Sean picked it up, whoever was on the other end would hang up. That happened about five times before he called the police. He gave them the number that came up on the caller id; it was traced to a payphone across town. The police took fingerprints from the phone on the chance that maybe; there weren't too many prints there. They wanted to match it to the ones they lifted from Bains' home. Detective Hamilton sent some officers over to tap the phone line; they wanted Me'na to answer next time and keep him on the phone.

Everyone kind of sat around watching the phone, when it rang nobody was ready for it. Sean looked at the caller id and it was the hospital calling.

"Hello, Dr. Williams speaking." On the other end was his friend, Nurse Amanda Hathaway. She wanted to speak with Me'na about something confidential.

"Ms. Collins, I was the nurse that took care of you when you were in recovery. I want to tell you something. If you are near Dr. Williams, get up and walk around the room."

Me'na stood and pretended to be looking for something. "Go ahead, Nurse Hathaway; I'm not beside him now."

"Did you know that Dr. Williams' birthday is in two days? His birthday is on Labor Day. I wanted to tell you in case you didn't know. I have a very special gift for him myself."

"Oh thank you very much for telling me. I didn't know."

Nurse Hathaway hung up the phone feeling she had done her part for them. Now it was their turn. She would send Sean his gift the next morning.

It would give him enough time to look for clues, to check plans and to make sure she was not left alone again.

Me'na went into the kitchen to wipe the smile off of her face. She didn't want him to know she knew they would be married on his birthday. She thought, *I bet he's forgotten what the day is. Men, can't kill 'em, gotta love 'em.* She went back into the den to join him before he asked too many questions.

"Why are you looking so satisfied with yourself? What did the two of you talk about?"

"None of your business, Dr. Nosey." She just giggled at the look on his face when she called him nosey. The phone's ringing again broke the happy bubble.

Me'na picked it up, "Hello."

"Well, hello my little dove. It's about time you answered instead of your boyfriend." She pointed to the phone and Sean inched closer to listen. The policeman was listening on the other phone. "It's almost over now."

"What's almost over, you lunatic?" she asked him.

"You are almost over. Didn't I tell you before that if I couldn't have you, no one would?"

"Leave me alone. I haven't done anything to you. I hate you."

He laughed. "You know what they say, there's a thin line between love and hate."

He cackled like a mad man. The policeman signaled that they had traced the number and a unit was on its way to nab him. She kept him on the phone for several more minutes until she heard sirens in the background. The line went dead. She hung the phone up and Sean gathered her in his arms to comfort her. A car pulled into the driveway and Tristan went to see who it was.

"Sean, it's your brother. Let him in?" he asked.

"Yeah, I guess so."

Thomas walked in and was not prepared for the scene that greeted him. It looked just like a movie. He greeted his brother and asked Sean what was going on.

"We may have the stalker. We have to wait," he explained to him.

"How are you holding up, Me'na?"

"I'm fine, Thomas. Sean is taking good care of me." She sat down without another word. She just stared into space wanting this to be over, wanting to be Sean's wife.

Detective Hamilton arrived about fifteen minutes later. "Bains got away.

They think he was shot by one of the pursuing officers. Blood was found at the scene. he couldn't have gotten far."

Me'na left the room to go and make some coffee, she had to get up and do something. Sean followed her into the kitchen. While she was facing the cabinets, he pulled her against his chest and just held her for a moment. Me'na leaned her head on him and was thankful he couldn't see the fear on her face. Neither said a word, there was no need for it. Theirs was an age-old method of speaking; body language, no words were needed. She leaned because she needed support. He hugged because he needed her.

They walked back into the den. Sean carried the tray with the coffee. Everyone took a cup except Me'na. She didn't like coffee.

"Dr Williams, we will find him. I know you're worried, but I always get my man." He walked toward Me'na and took her cold hands in his. "I promise you, ma'am, I will not rest until he is behind bars. Please believe me. I want to help you in the worst way."

"Thank you, Detective. I know you will try."

Tristan walked him out to his car. There were two cars outside watching the house, one close and one farther down the street. Detective Hamilton told Tristan not to leave her alone no matter what happened. He assured him that she would be protected at all times.

Me'na stood and walked to Thomas. She bent and kissed him on the jaw and told him good night. She then turned to her Sean. "Babe, I'm going to go to my room and read a little. You stay and visit with your brother."

She draped her arms around his neck for a good night kiss. Thomas watched, envying his brother. "Thomas, excuse me for a minute. I'm going to see her to her room."

Thomas nodded his head. Sean walked her down the long hall to her room and opened the door. They stepped inside and immediately clutched each other as though they were dying of thirst. The thirst this time was not water, but each other.

"Kitten, I'll get rid of him so we can sit together."

"No, you don't have to. You've been with me all day. You have needs." He gave her a suggestive look. She hit his arm and laughed. "Not that kind of need, you need male companionship. You guys need each other. Go ahead." She was pushing him out of the room.

"OK, I'll go, but as soon as he leaves…"

Me'na finished the statement. "I expect to see you right back here." She stood on tiptoes and gave him a kiss. "Now go." Sean left the room with a smile that touched his eyes this time.

Thomas was channel surfing and couldn't find anything on TV worth watching. "Nothing's on the set, man," Sean answered the unasked question.

"I see. Bro, is she going to be OK? I mean this guy sounds like he's obsessed with her in the worst way possible." Thomas was actually concerned about someone beside himself.

"I will make sure she is if it's the last thing I do. Want a beer or something?"

"No, I'm on call tonight. I came by to find out how you and I are doing. Are you still angry with me? I'm really sorry. Here you are dealing with a life and death issue and I was being my usual jealous self. Can you forgive me?" Thomas asked.

"I imagine so. Me'na isn't upset anymore. We talked about it and she has forgiven you. That's why she kissed you as a brother. That was her way of telling you without making a big deal about it that y'all are cool again."

Thomas hung his head in genuine shame. He had actually come to see if they had broken up yet, he wanted to pick up the pieces. He would straighten his act up, if for no other reason than he owed it to Sean.

He stood."Well, let me go. You need to be by her side now. I understand that as your brother. Sometimes it's not about me."

"Thank you, Tommy. I appreciate it."

"Sean, before I go, what are you doing for your birthday this year?"

The look on his face was classic. Sean had forgotten that his birthday was in a couple of days. "Man, I forgot. With all this stuff going on about Me'na, I don't know. Maybe staying close to home this year, none of your wild parties again. We almost got arrested last year."

Thomas started laughing, remembering what a good time he and Sean had. It was a blast.

BOOK ONE
CHAPTER TEN

Cameron Bishop stood ringing the doorbell to Me'na's condo. He'd rung it for the last three minutes with no answer. *Maybe she's at work. Well, let me write her a note telling her, I'll come back later this evening.*

He stooped down and opened his briefcase to find pen and paper. While he was looking for his notepad, a large shadow loomed over him. He looked up and saw a very large man. Cameron stood up. The man asked him if he could be of service.

"Yeah, you can if you know Me'na Collins. I'm looking for her," he replied.

Me'na was sitting in the car with Sean. Tristan was standing on the sidewalk watching. She had never seen this man before. She had no idea what he wanted.

"Me'na, do you know him?" Sean asked her.

"No, I've never seen him before today."

Henry asked him, "And you are?"

Cameron stuck his hand out and Henry shook it cautiously.

"My name is Cameron Bishop. I wanted to ask her a few questions. Why all the cloak and dagger?"

Henry looked him over for a couple of minutes before he decided that this man didn't strike him as a danger to Me'na. He looked as if he could be a dangerous man if he chose to, but danger doesn't leave notes telling you they will return, not usually anyway. Henry trusted his instincts, they never failed him.

He took a deep breath. "Ms. Collins is in the car, but she is being stalked and I'm one of her bodyguards."

Cameron told him, "I'm sorry if I put everyone on edge, but I'm looking for family and I think Ms. Collins can help me. That's all. I swear."

Henry told him, "Wait here."

As Henry walked to the car, the movers were pulling into the driveway. Sean's house was big enough to take in her things. He didn't have all of the rooms filled yet. He'd been in this house for four years and the second floor was still pretty much bare. Decorating wasn't his thing, he was happy to have a recliner, big screen TV and a bed. Anything else and it was just icing on the cake.

As Henry got close to the car Sean got out and asked her to stay seated. "Well, who is he, Henry?"

"He said his name is Cameron Bishop and he's looking for his family. He hoped Me'na could help him. He's probably adopted or something."

Sean looked toward Me'na. "You want to talk to him for a minute, baby?"

She got out of the car. "Yes, Sean. He can come inside with us." She decided to tease him and lighten his mood. "Mmm, he is one good-looking black man." She could barely contain her smile until Sean looked at her as if she had suddenly lost her mind.

"What?"

"Gotcha," she laughed.

"Me'na, this is serious business, I'm trying to keep you alive and here you are trying to make me laugh." He smiled anyway.

"I'm sorry, babe, I truly am." She continued to smile.

"Yeah right. I can see you are behind the big grin on your face. Come here, woman." Sean stopped walking and pulled her to him.

"Sean, I love you so much. You know I'm a prankster. I do love you though," she said.

Henry stopped and looked at them, then continued to walk. Tristan had his eye on them.

"Give me a sample."

Me'na leaned against him and reached for his mouth. She gave him the best short kiss she had; it would have to do until they were alone. As she broke the kiss up and tried to move away, Sean reached for her.

"Where do you think you're going? I am not through." He tried to pull her back again.

"All you asked for was a sample, remember?" She laughed.

"Yeah, my fault. I had hoped you wouldn't take me at my word so literally.

I will have to watch what I ask for." Sean put his arms around her and held her tightly; being married to her was going to be a kick.

As they walked toward Cameron, Tristan took care of the movers. Henry went in front of them to unlock the doors for them and the movers. As they approached Cameron, he took the initiative. They were already on edge. He didn't want to get beaten up. He stepped toward Sean first since the big guy looked very protective of her. It was good to see. So far everything was as it should be.

With a smile on his face he said, "My name is Cameron Bishop, I'm from San Antonio. I came here to speak with Ms. Collins about helping me locate my birth parents."

Sean introduced her to him even though it wasn't necessary. He wanted to make a point that nothing happened to her without going through him first. She stepped forward and shook his hand.

"Come inside, Mr. Bishop, I'm moving but we can talk for a minute. This way please." He followed behind Sean and before Henry into the house. "Please have a seat if you can find a place to sit, I'll be right back."

Me'na went to give the movers instructions. There were ten of them altogether; they were packing and moving, Sean insisted that she do nothing.

Sean sat there, not trying to make conversation. He was too busy looking at Cameron. He wanted to see if he reminded him of anyone from his dreams.

Uh, maybe, he thought.

Me'na came back and sat very close to Sean. "Now, Mr. Bishop, how can I help you?"

"Call me Cameron please."

She smiled and nodded. "I'm Me'na."

"I was adopted when I was only a couple of months old and now I'm searching for any family I might have." He continued. "Did you live in Austin?"

While he was searching through his briefcase for paperwork, Sean gave him a thorough once over again. He couldn't be too careful with her life. She was the other half of him. He thought if he had to, he could take him on.

Me'na answered when he closed his case. "Yes, I was born and raised there then we moved to Houston."

He handed her a picture, "Do you recognize this man?" He was trying not to look as desperate as he felt she was his last hope. He too had his ghosts.

"Yes, that's a picture of my father. He died when I was a teen. That's why we moved to Houston. Why, did you know him?"

Sean had become very interested in what was going on. Cameron looked very familiar to him. He looked like the man from his dreams. He looked like the man who cried out loud when Me'na died. He sat up straighter.

Cameron had such a relieved look on his face Me'na thought he was going to cry. "Yes, he's my father also. He and my mother never married because she took me and disappeared, and then she placed me up for adoption."

Me'na reached over and touched his hand, which was all he needed. His eyes became glassy. A tiny tear cruised down his face. She stood, he stood with her; Me'na hugged him to her. Sean stood up behind her to show his support for her.

Sean went to get him a glass of wine, he drunk it down quickly. "There's nothing stronger here, Cameron. We have something over at our other house." Me'na reached over to him and kissed his cheek, she'd heard him say our house; Sean didn't realize what he said it came naturally to him.

"Are you two married?" Cameron hoped they were.

They hugged each other and Me'na replied, "Tomorrow we will be!"

"Congratulations, I got here just in time."

"Cameron, you think that we are sister and brother, just different mothers." Me'na was more than curious. This could change her whole life. She's never had much family, just her, her mother, and a few cousins in the Golden Triangle area.

He started, "Yes, we are. My adopted parents left me a letter when they died in a car crash several months ago. In it, I found both my parents names. Unfortunately, I found out that my mother died a long time ago and I was hoping my father still lived. But, I found a sister and that's even better." He had a big smile on his face it was contagious. Everyone was smiling, even Sean.

"Can I see the letter, Cameron?" Sean asked him. He handed the letter over without a second thought, he was ecstatic he had family he belonged to someone again. Cameron remembered everything, but he would keep his secret, unless things started to go wrong again.

They sat talking while the movers boxed and loaded everything in the truck. Me'na got up from time to time to make sure nothing was broken or left behind. She got to know her new brother and Sean remembered everything about Cameron from his dreams. Here was help, Cameron didn't mean them any harm in his dreams; so maybe his showing up was a good sign, he hoped so.

Everything was packed and loaded in both trucks and Henry led them to Sean's house. After Me'na locked up the condo, she walked down the sidewalk to join Sean and her brother. Cameron was just getting into his car to follow them. Henry had the security car so Tristan was going to ride with Sean and Me'na. Tristan was walking with Me'na. Sean went to the driver's side of the car to get in. The passenger's side was facing the street.

As Me'na stepped off the sidewalk into the street, Bains' car came bearing down on her. Tristan saw him coming and only had time to knock her to the ground. Cameron saw the car coming and tried to jump out to help. Sean had a premonition when he opened his car door. He turned and saw the car speeding directly toward her.

"ME'NA! Look out!" he screamed.

Sean made it to her before she hit the ground. The car that kept going hit Tristan. "Cameron, come get Me'na and call 911. I'm a doctor I can take care of Tristan." Sean opened his trunk and got his bag out. He made Tristan comfortable until the police and ambulance arrived. He had a broken leg and it appeared that maybe some ribs were broken; he would need x-rays.

The ambulance arrived within minutes and the police not long after. Sean had him stable and gave the medics instructions on his care. He looked at Tristan. "Do you need me to ride in the ambulance with you and make sure you're taken care of?"

Tristan stopped him. "No, Doc, you go with Me'na. She needs you more than ever now. I'll be OK. You've seen to that and don't let this hold up the wedding," he shouted as he was put into the ambulance.

Sean turned around to see Me'na waiting for him to come to her. They rushed to each other and clung together as if dying. Cameron, unbeknownst to Sean, had a hunch that Bains wanted to hurt his sister again. That was part of the reason for the urgency to find her. When he first saw her, he knew it had to be the same Me'na. Everything and everybody was the same, she and Sean still loved each other to distraction, which was good. Bains or whatever his name is now, would not win. Not this time.

Cameron followed them back to the house where Detective Hamilton was waiting for them. Henry and the movers were through unloading the truck. Henry heard what happened to Tristan, he called the agency and they were sending over a couple of extra guys. The police was waiting for them in the house.

As soon as they walked into the house Detective Hamilton started speaking. "Ms. Collins, Dr. Williams, I heard what happened and rushed over. I now have an arrest warrant for Richard Bains. We're putting his face on TV tonight. Ms. Collins' name will not be released. We are just saying that he is armed, dangerous, and wanted for questioning. That will bring him in." The phone rang and Sean went to answer it.

"Hello."

"Sean this is Kristoff. One of Me'na's body guards just arrived in the emergency room. Is everything all right? Did anyone else get hurt?"

"No, Kris, just Tristan. Will he be OK?" Sean asked.

"Yeah, man, you did most of the work for me. He's going to be fine. How are you holding up? This must be torture for you."

Sean whispered, "I'm OK. I'm just worried about Me'na. She's not saying much. She's too quiet."

"You think she might be in shock?"

"Yeah, I'm afraid so. After the detective leaves, I'll give her a sedative so she can rest."

Kristoff as always was a good friend to Sean. "Say, if you need anything, call me. Hit me on my cell."

"OK, see ya'" Sean hung up the phone and walked back to Me'na.

Detective Hamilton was preparing to leave. Henry walked him out, asking if there was anything else they could do.

"Cameron, make yourself at home, I'm taking Me'na to her room, she needs to lie down."

"Go ahead, Don't worry about me. I'm fine." Cameron would be fine, but Bains would not be if he caught him before the police did.

Me'na let Sean guide her to her room, put her to bed and give her a sedative without complaint. He sat on the side of her bed holding her hand until she went to sleep. Sean then tiptoed out of the room so he could blow his top without waking her up.

He was so angry that he couldn't see straight. He wanted to kill Bains with his bare hands nothing could stop him. He would get him or die trying. He walked back toward the den and his new brother-in-law to be.

Sean stuck his head in the den. "Cameron, give me about a half hour I need to blow off some steam. I'll be in the gym if you need me." Sean went to his training room it was located on the vacant second floor. He changed into his gym shorts and started hitting the punching bag the way his trainer taught him. He worked on the bag until he was physically exhausted. For now the anger and rage was simmering, not boiling over.

The new guys arrived and Henry filled them in on their duty and shifts. Sean asked Cameron to come outside with him to talk. He needed to know more about him. He had to be sure he was on the up and up. He would allow no one near his precious Me'na that he didn't personally approve of while all the trouble was still going on.

"Cameron, as you can see there is a lot of stuff going on in our lives right now. I have to be sure that you are who you say you are. My Me'na is very trusting and loving; she's easy to hurt and I'll not have her hurt again."

They had stopped near the vegetable garden. There they sat on a bench to have a private conversation. Cameron was not offended; he would behave the same way if it was his lady in danger.

"I understand what you're saying. I'd feel the same way. Here are my credentials. I'm something of a Renaissance man. I do a little bit of this and a little bit of that." Cameron reached into his pocket and brought out his ID and birth records. "I am an architect by trade and I also work for the government when there is a need for one of my specialties."

Sean asked him, "What type of government work is that?"

"Well, all I can say is that I was full time in the intelligence community, but I'm sort of burned out. So now I just work for them on special projects." Sean looked at him with interest. Cameron continued. "My passion is design. It's what keeps me sane. I have been more of a freelance architect lately."

Sean looked him over and Cameron just sat there. He didn't mind. Me'na and Sean were deeply in love and he must protect her.

"Do you have a place to stay?"

Cameron shook his head no. "I just drove in from Austin and straight to Me'na's place. I didn't have time. Don't worry about me though. I'll get a room in the nearest hotel."

Sean raised his eyebrows up quizzically. "I can tell you don't know your sister. Man, she'd have my head on a platter if I didn't get you to stay with us at least for a while."

They started to laugh together. "Is she a little firecracker?" he asked.

"Man, is she, she's tough, strong, caring, and loving. I could just go on for hours. She's the best of all things to me. Me'na taught me to laugh again. So much was missing in my life. I love her with every once of my soul." Sean looked thoughtful for a moment.

"She told me she saw a promise in my eyes, a promise to love her and cherish her. She demanded that I give her these things." He chuckled a little. "She told me she was worth it and that I already knew it to be true."

Cameron asked him, "Did you know it?"

"Yes, I have always known it. I was merely waiting for her to come into my life so that I could begin." Cameron thought everything was as it should be; their love for each other was unbreakable.

"You know, Sean, I'm glad my sister has someone like yourself to care for her. I plan on staying here in Houston and getting to know Me'na and you, y'all are my family."

Both men went back into the house, Sean showed Cameron to his room. The phone rang and it was Thomas calling from the hospital.

"Sean, are you and Me'na OK? I saw Tristan in the emergency room and he told me what had happened."

"We're fine, Tommy. It was a close call though. Why don't you come over when you finish your shift? I want you to meet Me'na's brother."

"OK. I get off in a couple of hours. Do you have any more of that special gin that you keep hidden away from me?"

"Yeah, I do. How do you know about it?"

"My secret. You are so open, Sean. I have always been able to read you like a book. You always look toward whatever it is you don't want me to know about." Thomas started laughing at his brother.

"Ha ha ha, very funny. I'll see you when I see you." He hung up.

Sean went to check on Me'na. He wanted to make sure she didn't sleep too long.

Me'na was sitting up in bed with the remote in her hand. She looked up, as he entered. "You know, with cable there's still nothing to watch."

He smiled and went to sit beside her. "How are you feeling?"

"I'm fine. I feel stupid but I'm alright. I have you, don't I?" Me'na reached over and rubbed his face, she loved the beard. "Why are you smiling like that, silly?" she asked him.

"In my dreams you used to rub my face like that, and then plant a big kiss on me."

She leaned toward him and kissed him, "like that?" Sean pulled her down on the bed and passionately kissed her until she couldn't breath.

"No, like that," he said meaning his kiss to her.

Holding his face over hers she asked, "Show me again." He was delighted to comply.

Detective Hamilton called and spoke with Henry to tell them Bains had been spotted down town earlier that day. They were closing in on him. When Sean and Me'na came out of the room, Henry gave him the message when she wasn't around. Sean was grateful he waited for her to leave the room.

There were no leftovers from Me'na's Creole dinner the night before so they ordered pizza later that evening. The doorbell sounded and Henry answered it to find a messenger with a package for Sean. Me'na was talking with Cameron, giving him some background on the father they mutually shared in the recreation room. Sean accepted the package and gave the messenger his tip.

"Uh, I wonder what this could be?" he thought out loud.

He walked into the kitchen for a bit of privacy and opened the wrapper. It was from his friend Amanda Hathaway at the hospital, a birthday gift.

"Well, what do you know about that."

He was pleased she remembered his day was tomorrow. Opening the package, he sat down at the breakfast table. It was a rare book, looked like it dated back about five hundred years or so. He enjoined reading, it was one his favorite hobbies.

This had to have been a very expensive gift for her to give me, he thought. Inside the card said:

> *To Dr. Sean Williams,*
> *This book holds an insight into your past. Please read with an open mind and remember.*
> *Amanda Hathaway.*

"Mmm," Sean opened the book and carefully thumbed through the ancient pages, they were fragile.

On one page, he found a letter that was pressed with flowers to give it the scent of gardenias. He picked it up, started reading it, and almost tore the page in his excitement. It was a letter from Me'na to her fiancé, Sean.

"Oh my God! Oh my God!" he repeated. He read it aloud.

> *"My dearest love,*
> *"I want you to know my life changed when I met you. You made me want to wake up in the morning and not go to sleep in the night. Visions of you are constantly in my head and heart. I think I have loved you all my life; you have completed me*

and made me whole. I am going to try to find Thomas for you. I know the duke better than most and have seen what he is capable of. He is an evil man and would kill your brother just to have something to do. You have given everything to me, and I have nothing to give in return. Freeing the prince will be my gift to you. I am going to make it back to you with the prince in tow. I am not trying to die; but I am leaving this note for you in case things do not go as planned.

"Please do not be angry with me; I do this out of the great love that I bear for you. You are the best thing that ever happened to me in my life. If I don't make it out alive to you, I will be waiting for you on the other side with my arms open wide. I love you with all my heart and soul. We will find each other again and renew our love.

All my love,
Your Me'na."

Sean fell back against his chair the past was very real. It seemed as though Amanda Hathaway was not who she appeared to be. He saw a note from her telling him to look through the entire book. He shook his head and continued to go thorough the book very carefully so as not to miss anything. In the center of the book he found a red ribbon and another gardenia. Close to the last chapter, he found another letter from Me'na. This too he read aloud.

"My dearest Sean,

"There aren't enough words in the world for me to express the love that I feel for you. It is so much that I am near bursting. I had to write how I feel about you before this passage of time elapsed. Each day my love for you grows larger, sweeter and consuming. I love the way your hair falls in your eyes and you impatiently brush it aside. I could not live without you if I tried to, it would be like living without a heart and soul. You are so precious to me; every move you make is remembered. This is the way that you make me feel all the time. So the times that we are apart, I have so much love to carry with me that I am never alone anymore. You have secured your place in my heart and soul for eternity.

"All my love,
Me'na."

Sean was speechless. The letters were to him from Me'na in the past. There was a final note from Amanda Hathaway.

Remember your past, Sean. It will unlock your future. Listen to your heart this time. It will never lead you astray. Remove the tape from the spine of the book carefully, the contents belong to Me'na.
Fondly,
Amanda

Sean carefully turned the book on its side to remove the tape. As he removed the last piece of tape, he gently shook the book with one hand. He placed his other hand underneath and a solid gold locket fell into his palm. It was very old and heavy. The engravings on it were beautiful. There was also a very fine gold chain attached to it. Sean took a deep breath and opened the locket. Inside he found a picture of himself and a lock of hair. He sat there and remembered exactly when he gave it to Me'na. It had belonged to his mother. He sat in his chair, just holding the locket tightly in his hand. He once again thanked God for the chance to save Me'na.

He picked up the phone to call her at the hospital. He was told she had retired and headed for parts unknown. He remembered he and Thomas had an aunt named Amanda in his dreams. Was she the same person? he wondered. He was sure that she was. Everything else was the same. He sat there for a long time until Me'na and Cameron came looking for him.

"What's that look about, babe?" she asked him as she pulled out a chair.

Cameron sat down across from Sean. Instead of answering her question, he passed the letters to her. She read them aloud. She was as amazed as he was.

"You know, Sean, this looks like my handwriting, but I don't remember writing them." She passed them to Cameron.

Sean reached across the table for her hands. "I remember receiving them, in my dreams."

She looked at him with confidence. She knew he would know since he was the one with the dreams. All she had were images in her head of Sean, and a vague sense of knowledge of him. He was her measuring stick for all men and everyone fell short. She had always felt she was looking for her Prince; but according to the earliest letter, it must have been her King. Sean looked toward Cameron and tried to explain as best he could without sounding like the village idiot.

"Cameron, I've had dreams since I was twenty about your sister and me before we met. She and I have come to the conclusion that we lived and loved before. Before you ask me if I'm crazy, this book was sent to me as an early birthday gift from Amanda Hathaway." Sean showed him the notes from her. "The notes leave me to believe they are trying to show us the way. According to my dreams, Me'na was trying to help me recover my brother in the first one." Me'na reached over and touched his hand for support.

"She went missing in the second one. My brother who wanted her also supposedly rescued her. But, before each occasion, I felt something was going to happen to her. I as King relied on logic to rule effectively, but I should have used my heart to love successfully." Me'na got up and sat on his lap. She didn't want him blaming himself for the past.

"Baby, you did what you thought was necessary. Do not place blame on yourself." She hugged him tightly.

"No, I should have used my heart Me'na. I will not make that mistake again, I promise you."

Cameron watched the loving and giving taking place across from his with pleasure. "Sean, Me'na, I have never believed in past lives. But I knew I had to find my sister before it was too late. I didn't know too late for what. I just knew that it was imperative I locate her."

He remembered the past. He also remembered there were some things he'd rather forget. He was not sure if he should share this secret with them. Maybe it would be enough for them to know that he believed and supported them.

"Thank you for at least not thinking we're nuts. I can't explain it," Sean told him.

"There's no need to. You love and cherish my baby sister. That's all I want to hear," Cameron assured him.

"On that point you have nothing to worry about. She is my everything." Me'na laid her head on Sean's shoulder as he hugged her tightly.

Cameron stood up from the table. "I'm going to go and find myself some more of that cold pizza and get a beer, maybe watch a little TV. Let me know when your brother arrives, I really want to meet him." He thought, *Thomas,*

I am ready for any of your tricks, just try and pull something this time. You'll die in one of the many ways I've learned through the ages.

Sean and Me'na went into the recreation room to listen to some soft jazz. He had an extensive collection of everything that was made from the mid seventies until now. His favorite song was playing and he asked Me'na to dance with him.

"I am not a good dancer, Sean, I have two left feet."

He laughed. "Don't worry; I'm not much better myself. Just protect your feet."

He grabbed her hand and away they went. Regardless of what he said, he was an excellent dancer; Me'na found it easy to follow him. Then again, she would follow him anywhere he led.

"Sean, you're wonderful, I think I would love dancing with you all the time."

With Sean being left-handed, it was a little awkward when he grabbed her hand and spun her around. But she made the adjustment so that she didn't knock him down. They finished with laughter and much hugging that led to other good things.

"Oh my, Dr. Williams, you do take my breath away. Is there a cure for this aliment I suffer from?" she asked him.

His eyes were heavy lidded as he looked into hers. "No, it's a life long disorder there is no cure for. But, I will keep trying to research it with your help."

"Mmm, whenever you're ready, Doctor," she murmured.

Thomas arrived while they were in their own world. Cameron introduced himself to him. He looked Thomas over very carefully. He still looked like the same clever character he always was. He did appear a little different somehow; Cameron couldn't put his finger on it yet. He would watch him for any unhanded dealings.

"Hi, I'm Me'na's half-brother from San Anton. My name is Cameron Bishop."

"Pleased to meet you, Cameron. I'm Thomas, Sean's younger and only brother."

"Thomas, I'll be right back. I promised Sean I would come and get him when you arrived." Cameron wasn't telling the exact truth. He bent it a bit, but who cared? He walked in on his sister and Sean ending their kiss.

"Say, man, your brother's downstairs." He turned and went back down with the two of them following.

Thomas walked toward Me'na with open arms and kissed her on the cheek.

Sean was surprised but tried not to show it. Cameron watched the scene; he could tell Sean was a little apprehensive when Thomas kissed her. *Good*, he thought. *He doesn't necessarily trust his brother around her. Third time will be a charm this go round.*

"Thomas, have you met Me'na's brother Cameron?" Sean asked his brother.

"Yeah, he answered the door and introduced himself."

"Sit down, man. Relax."

Me'na asked him, "Thomas, are you hungry or thirsty? We still have some pizza left. I can get you some."

"Don't bother. I can get it." Saying so Thomas got up and went into the kitchen.

"Excuse me," Sean followed him. "Are you OK, Tommy? You seem different somehow?" Thomas got a plate and picked several pieces of pizza to warm in the microwave.

"Yeah, I'm fine, just tired. You know, I've been doing some soul searching about myself and I don't like what I see."

Sean asked him, "What do you mean, you don't like what you see?"

"I'm selfish and egotistical and not as nice a brother as you deserve." Sean tried to interrupt him, but Thomas waved him off. "No, it's true, Sean. You've been nothing but good to me my whole life and I've repaid your love for me with jealousy and mockery. I am sorry; you should have a better brother than I."

"Thomas, I don't know what to say." Sean was shocked by his disclosure.

"There is nothing to say. It's the truth. I am a bad friend and an even worse brother. Kristoff is a better brother to you than I am."

He kind of just hung his head and stood there waiting on the microwave to ring, not wanting to look up at Sean. His brother was speechless. Sean wasn't sure how to respond to this revelation. But it wasn't enough of a revelation to make him tell Thomas about his wedding plans on the morrow. Too many things had gone wrong before in the past. He would not take the chance. The best that he could do would be to call Tommy after the ceremony and invite him to join them at the club.

"Well, Tommy, the only thing I can say is thank you for realizing that I have tried to love you in spite of yourself." Sean placed his hand on Thomas' shoulder.

Thomas chuckled. What Sean said hit the mark dead-on. It was truthful. His brother was a bigger man than he was. Thomas had promised himself he would be the brother Sean deserved

They walked back into the den with smiles on their faces, Me'na was worried that Thomas would say something stupid to make Sean upset. Everything appeared to be OK. She was relieved for his sake.

For the first time in a long time, the brothers Williams had a mutually satisfactory visit. Cameron let his guard down just a mite. He didn't want to appear unfriendly to his host's brother. He remained ever vigilant for his sister's sake. Thomas stayed for several hours and went home when it became late.

"Thomas, what shift are you working tomorrow?" Sean wanted to know.

"Actually, I'm working until noon. I was supposed to be off but the hospital is short handed again."

"Are you a doctor too?" Cameron wanted to know.

"Yes, I followed my big brother into medicine after I got hurt playing football."

"Did you play professionally, Thomas?" This time Me'na asked the question.

"Yeah, I played for the Dallas Rustlers for two seasons. They really wanted Sean here, but he has always wanted to be a doctor."

Me'na smiled at Sean. "Babe, I didn't know you played professionally too."

"No, I was drafted by them, but medicine has always been my calling. When Tommy and I were in high school, they used to call us The Assassins. If I didn't get the opposing team for a touchdown, Thomas here did. Weren't we awesome, man?" They gave each other the sports high five, and then stood up to do their high school shuffle. They collapsed into laughter.

Thomas left feeling good about what he told Sean. He meant every word of it. He would try as long as humanly possible if he could. He might even surprise himself and remain a good guy.

It was lights out for everyone but the bodyguards. They maintained their watch. Sean walked Me'na to her room after Cameron went to bed.

"Come inside, babe," Me'na was trying to pull him by the arm.

"Kitten, you know how I feel tomorrow night is our wedding night. We've come this far..."

"Sean, you misunderstand me. I want to talk about something else."

He had the decency to blush. Of course his mind was thinking about something else. There was nothing wrong with his virility. She knew he couldn't resist her anymore.

"I understand, Sean, but things have fallen into place so perfectly that I don't want to let you go just yet. I want to talk about your house and if you mind if I redecorate it once I'm Mrs. Williams." He hoped he hadn't heard her correctly.

"What's this stuff about my house and me letting you decorate? This is our house and don't you forget it." He was upset.

"Sean, I should sign a prenup for your protection also."

"Kitten, this is the first time that you've made me upset with you. That is the worse thing you could say to me. After all we've been through, all the hurts and death experiences and now you ask me this. Man, I never…"

The only way she could shut him up was to kiss him until he couldn't speak. Her lips worked their magic on him he soon forgot his argument.

She raised her head. "What were you saying, baby?"

"I don't remember now. Yes, I do. Why would you ask me about a prenup?"

"I just wanted you to know I am willing to sign and that it will not diminish my love for you whatsoever. I want to protect you as much as you want to protect me."

"Well, thanks but no thanks. That would mean we would have to divorce and that is not going to happen. So I don't want to talk about it anymore OK?" Sean was still upset.

"OK, love, just kiss me good night." He did for about the next five minutes, knowing that by one o'clock the next day, she would be his legally.

As he turned to go, Me'na stopped him. "I like the nickname. I like kitten."

"I called you that in our dream life. I didn't remember until now. Good night, kitten." Sean gave her a quick good night kiss and went to his room.

Sean slept a good sleep that night, but Me'na was too keyed up to do anything but toss and turn until she was tired. Around three in the morning she left her room, climbed in Sean's bed, and lay down beside him. She put her arm around his middle; he mumbled and held onto her hand the remainder of the night.

BOOK ONE
CHAPTER ELEVEN

Sean awoke to find Me'na lying next to him. He gingerly got out of the bed. He didn't want to wake her up. He stopped and looked at the top of her head to make sure she had healed as expected. She didn't complain much, but he could tell she still had headaches. He stepped into the bathroom to wash his face and brush his teeth.

After splashing cold water on his face, he turned on the radio. Since Me'na was still sleeping, Sean thought he would go for a jog. He hadn't jogged since he brought her home and he was starting to feel it. He quietly got his jogging shorts and shirt together and went back into the bathroom to dress. Trying to find his favorite running shoes was more difficult than it should have been. He finally found them in the last place he would have looked, where they belonged. He usually just threw them in the closet.

He got his headset, and his cell phone. He was now ready to go. Sean prepared to run his customary five miles. He left Me'na a note so that she would not worry. He told the guards he was going for a run and to watch his bride carefully until he returned. He was off running down the street. The house was situated in one of Houston's wooded community's; there were plenty of jogging trails. Cameron watched him go out of his bedroom window; he didn't see anyone following him.

As Sean jogged, he thought about his dreams and real life being on the same collision path. Twice before, he had failed to save her, but this time things were slightly different. For one, there was Cameron; this time he was her brother. Previously Cameron was on his side, but he remained an enigma. He was sort of the same way in the present time. A part-time architect and part-time government man just didn't fit. Could he be a spy or some other sort of skilled operative for the CIA or NSA? Sean was going to have him investigated to be sure that he was who he said he was. The only things he and Me'na had similar were the eyes and the same coloring. Time would tell. Sean had started back to the house when the ballad "Now is Our Time" came on the radio. He had never been a sappy or sentimental person before he re-met Me'na, but danged if his loving her didn't change him a bit. Now this song that he had previously thought was an alright song before, now it meant something to him. He would have to be on his guard around Thomas and Kristoff before they called him a woman. He smiled at the thought.

Me'na woke up reaching for Sean, but found an empty space. She got up and checked the bathroom but he wasn't there; as she was turning to leave, she spotted the note.

> *Kitten, I've gone for a jog, should be back in a few. Please don't worry about me. I usually jog as much as I can. I have my cell phone if you need me.*
> *Love Sean*

She smiled when she read Love Sean. She took the note with her to her room and placed it amongst her keepsakes.

After she took her shower, Me'na went to find Cameron and ask him if he was hungry. She knocked on his door but he didn't answer, she opened the door but he wasn't there.

Um, where is he?

When she got to the kitchen, she found her answer; he was preparing breakfast for the two of them. He had his sleeves rolled up and looking very much at home in the kitchen. She stood there watching him for a moment then went to give him a good morning kiss on the cheek.

"Ah, Me'na, I was hoping to have this ready before you woke up, Surprise!" He sounded disappointed. She sat down at the breakfast table and watched him.

"What are you preparing for us?"

"Well, for starters," he began, "I have some bacon and sausage. It's almost done. Then I am going to cook you French toast. I hope you like French toast." He looked so hopeful she started laughing at him. "What's so funny, little sister?" he asked her.

"Well, when you asked me that, for a minute, you looked like a sad little puppy. I'm sorry I laughed." She couldn't stop.

"Sure sounds as if you're enjoying yourself to me." She got up and kissed his cheek again smiling.

"You know, Cameron, our dad used to call French toast 'lost bread'. I don't know why. he said that was what his mother called it."

"It's nice to hear something about him. It means a lot to me." She asked him if there would be enough for Sean when he returned from his run.

"There's plenty. I wasn't going to cook his until he got back. I watched him leave a while ago. He should be back soon." He looked at her. "You really love him with all your heart and soul, don't you?" It's wasn't a question really. It was more of a statement.

She answered quickly, "With all my heart and soul and then some."

"Well, that's good to hear since we're getting married later this morning," Sean answered the both of them.

"Happy Birthday, babe!" she exclaimed.

"Thank you, baby" He bounced over to Me'na to give her a kiss on the cheek and told Cameron good morning.

Me'na wrinkled her nose. "You smell. It's off to the shower for you, lover boy."

"Ah baby, don't you love a smelly me as much as a clean me?" He started chasing her around the kitchen with her screaming and laughing at him. Henry ran into the kitchen to see what was going on.

"I'm sorry, Henry, it's my fault. I was teasing, Me'na. We didn't mean to alarm you."

"That's fine, Sean. Women should be teased sometimes." That was a lot coming from the usually quiet Henry.

"I'm going to go and take my shower. Save some of that for me too."

Cameron was pleased to watch them play together. They were a perfect couple. *Only a few more hours and they will have forged new territory in their relationship. Good,* he thought. "Me'na please check to see if any of the guys want anything to eat while I'm cooking."

Cameron cooked breakfast for six people. His sister had to help him. The bodyguards took their food and ate while they watched. Sean was soon through showering, came up behind Me'na, and hugged her around the waist. She leaned into him as she had done before in previous lifetimes.

"Now this is much better. Hi, sweetheart. Did you have a pleasant run?" she asked him.

He turned her around to face him. "Yes, your face was before me the entire time." He kissed her slowly.

"Do you two mind taking that to the table please so I can serve your breakfast while it's still hot? Gee," Cameron teased. Both looked up at him with childish grins on their faces. The breakfast was good. Cameron really was a renaissance man, he could do many things well.

Me'na finished her food and took her plate to the sink. She walked behind Sean's chair, put her arms around him and started to sing "Spectrum of Love."

"You've always been beside me, little more than a shadow, keeping me company on nights that could have been unbearable. You were there, always there, I just had to see you. The shadow has become you; you were the shadow. You have always been beside me, now we are one…"

Sean didn't let her finish her song, there was no need to. Cameron got up and left them in privacy.

Cameron went to his room to make sure his weapons were prepared and ready to use if necessary. They would be leaving soon to go to the justice of the peace for the ceremony. They had to be there at noon. It was ten thirty and he was ready to take Bains' life if necessary. Cameron stood looking out the window, he vividly recalled the first time he had seen Sean and Me'na together. He caught up with them on a field of battle long ago…

"Who's that knight on the gray destrier charging this way?" the King asked.

The men looked in the direction the King was pointing. The figure on the horse could have passed for a smallish man. He wore a breastplate, leggings, chain mail and an old helmet that looked as if it belonged to a young boy. The rider and horse stopped midway with the horse rearing up and thrusting out its hoofs. Whoever the rider was, he could handle the destrier with much skill. While the horse was standing, he turned in menacing circles. The King's men gathered around him forming a tight circle.

Sean told his men, "I'm in no danger from a lone rider no matter how good a horseman he is."

The rider threw down a lance with parchment tied to it and raced back to his camp.

"Kristoff, go get the lance. Let's us see what he has to say."

Lord Kristoff galloped toward the center of the field to fetch the lance. He didn't stop his horse to grab it; he simply leaned over, pulled it out of the ground, and headed back to the King. The men made way for Kristoff's return to them. The King reached for the parchment and untied it from the lance.

The note read:

> *King Sean Winslow, King of Fastonia,*
> *Your castellan is being turned out of my castle. I will not yield to him or you. This land does not belong to Fastonia. I am lord and heir here. I need no spy from your court here. It was signed Lady Me'na Lord and Mistress of Upper Lakeland.*

Sean thought he was going to explode he was so angry. His men wondered at the gall of the letter writer, to offend the King was punishable by death. They could tell from the King's expression it was not a nice welcome note. Prince Thomas came forward and asked to read the letter; Sean wordlessly handed it to him.

Thomas raised his brows and whistled. "Oh no, who wrote this? Do you think it was Lady Me'na?" he asked his brother.

"Certainly not. I couldn't imagine a lady even knowing how to write let alone having this much brass," Thomas answered his own question.

"Evidently, this one does or she is being held against her will by an errant knight. Maybe he is marrying her to get the principality for himself. According to the terms, the old prince's father signed, when his son died, the principality would revert back to Fastonia and it will."

The King was determined he would prevail. A lone figure started walking from the enemy camp. It was the castellan.

"Connor, send someone to get him or we'll be waiting all day for him to get here," the King ordered. "Back to camp."

Everyone turned around and followed the King and prince back to camp.

Sean jumped off his destrier and marched angrily into his tent, the prince followed him in.

"Sean, you don't really think Lady Me'na is actually going to try and prevent us, do you?"

"We'll soon see what Sir Neil has to say about the matter."

Sean threw his long frame into the nearest chair and stretched out to his full height of six feet four inches tall. While he waited, his brother poured them some wine, he handed Sean a goblet, which he drank straight down. Sean was an extremely handsome man with green eyes that were heavily lashed and sensuous lips finished the portrait. He was broad of shoulder with a slim tapered waist and long muscled legs. He was the perfect warrior king for his time.

Lord Colin begged for entrance. Sir Neil had arrived.

"Send him in Colin," Thomas responded.

Sir Neil walked in and kneeled before his liege.

"Sir Neil, what has happened here? I sent you to govern this principality until it was securely in Fastonia's possession. What went wrong and who is in control here?"

The King was very upset, he looked calm. There were no outward signs of anger; but the prince knew his being so calm meant trouble for someone. This time it was not himself, which was a good thing.

Sir Neil stood. "Your Highness, Lady Me'na is a hellion, I cannot control her. She tried to kill me when I first arrived, but changed her mind. She had me placed in the dungeon until you arrived this morning. I feared for my life."

It was a crime to imprison the King's agent when he was on the King's business.

The King stood and towered over him. "How could a woman make you fear for your life? Is she a big woman or a tall woman. Does she have the face of a man?" Neil backed away from the King.

"No, sire. She is small of stature but is strong-willed."

Sean narrowed his eyes. "What of her face?"

"She has the face of a temptress with the body to match. She tried to bewitch me but I resisted," he boasted.

"Um," the King doubted she tried to seduce his plump body. Sean turned and went back to his makeshift throne. He thanked Sir Neil for trying to do his duty and released him from his service for now.

"Thomas, would you be so good as to ask the men to come in?" Thomas went to the tent opening and motioned for them to come in. Sean waited for them to all come in before he began to speak.

"We will not leave this place as you have probably surmised, this is my kingdom and I will not be dissuaded. William, have the infantry prepared for battle. Connor make sure the fealty knights are ready for they often lag behind. Henry, have the palace knights prepare for they are my best fighters. I want them in the middle of the fray." Each man in his turn bowed to the King and left to do as he was bid.

Thomas asked his brother, "You mean to take the castle now?"

"Now, there is no better time than the present, is there?"

The prince merely hunched his shoulders.

Across the field, they could see the King preparing for battle. She stood with hands on hips. "Good let's finish this business once and for all," she said to Sir Benjamin. She had remained dressed for battle after her initial ride to deliver the lance and message. She smiled as she remembered her bold ride to the center of the field.

"Sir Benjamin, what does the King look like. You have seen him, right?" she asked.

"My lady, he is very tall has blond hair and I think his eyes may be green or some such color. Why do you ask?"

"Just wondering in case I meet him on the battlefield. I want to know what an arrogant king looks like." *Though, it would be better if he were fat*, she thought. *Anything but green eyes.* That eye color was her downfall. She couldn't resist them.

Me'na gave an elegant shrug of her petite shoulders. She piled her curly hair high on her head and placed her helm on. Sir Benjamin helped her to mount her horse. This was her father's warhorse, Torment. He used to let her ride with him when the horse was being trained, she was not afraid of him; she just couldn't get on him by herself.

Behind her rode several mercenary knights that she did not totally trust. They kept a close eye on her whereabouts especially Sir Richard and his cohort Sir Martin. Richard and his men had a plan to force her to wed with him and thereby take control of the principality. He did not think the king would get here so quickly. Her stubbornness was ruining his plans. After he smothered her father in his sleep, his plan was to force her to wed him by first bedding her and getting her with child. Now all those well laid plans were for nothing. He'd have to satisfy his greed by raiding the castle during the battle.

Sir Benjamin rallied her troops together to answer their lady's call to arms. They met the King halfway on the battlefield. Sean stared at her the whole time. He didn't know it was a she. He thought she was the captain and if the captain were taken down, the battle could be over. With luck, her infantry would disintegrate and there would be minimal lost of life. Then he would storm the castle and find her. He wasn't sure what he would do to her since she was a lady. But her disobedience would be dealt with severely. He should probably marry her to an old fat man, which would be a good punishment for a lady as young as she was.

"What are you smiling about, Sean?" Thomas asked.

"I was thinking about marrying the Lady Me'na to Sir Charles." He grinned.

"That would be a horror for her. That would be too much punishment for the crime. Isn't she about nineteen or so? Lord Charles has to be about sixty-five." Thomas had joined his brother in laughter.

"Sixty-five at least." Sean continued to laugh.

Lord William looked toward the King to see if he was ready for battle, he was. Sean nodded his head to begin.

"Well, let's get to it," Lord William shouted to his men. The King's standard-bearer was in front of him along with the heralders blowing the horns. The infantry marched forward behind the archers. Archers prepared their bows to fire. Knights were in formation and poised to fight, the fealty knights just wanted this to be over so that they could go home.

Across from them Me'na's men were preparing as well in a similar formation. Sir Benjamin tried to appeal to her common sense. "My lady, could you go back to the camp at least, please do not join in the battle. You could get killed."

"I am willing to take my chances, Sir Benjamin. I am not afraid." She left him there.

He shook his head and thought, *I am afraid. If the King finds out I allowed you to be in combat, he'll skin me alive*. He followed her to the front of the knights' column. Her standard-bearer had her colors.

The archers marched a little closer and prepared to fire their arrows. Sir Benjamin gave the order for them to fire. "Fire!"

The front row of archers released their arrows, knelt for the second row to release theirs and then the third group to release their arrows.

Across the field, the King's men knelt with their shields held in front. While Me'na's archers reloaded, Sean's archers fired their arrows and her men shielded themselves. It went back and forth this way for several minutes. Sean sent his infantry racing forward to clash with hers. He wanted this over with as soon as possible. Her men held their positions and tried to push forward. Both lines of infantry were fighting fiercely until the king released his knights to run over her men.

Sir Timothy was second in command, he raced forward with his knights; only the mercenary knights held back a bit. They were waiting for a chance to double back to the castle to pillage and rob her blind. Richard and Martin stayed close behind her most of the way. Sir Benjamin was trying to fight his opponent and watch out for her at the same time.

Me'na charged forward screaming her battle cry. She was going straight to the king. Thomas, Connor and Kristoff were on his tail trying to watch his back as he brought the fight to her. Richard motioned for Martin to get behind her and stick her in the ribs with his blade. Her back for now was unprotected; Benjamin was engaged and could not assist her.

Sean saw one of her own men try to kill her. He hollered for Kristoff to cut him down. Kristoff raced toward Martin and split him down the middle of his face; an arrow came out of nowhere and struck him in the throat at the same time. He fell from his horse onto the blood stained ground. Sean briefly glanced in the direction the arrow came from. There was a knight on the hill, he moved his bow and put it out of sight. He was coming down the hill; Sean couldn't tell whose side he was on.

After Lord Cameron shot the cowardly knight in the neck, he put his bow on his back and prepared to go down the hill. He was thankful he was an accurate shot; for the bow was not his weapon of choice.

Me'na was vaguely aware that Kristoff raced around her back. She was too busy trying not to be afraid of Sean's charge. The King looked larger to her the closer he got. She wasn't so sure anymore, but she would stay the course.

The King took notice that the person he thought was the captain looked a little smaller than he first thought. Instead of cutting her throat with his first swipe, he knocked her off of her horse. To the King's thinking, if this was a squire, he showed much courage under fire and was very bold. He was looking for a new squire. This young man would do nicely.

Me'na fell hard on the ground, jolting her spine. She quickly got up for Sean jumped off his horse, and came straight for her. Me'na put both hands on her sword and prepared to defend herself. Sean noticed his men had surrounded him so that he could finish his combatant off at his leisure.

Me'na looked up at Sean and he seemed a giant to her. She held her ground for she was brave if not foolhardy. Their swords clanged together and the shock from the action vibrated through her arm. Sean watched her curiously. He wasn't so sure about his opponent. He pushed her sword back with his and knocked her down again. He stepped quickly to her to prevent her from rising. Sir Richard galloped away quickly. Sean did not notice him leave.

"Let's see what manner of man we have here," he said to no one in particular.

She was trying to get up but his foot held her fast. He allowed her to rise up on her elbows a bit. The King reached down and removed her helmet. To their surprise, it was a woman. He looked down into her eyes, amber eyes met green eyes. It was as if time stood still for a moment.

"My Lady Me'na, I presume," he stated.

"Your Highness," she responded. She was mesmerized.

Sean gave her his hand so she could get up, he pulled his helmet off. The fighting around them had ceased, all eyes were watching this encounter. Conqueror and conquered, neither could do more than stare at one another for a moment. Sean came out of his trance first.

"William, Kristoff, Connor, and Colin, check the wounded and prepare to go to the keep." He watched her narrow her eyes at him, "What say you, lady? Do you join us?" He didn't wait for an answer. Sean's horse was brought to him and he mounted. He then reached down and picked Me'na up.

"Let me go, Your Highness." Sean had her sitting sidesaddle in front of him.

"You don't want me to do that, do you?" He hugged her to him on pretense that he was keeping her from falling off. Her heart was beating fast. She couldn't think of anything that she should say. *I need to put up some kind of struggle. It's those blasted green eyes of his. I just can't give in like this, not without a fight no matter how handsome he is.* Instead, she said nothing, better to be silent than tell an outright lie.

She felt his chuckle vibrate deeply in his chest. He was holding her as if she belonged to him. *I know I'll sit as if he is not affecting me. I'll not surrender this battle.*

"Give over, lady. It's over," he gently murmured.

She sighed, and relaxed against his hard chest. There was something about him she could not resist. He wasn't even trying to be charming and she melted against him anyway.

The King had come to the same opinion about her. *I will have her as wife, which will be the best way to settle this dispute and besides I desire her. Why not?*

While his horse trotted smartly to the keep, Sean tipped her face up for a kiss. He had to taste those red lips and nuzzle that long golden neck of hers. Surprisingly, Me'na kissed him back with more passion than he expected. Sean put one arm around her and brought her as close as he could get her to him, he deepened the kiss and heard her moan softly. He had lost the battle to her as she had to him. *Ah yes,* the King thought, *there should be a cleric at the castle. She will be mine before nightfall.*

Cameron shook his head to clear it of the past. This was his sister and he would make sure she won this time no matter what it cost him. He turned from the window and his musings.

This would end now, today. It would go no further. He placed his federal badge in his pocket, just in case he needed it to stay out of jail. He chose his brick red shirt to go with his black suit, no tie today, he needed to be casual. He placed one gun in the small of his back the other in his shoulder hostler. He was ready. All he needed was time to finish what had begun a long time ago.

Me'na was in her room showering again, she was extremely nervous. She and Sean had never gotten this far before; he had warned her not to try to do anything for him that took her out of his sight. Each time she died, she was separated from him. Not this time, he was next door to her.

She picked up the phone book and looked for the number to a florist friend of hers. Since this was Sean's birthday, she couldn't go out and buy him anything; so, she would make their wedding night a night to remember. She ordered six dozen yellow roses and pink and yellow combination roses. She also asked her friend to buy as many vanilla scented candles that she could find at the shop next door to hers. She had checked earlier that morning to make sure champagne was in the house. She and Henry arranged for someone from his agency to be there to let her friend inside. Once her girlfriend Cherry arrived, she would leave a trail of roses to the master bedroom and make a bed out of some of the flowers. She would place the candles around the room and dim the lights. The champagne was chilling in a bucket. Henry told the policemen outside what was going on, so they would not delay the delivery. All was in readiness and she was finished dressing.

Sean was not nervous one bit. He had lived his entire life to get to this moment. He knew they'd never gotten this far, but he had faith that this time they would succeed. He couldn't explain it, he just felt it. There was Cameron. This time he was her brother, and miracle of miracles, Thomas was actually changing. Though he didn't put much stock in it, he had to see it with his own two eyes to believe it. They hadn't heard from Bains in at least twelve hours, maybe, just maybe this time was a go. He would kill Bains with his bare hands if he caught him near Me'na. No one would be able to stop him this time, not even the police.

Sean was a big and powerful man. He worked out regularly with free weights. He had a black belt in kickboxing and several different varieties of martial arts. He hadn't worked out the previous week because he couldn't leave Me'na alone. This led to the idea of using one of the empty rooms on the second floor as a gym. So for, all he had up there was a punching bag and a treadmill. He'd pass this by Me'na to see which room she could do without once she started decorating their home. Their home, it sounded good and right. Sean never realized how ready, really ready he was to settle down until the day of her accident. It seemed a lifetime ago, it was several lifetimes ago.

Cameron and Sean were in the den waiting on Me'na to appear when the phone rang. He looked at the caller ID and it was an old flame he hadn't heard from in ages.

"Hello."

"Hi, Sean, it's me, Monica. How are you doing?" she asked.

Cameron stood close to Sean. He stepped away from him so he could talk. He really wanted to watch him handle this caller. He knew Sean loved his sister to distraction. It would be interesting to see how he handled it. Cameron had been in a similar situation with a new girlfriend when his old girlfriend called. It was not a pleasant scene.

"I'm fine, Monica. I'm getting married in about an hour.

"Congratulations, Sean, I didn't know, but I do wish you the best. You deserve it."

"Thank you. We are happy," he told her.

"Well, don't let me keep you, bye." She hung up so nice and easy.

Cameron stood there smiling his congratulations to him for getting out of a potentially sticky situation.

"That was sweet, man. You didn't bungle it like I did," Cameron said as Me'na walked in the room.

"Didn't bungle what?" She was looking from one to the other.

Cameron told her, "It's a guy thing. You wouldn't understand, sis." She walked over to him and hit him on the arm.

"Ouch! What was that for?" he asked. Sean stood there waiting to erupt into laughter.

"It's a woman thing. You wouldn't understand," she countered.

"Man, if I have to put up with this kind of abuse, I think I'd rather have a brother." Sean couldn't hold it in any longer. He exploded into laughter.

"Well, how do I look, you two guys?" she asked them.

"You look beautiful, baby. I'm sorry it took me so long to say it. I was enjoying watching you and Cameron."

Me'na had on an ivory dress that stopped above her knees. It was low cut and she wore the gold locket Sean gave her from the past. It was nestled between her breasts. Sean walked over to her and picked up the locket. It was warm to his touch. His eyes met hers and he slowly placed it back in its nest. Her hair was up with tendrils trailing down her neck. It was a very soft and sexy look that she wanted to paint and did portray. She had her legs sheathed in ivory stockings and four-inch heels completed her look. She couldn't go shopping so she had to find something to wear out of what she already had. She was stunning, Sean was very proud that in about forty-five minutes she would be his wife.

"Me'na, once we're at the restaurant celebrating, I want to call Thomas to join us if that's OK with you?"

"Sure, babe. He's your brother. Mine will be there. The more the merrier."

Before they could leave out of the door, the phone rang again. Cameron walked on outside while Sean answered the phone.

"Hello," he said. Me'na was standing on the side of him. Sean became uncomfortable with her being so close to him and another ex-girlfriend on the phone.

"Sean, it that you?" This time it was LaKesia on the phone, putting him in the hot seat.

By the way he squirmed, Me'na could tell it must be a woman. She had been wondering about ex-girlfriends, someone as handsome as he was, had to have a lot of female friends. He reached over and grabbed Me'na's hand.

"I'll see you in the car, Sean." She left him alone. She kissed him on her way out.

Me'na was not insecure in her relationship with him. This was her way of showing it to him. If she didn't trust anybody else in the world, she would always put her life in his capable hands. She left the room with a smile on her face. Sean turned his attention to LaKesia.

"Hi, LaKesia. It's me. I can't talk. I'm on my way out the door to get married this morning."

"Married, to who?" she asked.

"To the love of my life, my best friend." He went a little overboard but he wanted her to pass the word along that he was unavailable. "Her name is Me'na. You should meet her one day."

"Uh, Sean," she stuttered, "I don't think that would be a good idea. I wish you well even though I wish you weren't marrying. Good luck, see you around the playground," she finished.

"Bye, thanks for the well wishes." He hung up also.

Sean left out of the house with a smile on his face. He realized what Me'na had done. She showed him she didn't fear his past social life. He only wished he'd feel the same way if an old boyfriend showed up. He didn't think he would though; men had this thing about territory they didn't like admitting to women.

As he walked to the car, he looked toward Cameron, hunched his shoulders and Cameron started laughing.

Everyone had already headed outside towards the cars. There were more police outside parked all along the road. One would follow them to the justice of the peace. Sean opened the door for Me'na to get into his two-seater Jaguar. He went around to get in and pulled some flowers out of the back. He gave them to her for a bouquet; he'd had a big bouquet of gardenias prepared for her. Sean peeled out of the driveway and was gone; he slowed down because he forgot cops were following him.

He looked toward Me'na and told her thank you. "What for, babe?" she wanted to know.

"For leaving me in the room with another woman on the phone. You showed you trusted me. I appreciate it, another woman might have had my scalp." He grinned.

"Sean I have loved you for hundreds of years and never lost you to another. If I can't trust you, I don't need you. We have to trust each other above a lot of other nonsense, without trust, we have nothing." She leaned over and kissed his cheek. "And besides, I know you're not a monk, I don't want a man I have to show the ropes to." She started laughing at the astonished look on his face.

"What, woman! Just wait until you're legally mine and sass me again…" He was grinning too much to finish his mock threat to her. She just leaned over and smacked him on the lips again. Sean threw his car into the fifth gear and hit the freeway zooming. The only thing he wanted to do was get to the justice of the peace as soon as possible. He had to have this saucy woman for his very own and yesterday wouldn't have been soon enough for him.

They arrived at the justice of the peace in record time with Cameron screeching to a halt right beside them. Henry and the rest of the bodyguards arrived in a couple of minutes. The police were the last to get there.

Officer Broussard walked up to Sean. "Say, Dr. Williams, if this wasn't a special thing you and Detective Hamilton have going here, I would have had to try and catch you to give you a ticket. But I don't think I could have made it. Be careful." He walked to the building.

Me'na whispered, "He wouldn't have caught us." They both started to laugh.

Inside, the justice of the peace was waiting. He was familiar to Sean. He looked like a knight that was Thomas' friend back a lifetime ago.

He introduced himself to them. "My name is William Chaney. I'll be marrying you two today. Please come in, have a seat while I get the papers ready."

Sean was startled at the name and face of the JP. Cameron looked over to him to see if Sean showed any knowledge of him. *Yes,* he thought. *He remembers. That's good. William is no threat to Me'na.*

Sean put his arm around her and helped her to a seat while the men stood. The justice's assistant came to get them. His honor was ready. The policemen were standing outside the small building making sure Bains did not enter. Hand in hand, they walked toward their future.

Cameron stood up with Sean as his best man and as Me'na's bridesmaid to much snickering from the guys. He took it good-naturedly. It was fun amongst newfound friends and a new sister.

Justice Chaney started the ceremony without a hitch; never had they gotten this far. Sean tried to look solemn but couldn't wipe the smile from his face; Me'na's eye's glistened with unshed tears.

"Dearly beloved, we are gathered here to wed this man and this woman…" he went on. They exchanged rings and vows looking at each other steadily, green eyes into amber eyes. "If any man knows why this couple should not be joined together, let him speak now or forever hold his peace," the justice asked.

A brief silence followed, Cameron was vigilant. He didn't want to have to silence someone at his sister's wedding. They had all lived for this point in time. "I now pronounce you husband and wife. What God has joined together, let no one put asunder. You may kiss your bride."

Before the words were out of his mouth, Sean had a death gripe on her lips. Everyone applauded them. Success at last, reigned in his mind and heart. She was finally his wife as she should have been many years before. Me'na was kissing and clutching him all at the same time, she was so happy. Well wishes and hugs were given to everyone present. Cameron hugged his new brother-in-law and swung his sister around. He tried not to look grim; he knew the day was not yet over.

BOOK ONE
CHAPTER TWELVE

Everyone was asking Sean where they were going to celebrate. He pulled out of cell phone and called Robert Langston owner of his favorite restaurant and club.

"Say, Rob, man, this is Sean."

"Hey, what's going on?" Robert asked him.

"Man I just got married and I wanted to know if you're serving now."

"What? You got married? To Me'na?" he asked.

"Yeah, man, to her." His eyes softened when their gaze met.

"The chef and staff are here, we'll open now for you and Me'na if you don't mind a couple of amateur waiters." He was happy for them.

"We don't mind anything right now. We'll be there in about thirty minutes. Thanks, I won't forget this." He hung up and told everybody where to go.

Next, he called his brother. "Tommy, can you get down to Capricorn in about a half hour?"

"Yeah. What's the hurry?" Thomas was curious.

"We just got married and I wanted to share our happiness with you. Please say you'll come." Sean pleaded for understanding from Thomas. The old Thomas wouldn't understand.

The new one surprised him. "I'll be there in twenty minutes." He hung up and changed clothes quickly. Thomas wanted to show his brother he had finally grown up; he would stop all his juvenile behavior and be the man he should be.

Sean smiled a happy smile, Me'na asked him if everything with Thomas was OK. "Thomas will be joining us and I'm hoping for the best where he is concerned. He has always begrudged me any happiness, we'll see."

She rubbed his arm and thought, *Not this time. I am watching out for your best interest. I'll not have him hurt you again.*

Outwardly, she merely smiled, he was hers at last and nothing would change that. Sean headed downtown toward Club Capricorn at a modest speed for him. He had precious cargo on board, his beloved wife. Everyone including Thomas arrived at the same time. Thomas rushed to his brother's side and gave him a big bear hug.

"Man, look at you, married. It's about time you and Me'na married. I'm happy for both of you!"

Sean returned the hug. It meant a lot to him. Thomas hugged Me'na and welcomed her into the family. He and Cameron shook hands.

Thomas was in such a hurry he failed to notice a car followed him. It stayed a few cars behind him and parked down the road when he stopped.

Bains was in a rental car this time. He knew the police were looking for him. The officer with the wedding party went inside also.

Robert and his head chef Patrick Hadley greeted them. The chef was world renown and attracted a large clientele. He and Sean often played basketball together on the off chance they were available at the same time. When he heard Sean had gotten married, he wanted to meet the bride.

"Me'na, this is Patrick Hadley; basketball player and sometime chef," Sean introduced them.

"Hi, Patrick. I'm happy to meet you," she replied.

"Ah, Mrs. Williams, the pleasure is mine I assure you."

She giggled like a schoolgirl, this was the first time she was referred to as Mrs. Williams in public, and it felt good. The chef and his staff out did themselves. Robert served them personally along with one of the sous chefs. There were many toast raised in their honor. Sean only drunk one glass of champagne, and Me'na merely tasted it. She wasn't a big drinker and wanted her wits about her for later. It was time to leave, they had been there for about two hours and the couple was ready to be alone. Sean thanked Robert for all he had done and Thomas pulled out his credit card to pay the bill.

"No, Thomas, it's on the house," Robert tried to tell him.

"I need to pay for this, Rob. I owe my big brother a lot and I'm starting now." Robert took his credit card and charged him. Sean noticed what was going on and walked over to his brother to thank him.

"Don't thank me, Sean. I'm your brother and I'm going to start acting like it. I really am happy for y'all." They shook hands and everyone prepared to leave.

Sean's guard was only slightly down due to his happiness, but Cameron's was more fine-tuned than ever. Things were going too good for him. Bains had to be somewhere lurking around. He looked up and down the street and saw parked cars and traffic going by.

As Sean opened Me'na's door they stopped to kiss each other, a shot rang out of nowhere. Everyone ducked and Sean pushed her into the car. The bullet barely missed the both of them. The police ran across the street looking while Sean sped quickly off into traffic. Thomas followed closely behind them with Henry on their tail. Cameron delayed his departure. He was looking for the assailant. He couldn't see anything and chased after his sister. He pulled his gun out and rechecked it to make sure it was loaded.

Bains managed to elude the police again and he was chasing them. Sean had made it to the freeway and was driving at least a hundred miles an hour.

Me'na was of course terrified.

"Stay down, baby. I'm used to driving this fast. We'll be OK." He tried to reassure her.

Thomas kept up with him. Henry saw Bains in his rearview mirror and was trying to cut him off. But insanity breeds more than madness. It gave Bains the skill to out drive Henry. They were going extremely fast in and out of cars. Drivers were blowing their horns and pulling over to the side of the road.

Bains started shooting hurriedly at them again. He didn't want to miss his target. Thomas could see him in his mirror and he kept getting in his way. He tried to keep him from getting to his brother. Bains shot at him also. Thomas ducked and dodged bullets. Cameron came up fast and shot at Bains. He thought he hit him but he wasn't sure. Bain's car jerked to the side a little.

"Yeah, I must of winged him," Cameron said to no one in particular.

Henry came up on Bains blind side and tried to side swipe him. Bains turned the gun on them and shot Howard in the shoulder. You could hear police sirens in the background. Sean jumped off the freeway with Thomas on his tail. Bains followed a close third. Cameron was closing in again on him. They raced through the neighborhoods when Bains' car slammed into the rear of Sean's.

The Jaguar did a three hundred and sixty degree turn in the middle of the street. Finally, the car stopped spinning and Bains jumped out of his car with his gun pointing at an unconscious Sean. Thomas stopped at the same time. He saw Bains raise his gun to shot his brother. He hurled his body at Bains and knocked him down. He grabbed Bains legs trying to reach the gun first. The madman turned and hit him in the head with the gun butt.

Sean was coming to when Bains managed to kick Thomas' body off of him. He stood up to fire the gun at Sean when Cameron's bullet got him in the head. He unceremoniously fell forward.

The police had finally arrived and told Cameron to drop his weapon. When the officers approached, he told them to check his ID. Cameron was told to reach in his jacket and throw it down. Officer Statton picked it up and looked towards Cameron. He gave it back and told him to holster his gun. Cameron put his gun back in his shoulder holster.

The officers had called several ambulances to the scene. Thomas was starting to come around; Cameron went to help care for him. *At least one positive came out of this,* he thought, *Thomas changed, and that's a plus for Sean.*

Thomas sat up holding his head. He looked toward Bains and thought the police had shot him. Cameron didn't correct him.

Inside Sean's car, the medics were helping them out. He came around to Me'na's side and grabbed a hold of her as soon as she was free. She was crying hysterically. He just held her in his arms, and kept kissing her head until she settled down. His favorite car was ruined, but this time, he had won the girl.

They walked over to Thomas. When Sean reached his brother, Thomas grabbed him and cried on his shoulder. He had come so close to losing the brother, whom he'd just started learning to appreciate.

"Thank God you're OK, I don't know what I would have done if I lost you, Sean," he sobbed.

Me'na stood back with Cameron's arms hugging her for support. Through all the terror she and everyone else had gone through, she was able to smile at this miracle. Thomas meant the world to Sean; it had taken his brother at least two life times to feel the same way.

Howard was taken to the hospital and Sean insisted that Thomas be checked out. Cameron followed the ambulance to the hospital. Before he left, he told Sean he would be staying in a hotel that night, he and his new bride deserved some time alone. He'd see them later the next day. Officer Statton drove them back to the house, while he was driving them. Detective Hamilton called to wish them good luck.

Sean open the kitchen door, he stopped to pick up his bride to carry her over the threshold. He hurriedly used his foot to push a broom that he had decorated with satin ribbons on the floor; he wanted to honor her heritage. Back in the slave days, they were not allowed to marry so they started their own tradition of "jumping the broom". He put her down so they could jump together. She was happy her Sean was so thoughtful.

He told her, "We are now married to each other two different ways. Nobody can break us up." He kissed her to seal the bargain.

They followed the trail of roses to the bedroom. He was pleased she had found a way to have this done. Inside their room, the light was dim. Candles were waiting to be lit.

"Sit here in the chair, husband, while I light the candles." She blushed.

He sat back with his arms spread over the chair admiring his wife. Once all the candles were lit, she went into the bathroom to change into the best outfit she had. About a year ago, she had purchased an expensive two-piece teddy. She didn't know why she bought it at the time. She just had to have it. Now she knew why. Sean had always been in her future.

She walked into the room where he was waiting; he sat up as she approached him. Me'na turned off the lights so only the candles burned low and seductively. As she got closer to him, Sean stood and opened his arms to her. She walked into them. She still fit perfectly as she always had. Me'na placed her arms around Sean's neck and lowered his lips to hers. As their lips touched, the long denial of passion they had suffered through was finally over. They devoured one another in the fire that raged within them. It didn't take long before both were lost in the magma-like wave of passion.

THE END

Printed in the United States
37746LVS00004BA/1-15

9 781413 765496